Into the Fading Twilight

CATHERINE COWLES

Bloom books

Cover and internal design © 2026 by Sourcebooks
Cover design © Mary at Books and Moods
Cover images © macrovector/Freepik, creativepack/Freepik, rawpixel.com/Freepik, Best Content Production Group/iStock, blueringmedia/iStock, GreenSkyStudio/Adobe Stock
Inside cover art by Elizianna
Internal design by Champagne Book Design
Internal images © tatahnka23/Depositphotos, Undrey/Adobe Stock

Published by Bloom Books, an imprint of Sourcebooks
1935 Brookdale RD, Naperville, IL 60563-2773
(630) 961-3900
sourcebooks.com

Cataloging-in-Publication data is on file with the Library of Congress.

Printed and bound in the United States of America.
LSC 10 9 8 7 6 5 4 3 2

Also Available from

CATHERINE COWLES

Starlight Grove

Across the Vanishing Sky
Into the Fading Twilight
Beneath a Midnight Moon
Through the Gathering Storm
Within the Starry Silence

Sparrow Falls

Fragile Sanctuary
Delicate Escape
Broken Harbor
Beautiful Exile
Chasing Shelter
Secret Haven

The Lost & Found Series

Whispers of You
Echoes of You
Glimmers of You
Shadows of You
Ashes of You

The Tattered & Torn Series

Tattered Stars
Falling Embers
Hidden Waters
Shattered Sea
Fractured Sky

The Wrecked Series

Reckless Memories
Perfect Wreckage
Wrecked Palace
Reckless Refuge
Beneath the Wreckage

The Sutter Lake Series

Beautifully Broken Pieces
Beautifully Broken Life
Beautifully Broken Spirit
Beautifully Broken Control
Beautifully Broken Redemption

Standalone Novels

All the Missing Pieces

For a full list of up-to-date Catherine Cowles titles,
please visit www.catherinecowles.com.

Into the Fading Twilight

Sometimes you just need a hug.
This book is for everyone looking for comfort, solace, peace, healing:
may you find it in both likely and unlikely places—
and consider this my hug to you in book form.

Prologue

NOVA

Everything hurt. So much that I couldn't identify all the places the pain had made a home in me. And maybe that was for the best. The agony had become more of a dull ache because it was so ever-present.

My stomach cramped as if to call me a liar. Hunger. I could still feel that. But the food the man had left me was long gone now. Days ago. And the water... *Did I drink the last of that?*

I thought I had, but it was too much effort to roll over and see. Some part of me knew I needed to fight. To harness that spirit within me—the one that had carried me through the days and nights of fear and torture. But it felt like a ghost now.

I rolled to my back on the forest floor, the chain clanging with the movement—the same chain I'd carried with me for countless days and nights. They hadn't started out immeasurable, though. At first, I'd been meticulous about marking the moments, never losing sight of the time that had been stolen from me.

I'd memorized the tally of each dusk and dawn by the slivers of light around my prison door, the count branded on my bones. But I'd stopped at some point. I thought it was at three hundred and twelve—the number that had beaten me. Maybe because it was so close to a year, and that fact had been too difficult to bear.

We'd passed the year mark now, for sure. And my captor bringing me out to the woods and leaving me chained to a tree wasn't exactly a good sign.

He'd left me before, but it was always in the underground cell. It was a hell of a mindfuck when you started wishing for the person who'd stolen everything from you to appear again—when the master of your pain was who you hoped to see.

Then he'd show up, and I'd swallow those words whole. His torment wasn't always physical, though he did like to use his fists. But where he really shined was in the emotional. Letting me know all the ways everyone had moved on without me. My friends. My family—not that they'd ever cared.

His manipulations were his true weapons—the kind of manipulations that made you want to give up.

I squeezed my eyes closed, trying to force the memories from my mind. I thought about my best friend, Brae, and her son, who was like a nephew to me. I tried to imagine Owen a year older now. What teeth had he lost? What color were his new glasses?

I held the last images I had of them in my mind as my eyelids fluttered open. The light hurt after all my time in the dark, but I stared up through the tree branches. Little particles of light twinkled and danced in the twilight like they were floating on air.

Or were those snowflakes? Was it snowing?

My mind struggled to process that. It didn't seem right. I was hot. My skin felt like it had been fried and burned. But those looked like snowflakes. All around. Like I was in a snow globe.

A sound pierced my ears, and I tried to lift my head but couldn't quite make it happen. Everything was too heavy, which was probably a good thing. I didn't want to see the man again. I didn't want to hear his cruel words or feel his fingers tightening around my neck as he squeezed.

A twig snapped. I heard footsteps.

Maybe it was a bear. Part of me hoped it was, that this would all be over.

Snowflake lights danced around me. *Beautiful.* It would be a beautiful way to go.

A curse sounded, and the footsteps quickened. And then a face filled my vision. Not the man. Someone else.

This was a man, too. But breathtaking. He didn't have hate in his dark-hazel eyes, even as they sparked with anger. His dark hair looked as if he'd run his fingers through it countless times. And his skin was the kind of golden color that spoke of many hours spent outdoors.

"Nova?"

The single word was deep. Gruff. Ragged.

And it was also my name. How long had it been since I'd heard it? The man didn't call me by my name. Maybe because he didn't consider me human.

But *this* man? He said my name. Said *Nova*. He knew who I was.

Another few curses slid from his mouth, but they somehow managed to be beautiful. Breathtaking, just like the man.

A backpack slid from his shoulders, and he pulled something from it. A device. He hit some buttons on it, then pressed it to his ear. A phone. But it had a long antenna, as if it were from the nineties or something.

A second later, he was barking orders. "I've got an injured female. Late twenties."

He pressed two fingers into the side of my neck. I wanted to thrash. *Not my neck.* But the pain didn't come. Just gentle pressure.

"Pulse is slow. She's critical." That dark-hazel gaze roamed over and past me. "Bring bolt cutters. She's chained to a goddamned tree."

He listed off a series of numbers, and my eyes started to flutter again. The snow that I knew *wasn't* snow danced now, and it really was stunning.

"Nova!"

My name was a command, a demand for my presence.

My eyelids flipped open, and I took in the beauty above me.

"You stay with me, okay? Don't go to sleep. Help's on the way. You just stay with me."

Everything was heavy now. It was all too much. "Let go."

It was the first time I'd heard my voice in months. And the lack of use rang through in the two syllables. Like a door rusted closed now forced to open.

"What?" His voice was quieter. Softer.

"Let…me…go." It was what I needed. To finally be released. To go with the snowflakes. They would carry me away, and I would finally feel peace.

A hand slid through mine. "Nova. You're going to live, okay? You're alive. You're breathing. And you're going to fight for that. You've got so much to live for."

But I didn't feel that. I didn't feel it one bit. All I felt was pain. It was stronger now. And I couldn't bear it anymore.

He squeezed my hand. "Brae's been looking for you. She never gave up. Never stopped."

My best friend's name. The promise of her. The one person who'd stuck by me through thick and thin. It sparked something deep inside me.

The kind man gripped my hand even harder. "You're alive. You're breathing. Just keep breathing, Nova. Keep breathing."

Something about the desperation in his voice, the pleading there, made me want to fight. But it was too little too late. I was too far gone.

I slid under, but the snowflakes met me there. And they carried me, just like I knew they would.

Chapter One

NOVA

FOUR MONTHS LATER

THE WIND LIFTED MY HAIR, SWIRLING THE DARK-BROWN strands in front of my face as I stared out at the water below. Soon, it would be too cold for anyone to consider this endeavor sane. Who was I kidding? People *already* thought that ship had sailed when it came to me.

I'd heard the muttered *"crazy."* Or the tsking and *"Poor dear. She'll never be the same."*

They weren't wrong. I *wouldn't* be the same. But I was okay with that.

I eased out of my sneakers, tossed them down the cliff to the lakeshore below, and slipped out of my shorts and tee. I'd leave those up here. With my luck, they'd land in the water if I dropped them.

Taking a step forward, I inhaled deeply, the straps of my swimsuit cutting into my shoulders. The scents of pine and lake water swirled as I placed my palm directly over my heart, not opening my eyes. The steady beat against my hand was just another reassurance I desperately needed.

Blood roared in my ears, and it felt like my muscles might tear free of the skin encasing them. Everything was so loud: the voices, the concerns, the whispered worries.

"You're alive," I croaked. "You're breathing."

And then, I jumped.

I didn't look. My body had already memorized exactly what it needed to do: Hurl myself out over the rocks and wait for the miracle.

The wind whipped against my body, colder now that we were in late September. And then it hit. Pain and sheer pleasure all at once. The water smacked against my skin—the kind of slap that assured me I was most definitely alive.

The shock hit me like a freight train, but I welcomed it. I let my body go down, down, down, without trying to swim for the surface. Instead, I tipped my head back and stared up.

The water was a dark, blueish-green haze. The sun sparkled through the surface, and I watched it all—the way it felt like I'd watched so much during my *coming back*, being on the outside looking in. But unlike all those other moments, this was the one place the world went quiet.

My lungs burned, but I held on for one more moment, needing more of the silence. My chest raged, ribs squeezing painfully, and I finally kicked for the surface. It was harder. Everything was. I'd lost too much muscle and bone density while in captivity. But I'd gained fight. And I knew how to use it.

I broke the surface, sucking air into my lungs. It was pain and relief all at once, and I knew in that moment that I was still here. There was no doubt in my mind—no waking from a nightmare, wondering if I was dead or still locked away. I was alive, and I was breathing.

I took in a few more lungsful of air and then flipped to my back, floating. The sun was so bright that I had to shut my eyes. Something about the lack of light and vitamin D while I'd been locked away had injured my eyes. The doctor told me they'd likely heal with time, but for now, sunglasses were my best friend.

Which wasn't necessarily a bad thing. They could hide the things my eyes revealed.

I floated for a few more minutes until the cold seeped into my bones. I never let it fully set in. That brought snippets of memory: shivering on the thin mattress on the floor, the stale air.

I shoved those memories back down to where I'd locked them away.

There'd been nothing but sweet relief when I woke in the hospital, unable to remember the details of my capture or confinement. But the numbness hadn't lasted. I was starting to get brief snatches of things.

But based on the little information I had about my time in captivity, there was no way to know if they were truly my memories or something my imagination had conjured up. It was a hell of a thing, not being able to trust your own mind.

Flipping over to my stomach, I swam toward the shore. By the time I reached the beach, my muscles ached and my arms felt like they weighed a ton each. It didn't matter how hard I tried to ease myself back into working out or how diligently I followed the plan the nutritionist had laid out for me, the strength always seemed just out of reach.

"You're alive. You're breathing."

His voice—the one that always seemed to keep me going—echoed in my head. The voice of a man whose life had ended up inextricably linked to mine. Someone who had no idea that he drowned out the sound of my monsters.

I held on to those words. It was one thing my memory *hadn't* let go of during my seventy-two hours in a coma.

I could still hear those words as if Kol Archer were standing right next to me and making the command all over again.

Climbing out of the water, my skin pebbled as I headed up the beach. I didn't let the cold settle in as I slipped on my shoes. "You're alive."

I needed that reminder even more today.

I climbed the steep path to the top of the cliff in nothing but my bathing suit and sneakers. My limbs trembled with the effort, but I kept right on pushing. By the time I reached my clothes and the bike I'd snagged at a yard sale for fifteen bucks, my heart was hammering in my chest and my lungs ached.

Quickly drying off and pulling on my clothes, I reached for my sunglasses. Even with the sun not at its peak, I still did better with them on. Adjusting the frames, I jumped on my bike and headed for home.

Home.

That's what Brae wanted it to be. My best friend had worked so damn hard to make it that for me. A room painted a deep purple—one of my favorite colors. My old bedding, photos, and other belongings, my favorite candle.

But none of it…fit.

Or maybe *I* didn't fit. Because while a madman had kept me locked away, the rest of the world kept spinning.

Brae had started over here in Starlight Grove, and that had included falling in love. Dex Archer wasn't what I would've expected for my best friend, yet he was completely perfect for her. And I was over the moon that she and her son, Owen, had found the love they deserved.

Yet it made me feel like I was on the outside looking in. The third wheel—or technically fourth I guessed—throwing their routine into chaotic disarray. But I didn't know how to make it better.

I pulled my bike up to the three-bedroom cabin on Briarwood Lane. It was so incredibly different than the small house we'd rented several hours south of here, in Oakland, California. There were no honking horns or music drifting out of windows. No crowded streets with an array of shops for anything you might need.

But, God, it was beautiful here in Starlight Grove. The small town, a mere hour south of the Oregon border, held endless forests and meadows and a staggering mountain peak. The babbling sound of the meandering Clover Creek, which lay behind the cabin, was calming. And the air… I inhaled again, Kol's words echoing in my mind.

"You're breathing."

This air reminded me of that. No smog or trash. Just trees and freedom.

The screen door slapped against the frame, and my eyes flew open. I was thankful for my sunglasses because I knew I winced at the look on Brae's face as she stood on the front porch. Waiting. Worry creased her brow, but there was a hint of annoyance I could only place because we'd known each other for practically our entire lives.

From the preschool sandbox to now—and everything in between. When my family showed they were a complete waste of space, Brae made sure I was okay. She shared her lunch with me when my mom forgot to send one. She always invited me over after school so I had a safe place to do my homework. And she picked up the pieces every time my parents broke my damn heart.

So when she needed me, I hadn't even paused to think it through. The answer was always yes. I'd moved cross-country with her when she ended up pregnant at nineteen and the father proved he was a douche of epic proportions.

And we'd built Owen a beautiful home. I'd helped her with diaper changes and three-a.m. feedings. Had been there for his first steps and first words.

We were a family. But it suddenly felt like I no longer belonged.

"Hi," I said dumbly as I got off the bike and headed for the front path.

Brae's amber gaze swept over me, taking in my wet hair and damp clothes. "Swimming?"

That's all I'd told her about my sporadic disappearing acts: that I liked to go swimming. I knew it confused her because I'd never been one for the activity before, but she'd gone for it.

I nodded, forcing a smile. "Beautiful morning for it."

My so-called swimming trip had nothing to do with the sun or the morning and everything to do with the fact that I was starting a job after months of little contact with anyone but a handful of people. My nightmares and anxiety were raging like the creek after a thunderstorm.

Brae's mouth thinned into a tense line. "It's cold. I'm not sure it's good for you to be doing it so late in the year. There's a YMCA a couple of towns over. I could drive you and—"

"That's okay," I said quickly. "I'm not cold."

The goose bumps on my skin said my words weren't exactly truthful.

"I just don't want you to get sick. You're still getting your strength back," Brae argued.

I tried not to recoil at her words, but it was as if she'd reached out and slapped me. I didn't need the reminder of how far I'd come, how far I still had to go, or how precarious the doctor warned me things could be for a while.

"I'm good," I ground out, sidestepping her and heading inside.

I hated myself for the frustration I felt, directed at the one person who *truly* loved me. The one who'd never given up on me.

When my parents and brother found out that I'd gone missing, they hadn't done anything. I'd learned later that they hadn't even bothered to leave Rhode Island to come out to California. They hadn't called for updates on my case. They hadn't even reached out when I turned up alive.

But they *had* taken $10,000 to do an interview on a prime-time news special.

The sound of Owen's happy voice drifted through the cabin. "More cookies in the batter, Dex!"

A low, rumbling laugh sounded. "Any more cookies and you're going to turn into the Cookie Monster."

Tipping my sunglasses to the top of my head, I made my way into the kitchen and toward those joyful sounds. Though I often felt like I was on the outside looking in, but it helped to know that the people I loved most had found happiness.

Owen beamed over at Dex from his spot atop a stool, where he was helping with some sort of cooking project. "I'm down with being a cookie monster."

Dex's gaze flicked to me from behind his tortoiseshell-framed glasses. It didn't stay long, but I knew he registered everything about me in those brief moments, from my wet hair to the dark circles under my eyes. “Morning, Nova.”

I forced a smile again and hated myself for it a little more. Dex had been nothing but nice to me. *More* than nice. He’d been kind and understanding. He never got too close—always gave me a wide berth. He’d welcomed me into the house he shared with Brae without a thought. And he eased Brae as much as possible, given the situation.

It wasn’t just him, either. It was his whole family. The Archer brothers and their great-uncle, Waylon, had pitched in more than was expected. One brother in particular.

Kol.

The second eldest of the bunch had been the one to find me that day. The one I’d learned had kept looking, even though every law enforcement officer thought I was dead. He’d kept searching because something hadn’t sat right with him. *He’d* been the one to save me—in more ways than one.

“Morning,” I finally forced out. My voice still sounded a bit rusty, as if I’d taken up smoking while being held captive.

Owen grinned at me. “Supernova. We’re making cookies and cream strawberry pancakes. They’re my favorite! Have you ever had them before?”

My smile came a little easier then, felt a little more *real*. It always did with Owen. Because he was the coolest kid around. “I haven’t, but—”

“I’ve got a green smoothie and scrambled eggs for you,” Brae hurried to say as she moved around me in the kitchen, careful not to come close to touching me.

No one ever touched me now.

My mouth pursed as I tried to hold back the words I wanted to spew. Instead, I simply said, “I think I’ll do the pancakes.” My gaze flicked to Dex. “If there’s enough.”

He shot me a grin, even if it was a little strained. “There’s a mountain here. I’d love some help demolishing them.”

“But the doctor said you should focus on nutrient-rich foods and nothing too heavy—”

"Hellion," Dex said softly, giving my best friend a gentle-yet-pointed look.

A muscle fluttered in Brae's cheek. "I just want her to follow the doctor's instructions and get back to full strength. A green smoothie and scrambled eggs are healthier options, and—"

"Strawberries are super healthy," Owen pointed out helpfully.

I'd made the mistake of letting Brae stay during my final doctor's visit at the rehabilitation center. She'd taken notes like she was about to be grilled on every piece of information. Now, she wouldn't let me bend a single guideline. So much so that I'd even taken to hiding my favorite wild berry Skittles in my bedroom.

"B," I said quietly. "I can handle my meals. And I don't think having pancakes is going to send me hurtling backward."

"But—"

"Pancake party, it is," Dex said, cutting Brae off again.

She sent him a look that had more guilt swirling inside me. The last thing I needed was the weight of knowing I was putting a strain on my best friend's relationship.

Owen started sing-chanting, "pancake party," over and over.

"I'm just gonna shower real quick." I turned and hustled out of the kitchen before Brae could ask if I needed help.

I knew she meant well, but the constant micromanaging was stifling. Some days, it felt like there wasn't a single moment when there wasn't eyes on me, no time when I didn't have to keep my guard up.

Except when I went flying. When the adrenaline poured through my system and the freezing-cold water reminded me that I could breathe. That I was alive. Just like Kol's words promised.

Slipping into my bedroom, I closed the door behind me and tried to settle. It didn't work. I could hear Dex's and Brae's muted words in the other room, feel the strain in them. The walls seemed like they were closing in on me. All the belongings that had once been mine but now felt like a stranger's were strangling me.

I wanted to scream. I wanted to let loose one so loud it would tear down the forest and break the sound barrier. But I didn't.

I swallowed it all down and just leaned against the door.

A flash of something flared in my mind: hands around my throat. Squeezing. Cutting off my air. Making dark spots dance in front of my vision.

"No one's even looking for you. You're so forgettable, they don't even care."

A wave of dizziness swept through me as I struggled to keep my balance. I couldn't breathe. Everything was too tight. Too close.

I tore at my clothes, but they stuck to my skin, the wet material feeling like suffocating cement. I clawed, nails raking over my flesh until the T-shirt slapped against the wood floor. I fitfully yanked at my bathing suit top. The straps and ties were too complicated for my brain to process, so I tore at it until something snapped and it fell to the floor.

My chest heaved, breaths coming in short pants as everything burned. "You're…breathing…you're…alive…"

But I didn't believe the words this time. They didn't feel true.

The only thing I could feel was those hands around my throat. I just didn't know if it was a nightmare or a memory. But maybe it didn't matter. Because some days, it felt like I was walking through a living nightmare anyway.

Chapter Two

KOL

"Are we ready to rock?" I asked, looking down at my daughter, who always kept me on my toes. Especially when it came to her attire.

Skylar hadn't disappointed this time. She wore a plastic tiara, complete with pink and purple gemstones, paired with tactical goggles, making her blond hair stick out in a haphazard array. She had a magenta feather boa over her camo shirt that read: *Don't Mess with Me, I've Got Uncles*. And she did. Four, to be exact. And any one of them would do anything to keep her from harm.

She'd completed the outfit with a purple tutu and combat boots. Equal parts princess and warrior. And 100 percent Skylar.

She lowered the goggles over her eyes. "Let's smash some stuff."

I swallowed back a chuckle. "I hate to break it to you, Little Princess, but we are past the smashing phase and into the rebuilding one."

"Aw, man," she complained.

This time, I couldn't hold back my laugh as I crouched to her level. "But look at all we've accomplished."

I scanned the garage attic, trying to see it through my girl's eyes. She'd helped me in fits and starts before getting bored and seeking entertainment with her besties: Tink, the mini-Highland cow, and Pepper, the goat. But I was damn proud of all we'd accomplished.

"It looks..." Skylar's nose scrunched. "Empty."

My mouth curved. "That means it's time to build it back up." And I had a specific vision in mind. Just in case.

Sky looked up at me with mischief in her eyes. "Do I get to use the big saw?"

I tried not to let my overprotective streak strangle my response. Letting out a breath, I studied my eight-year-old. "What are the rules?"

She instantly stood at attention. "Hands only where you say. Goggles on. Never use power tools with Uncle Mav."

I pressed my lips together to keep from laughing at the last rule, even though it was probably the most important one, given my youngest brother's reckless nature. "All right, then. Let's do this."

I helped Skylar onto the stool where she could help me position the two-by-four. Her hands wouldn't be anywhere near the table saw blade, but she would still feel like she was a part of things. Empowering her with knowledge and skills that she could carry with her for the rest of her life was one of my favorite things.

"Let's chop it, Daddy!" she said gleefully.

Grinning, I started up the saw, and we began sliding the piece of wood across the table, perfectly in line with the mark I'd traced. The moment we made the cut, I flipped off the saw. Sky took one half, and I took the other.

Setting the piece on the floor, she flipped her boa over her shoulder. "Teamwork makes the dream work."

"Couldn't do it without you."

She beamed up at me. "That's because I'm the best helper around."

"That, you are."

And she proved it by helping for the next hour until she got bored.

"Can I go play ninja warrior with Tink and Pepper now? I put in a hard day's work."

I coughed to cover my laugh. "A *real* long one, huh?"

She blew out a breath. "The longest."

"Go play. I'll have an ice-cold chocolate milk waiting for you when you're done."

"Better make it a double."

That had me groaning. Having an uncle who owned a bar had its downsides.

But Skylar was already grabbing her Nerf gun and running down the stairs.

I knew the sounds by heart: her footsteps on the staircase, when they hit the final landing, the back door to the deck slamming.

A peal of laughter lit the air then, a different sort of noise—the kind I always loved to hear. I straightened to peer out one of the back windows. My natural inclination was to check on my daughter, but her laughter always called to me. I never knew what I'd find.

Tink, the mini-Highland cow, let out a bellowed moo and raced in a circle. Sky dropped into a roll, letting a Nerf dart fly at the target across the yard. It hit the center of the bull's-eye.

The roll itself hadn't been careful. She'd hit the ground with enough force to jar her tiny form, making me wince. I crossed to the window and leaned out of it. "Careful, Little Princess. Precious cargo, remember?"

Sky flipped up her tactical goggles. "Gotta roll with the bumps to get where you're going."

My eyes narrowed. "Says who?"

"Grampa Way Way."

Of course he had. My great-uncle, Waylon, was many wonderful things. The kind of generous that meant giving a home to five brothers whose world had been ripped apart in the worst possible way. The sort of protective that meant putting any townsperson in their place without a second thought for sending one of us Archers a side-eye. The type of caring that meant making sure all of us had the kind of support we needed as we healed.

Even to this day, his home, Twisted Oak Ranch, was a refuge for most of us. Orion, Maverick, and I all had homes here. And Dex was in the process of building his with Brae. The only holdout was Wylder, who had an apartment over his bar. But Waylon had truly given us all a place where we could simply be, without fear or prying eyes.

He was also reckless with a side of being a character and a half. And I constantly had to make sure he wasn't getting my daughter involved in something that could result in broken bones or an arrest record.

"Grampa Way Way also had you combing the woods for Bigfoot tracks for three hours yesterday. Maybe he's not the best person to be taking advice from."

Sky grinned, exposing a missing tooth that was just starting to grow back, and made some sort of *Star Trek* sign. "The truth is out there."

"You sound like Uncle Mav," I shot back.

"You mean she sounds like a *genius*," a new voice cut in, and I turned to find my youngest brother, Maverick, filling the entryway to the garage attic. We were just about the same height, hovering around six foot four, but Mav's form was slightly leaner than mine. It came from his hours working on wildfires and house fires alike—all that gear weighing him down day after day.

"Uncle Mav!" Skylar shouted from below. "Come play target practice with me and Tink."

Mav grinned as he joined me at the window, eyeing the target. "Sweet shot, Little Princess. I'll be down in a minute."

Sky gave him a salute and headed into another roll that made my spine ache.

Maverick shook his head. "You know, she scares me a little."

"She should," I grumbled. Though I was grateful for it in many ways. My girl could protect herself. Being raised by six men with no feminine influence to speak of meant that Skylar was a commando with a glittery twist. The blend was uniquely her. But I couldn't help but fear that I wasn't giving her something she needed.

It was just one of the many worries that kept me up at night. What would happen when she got her period or had her first crush? Would she feel comfortable talking to me about that sort of thing? Would she resent me if she ever found out why her mother had really dropped her on my doorstep and refused to be a part of either of our lives?

"Earth to Kol...are you having some sort of stroke?"

I snapped back to the here and now at Mav's voice. "Sorry. Spaced."

One corner of Mav's mouth lifted as his dark-hazel eyes—the ones we all shared—sparked with mischief. "I really hope you don't space while holding power tools."

I scowled in his direction. "Only with your hand in the path of the saw."

Maverick shook said hand as if he'd hit it. "Sky must get her ruthlessness from you."

My gut twisted. That's what her mother would've said.

"It should serve as a good reminder not to mess with me."

"Who says I'm here to mess with you?" Mav asked, affronted.

"Your general presence at any given time."

Maverick was always on the lookout for trouble. It usually came in the form of some adrenaline-inducing sport. Everything from BASE jumping to free climbing to skydiving. He was on a mission to live life to its fullest. Some part of me knew it was because he'd come so close to losing it. But I shoved that thought down. Because if I thought about how close Mav had come to dying, how close *all* my brothers had, I'd be forced to think about how I'd failed them all.

"I was coming to check on my big bro. Wanted to see what he's been locking himself away with during the *rare* moments he's not working these days," Maverick challenged.

I couldn't help but wince. I'd been logging some seriously long hours as of late. Ever since that day—the day I'd found Nova.

The image haunted my waking hours and the few sleeping ones I managed to grab. Her emaciated form *chained* to a goddamn tree. Her pleading words: *"Let me go."* They were etched in my mind forever.

And all of it together was the reason I was working those long hours after Sky went to bed. The monster who'd tortured Nova might've been dispatched to hell where he belonged, but that wasn't enough for me. I needed *all* the answers, to know everyone Travis Moore had hurt. Killed. Whether there were more victims we had yet to find.

I was just grateful that my role as a Forest Service investigator allowed me to stay on the case. The truth was that the nearest California State Police office was an hour away, which made it hard to have boots on the ground. And our Juniper County Sheriff's Department was in disarray after one of their officers had turned out to be a serial killer and their sheriff had been involved with an illegal drug operation. I'd become the best—and really, the only—option for continuing the investigation.

I sent Mav a pointed look. "You know why those hours are long."

"I'm just giving you shit," he said quickly. "You got anything new?"

He wasn't quite as invested as I was. No one could be. Not when I was the one who'd found her. I was the one who'd held her hand as she slipped into unconsciousness. The one who'd filled her lungs with air when they stopped working. No one could feel the weight of this case as much as I did.

But my brothers were trying to help. In the ways they always did. Ways that skirted the legalities of the system but were necessary to help those who had disappeared and been forgotten.

It was our way of atoning for crimes that had never been ours. Our way of helping to balance out the atrocities our father committed.

We never talked about the *why*. But that didn't mean we didn't understand it. We'd each come to terms with our trauma in our own way, dealing however we could. But this was the one thing we did together: Looking for people who'd been lost. Trying to bring closure for them and their loved ones—something our father's victims never got until it was far too late.

"I'm looking at a new unsolved case." I leaned the two-by-four against the bare drywall. "Missing hiker. Twenty-six. Similar look to Nova."

Just saying the words had fury flaring back to life inside me. I could see her in my mind—the Nova she was today. She'd slowly been putting on weight, looking healthier. Her dark, nearly black hair gleamed when the sun hit it now. Her silver-gray eyes had a spark in them, reminding me just how much of a fighter she was.

"Shit," Mav muttered.

"Swear jar," I warned.

He rolled his eyes. "Sky can't hear me. And I hate to break it to you, but I'm pretty sure she's heard the word *shit* before."

I glared at my brother. "Just because she's heard it before doesn't mean she needs to memorize it."

"Yeah, yeah." Mav waved me off. "Missing hiker. You upload the deets to our app?"

The app was something our computer-genius brother, Dex, had designed. It was a place where we could organize our case files—and house all the tips about those cases. We called the app and the shadow organization the Hourglass Network.

"Not yet. I need to verify she's a possible."

Maverick nodded. "And, in the meantime, you...what? Became Bob the Builder?"

That glare was back on my face. "I like building stuff."

He arched a brow. "I mean, you made a mean playhouse for the little princess, but this is kind of next-level."

My gaze swept across the space over the garage. I'd brought it down to the studs and was building it back up, complete with larger windows and a skylight. Things that would make it feel open and the opposite of confining.

"I needed a project. It helps me think," I said, defending myself. And that was true. I just didn't want to think too much about what my other reasons might be.

"What are you going to use it for? Sky moving out?"

Just the reminder that my girl would indeed do that one day had my stomach lurching. "Don't say that shit."

Mav barked out a laugh. "Dude, I can't wait until her first date. You're gonna stalk that kid."

A scowl twisted my lips. "She's not dating until she's twenty-five, at least."

His laughter only intensified. "Good luck with that. Your girl is adorable and funny as fuck. She's gonna be asked on a million dates before you know it."

Nausea rolled through me. "Take that back."

Mav just shook his head. "Prepare now."

I shot forward, trying to trap him in a headlock, but Maverick dodged my arm. He wasn't as successful when it came to my fist, which hit him in the kidney.

"Oh shit! That hurt, asshole." Mav hit me with a hook to the ribs.

I grabbed for his tee, trying to pull it over his head so it would blind him. "Don't talk about my daughter dating."

Maverick snort-laughed as the T-shirt covered his eyes. He twisted, trying to escape the offending fabric. "Fine, fine. Jesus. That's your trigger. I get it."

It and so many other things, for so many reasons. But that was the case for all of us.

Mav pulled his shirt back down as he straightened. "I was just stopping by to see if you heard that Nova got a job."

I bristled, every part of me going on alert. Nova was on a long road to recovery. Two weeks in the hospital. Three in a rehabilitation unit that worked on physical and occupational therapies. And now, outpatient treatment. "It's only been four months."

Maverick shrugged. "Dex said she's been dying to get back to some sense of normalcy."

I understood that: needing to find routine again. But this seemed a little quick.

"Wylder hired her at the Boot," Mav went on.

That had ice sliding through my veins. Our eldest brother owned a bar and grill in town. It was mostly safe, but in the later evening hours, things could occasionally get dicey. The idea of Nova in the midst of that didn't exactly sit right with me.

"When?" I growled.

Mav's lips twitched. "She starts today."

I was already moving. "Watch Sky."

"Where're you going?" Mav called, as I snatched up my keys and headed for the door.

When I didn't answer, he shouted after me, "Tell Supernova I said hi."

I just flipped him off. "Do not let my kid jump off the hayloft or ride in the pasture with no tack, understood?"

"Who me? I would never."

The hell he wouldn't. But it was a risk I was willing to take because something had created a bond between Nova and me that day. And now, I couldn't handle the idea of her being at risk. Not being okay. I needed to check for myself—even if that made me reckless. Because getting involved with a victim of a case in any personal capacity? It broke every rule in the book.

Chapter Three

NOVA

I FELT EYES ON ME. AGAIN.

I ignored the sensation. Even though it was like nails on a chalkboard. I stayed focused on the wind drifting in through the open window as Brae made the turn onto Mountain View Way, the street that would lead us directly into downtown Starlight Grove.

The main drag through town was aptly named because the moment we turned onto the street, Mount Lupine came into view, popping up in the distance. Snow already dotted its craggy peak, and the bracketing forests made it seem even more imposing.

But there was something about its beauty. The largeness of it. It reminded me that there were forces out there so much bigger than me.

I relished the realization that those forces ruled the world. They weren't good or evil; they were simply *life*. And life went on. Just like my breath did.

I felt eyes on me again, those nails scraping down the chalkboard.

"How are you feeling?" Brae asked as the sensation abated and she turned her gaze back to the road.

"Good." The answer came automatically, with zero check-in as to how I was *actually* feeling. An easy lie. Or maybe not. Though compared to what I'd been through, I *was* good.

Brae was quiet for a moment—the kind of silence that made me realize a chasm had erupted between me and my best friend. The one who used to know me better than anyone. Now, it felt like no one knew me…not even myself.

"Your eyes?" Brae pressed.

My sunglasses were firmly in place at the moment, but they still allowed me to take in the town around me. There were about twenty or so shops and restaurants in the downtown area. Starlight Grove was an old mining town that had made the switch to ranches when the gold dried up, but it still kept some of that Old-West aesthetic.

There was a mix of that western vibe, with aged brick buildings and ones that had an antique farmhouse feel. But all of it carried a clear sense of pride in the décor. Flowerpots and baskets. Some fall designs with leaves and pumpkins. Plenty of advertisements for town events.

The bookstore had a sign for an upcoming book club meeting. Several tourist shops advertised the homecoming football game. The bakery told folks that their s'mores pie was back.

"We should hit up the bakery after work," I said.

Brae's brow furrowed at my abrupt change of subject. "The bakery?"

"It says they have s'mores pie. I'm down for that."

Her mouth pursed, lines of disapproval etching themselves there. "Maybe."

Brae had transitioned from best friend to mother somewhere along the line, and I missed the hell out of my bestie. We'd worked summers at the same bar and grill in Rhode Island and had a blast. I wasn't sure I'd be able to say the same about working with her at the Boot. But I had to try.

"Or we could do boysenberry milkshakes at the Grove Griddle." There was a hint of desperation in my tone that had nothing to do with wanting to visit the town diner and everything to do with missing my partner in crime.

Brae made a humming noise as she pulled into a parking lot behind the Boot. The building itself was a stunner. It was made of aged wood so dark that it was almost black, but that only made the flowers potted in water troughs pop all the more. And the swinging doors on the front made it look like an honest-to-goodness saloon.

Brae swung into an empty parking spot but didn't turn off the engine. I braced as she turned to face me. She reached out as if she was going to place a hand on my forearm, and my breath caught in my lungs. I wasn't sure if I wanted her to touch me or if I was terrified by the idea of it. But it didn't matter because as quickly as she reached out, she snatched her hand back.

It hurt.

Even knowing *why* she'd retreated, it still felt like a dagger to the ribs. Dex had let it slip that I'd screamed bloody murder when Brae tried to hug me in the hospital and hadn't stopped until they sedated me.

I had no memory of the incident. Not even a flicker. That time was spotty at best. And I wasn't sure what was the truth and what was my imagination. Just like my time in captivity.

Now, no one touched me.

It only added to the tally of how long it had been since I had felt any sort physical kindness: A pat on the back. Fingers woven through mine. A hug.

I missed it.

But I was too scared to ask for it all the same. Because what if I freaked out again? That would seriously hinder my *I'm totally fine and don't need to be sent back to therapy* story.

"Nova?"

I jolted in my seat. "Sorry. Space cadet city."

Brae frowned. I swore she'd donned that expression more in the four months I'd been back than during the rest of her life combined. "Are you sure you're ready for this?"

The doubt etched into her face hurt just as much as her pulling back from the touch, but I just battled it with a smile. "Why wouldn't I be?"

Brae only stared back at me.

The blank stare hurt, too. More evidence of the distance between us.

Shoving open the SUV's door, I stepped into the sunlight. It still felt decently warm for late in September, but there was the slightest bite to the air that hadn't been there even a week ago. "Come on, these tips aren't going to earn themselves."

Brae hurried out of the vehicle. "You know I can cover you."

I hated the annoyance that flickered deep. Brae couldn't cover me. But Dex could. And that somehow made it worse, that this person who barely knew me had been paying my way. Pity money.

Heap it onto the pity job his eldest brother, Wylder, was giving me, and I owed the Archer brothers big-time. The family might've had a reputation around town, but they were all generous to a fault. One more generous than all the rest. The one who had given me hope when all of mine had vanished.

I turned to face my best friend, trying like hell to make her *see*. "I *want* to work. I'm ready. And if I have to sit in that house one more day twiddling my thumbs, I'm going to lose it."

"You don't sit in the house. You disappear and don't tell anyone where you're going."

There was an edge to Brae's words that hadn't been there since my return. But I understood. My disappearing acts had to be triggering. But sometimes, I needed to *breathe*. And I couldn't do that at the cabin, surrounded by people who were constantly wondering if I was okay.

She reeled in her reaction. "I'm sorry. I—"

"Don't apologize," I said quickly. "I get it."

But I didn't tell her that I wouldn't do it again. Because I knew I would. It was the only thing holding me together at the moment. Instead, I headed toward the back door with a *Staff Only* sign above it.

As I walked, I tugged on the sleeves of my blouse, making sure they covered my wrists—skin littered with scars. Marks left behind from shackles. At least, that's what the doctor had told me.

They ringed my wrists and ankles, evidence of what had happened to me. Proof that it hadn't been a nightmare. But it was just one more reason for people to wonder if I was okay. So I hid them the best I could.

My fingers closed around the door handle, and I pulled hard. My biceps struggled with the effort, but the door gave way, and I stepped inside, holding it for Brae. Her face was a careful mask now, but I did my best to ignore it. Instead, I followed her down the dimly lit hall, passing a stockroom, an office, and two bathrooms before stepping into the bar and grill's main room.

I wasn't sure if Wylder had had a hand in the décor or if he'd inherited the place as it was, but if he *had* been a part of it, he had a gift. The large space had booths lining three walls and tables in the middle, all of which were made from dark, warm wood similar to that on the outside of the building.

The walls were dotted with local signs and posters on two sides, most of which had a vintage feel to them. Another wall was covered in license plates from all over the country. I even saw Hawaii represented. And finally, there was the bar. It was a stop-you-in-your-tracks piece of woodworking, a true art form, made all the more striking by the beautiful array of bottles lining the shelves behind it.

Music filtered out through the speakers and into the mostly empty space, a blend of country and rock that fit the patrons I assumed would be there. It was my first time inside, so I couldn't be completely sure, but it fit with the locals I was starting to get to know.

"Nova." A deep voice greeted me.

I turned to see the eldest Archer brother striding across the space. Wylder didn't exactly fit his name. There was a quiet steadiness to him. He certainly wasn't shy, but he also didn't speak unless he had something he truly considered worth saying.

But that didn't mean he wasn't paying attention. I'd learned over dozens of family dinners, movie nights, and other occasions that Wylder's brain worked faster than the rest of ours. It made connections many of us missed. I'd be sitting around a dinner table with him not saying a word, and then he'd come out of left field with a zinger that said he'd been following the whole convo.

I grinned at him as he approached. "Hi. Thanks for hiring me."

"You don't have to keep thanking me," he grumbled as he ran a hand through his rumpled, dark hair.

My lips twitched. "I like to thank people for the nice things they do."

"I needed another waitress," Wylder argued.

"It's still nice that you let me be that waitress," I shot back.

"Yeah, yeah," he mumbled.

My brow arched. "Not one for thank-yous?"

A hand slapped down on Wylder's shoulder as a man in his mid-thirties appeared at his side. "Hates thank-yous and praise of any sort. But I'm going to thank him anyway." The man turned to Wylder. "Thank you for hiring this absolute bombshell of a babe, boss. Especially since Brae got engaged to your brother and broke my damn heart."

"Aidan..." Wylder warned.

But I couldn't help but laugh.

"At least you're still hot and single." Aidan's blue-green eyes danced as he winked at Wylder and then turned to me. "Nova, I'm Aidan. Let me be your guide to the Boot. I will set you on the path to big tips with as little work as possible."

Brae let out a choked sound of amusement. "What he means is, if you flirt with every human that enters the premises, your tips will be huge. Or you'll end up with a beer dumped on your head."

Aidan shook his head. "Come on now, B. You know I never get a drink dumped on me. My skills are too good for that."

"I don't know," Wylder argued. "That elderly lady tossed her sweet tea on you when you flirted with her granddaughter."

"And don't forget the couple that came down from Portland. Wasn't his name James? He did not appreciate you asking for his husband's number," Brae added.

Aidan winced. "I might've miscalculated there. I thought they were brothers, not married. I'm still trying to get the grenadine out of that tee."

I pressed my lips together to keep from laughing again. "It's nice to meet you, Aidan. I'll be sure to take no dating advice from you."

"Oh, you should definitely take dating advice from me. Like letting me take you out dancing on Friday night—"

"Aidan," Wylder clipped. "What's the rule?"

Aidan scowled at his boss. "No dating anyone employed by the Boot or you."

Wylder let out a huff. "Correct." His gaze flicked to me. "I lost too many good people because of their broken hearts."

Aidan sighed. "Too handsome for my own good."

"You and Maverick need your egos examined," Brae muttered.

"Ain't that the truth?" a new voice cut in. The woman who entered our huddle looked to be in her early sixties, with ruddy cheeks and a warm smile. Her dark hair was threaded through with silver, and the lines around her green eyes said that warm smile appeared often.

Brae grinned back at her. "Fiona, meet my best friend, Nova. Nova, this is Fiona, part-time cook, part-time waitress."

"All-the-time keeper of these fools," Fiona amended. "Nice to meet you. Call me Fiona or Fee. I answer to both."

"Lovely to meet you, Fiona."

I expected her to move forward and extend a hand for a shake, but she didn't. Neither had Aidan nor Wylder. And I knew then that warnings had been given. No touching.

Embarrassment washed over me, the emotion tinged with shame. Like every person here had seen my deepest, darkest secrets—things that even I didn't understand. I suddenly felt a little nauseous.

Keep it together.

I chanted the words over and over. Because if I lost it now, Brae would lock me up in the cabin for sure. There'd be no job, no outings, and she'd drive me back to that damned therapist, who looked at me like I was a science experiment.

You're alive. You're breathing.

I held on to that refrain like a lifeline.

"Where's Cora?" Brae asked.

The vibe in the group shifted, the air going charged at the name.

It was enough to bring me back to the here and now. Because I'd been bracing for this, too. Meeting the woman.

Wylder's gaze shifted slightly. "She might be running a little late. I'm sure—"

"I'm here," a new voice interjected—a little too brightly. "Sorry I'm late. I spilled coffee on myself and had to change and put my shirt in to soak, but it might be too late for that one." She sucked in air as she came to a stop outside our huddle, her green eyes coming to me.

I didn't miss the way Wylder took in everything about the woman as if checking for invisible injuries.

"Hi," Cora greeted, but the single syllable was more of a squeak than anything.

"Hi," I parroted. It was all I could get out as I surveyed her. Cora was probably around my age of twenty-seven, give or take a year or two. Her light-brown hair was pulled back into a loose braid, and while she wore light makeup, I could see the dark circles peeking out.

Lack of sleep. Something I knew well. And then I saw it, the emotion brewing in her eyes. The thing she was trying so desperately to cover with that warm smile.

Guilt.

Because my captor, my tormentor—the man who'd kidnapped and killed at least eight people—had been the love of her life. The one who'd gotten off on watching the loved ones of those missing persons fall apart. Used his role as an investigator with the sheriff's department to insert himself into every investigation so he could watch it all up close and personal. A monster.

But as I looked at the woman opposite me, I realized something. I wasn't the only survivor of Travis's reign of terror. Cora was, too. And just like me, she was trying to pick up the pieces.

That eased something in me, but at the same time, it broke my heart. Still, it made my smile turn more genuine. Because I wanted to reassure her somehow. "It's really nice to meet you."

Breath left Cora's lungs in a visible exhale. Relief. "You too."

Wylder watched the exchange. "Well, now that everyone has met, let's get this show on the road. Nova, you'll shadow Brae for the first couple of hours, and then you should be able to start taking tables on your own. I'll be behind the bar if anyone needs me."

"Aw, man," Aidan muttered. "I wanted Nova to shadow me."

"I want her to learn *good* work habits," Wylder shot back.

Aidan just shook his head. "Harsh, boss man. Harsh."

Cora chuckled, the sound a little rusty but like she was trying to find the light around her. I understood that, too.

I followed Brae to a cabinet behind the bar, where we stashed our belongings. As I secured my sunglasses case in my purse, I hoped my eyes would hold up okay. The bar wasn't overly bright, but I'd never gone more than a few hours without giving my eyes a break.

Because I was used to living in the dark. And I couldn't go even a few hours without a reminder of that.

Straightening, I steeled my spine and followed Brae to unlock the doors.

Today's crowd probably wouldn't be *that* huge—it was past the heart of tourist season in Starlight Grove. People mostly came to town for the outdoor activities: fishing, rafting, biking, rock climbing, hiking.

That's what had brought Brae and me here originally. A girls' weekend of eating, wine tasting, massages, and what was supposed to be a beautiful hike. One that had ended with Travis Moore kidnapping me.

I shook off the reminder and followed Brae around as she started her duties, getting a few folks seated and starting drink orders. After we dropped off two Cokes to a couple of tourists, we headed to a table of what looked like locals: two women who appeared to be in their eighties, assessing me with a single-minded focus.

"Good afternoon, ladies. How are you doing?" Brae greeted.

One of the women wore a shirt that read *Knitting So I Don't Stab Someone.* She set her menu down and grinned at Brae. "Just lovely now that things are cooler. How are you, dear?"

"Just fine, Miss Patricia. This is my friend, Nova. She's shadowing me today to learn the ropes," Brae informed her.

The second woman's eyes narrowed on me—not in a mean way but in an assessing one. "Nova? Are you the girl that—?"

"Maisy," Patricia hissed.

Maisy let out a huff. "I'm just surprised she'd want to work *here*. That's all."

What the heck did that mean? She didn't think I'd want to work in a bar? I guessed it made sense. Maybe she thought I needed to work in a library or at an accounting office. Somewhere quiet, where I wouldn't startle. I'd have to get used to people making assumptions about my recovery.

Brae's mouth thinned into a hard line. "Can I get either of you something to drink while you're looking at the menu?"

Patricia's cheeks reddened, clearly embarrassed by her friend. "I'd love an Arnold Palmer. Thank you, Brae."

Maisy clearly gave zero fucks and simply tapped her fingers on the table as she stared at me. "I'll take a Coke. Glad you're okay, Nova. That must've been quite an ordeal—"

"All right, then," Brae cut in. "We'll get those right out to you."

I followed Brae toward the bar.

"This is exactly what I was afraid of," she mumbled. "People are going to hound you the second they find out who you are."

"Maybe I should come up with a fake name. I always thought I'd make a good Sharleen."

"It's not funny," Brae spat.

I shrugged. "People are curious. I get it. I probably would be, too. I know how to dodge folks if I need to."

"Good luck with Miss Maisy," Brae grumbled.

"I can handle her. Let me prove it." I moved to the waitstaff end of the bar and gave Wylder the ladies' drink orders. He filled them in a matter of seconds, and then I was off to the table.

"Here you go, ladies," I said, depositing their glasses. "Do you know what you'd like to order?"

Maisy's gaze roamed over me. "How long have you been out of the hospital?"

She was bold, I'd give her that. "I can tell you one thing: The food here is a heck of a lot better than what they serve there. I especially recommend the bacon cheeseburger."

Patricia's lips twitched, knowing exactly what I was doing. "You know, that sounds perfect. I'll do the bacon cheeseburger, medium, and sweet potato fries."

"You got it. Miss Maisy?"

The second woman let out a huff of annoyance. "I'll do the chicken bacon ranch salad and curly fries."

"Coming right up," I said, taking their menus and heading to put in the order.

Brae watched me as I moved. I just had to hope that, with time, she'd trust that I could handle this—and that I wouldn't turn out to be a liar.

Everything hurt. It had only been three hours, and my entire body felt like I'd run a marathon. I was happy as hell that I'd opted for sneakers, but my feet still felt like they'd taken a pounding. My lower back. My arms. My head. My eyes. Everything throbbed.

But I wasn't even close to being done for the day, and I wasn't about to let anyone know I was dying.

Cora had been keeping her distance, but I didn't miss how her gaze flicked to me every so often. Checking in? Or maybe just wanting to know more about the woman her fiancé had held captive for over a year. But now, she finally crossed my way.

"Insoles."

My brows drew together. "What?"

"Insoles for your shoes. They save my back. I can show you the ones I order when we're done with our shift or things quiet down."

Things had been surprisingly busy. But after an hour of working with Brae, I had been ready to go out on my own. And that was a relief and a half—just like this small act of kindness was.

"Thank you," I said, giving Cora a small smile. "You're a lifesaver."

Something flickered in her expression. Pain, I realized. I wanted to kick myself for my choice of words.

"Hey, babe," a voice called out.

I winced at the moniker. The table of three guys who were packing away some beers with their lunches was my least favorite table of the day.

"I'd better get that," I mumbled.

Cora nodded, turning back to her own table.

I straightened my shoulders and turned to the three guys who wore T-shirts for a landscaping company. The idea of them pounding beers and then operating heavy machinery didn't fill me with joy. But maybe they had a half day.

"What can I get you?" I asked the man who'd bellowed. They all had their food, and no one had an empty glass.

His gaze raked over me in a way that had me fighting a shiver. "I missed you, babe. You're leaving us hanging."

My back teeth ground together. "Well, here I am. Do you need a soda or a water?"

The man's friend snickered, not helping the situation.

"Shot of Jack," man number one demanded, leaning in closer. "Don't make me wait. I wouldn't want to miss you."

Miss you.

Those two words clanged around in my head, shaking something loose.

Hot breath on my face. Hands closing around my neck. Squeezing. "No one even misses you. They're not even looking. They don't care at all."

A wave of dizziness hit me, right along with the memory. Or was it something my imagination had conjured up? I had no idea. And that only made the disorientation worse.

"Nova. Everything okay over here?" Wylder's deep voice cut into my spiral.

"All good," I forced out, the words sounding rough. "This gentleman needs a shot of Jack."

Wylder's dark-hazel gaze narrowed on the man, surveying the

beers and doing some sort of mental calculation. "I'll get you that as long as you'll also let me call you a cab."

The idea of a cab in such a small town was comical, but Brae had told me there was exactly one cab company with two to three drivers at any given time.

Bellowing man stiffened. "I can hold my liquor just fine, Archer."

"Might be the case, but I've got rules to follow." Wylder turned to me. "Why don't you take your break? I've got this table."

Shit. I didn't want Wylder thinking I couldn't handle myself. But as I opened my mouth, another wave of dizziness hit. *"No one even misses you."*

"Sure," I croaked, already moving despite the guys' protests.

I wove through the tables, my vision going a little blurry. *Shit. Shit. Shit.* I needed to breathe. But the air in here wasn't the right kind of air. Too warm. Too stale. The scents all wrong. I needed to get out.

I fumbled down the hallway until a voice pulled me up short. "Nova."

Two syllables, roughly spoken. Like a gruff command or a barbed lasso.

I turned as if I had no control over my body.

And there he was.

He tended to do that: show up exactly when I needed him. Like he had some sort of radar for my trauma responses.

He moved in closer. Just close enough that I caught the scent of him—pine and cedar and fresh air. Like the mountains clung to him. Maybe because he practically lived out there and rarely came inside.

I looked up into the eyes of the man who'd saved me. Some might think his dark-hazel eyes were identical to his four brothers, but they'd be wrong. His were different. There were flecks so dark they were almost black, and then flecks of light. The kind of gold that held hope. He was a balance of both—the light and the dark.

Kol Archer. His name had that same balance: the light and the dark. Everything about him was a blend. Brains and brawn. Gentleness and power. Stillness and movement.

"Are you okay?" His question was low, barely audible over the music and voices, yet deafening at the same time.

Maybe it was the powerful blend of all that was Kol that had me answering. Or perhaps it was the fact that he'd brought me back from hell itself and we'd bonded there. Either way, my lips spilled my secrets to the man with the haunted eyes.

"Everyone's watching." Another wave of dizziness hit me. "There are eyes on me all the time. I can't flounder for a single second without them all rushing in and trying to fix it. I know it's because they care, and I should be grateful, but I—" The dizziness intensified. "I—" The right words wouldn't come. "I can't even…"

"Breathe?"

It was a single word that Kol supplied, but it was the exact right one.

"I can't breathe."

It was the ultimate confession, and he was the only one I could admit it to. But it was the truth. I couldn't breathe.

Chapter Four

KOL

I WOULD'VE GIVEN ANYTHING IN THAT MOMENT TO GIVE NOVA back her breath. To give her air. To breathe for her.

"Come with me." The words were out of my mouth before I could stop them. It was a mistake. I knew it, but I didn't care.

I'd been careful not to be alone with Nova. Ever. I might've edged close to the rule line, but this took us into serious bending territory. You didn't establish a personal relationship with a victim. Especially when you were still working the case they were involved in. Travis Moore might be dead, but we were still untangling his web and making sure we identified all his victims.

But Nova's pain was too much for me to bear, and I'd do anything to ease it.

Her gray eyes flared in surprise at my soft command. A hint of silver flickered in their depths—the kind that promised that life and fight were still sparking there. And God, it was a beautiful thing to see.

She followed me down the hallway, sticking to my side. But I didn't touch her. I made sure there were at least six inches between us at all times.

I kept that space for more reasons than just keeping myself within the lines of rules and regulations. I'd seen what had happened at the hospital. I'd been just outside her room when Nova started to scream—the kind that sounded like she was dying.

I'd rushed into the room to see tears streaking down Brae's face as Dex pulled her away. But Nova hadn't stopped screaming—not until a nurse came running and slid something into Nova's IV that pulled her under.

"I just…I hugged her."

Brae's pained words had stuck with me. They'd stuck with us all. Now, we were careful around Nova. Careful not to cross any invisible boundary.

But the Archer brothers knew how to toe those lines. That's what happened when you had a brother who processed trauma by retreating, by not speaking and refusing any forms of touch. We found ways to meet Orion where he was. And we'd do the same for Nova.

I pushed open the back door that led to the small parking lot behind the Boot. Sucking in air, I relished the feeling of being outside again. I always felt more at home when not fenced in by four walls.

Holding the door for Nova, I waited. She stepped outside, instantly tipping her head back as if searching for the sun. The rays hit the apples of her cheeks and glinted off the nearly black strands of her hair she had pulled back in a braid.

I forced my gaze away from her and all that beauty and focused on the forest beyond the parking lot. It wasn't the kind of wilderness I typically lost myself in. When I needed wild, I went deep into the mountains. *That* was the kind of wilderness where you could go without encountering another soul for days. Where the silence was deafening, yet the one place I could finally hear my voice.

But I didn't have wild like that at my fingertips. I'd have to settle for this instead.

I strode across the parking lot, trusting that Nova would follow.

And she did. I could make out her lighter, sneaker-clad footsteps in between my heavier work-boot-clad ones.

The moment my boots hit the dirt, something in me relaxed. Just a fraction. But it was enough.

I took a handful of steps farther into the trees, stopping between an aspen and a spruce. I turned to take Nova in. Her face was a little pale, and her hands trembled at her sides. That shaking pissed me the hell off. The last thing she deserved was to be scared.

"Take your shoes off." A little of that pissed off slipped into my tone, even though I didn't mean for it to.

Nova arched a brow. "You know, you have a real bossy, grouchy thing going on right now. *Come with me. Take your shoes off.* Have you ever heard of the word *please*?"

My lips wanted to twitch. Hell, it was a relief to see that fire. To be so close to it. I could feel it licking at my skin. "Take off your shoes, *please*."

Nova crossed her arms. "Why?"

I sighed and bent over, unlacing one boot and then the other. I could feel Nova's eyes on me, watching every single movement. Even though we were in sight of the back door to the Boot and within shouting distance of main street, I knew that her being here with me, alone, meant trust. And I didn't take that for granted.

My fingers slipped into one sock, and I pulled it free before moving to the other. My feet pressed against the pine-needle-covered dirt, and I felt freer. I crossed to the aspen tree and placed my palm against the trunk.

If my brothers saw me doing this, I'd never hear the end of it. They'd call it woo-woo bullshit, but I knew the truth: Nature healed. It was more powerful than any other tool we had at our disposal if we just listened.

I locked eyes with Nova and held the stare for one, two beats, and then closed mine. I pressed my feet harder to the earth as I flexed my fingers against the tree bark. And then I breathed.

In and out. Over and over. I let the sound of the wind guide me, calm me.

And then I opened my eyes again.

Nova's silver gaze was rapt. Not focusing on my feet, hands, or even my face but on my chest. She was watching me breathe.

"Try it." My voice was softer now. Gentle. Coaxing.

Nova took two steps forward. She toed off one sneaker and then the other. Her socks were purple with pink polka dots. Happy socks. But when she pulled one off, I caught a flash of the scars in various stages of healing: from red and raised to silvery and slick.

That rage was back, the reminder that she'd been fucking chained to a wall for over a year before being chained to that tree for nearly a week with no food or water. I'd seen the cell. The makeshift bathroom with its shower and toilet. The stained mattress on the floor. The chains.

I shoved all the fury down. Because this wasn't about me. It was about Nova.

Her gaze flicked up to my face, humor lighting her eyes as she pulled off her second sock. "Do you have some kind of foot fetish I should know about?"

I shook my head. "Nova."

She dropped the sock to the dirt. "What now, Boss?"

I took a breath and met her gaze. "Palm on the tree."

"Bossy." But Nova still did as I asked and rested her hand just below mine with only about an inch separating our fingers. Hers were so much smaller than mine—delicate and slender. Mine curled around nearly half the trunk with gnarled knuckles that mirrored the knots in the bark. But we both had scars. Mine from countless construction projects and time spent outdoors. And hers? I wasn't sure I wanted to know.

"Close your eyes," I whispered.

A hint of panic lit those silver eyes, and the urge to touch her, to give some sort of comfort, was almost overpowering. But I didn't.

"Keep them open. It's okay. I just want you to feel—the earth beneath your feet. The energy there. Your palm against the tree, the life bleeding into you. And *breathe*. Let all that life force guide you."

Nova's fingers flexed around the tree trunk, pressing in. Her toes, painted a sunshine yellow, dug into the pine needles beneath her feet. I heard her inhale—sharp at first and then easier, in and out, her chest rising and falling. Everything started to even out. Steady. Deep.

"I'm breathing," she whispered.

"You're breathing."

Her eyes found mine. "Why does that help?"

I shrugged, my hand falling away from the tree, almost grazing hers, but not. "Makes you focus on things other than whatever's taking over your mind. It would be better if we were in an actual forest instead of at the edge of town."

A smile tugged at Nova's lips. Not one of the fake ones she wore so often but a *real* one. "I'm picturing you going all yogi out in the middle of the wilderness, Kol."

Fuck.

Her saying my name did something to me—something I did not need to acknowledge in any way, shape, or form.

"I don't bend that way, Phoenix."

Her eyes sparked at the nickname—one I'd never uttered aloud before. But a phoenix was exactly what I'd started to think of Nova as. She'd risen from the ashes, and she was more powerful than ever. People might not think of her that way. They might see her as damaged or broken. But I knew the truth.

She was a survivor. She'd crawled back from death itself. And she was still *here*.

"We all start somewhere," she said with a grin. "I could teach you a few pretzel twists."

Movement caught my attention—the Boot's back door opening, just beyond the trees. Wylder and Brae stepped out, searching.

Wylder's gaze found us first, instantly assessing in that way he always did. He said his years of working in a bar had given him insight into people. But I thought my eldest brother had some innate gift that allowed him to see more than the rest of the world.

Nova turned and followed my gaze. "I'd better get back to work before I get fired on my first day."

Some part of me wanted to tell her not to go. And what the hell was that instinct?

"Wylder won't fire you," I muttered.

Nova's lips pursed as if she didn't like that, which made no sense. But instead of arguing with me, she donned her socks and shoes and started walking.

I hurried to follow her, not bothering to tie the laces on my boots.

Worry lines furrowed Brae's brow as we approached. "Are you okay? Did something happen?"

"I'm fine. Why?" Nova replied, easy-breezy, as if her panic attack had never happened.

Brae frowned. "You were barefoot in the woods, looking all intense."

Nova tucked a strand of hair that had fallen out of her braid behind her ear. "I was trying to help Kol. He has a foot fungus. I heard pine needles help cure it."

My jaw went slack as I gaped at her.

Nova simply winked at me. "See you around, Boss."

Wylder let out a half laugh, half cough as he slapped me on the shoulder. "Good luck with that, buddy."

Chapter Five

NOVA

The wind ripped through my hair as I stood on the edge of the cliff. It was a violent kind of wind tonight. The kind that reminded you just how powerful nature was. I loved it.

The air battered my bare skin, nothing but the sports bra and underwear I wore protecting me. I hadn't put the swimsuit on. Told myself I didn't need it. I'd jumped that morning. It should've been enough of a fix for a few days at least.

But it wasn't.

Maybe it was all the half conversations with Brae. Or finally coming face-to-face with Cora. My first day at a job after so long. The memories or imaginings fighting against the walls of my mind.

It could've been any of it fueling that need. It could've been *all* of it.

All I knew was that I felt like I was going to crawl out of my skin. And the panic was swirling like an angry sea under a stormy sky, threatening to swallow me whole.

"I'm alive," I whispered into the wind. "I'm breathing."

And then I launched myself into the air, trusting that it would catch me. It did. Like always.

The air, colder now that it was twilight, whipped against my body. And then I hit the water, like a thousand tons of frigid force.

It was the kind that could drown you if you weren't careful. But I let it swallow me as it was the only thing that could beat back the panic. I submerged myself, going deeper and deeper, then cast my blurry gaze up to the surface. Broken light made its way through, but sometimes, that was all you needed—a fractured piece of hope to keep you pushing on.

My lungs lit like fire, spurring my legs into kicking. Harder and harder. But they were beyond fatigued after my first day of being on my feet for so long.

A hint of fear bled through the relief as my lungs seized. I broke the surface and sucked in air. The first breath hurt, but it did exactly what I needed it to. It reminded me that I was alive, breathing. That I was still here.

I didn't float this time. I kicked toward shore. My movements were awkward and jerky because my body was ready to give up. But I fought my way toward the beach.

Heaving myself out of the water, I slid my feet into my battered sneakers and made my way up the cliffside, my teeth starting to chatter as I wrung out my hair. An evening cliff jump might've been a mistake.

But as soon as the thought entered my mind, I knew it was wrong. Because even as my whole body hurt, the anxiety and panic were back down to that low hum, no longer threatening to strangle me.

I pulled on my leggings, tee, and sweatshirt, not exactly comfortable over my wet underwear, but the bike ride back to the cabin wasn't too terribly long. The wind in my wet hair wasn't my favorite sensation, but it punched that panic and anxiety even lower.

As I pulled up to the cabin, I saw movement behind the windows. Owen was jumping on the couch as Dex and Brae looked on, laughing. He held a video game controller over his head in some sort of victory dance. Dex wrapped an arm around Brae's shoulders and dropped a kiss to her temple.

She melted into him like it was the most natural thing in the world. Like it was exactly where she belonged. And it was.

I was the interloper.

Pain hit me hard and fast—the kind that stole your breath. And not in a good way like the water. This was a brutal sneak attack.

Because I wasn't sure *where* I belonged.

Swallowing hard, I leaned my bike against the steps and headed up them. I unlocked the front door and stepped inside to Owen yell-singing some made-up song about being the champion of an elven universe.

The second the door snicked closed, Brae was moving toward the entryway. Her gaze traveled over me, and her jaw went slightly slack. "You're soaking wet."

I shrugged, not having the energy to force one of those fake-ass smiles. "I went for a swim but forgot my towel."

"Nova. It's forty-seven degrees out. That water had to be freezing."

"It felt nice after a long day," I hedged, trying to sidestep my best friend.

"You could catch pneumonia. Your body's already fragile—"

"I'm not weak." The words whipped out of me like a slap.

Brae looked like I'd done worse than hit her. "I know," she whispered.

"I'm sorry. I..." There was nothing I could say. Everything I did seemed to hurt someone. Made them worry. I'd never felt more like a burden than in that moment.

Dex moved into the space, his arm sliding around Brae, giving the kind of comfort I wasn't sure I'd ever have again. "You should grab a hot shower. Nothing feels better after a lake swim."

He was trying to smooth the jagged edges for Brae and me. I appreciated it more than I could say, but it was like a Band-Aid on a bullet hole.

"Yeah," I croaked.

Owen leapt into the entryway. "We gotta go in thirty minutes."

I frowned. I never went anywhere. I could count on one hand the number of places I'd been. The local doctor's office for my check-ups. My physical therapist's practice. The grocery store. And now the Boot.

"I'm gonna teach you to feed the alpacas. Remember, Supernova?" Owen went on, practically bouncing in place.

I'd forgotten. There *was* one other place. Twisted Oak Ranch. Home to the Archer brothers. Well, their great-uncle, Waylon, anyway. And three of the brothers had homes on the property: Orion, whom I'd only seen once and who hadn't exactly been thrilled about my presence on the ranch; Maverick, the reckless Archer; and Kol.

Just thinking his name made my skin pebble. The cold and the wetness, that was all.

"I, uh—"

"Come," Brae said softly. "Waylon will be sad if you're not there."

"You gotta, Supernova! Maybe an alpaca will spit on you," Owen said hopefully.

Dex chuckled. "How can you say no to alpaca spit and whatever crazy Bigfoot story my great-uncle has up his sleeve?"

I couldn't. Not with Owen's hopeful eyes on me. I'd already missed too much of his life—a whole year. The first time I saw him after waking up in the hospital, he'd looked like an entirely different human. His blond hair was even lighter, thanks to all the time he spent outdoors here. His green eyes shone brighter because of how well cared for he was, and the blue glasses he rocked made him somehow look even more grown-up. I wasn't about to miss any more.

"I'll go get ready." Even if it meant lying to everyone around me that I was okay.

Chapter Six

NOVA

Dex's 4Runner handled the bumps in the gravel roads that snaked across Twisted Oak Ranch like a pro. And Owen, bless him, chattered the whole way, listing off facts about alpacas, telling stories about all the times he'd fed them with Skylar.

Nothing about Waylon Archer was typical, and that extended to the kinds of animals he raised. Most of the ranches around here were for cattle, with the occasional horse ranch. But not Waylon's. He raised alpacas, goats, some adorable, shaggy sheep breed, a small herd of yaks, and a handful of mini-Highland cows. He specialized in cheese and shearing for yarn and other fibers.

"Did you know that alpacas all poop in the same place?" Owen broke into my thoughts. "They have like one spot where they pile it."

My nose wrinkled. "I don't want to visit that spot in the pasture, okay, Bubs?"

He grinned. "It does kinda smell."

"Don't tell Waylon that," Dex said as he rounded a curve, the main ranch house coming into view. "He uses it for the garden."

"Gross," Owen muttered. "There's poop on our lettuce?"

Dex went on to explain fertilizer to Owen, but I was too busy taking in the house to listen closely. It didn't matter that I'd seen it half a dozen times now; I was still awestruck.

Waylon had built it with the help of a few friends. Apparently, they had kept adding on as time went by, leading to its sort of ramshackle look. But it worked. The sage-green siding. The wraparound porch.

But the scene stealer was the massive oak tree that erupted straight out of the house itself, making the home seem almost magical. And maybe it was. Brae had shared that the Archer brothers had come to live with Waylon when they were anywhere from eleven to eighteen. She hadn't shared what had happened to their parents, but I knew it couldn't have been good for them to end up living elsewhere.

Waylon had made a safe and secure home for the brothers, and you could tell by how close they all were that he'd done an amazing job of being a parent to them. And I had to imagine that growing up in a house like this one had been a trip and a half for a kid because the outside had nothing on the inside.

As we headed up the walkway, a massive Irish wolfhound ambled toward us. She came straight to me, leaning against my thigh. My hand instantly dropped to give her some scratches. No human beings touched me, but this sweet pup didn't have any such reservations. "Hi, sweet Lucy girl."

"You know," Dex began, "*I* used to be her favorite. But I guess her affections are fickle."

A laugh bubbled out of me, and it was so damn nice to feel it—the rumbling authenticity of a *real* laugh. "I guess she just has good taste," I shot back.

Owen snickered. "She got you, bruh."

Dex grinned, holding the screen door open for our group.

As we stepped inside, I smelled the scents of true home cooking and heard a bickering argument from the back of the house.

"I'm telling you. That sighting over in the Mojave Desert was the real deal," Maverick said.

"Please," Wylder huffed. "You're the prime target for all those supermarket gossip mags, aren't you? Do you believe Taylor Swift is the leader of the Illuminati?"

"I mean, if anyone would be the perfect cult leader…" Mav shot back.

Waylon grunted. "That song about players playing is a bop."

Wylder groaned, but Maverick just laughed.

We made our way through the house and toward the voices. Every time I came here, I discovered something new. It made sense because the interior was like a chaotic work of art with the countless clocks Waylon had made over the years covering the walls.

The furniture in the living space wasn't something any designer would've put together, but it somehow worked in a way that was all Waylon. A brightly striped chair paired with a pastel flowered couch and a couple of antique wooden chairs. A rustic church pew that had been refinished as a bench.

Today's discovery was a rainbow clock covered with different animals in every color—bulls, alpacas, goats, yaks, sheep, horses, dogs, cats—and tucked away in one corner was Waylon's true love…Bigfoot.

I grinned as we headed into the kitchen. This house was the coolest.

"I'm telling you, *something* went across that trail cam I set up in the northwest woods," Waylon said as he rested a hand on his rounded belly covered by his Carhartt overalls.

Wylder sighed and leaned back in his chair. "I'm sure something *did* go across your trail cam. A deer or a bear. Maybe a cougar."

Brae's whole expression brightened. "A sighting?"

"It's gotta be," Owen cheered. "He knows we believe, so he's not afraid to show himself."

Dex groaned. "Please, don't you three start."

Waylon narrowed his gaze on his nephew. "I will not tolerate Bigfoot disrespect in this house."

Maverick let out a low whistle. "You did it now. Grounded for sure."

Wylder snickered. "Maybe his punishment should be helping you set up Bigfoot trail cams."

"That's not a bad idea," Waylon agreed. He turned to me. "How was the first day?"

Waylon was the ultimate grandfatherly figure, complete with hilarious Bigfoot conspiracy theories. But his warmth and welcome were always like a balm.

"I think I did pretty good." I glanced at Wylder. "But you might want to ask the man in charge."

Wylder's lips twitched. "A-plus for sure."

A hint of relief washed through me at that.

"I knew it," Mav said, popping the cap off his beer with the edge of the kitchen counter. "Heartbreaker on the loose. Bet those tips were sweet."

I chuckled. "Not sure about that, but I definitely got to meet some characters. Did you know the owner of the Grit & Grove was abducted by aliens?"

Maverick grinned. "Hal? Oh yeah, he's a believer. Big-time."

The mechanic had told me all sorts of tall tales, but they were kind of amazing.

Wylder groaned. "The stories only get more outlandish when he has a couple of beers."

"Hey," Mav cut in. "If you got anally probed, it would stick with you, too."

"What's anally probed?" a new voice cut in.

I turned to see Skylar with a look of confusion on her face. She looked awesome with her combat boots, princess dress, fairy wings, and camo headband.

"Maverick," a deep voice growled.

That timbre had goose bumps rising on my arms, and my gaze instantly cut to the owner. Kol stood behind his daughter, glowering at Maverick. The muscle along his jaw pulsed, making the thick scruff twitch.

"Hey, man, I didn't say any bad words," Mav argued.

"You said butt probe," Owen cut in. "And stuff's not supposed to go there. Only come out."

Wylder started coughing in an attempt to hold back his laughter, his face turning beet red.

Skylar's nose wrinkled. "Joey tried to stick a race car up his pooper when he was four and had to go to the doctor to get it out. Lacey told me her mom told her."

Mav grinned. "Gotta be careful when it comes to—"

"Maverick," Kol thundered.

"What?" Mav asked with faux innocence. "What'd I say?"

I sat out on the back deck, watching Sky and Owen race around the yard with Tink the mini-Highland cow and Pepper the goat running after them. Skylar's fairy wings had made it onto Tink at some point, and Pepper wore a purple feather boa with sparkles. The land around us had descended into twilight, the sun sinking behind the horizon and making me just the slightest bit twitchy. But someone had hung patio lights around the back deck and on two of the trees, casting out the worst of the shadows.

I inhaled deeply, the scents of pine and fresh, clean air filling my nose. It was beautiful here. Peaceful. Even with the occasional shriek from Sky or Owen.

Skylar raced toward me. "You need some flair."

My mouth curved. "Tell it to me straight, sister."

"This!" She pulled off the bright-pink feather boa she wore and draped it over my shoulders.

I stilled for a moment, unsure if the contact would be too much, but it wasn't. Sky's hands hadn't grazed my arms, just the boa. And in a way, it felt like the closest thing I'd come to a hug in over a year.

I drew my hands along the feathers, relishing the tickling sensation. "This is the nicest thing anyone has done for me in a long time. Thank you."

Skylar beamed at me, sheer pride on her face. "You're welcome. You look happier now."

I looked happier. *Hell.* If even an eight-year-old was seeing the cracks in my façade, I needed to up my acting game. Or, better yet, find somewhere to let my mask down.

"You know, I think doing something to help another person find their happy is one of the best things you can do," I told her honestly.

Skylar's whole face brightened. "Really?"

"No lies detected."

She giggled and glanced over at Owen, who was trying to head-butt Pepper playfully. "He's happier, too, now that you're back. So I guess you give happy, too, Supernova."

And with that, she took off running back toward Owen.

I simply stared after her, leveled by a pint-sized princess with a badass commando streak. I wanted to be a happiness giver. But lately, it felt like all I did was induce stress.

My gaze dipped as my finger slid across my phone screen. A new phone. Because my old one was still in an evidence locker somewhere.

A chill skittered down my spine, but I steeled my muscles and fought it off. Instead, I focused on the listing in front of me. A studio apartment above one of the shops in town. No full kitchen but a kitchenette with a refrigerator and a hot plate.

Not ideal, but I could make it work. And it was only two blocks from the Boot. That was a plus. Then, I took in the price. *Nine hundred dollars a month.* And that didn't include utilities.

My shoulders slumped. I wouldn't be able to afford that anytime soon. Especially if I needed to hand over the first and last month's rent.

"Apartment hunting?" A low voice cut into my swirling thoughts.

I didn't jolt, a rarity for me when I got surprised, because it felt like I knew that voice like the back of my hand. My gaze flicked up to find those hazel eyes, the ones that held both darkness and light if you looked closely enough. "Snoopy *and* bossy? What a combo."

Kol grunted and lowered himself onto the deck next to me.

"And a true conversationalist on top of it." Amusement laced my words, but it was accompanied by a soft intake of breath. Because

Kol? While he didn't touch me, he got closer than anyone else. Not in a way that crossed boundaries but in a way that said he was comfortable, that it was easy being around me. And God, that was a gift.

"Apartment?" he asked.

"One word," I muttered. "Progress." I handed him my phone. It wasn't as if I had any secrets.

He scrolled down the listing, zooming in on the photos of the small space. As each second ticked by, his frown deepened. "Way overpriced."

"I think everywhere here is." It was surprising for such a small town, but landlords pulled it off because Starlight Grove was a tourist haven in the spring and summer months. They could make more with weekly rentals during that period than long-term leases year-round.

Kol offered my phone back to me, studying my face as I took it. There was something about his stare. It was as if he could see invisible truths tattooed on my skin.

"You ready to move out of the cabin?" he asked as I slid my phone into my jeans pocket.

He didn't ask if I wanted to. He wouldn't because he already knew. I'd confessed to him nearly a month ago that it was yet another place where I couldn't breathe. And Kol? He always remembered—even the tiniest of details.

I looked out at the twilight horizon, the stars coming out to play in the farthest corners of the darkening sky. "It's time."

Kol was quiet for a long moment. "You don't seem entirely sure."

Of course he somehow heard the uncertainty beneath those two words. And just like always, he pulled the truth from my lips. "I'm scared."

He was quiet again, letting that truth breathe between us. He waited for more, but he didn't fill the silence, afraid of some awkwardness. He just waited, like his superpower was patience.

"I know I need space, or I'm going to explode. I hurt Brae tonight, and I'm just going to keep doing it. But…"

"You're scared," he said, simply echoing my words back to me.

"I'm scared." Somehow, saying the words after Kol gave them a little less power. The shame they brought still coated my skin, but it didn't hold me hostage any longer.

Kol pushed to his feet, shoving off the side of the deck. "Come on."

"You know I'm not a dog, right, Boss?"

His lips twitched. "Come on, please?"

I let out a huff as I pushed off the deck, landing on the grass below. "Slight improvement."

Kol's gaze found his daughter. "Sky, I'll be back in fifteen minutes. You know the rules."

"No animals after dark unless there's an adult that's not Uncle Mav," Skylar began.

I snickered at Mav's banishment to the kids' table.

"Nothing sharp, explosive, or dangerous. Always stay in sight of the tree house," Sky finished.

The Archer brothers had dubbed the ranch house *the tree house,* thanks to the oak growing out of it, and it had caught on.

"Love you to infinity," Kol called.

"Infinity times infinity," Skylar yelled back.

Apparently, Kol's lack of conversational skills didn't pertain to his daughter. I absolutely adored that. And maybe I was a little envious, too. He spoke the L-word so easily when it always seemed to get stuck in my throat. Even for the people I knew I felt that way about.

I followed him around the side of the house to where an ATV was parked. It looked like a cross between a golf cart and a four-wheeler. It was military black, except for the glittery pink bow someone had affixed to the hood. I had a feeling I knew who.

Kol climbed behind the wheel and started it up with keys that had been left in the ignition.

I slid in next to him. "I like your ride."

He just grunted again.

"God, stop talking already, would you?" I complained.

I stole a glance in Kol's direction as he reversed out of his makeshift parking spot and swore that beautiful mouth twitched.

He was quiet as he drove us down a gravel road I hadn't been down before, deeper onto ranch property. As the darkening sky closed in around us, my fingers dug into the seat.

You're breathing.

It was both a command and a promise. I was breathing. I was alive. The darkness didn't hold me prisoner any longer.

Kol shifted as he made a turn, his body leaning ever so slightly toward me. That scent of forest and clean air filled my nose. And the fear eased.

Because that smell was uniquely Kol and would always mean safety.

As we curved around the road, a house came into view. No, a cabin. And it was aglow.

Lights dotted the front and shone from several windows, illuminating it just enough to let me take it in. Everything about it was perfect, from the dark, reddish wood of the exterior to the massive swing on the front porch. It was cozy and welcoming yet peaceful, as well.

Kol slowed to a stop in front of the cabin and turned off the engine. But my gaze was still locked on the house. A princess crown and fairy wings lay on the swing, making me smile. "Is this your place?"

He nodded and slid out of the ATV. "Come on."

"Please?" I challenged.

"Come on, Phoenix. *Please.*"

Phoenix.

A rumble of something slid through me at the nickname. Maybe because it was exactly what I wanted to be but didn't quite believe I could be yet.

I trailed behind Kol, stepping into the darkness because he made me brave. But he didn't go to the front door. Instead, he strode to the garage, which was connected to the house by a short, windowed walkway. Pulling out a set of keys, he unlocked a door.

I frowned. I wasn't exactly a car or tool girl, so I wasn't sure why Kol was leading us into a place that housed that sort of thing. But still, I followed.

Slipping inside, Kol led me around his Forest Service truck and toward a set of stairs at the back of the space. He took them one at a time, making sure I was with him every step. Then, he opened another door at the top of the stairs and stepped inside.

The scent of sawdust filled the air, and I took in the surrounding attic area. The walls were still exposed drywall, but a living space of sorts was beginning to take shape. A kitchen in one corner, a bathroom in another, and so many windows, the space would be full of light during the day.

"An apartment?" I asked, moving toward the massive window at the back. The moon illuminated the land just enough for me to see glimpses of the pastures and forest, with Mount Lupine in the distance. It was breathtaking.

"An apartment," he echoed.

I stilled, taking a second before I turned to face Kol. A buzz lit beneath my skin. "Oh." It was all I could manage to say at first.

Kol simply stood there, waiting for…something.

"And you're showing it to me because?"

"You should live here."

He said it simply. Like it was an undeniable truth.

"I should live here," I parroted. I knew the Archer brothers were protective of Twisted Oak Ranch. It only took a couple of visits to realize that. Outsiders weren't exactly welcome, and I got the impression the few dinners I'd been invited to were exceptions and not the rule. The fact that their middle brother, Orion, hadn't graced a single one was proof of that.

"It'll be ready in about two weeks. Maybe less if I can get my brothers to help," Kol went on.

"Are you serious right now?"

Kol stared at me, those eyes stormy with flecks of light in their depths. "Phoenix. Sometimes, we have to walk before we run. Here, you'll know you're safe but will have your space. No one breathing down your neck."

"Kol," I croaked.

"I've got you."

My eyes burned. Because I knew those words were the truth. He *did* have me. I didn't know why the universe had brought him into my path, but I knew I'd be grateful for the rest of my days.

"You don't even know me," I rasped.

Kol didn't look away. "I know enough."

The words burned with the most beautiful, scarring heat. "Okay."

His mouth curved into one of those rare smiles. "Okay."

Chapter Seven

KOL

The words blurred as I stared at the computer screen, the fluorescent lights in my office only making it worse. It was too early in the day for that, but burning eyes and hazy vision were the consequences of barely managing a few hours of sleep.

"You don't even know me."

Nova's words echoed in my head as an image of her face played on repeat. The way those gray eyes filled with pain, gratitude, and hope. She was so damn strong. And she deserved a hell of a lot more than just a tiny apartment over a garage. But I'd still make it the best it could be.

I snatched up the eye drops in my desk drawer, depositing more than a few in each eye. It helped a little. At least enough that I could see my phone screen clearly. I pulled up the group chat with my brothers and scowled at the name.

Every time someone changed it, Mav changed it back to his group moniker of choice: *50 Shades of Slay.*

We all dealt with what our father had done differently. It marked us all in different ways. And Mav's tool of choice was laughing in the face of trauma. But I knew that humor hid his scars, both physical and mental.

> **Me:** *Anyone up for helping me with the apartment this week? Close to the finish line and would love to get it done.*

I wasn't quite ready to share who would be inhabiting the space.

> **Wylder:** *You jammed on this project. I can help after six.*

Wylder worked a mix of days and nights at the Boot, wanting to have his finger on the pulse of how his staff was handling things.

> **Maverick:** *What's my payment?*
>
> **Me:** *Pizza and me not telling Uncle Waylon that you're the one who broke his Bigfoot grandfather clock in high school after coming home drunk and trying to fight it.*
>
> **Maverick:** *Hey, it looked like a bear.*
>
> **Dex:** *A bear in the house?*
>
> **Maverick:** *It could happen. Those cute fuckers are resourceful.*
>
> **Wylder:** *Let us not forget that Mav lost the fight to that inanimate object.*

I couldn't help the snicker that left my lips.

> **Me:** *Remember? He started bequeathing us all his prized possessions.*
>
> **Dex:** *I'm still holding on to the hope of getting his prized Derek Jeter rookie card.*
>
> **Maverick:** *None of you are getting shit for making fun of my trauma. I still have a scar from where Bigfoot's fist hit my jaw.*

Wylder: *What do you tell people it's from?*

It wasn't the only scar Mav carried, and we all knew he never told the truth about where they came from.

Maverick: *A fight with a grizzly, where I saved a kid from being attacked. Obvi. Gets me laid a lot.*

Me: *TMI. Are you guys coming to help or not?*

Dex: *You had me at pizza.*

Maverick: *Throw in garlic knots, and I'm in.*

Me: *So high-maintenance.*

Maverick: *I know my worth.*

I waited for a moment, hoping Orion would jump in on his own, but he'd been quieter lately. Especially after everything that had happened with Nova and Brae. Having a monster in our midst yet again had reminded him too much of our past. Of our monster. The one he'd killed to save us all.

Me: *Orion? You in?*

Maverick: *He's too busy brooding. Planning booby traps should anyone dare to approach his house. Scowling at puppies.*

Mav's way of dealing, through and through. Needling Orion into a response.

Orion: *I'm working.*

He was always working. Orion had turned his talent for mapmaking into a true art, creating pieces that often went for over six figures. But he used his skills for our brother venture for free. He was the one who mapped out the locations we searched for missing persons, and over time, he'd become skilled at geographical profiling as well.

Dex: *Take a break so you don't get carpal tunnel.*

Wylder: *You know if you hit the two-week mark, one of us is coming over for proof of life.*

We all waited for a moment.

Nothing.

> **Maverick:** *Okay, change of plans. Family dinner at Orion's. Invite Little Badass and Supernova.*
>
> **Dex:** *Don't call my fiancée Little Badass.*
>
> **Maverick:** *What? I didn't say HOT Little Badass like I wanted to.*
>
> **Dex:** *Mav, I will empty your bank accounts, post photos of you dressed up as a fairy for Sky's birthday all over your social media, and change your ringtone to "Baby One More Time."*
>
> **Maverick:** *Those fairy wings make my biceps look huge. I'm down with it. And I love a little Britney Spears.*

I shook my head.

> **Me:** *Stop trying to use my kid to get laid.*
>
> **Orion:** *If you all shut up, I'll come for an hour.*

Victory was ours. It just worried me how hard it had been to make it happen.

Sliding my phone into the dock on my desk, I got back to work. Clicking on the file that read *Travis Moore,* I took in all the subfiles: *Confirmed Victims. Suspected Victims. Evidence Results. Photographs. Maps.*

It went on and on. We had nine confirmed victims, all of them deceased—except for Nova.

My back molars ground together at the reminder of how close she'd come to not making it. *"Let me go."* Her voice was the barest whisper in my memory.

Because Travis had become obsessed with keeping one of his victims alive. He wanted the high of knowing she was still out there, right under everyone's noses. And he'd used that life to mess with Brae, leaving a bloody locket on her door, recording Nova screaming. It had been a study in different kinds of torture.

I shoved that down and clicked on the *Suspected Victims* file. I had dossiers on about a dozen possibles—ones I had found while working in my official capacity here at the Forest Service and others my brothers were helping me gather on our less-than-official mission with the Hourglass Network.

The work I did for both was fairly similar; it was just that the Hourglass Network had far fewer rules and paperwork. While Dex was more than happy to walk the morally gray line of hacking into any databases we might need, I never crossed that line. I had access to countless law enforcement registries, but I never used them for any unofficial means. I could ignore how Dex *happened upon* certain information, but that was as far as I was willing to go.

That didn't mean I didn't contribute. I brought a law enforcement eye to the cases, along with my tracking abilities. And when it came to this particular case, I also knew what avenues had already been explored so we didn't have to cover them twice.

Of the nine confirmed victims, seven had been buried across Travis's property or nearby, nestled in the national forest outside of Starlight Grove. He'd lived in one of the handful of properties grandfathered into having land rights, and the fact that there were only about five cabins within a hundred-mile radius had given him the privacy he needed to create a house of horrors.

But we'd found one farther away—a solo camper, backpacking through an area we thought might've crossed with Travis's hunting grounds. My brothers and I had combined our skills, using geographic profiling, victim profiling, computer history, and my on-the-ground tracking to find a burial site. It had been so off the beaten path that I was sure Travis had thought no one would find it. So he'd left more than a little DNA behind.

And that victim told me we could have more.

A knock sounded on my open office door, and I swiveled to take in my boss. Sherri Goodwin was a take-no-shit leader who cut right to the heart of things. And it didn't hurt that she had the kind of intelligence that brought about more case closures than any other officer in the Forest Service's history.

"Morning," she said, greeting me while cupping a mug in her hands and looking just a little tired.

One corner of my mouth pulled up. "Still on the herbal tea kick?"

Sherri scowled at me, her brown eyes narrowing. Her features hinted at her Karuk ancestry, one of the tribes indigenous to our Northern California area. "Don't remind me. I'm trying to convince myself that this is black coffee with all the caffeine in the world."

I chuckled, leaning back in my chair. "Don't look in my cup. It might tempt you."

Her scowl only deepened. "Why'd I make Russ this stupid promise?"

"Because you love him, and he cares about you living a long, healthy life?" I supplied.

"Love and marriage. Stupid," she grumbled.

I shook my head. "As soon as you wake up a little, you'll remember all the reasons that isn't true."

Sherri's expression softened a little. "We have made some pretty damn cute kids."

"You have."

She took a sip of her tea. "Catch me up to where you are."

I nodded, slipping into official mode. "I'm still working through the list of possible victims. While we were able to narrow the scope to those within the five-county radius Travis could've potentially had case access to, we also have to expand the victim profile."

Travis Moore, a sergeant in the Juniper County Sheriff's Department, had gotten a kick out of inserting himself into every missing person's case he'd perpetrated. But the problem was that he didn't have an exact victim profile. While he'd certainly favored women in their twenties with dark hair, he'd also skewed outside that. He'd taken men, women with other hair colors, and a diverse range of races, ages, and backgrounds.

Sherri nodded slowly. "I want you to take Pete on to help you work through everything."

It was my turn to scowl. "I work alone."

"Yeah, yeah. You are loner, hear you roar," Sherri muttered.

I'd worked my way up the ranks as a Forest Service investigator and had proven myself, case after case. "You think I can't handle this?"

She shook her head instantly. "You know that's not it. I'm getting pressure from higher up. They want this one put to bed."

I got that. The media coverage of Travis's crimes had spread far and wide, from local and national news to prime-time specials and podcasts. And I'd even heard there was a movie in production—everyone making the most out of others' misery.

Sherri scrubbed a hand over her face. "Listen, I know Pete's an asshole. Everyone in this office knows Pete's an asshole. But he's an asshole who does good work. And if I can deal with him being a misogynistic prick, you can deal with him being an asshole."

Hell. She had a point. Pete was always dropping little comments that undermined Sherri, things that were just shy of getting him in trouble. But Sherri dealt. I could, too.

"You're the senior officer," she went on. "Utilize him for what he does best and don't let him walk all over you."

That was easier said than done because Pete did whatever the hell he wanted and walked over the rest of us to claim whatever credit he could.

"Sherri—" I began.

"How many possibles do you have?" she cut in.

My mouth thinned. "Thirteen."

She shook her head. "You need to take care of yourself, Kol. I know you care about this one, but don't let it drive you into an early grave."

"I'm not," I clipped, but I could feel the muscle along my jaw beginning to flutter.

Sherri studied me for a long moment. "Is this one getting too personal? I know Nova is close to your brother's fiancée. I can do a full reassign if—"

"I know the rules." Tension wove through my muscles, turning them to stone. That wasn't a lie. I *did* know the rules. Just like I knew a victim of a case living above my garage could be considered a *personal relationship* that broke more than one of them.

Fuck.

But I couldn't let Nova slowly drown while living in Brae and Dex's cabin. Not when I had the ability to help. It went against every fiber of my being. Sometimes, breaking the rules was the risk.

And it *was* a risk. Sherri didn't mess around with conflicts of interest. We'd had cases go sideways because of an investigator's relationship with a victim, and she'd never forgotten it. She wouldn't hesitate to discipline me. Or worse, fire me.

Sherri was quiet as she continued to watch me, taking stock of everything under my words. But if she saw through to my secrets, she didn't say anything. "Fine. But you can't investigate thirteen cases on your own. Divide and conquer. Give Pete a few to look into and start there."

"Did I hear my name? Talking about how invaluable I am?" Pete cut in, moving in beside Sherri in my doorway.

That now-familiar scowl was back. I stared at the douchebag extraordinaire. In his late forties, I had no idea how Pete had ended up working for the Forest Service. While I hated logging time in our office, preferring the forest as my backdrop, Pete's idea of camping was a luxury lodge with every amenity known to man, and his carefully coiffed hair showed it.

Sherri's mouth thinned. "Pete, we're going to add you as a second on the Travis Moore case. You'll answer to Kol on this one and take your orders from him."

A war of emotions played out over Pete's expression. A flash of excitement in his brown eyes, followed quickly by more than a hint of annoyance. "I could always take half the cases and Kol the other. Then, we won't get in each other's way," Pete suggested.

"This is Kol's case," Sherri said with finality. "You want on, you're support to him."

A muscle pulsed beneath Pete's eye. "Yeah. No problem." His annoyed gaze flicked to me. "I've been over your notes. I've already got a few ideas of where I could strengthen things."

Already undermining. Typical Pete.

"I'll be sending you five cases to look into," I said, ignoring his suggestion. "Put your case notes in the portal."

What I wouldn't tell him was that they were five cases my brothers and I had already looked into. I wasn't a pompous ass—a second set of eyes never hurt, and there was always a chance that Pete could find something we'd missed. But I wasn't about to trust him completely. Not on a case this important.

Pete's eyes flashed with a hint of fire. "Make sure you send me all the files you have on each."

"You know I will," I shot back.

Sherri sighed as Pete stalked away. "Do me a favor and try not to kill him on the way to closing this case."

"I can't make any promises," I grumbled, turning back to my computer to send the douchebag everything I had on the five possibles I was assigning him.

I cracked my neck and focused on the other eight cases. Highlighting a missing backpacker, I sent the file to my phone. I needed to get out of this claustrophobic office and into my real workspace. I always did my best work in the forest, in the quiet.

Checking to make sure the files had made it to my phone—tech was *really* not my thing—I grabbed it and my keys. As I headed for the door, my cell dinged.

Nova: *I think you gave me a foot fetish, Boss.*

Below the text was a photo of Nova's feet in tall grass, her toenails, still a sunny yellow, peeking through.

How could toes manage to be cute? Maybe I'd taken a hit to the head when I was working on the apartment and didn't remember it.

Me: *You know this means Brae and Wylder will think you have a foot fungus now, too.*

Nova: *Naw, my feet are too cute to be fungusy.*

Me: *Fungusy isn't a word.*

Nova: *I made it one.*

That was Nova, through and through, making her own rules. And she should. She'd lost a year of her life. She should live exactly as she wanted to now.

Me: *Give 'em hell today.*

Nova: *You wrangle those trees into submission, Boss.*

I chuckled, slipped my phone into my pocket, and headed for the front door of our office building. The moment I stepped outside, I inhaled the fresh air. There was something about being stuck inside an office: the recycled air with no open windows, thc artificial light. I hated everything about it. The only reason I could manage what I did was because I got to spend so much time outdoors.

It hadn't always been like this. There was a time when I thought I would be a lawyer or maybe go into finance, possibly take over my father's import/export business. But all of that had changed when we discovered who our father really was. That he was a monster who preyed on women who looked exactly like our mother—a woman who had disappeared years before. That he stalked and killed them, burying them in the orchard on our property and saving trinkets from his kills that allowed him to relive them over and over again.

Everything changed when Dex and Mav found those IDs and locks of hair—and then Edmond Archer had found *them*. He had nearly killed Maverick and only stopped because Orion ended him. And I came to terms with the fact that I hadn't been there when my brothers needed me the most.

Too caught up in my own bullshit. Too cool to stay back and watch my little brothers like I should've. I just *had* to take my girlfriend out to that movie she was dying to see. Too selfish.

And when I came home to find it crawling with police, FBI, and paramedics...I lost the ability to breathe. Everything in the house felt like it was closing in around me. And the only place that gave me respite was the forest.

It had stayed my refuge. The forest was my home now, in every way.

"Kol." A deep voice cut into my swirling memories as I crossed the parking lot.

I looked up to see a familiar figure in a Juniper County Sheriff's Department uniform. Roger Oakley wore the evidence of what he'd been through in the past four months. A best friend who'd ended up being a serial killer. A boss who'd turned out to be involved with a cartel pot–growing operation and had gotten himself killed.

And he also wore the pressure of trying to clean up a department completely wrecked in the wake of those discoveries. He looked older than his thirty-one years. Dark circles rimmed his blue eyes, and his sandy-blond hair desperately needed a cut.

"Hey," I greeted. "What are you doing here?"

"Coming to find you, actually."

The Travis Moore case had been handed off to the state police and the Forest Service in a joint investigation, with the sheriff's department serving as support. There were too many conflicts of interest for them to run point, and they needed time to pull themselves together after all the upheaval.

"Travis's case?" I asked.

Shadows passed over Roger's face, the pain that came with having someone close to you betray you. And God, I knew what that felt like. Roger swallowed, his throat working with the action. "No. The election."

My brows rose. Roger was filling in as interim sheriff, but there was an official election coming up in a couple of months to permanently fill the seat. "You need an endorsement?" I asked, wondering why the hell he'd want one from me. It wasn't as if my brothers and I had a great reputation. Not with who our father was.

"I was actually coming to see if you might be interested in running."

I came to a full stop, my keys dangling from my finger. "I'm sorry, what?"

Roger shot me a grin. "I was coming to see if you might be willing to run for sheriff."

"Have you been drinking this morning?"

He let out a low chuckle. “No, I have not been by the Boot for morning shots. I’m serious, Kol. People respect you, especially after you stuck to your guns and found Nova when everyone else gave up.”

When everyone else gave up. Those words echoed in my mind like a cannon being shot off in an empty room. Because the rest of the world *had* given up. When her friendship bracelet was found in a grave with a decomposing female body of the right age, they’d thought it was her.

But a little niggle of doubt had grown inside me—one that reminded me of the joy Travis had gotten out of messing with people in the worst possible ways. So I’d wondered if maybe she was still alive.

I’d studied the maps and started working outward from his property, day after day, until I found the signs: a worn path, evidence of footsteps, drag marks. And then, I’d found *her*.

Nova.

Barely alive. A shell of a human. Someone who hadn’t wanted to keep fighting.

But she had.

She’d become a phoenix.

We still didn’t know exactly *why* he’d taken her out of her cell. To heighten the game? To leave her to die once he planned to take Brae as a replacement? There were so many unanswered questions, and each one was darker than the last.

I cleared my throat as if that would clear all the memories. It didn’t. They would be burned into my brain for the rest of time. “I have no interest in playing the political game of sheriff. And even if I did, you know at least half this town either despises me and my brothers or is terrified of us.”

Roger’s mouth thinned. “Half this town are idiots.”

My lips twitched. “Likely. But it still takes them to get elected.”

He ran a hand through his hair, tugging on the ends of the strands. “Fuck.”

I could see it then, the true strain. “What’s going on?”

Roger let out a sigh that carried a massive weight. “Some asshole from Deer Creek is running. From what I’ve heard, he’s Miller two-point-oh.”

Someone like our power-hungry ex-sheriff was not something any of us wanted to repeat.

"Why the hell aren't you running?" I asked. "You're the one who's been putting the department back together, making sure people have the support they need, going back through Travis's and Miller's cases."

More shadows swirled in Roger's eyes. "He was my best friend."

I knew Roger wasn't talking about Miller. As much as people were angry about the ex-sheriff's involvement in the drug ring, that had nothing on Travis's actions.

Travis had not only kidnapped and killed citizens of Starlight Grove, but he'd also embedded himself in the lives of their loved ones. He'd pretended to provide comfort when *he* was the source of their agony.

"You didn't know," I said quietly.

Roger shrugged. "Maybe not. But I should've seen something."

I knew that feeling so damn well. And it messed with your head something fierce. "Roger. He was a psychopath. He knew how to assimilate. How to charm and manipulate. Not a single person in his life saw it. Not even Cora."

Roger jerked at her name. Because we all felt what she'd endured. The ultimate betrayal. It was something I wasn't sure she'd ever recover from.

"A part of me still doesn't believe it," he whispered hoarsely.

"I know how that is. Trust me, I do. But we just have to keep moving forward. And the Juniper County Sheriff's Department deserves someone like you leading it. Someone like you putting the pieces back together so we can have a department we trust."

Roger nodded slowly, jerkily. "I want to do it. I just…"

"Don't know if you can?"

"Don't know if I can," he echoed.

"You'll do it. It'll be hard as hell, but you'll do it." I had no doubt.

Roger nodded again, this time with a little more force and certainty. "How are things going with the case?"

I let out a long breath. "Sherri just put Pete on as my second."

"Hell," Roger muttered, knowing exactly what a douche Pete was.

"Sorry about that. Let me know if I can help. I'm flagging any potential case matches as we revisit everything."

"Thanks. That's all you can do right now." But I prayed he wouldn't find any more matches. Because with every additional victim came a new firestorm of media coverage and another chance for it all to be thrown in Nova's face.

Chapter Eight

NOVA

"Here's your check. Take your time and let me know if you need a refill," I said, sliding the bill holder onto the two top.

The man looked up at me as he pulled it toward him with two fingers. Everything about him was just a little too slick. He'd been nothing but quietly polite as I took his order and served him a chicken bacon ranch sandwich. But his outdoor gear was a little too perfect. His haircut, too. And it put me on edge.

Dark-brown eyes studied me as he flipped open the bill holder. "And how much of a tip would it take to get you to accompany me to dinner tonight?"

And there it was.

I was almost relieved by the douchebag move after being on edge over nothing for the past hour. It proved that just maybe I *could* trust myself and my intuition.

I didn't mind a patron hitting on me every now and then. Asking me out. Shooting their shot. Even if the answer would always be no. It had happened back in Oakland when I worked at the coffee shop and yoga studio, and I'd mastered the polite decline if I wasn't interested.

I wondered what this guy would say if I replied honestly. *"No one's touched me in almost a year and a half. The only person who tried sent me into a breakdown so extreme that I had to be sedated. But if that's cool with you, let's get a drink."*

But he went straight to the buying-me approach, and I wasn't down with that.

"I can get you some boysenberry pie for dessert or a cup of coffee, but I'm afraid I'm not on the menu, and no human being is for sale." I delivered the line with a beaming smile.

The man scowled at me.

I just smiled wider. "You let me know about that pie."

Turning, I headed back toward the bar.

Aidan moved in alongside me, fighting not to laugh. "That was a thing of beauty. '*You let me know about that pie.*'" The laughter found him then. "What a douche canoe."

Piper, our youngest waitress at just twenty-one, flicked her dark-brown locks over her shoulder before reaching for her tray of drinks. "I definitely want to be you when I grow up."

"I don't know about that," I said with a laugh. "I probably just smart-assed my way out of a tip."

Wylder's dark brows pulled together as he moved to our end of the bar. "What happened? Is everything okay?"

Aidan waved him off. "Don't worry. Nova has it covered. She just put a douche canoe in his place after he all but asked her how much a roll in the hay would cost."

Wylder's dark-hazel eyes flashed. It wasn't the same way Kol's did, though. This was different. His went stormy black—the only sign of his temper. He watched as the Slick Rick rose from the table and tossed a few bills on the surface. "I'll ban him—"

I held up a hand. "I'm fine. It honestly felt kind of good. Something about him was off, so it felt vindicating that I was right."

Wylder took that in, and then a small smile curved his mouth. "Always good to know you can trust yourself."

Of course he instantly understood. Because Wylder could read people better than anyone I knew.

The sound of uproarious laughter filled the air, making me turn to see Cora walking away from a table with a few people I recognized as locals. Her mouth was set in a tight line, but I didn't miss the slight tremble of her tray.

My gaze narrowed on the patrons at her table. Was it douche canoe season? It didn't look like they were drinking anything but sodas, yet I could see the way a few of them looked at Cora. As if they were laughing *at* her, rather than with her.

One woman, who looked to be in her early thirties, flicked her brown hair over her shoulder as she lifted her voice. I could just make out the words.

"You're telling me she didn't know about her psycho fiancé? Please. Some women are so desperate they'll do anything to keep a man."

Cora's cheeks turned bright red, but she kept right on walking toward the bar. "Can I get a lemonade, please?"

Her voice was soft, her gaze downcast.

"Why don't you let me take that table?" I offered. "I've only got one now."

Cora shook her head, not looking at me. "I'm fine."

Other than her offer of insoles help, she'd basically avoided me since I started. She'd give me a polite hello and then do everything she could to keep her distance. I understood, but it still smarted. More than that, it had guilt digging in deep. If my being here was too hard for Cora, then I needed to look for another job.

Wylder filled the lemonade, but his gaze didn't stray from Cora. A muscle fluttered along his jaw as his fingers tightened around the soda gun. "Why don't you take your break? My office is open." His voice was so incredibly gentle, and there was something almost tender in the way he focused on Cora. Like he would do anything to take away her pain.

Piper sidled up to the bar between Cora and me. "I've got this, Wy."

She grabbed the lemonade and strode toward the table of assholes. Her smile was bright as she approached. "I've got one lemonade for the jerk-face who felt the need to make fun of a woman who's been through hell. I'd take the drink because it's clear this may be the only good thing in your life, if you feel the need to kick someone when they're down."

The brunette at the table gaped at Piper. "You can't talk to me like that."

Piper only beamed wider. "Oh, I can. Because my boss looked like he was two seconds away from eighty-sixing your asses. Really, I saved you."

The woman's gaze flicked to the bar, where I could *feel* Wylder's wrath pouring out of his expression. She paled slightly.

The guy across the table snickered. "Guess your big mouth is finally coming back to bite you, Beth."

"Shut up, Deacon," she hissed, snatching the lemonade from Piper.

Our youngest waitress strode back to us, a huge grin splitting her face. I answered it with one of my own. "The student becomes the teacher."

Piper's eyes sparkled. "I learned from the best."

"I'm going to take that break." Cora made a beeline for the back hallway.

Piper's smile fell. "Did I fuck up?"

"No," Wylder said quickly. "She's just going through a lot. I'm going to check on her."

"Can I?" I asked, cutting in.

He looked back at me, uncertainty in his expression.

"Please," I said softly. "I need to say some things. If they don't help, I'll steer clear of her from now on."

What I didn't say was that *steering clear* would mean finding a new job. But I knew Wylder would understand. He was the most empathetic person I'd ever met.

"Okay," he agreed. "Let me know if you need anything."

I nodded and started for the back hallway. The bar was only about a third full, so I knew Piper and Aidan could handle the tables for now—though it would pick up again when happy hour hit in about forty-five minutes.

Making my way down the quiet hall, I stopped in front of Wylder's office door. I took a second to steady myself, remembering how it felt to have my bare feet pressed to the earth, my palm against the tree trunk. I *breathed*.

And then I twisted the knob to the office door and stepped inside.

Cora's head snapped up the second the door opened. Tears glistened in her eyes, and her face had gone pale.

Shit.

I quickly closed the door and moved deeper into the room. Cora sat on the leather couch Wylder had shoved up against the wall, but I didn't want to corner her, so I opted to balance on the side of the desk.

"Hey," I said softly.

Cora's gaze immediately dropped to her hands.

"That woman was a bitch."

Nothing.

"No, that's an insult to female dogs. She was an asshole."

More silence.

I took a deep breath. "No one believes what she was saying."

A tear fell from Cora's eye, splashing on her joined hands. "Yes, they do," she said, so quietly I could barely hear her.

Even though her words were barely audible, I felt the pain in them. "None of what happened is your fault."

That was what I'd wanted to say to Cora for months. Ever since I overheard Wylder talking to Dex at an Archer family dinner about how much she was struggling.

Cora still didn't look at me. "I should've known. I went to that cabin more times than I can count. I walked that land. I probably stepped on the places he buried people. People I helped search for."

Flashes of *something* coursed through me. Hands tightening around my throat. Lungs burning. *"No one's looking for you."*

I shoved it all down. It didn't matter whether it was a memory or my imagination.

"If you'd known, you would've stopped it," I croaked.

Cora's head lifted, finally meeting my gaze. There was so much pain in hers. "He *tortured* you. Almost killed you. He kept you in a goddamned hole for over a *year*."

I fought off the images that wanted to surface. "But *you* didn't. This isn't your fault. And if my working here is too hard, I can find another job."

Cora's jaw went slack, but she quickly recovered. "No. Please, don't. That would make it all worse."

I let out a long breath. "We can't let him win."

Defiance lit up Cora's features, giving life to just how beautiful she was. "You're right." She rubbed her palms over her jeans-clad thighs. "But I have no idea how or where to start."

"We start together. When the assholes show, we've got a united front. And I'm not afraid to pour a lemonade over someone's head."

A soft laugh escaped her. "Why am I not surprised?" As the laughter died, Cora studied me for a moment. "How are you doing it?"

I understood what she was asking: How was *I* facing all the people who knew things about me I never wanted a soul to know? "I already lost a year of my life. I won't let him take anything else."

Cora nodded slowly, sending her light-brown hair sweeping over her shoulders. "You should come to a Compass meeting."

My brows pulled together. I was familiar with the organization's name, thanks to Brae. It was a nonprofit support group for the loved ones of missing persons.

"I don't know anyone who's missing," I said gently.

Cora shook her head. "It's more than that. We also help those who are still looking for their family or friends. It might give you a little purpose. And it might help to be around people who get it, in a way."

I knew from my interviews with law enforcement that Cora's mother had disappeared when she was in high school. And it was her involvement in the group that had given Travis his in. He'd gone to meetings, gotten updates from Cora, and all to get information about the families he'd torn apart. It was like a drug for him.

"Sure." The single word was out of my mouth before I could stop myself. I wasn't sure how I'd react to people talking about all the losses in their lives. But Cora was reaching out, and I wanted to meet her halfway.

"Good," Cora said quietly as her gaze met mine. "And thank you. I'm not sure many people would be able to manage the kindness you have. It just shows how incredibly strong you are."

I took those words to heart, letting them settle in and become a balm to the wounds I didn't show anyone. "Thanks for letting me."

We didn't say anything else, just sat there in the silence for a moment before rising to head back out to the bar. As we stepped out of the office, Wylder was there, waiting.

His gaze flicked to me. "Can you handle the bar for a minute?"

I knew he wanted to check on Cora himself, make sure she was okay. I shot him as much of a grin as I could manage. "As long as no one orders a crazy cocktail like a Harvey Wallbanger."

Wylder's lips twitched. "That's basically just vodka and orange juice."

My grin came a little more naturally now. "Then I guess I've got it handled."

I headed back out to the main area, which was already a little more crowded, and moved straight to behind the bar just as a familiar face headed my way.

Those hazel irises, a study in dark and light, locked on me, making my heart do some sort of stutter step. My doctor in the hospital had told me to be aware of heart palpitations because of the strain my heart had been under due to the conditions of my captivity. But I didn't think these had anything to do with that.

Kol was dressed in his Forest Service uniform—something I hadn't seen him in all that often. But he wore the hell out of it. The dark-green pants and tan shirt shouldn't have had me almost drooling, but they definitely did.

Kol's thick thighs strained against the dark-green pants as he crossed the bar. His shoulders looked impossibly broad in the tan fabric of his shirt. And the uniform gave him an air of authority.

He slid onto a stool in front of me. "Working the bar?"

"Wylder needed a minute." My voice sounded almost hoarse, and Kol's eyes narrowed ever so slightly.

"You okay?"

"All good, Boss." I straightened my shoulders. "You know what you want, or do you need a menu and a minute?"

One corner of Kol's mouth kicked up. "It's my brother's bar. I know the menu."

"Then tell me what you want, smartass," I challenged.

That dark-brown scruff around his mouth twitched. "I'll take the cheeseburger, medium. Add avocado and onion straws. And a Coke."

"What kind of fries or salad?"

"Steak fries."

That fit. The manliest kind of fries on the menu.

I scribbled the order on my pad and stuck it on the wheel in the open pass-through window. "Order for Kol, Fee."

She grinned at me from the griddle. "Tell that troublemaker I'm gonna put some hot sauce on it for him."

I sent her a salute, turning back to Kol. "Fee said she's putting hot sauce on your burger."

"She always treats me right," Kol said, his voice rumbling in something as close to a chuckle as I'd heard from him.

Why did that have jealousy rising? Fiona was old enough to be Kol's mother, yet the thought that they shared knowledge about each other that I didn't stung. It was ridiculous.

Piper elbowed up to the waitstaff end of the bar. "Two Aspen Ales and a Diet Coke."

I moved to grab her drinks as more people slid onto stools, hoping to take advantage of the happy-hour specials.

Wylder appeared at my back, shooting Kol a grin. "My second most antisocial brother is becoming a regular. Love to see it."

Kol scowled at him as I slid the last drink onto Piper's tray.

"I'm hungry," Kol grumbled.

"Mm-hmm," Wylder hummed.

Kol flipped him off, which only made Wylder laugh. Then my boss turned to me. "Want to handle the diners behind the bar, and I'll do drinks?"

"You got it," I said, moving down the bar to where a new face sat.

The man looked to be in his late twenties or early thirties. Everything about him read hipster, from the mustard beanie and black-framed glasses to the flannel and blond beard.

I grabbed a menu and slid it across the bar. "Welcome to the Boot. Can I get you something to drink while you look at the menu?"

He shot me a grin that revealed two dimples. They made him look younger, almost boyish, and had his light-blue eyes twinkling. "You got any local ales?"

"More than I can count," I said, gesturing to a skinny chalkboard to my left. "I'll just need to see some ID."

The man shifted on his stool and pulled out his wallet as he studied the menu. "Got a personal fave?"

I quickly scanned his driver's license; Reese Gatlin was twenty-nine and from Michigan. "I like the Fall Creek Ale. But the Aspen is also a local favorite."

I'd done a tasting to familiarize myself with our menu, and I was glad I had.

"Let's go with your number-one favorite," Reese said, putting his license back in his wallet.

I grabbed a pint glass and lowered the tap, tipping the glass at an angle. "Far from home. You on vacation?"

Reese smiled again, those dimples popping. "A little work, a little play."

"Always a good combo." I set the glass on a cocktail napkin. "Just flag me down when you're ready to order."

I moved to the next patrons, a couple from Nevada, in town for some hiking and wine tasting. I found a rhythm in the steady stream of customers the afternoon had to offer, but I still felt the heat of Kol's gaze flicking to me every so often as I worked.

It didn't feel like the gazes of others. It didn't make me twitchy or anxious. It felt…comforting. As if there were no way I could disappear when he was around.

"So," Reese said, pulling my attention, "any recs for spots to hit up around town?"

I was really the wrong person to ask about that, but I didn't welcome the conversation that would come with saying I was new in town—sort of. How did you explain that you'd been in Starlight Grove for over a year yet had only been to a handful of places?

Instead, I filled in what I knew. "The Grove Griddle has the best pancakes I've ever had in my life. Hit up the Cozy Cup for an excellent latte. And you can't go wrong with any of the wineries in the area."

"What about hikes?" Reese asked, his focus staying on my face. "Any recommendations there?"

A chill skittered up my spine as I remembered the last hike I'd been on. "Not much of a hiker. Can't help you there."

"What about Three Creeks Canyon Trail? Heard it's pretty."

A wave of dizziness swept over me. It was the place I'd been taken from. I only remembered bits and pieces: driving to the trail with Brae, being annoyed that she went off trail to look at more wildflowers, and then…nothing. It was one big blank.

"Not sure," I forced out. "You'll have to ask someone else."

I felt Kol's gaze on me, his radar for my trauma and anxiety as astute as always.

I tried to move down the bar to check on the Nevada couple, but Reese stopped me.

"Nova."

I froze. I hadn't told him my name. And none of us wore name tags.

My gaze snapped to him as I went instantly on alert. For what, I didn't know. It wasn't like I had the skills to defend myself. I'd taken one self-defense class at the local YMCA with Brae, and that knowledge was rusty at best. That was something I needed to change. I caught sight of the tiny knife used to prep lemon and lime wedges. My fighting instincts were there, at least. That was something.

"I know who you are," he said, his voice gentle.

"So do a lot of people," I clipped.

"I was one of the people who helped. I'm a journalist. I covered the case from nearly the beginning. And now, I'm making a documentary. I really want to dive into the mind of the monster and how you survived."

The dizziness intensified, and I gripped the edge of the bar to steady myself. "Good for you, but I don't do interviews."

"Come on, Nova. Not even for someone who helped find you?" Reese pushed.

Helped find me?

He hadn't helped find me. Brae had helped find me. Dex and all the Archers. Kol.

Kol was the one who never gave up. Even when everyone else thought I was dead. He believed I was still alive. Still breathing.

"Everything okay?" His deep voice found me even now.

I hadn't noticed him rise from his stool or cross to us. I hadn't heard the footsteps. But that, too, was Kol. Not showy about his dominance, his protection, but always acting when it was needed.

Annoyance flashed over Reese's face. "All good, bro. Just chatting."

Kol didn't move, didn't look away from his target. "Nova?"

"He's a reporter," I croaked.

I hated that I couldn't pull it together. That I couldn't tell the damn journalist to get out myself.

Kol's hazel eyes darkened, the glimmers of darkness nearly snuffing out the light ones completely. "Is he, now?"

Reese shoved back his stool. "Hey, I don't want any trouble. I was just telling Nova I was making a documentary. Giving her a chance to be a part of it."

"You *want* to be a part of that?" Kol asked me without taking his eyes off Reese.

"No." My lungs were so tight, just that single syllable hurt.

Kol took two steps, his massive, six-foot-four frame towering over Reese. "Then kindly get the fuck out. And stay out," he snarled.

Chapter Nine

KOL

Fury coursed through me in scalding waves. It had blood rushing in my ears and that vein in my neck pulsing. A fucking reporter. I knew all about those snakes in the grass.

They'd hunted my brothers and me after our father's death and the discovery of who he really was. They'd surrounded our property in Connecticut, some photographers even going so far as to scale walls to try to get a shot of us. They screamed their questions as we drove by in tinted-window SUVs.

Hell, Mav had only been eleven at the time, recovering from wounds that had almost ended his life, and they didn't give a damn. They followed us across the country to Starlight Grove, waited just off our schools' premises with long-range lenses, and sensationalized everything that happened.

And it only got worse when they started speculating about our mother's disappearance. Had she simply had enough and needed a fresh start like her email had said? Were the pressures of being a mom to five boys and the wife of a prominent businessman too much for her to handle? Or was it something darker? Had our dad killed her? We still didn't know. But assholes like this reporter loved to speculate.

I wasn't about to let this piece of shit do that to Nova.

"Get out now, or I will *help* you out, and you won't like that very much," I snarled.

There was a flicker of fear in the man's eyes, but he made the stupid move and doubled down. "Try freedom of the press. And you'd think there'd be a little gratitude. I pushed for coverage of Nova's case. Even before anyone knew about Travis Moore."

My teeth ground together so hard that an ache took root in my jaw. "I don't care if you have a psychic connection to Elvis himself. You have no right to harass the victim of a crime."

"This is a private business, and I'll have to ask you to leave," Wylder cut in, his voice going cold.

The reporter's eyes flashed with anger, but he didn't move.

"And you'll need to leave *now*, or I'll have you arrested," Wylder went on.

"I'd be happy to do the honors," I gritted out.

The reporter's gaze cut to me as he pushed off his stool. "You're a cop?"

He obviously wasn't a very astute reporter, given the fact that I was in uniform.

"Forest Service."

The man scoffed. "Tree cop?" But then his expression lightened, something dawning. "Shit. You're the one who found her, aren't you? I heard someone in the Forest Service did. I—"

"Out," Wylder barked, rounding the bar to physically remove the reporter if he had to.

The man held up both hands and backed up. "I'm going." He pulled a card out of his pocket. "I'd love to interview you, too."

I didn't take the card, so the reporter dropped it onto the floor. "Call me. You deserve some accolades for all you did."

My lip curled in disgust as I turned back to the bar.

Nova stood there motionless, her face pale.

Fucking hell.

I moved then. "Come on."

"Not a dog, Boss." She forced out the words, but there was a slight tremble to them.

"*Please,* Phoenix."

She started to move then, crossing to the end of the bar.

"Wy's office," I clipped.

Nova moved, falling into step beside me. She tangled her fingers in front of her, braiding and unbraiding them, knuckles bleaching white before color rushed back in.

God, I wanted to reach for one of those hands. Let her strangle *my* fingers if she needed to. Let her pour her pain into me.

But I didn't. I wouldn't cross that unspoken boundary.

For so many reasons.

I held the door open for Nova, and she slipped inside. The moment the door was closed, quiet reigned. Wylder had gotten the room soundproofed so he could escape the noise when he needed to. But now, it was almost too quiet.

"They can just…find you, drag everything up," Nova spat, a little of the color coming back to her cheeks.

"It should be illegal."

Those gray eyes cut to me and turned silver. "It should be more than that." She sucked in a breath. "I know they aren't all that way. Dex's friend, Ridley, wasn't. I listened to her podcast. She was kind, trying to help."

There were good eggs out there, just like with any profession. But something about reporters covering certain kinds of crime lent itself to predatory behavior.

"It feels like they're cutting you wide open, and no one can do a thing to stop it." My words came out just a little hoarse, because giving her that truth cost me.

Nova stopped pacing and stared at me for a long moment. "You say that like you know how it feels."

I struggled to swallow, my throat sticking on the movement as if I hadn't had anything to drink in hours. "I do."

She was quiet. Waiting. I knew she wasn't a stranger to silence. She'd had to live with it for countless hours during the year Travis held her. But this was different. Her silence now was a gentle request with infinite patience on the other end.

She deserved to know. For so many reasons. First and foremost because she'd be moving into my house. And some people didn't want to risk being in the same vicinity as someone who shared DNA with a killer. Skylar's mother certainly hadn't. Maybe my mother hadn't either.

"Brae hasn't told you about our father, has she?"

Dex had shared that she wanted to wait. Not burden Nova or frighten her when she was still getting her sea legs. But it had been four months now. And it felt like a lie more than anything at this point.

Nova's brows pulled together. "I know that you and your brothers came to live with Waylon when you were kids."

I nodded, but the movement felt robotic. "When I was seventeen. Mav was eleven. Dex was twelve. Orion was fifteen. And Wylder was eighteen. After we found out our father was a serial killer."

Nova sucked in an audible breath, but she didn't move. She didn't run. Or scream. Or look at me with horror in her expression.

Instead, her gray eyes filled with sorrow. "Kol. I'm so sorry. I can't imagine."

"So I know all about reporters. Ones who will do anything for a headline. For their name above the fold."

Nova did something I never would've expected. She moved closer. For a second, I thought she might reach out and take my hand. She didn't. But she got so close I could feel the heat coming off her body, see the faintest smattering of freckles on her nose.

"I hate that you know how it feels," she whispered. "That you lived through that."

I stared down at her in wonder. "Why aren't you running?"

Her mouth puckered in an adorable little frown. "Why would I run?"

"Because I come from the same kind of monster that nearly killed you."

Nova didn't look away from me as she spoke. "You lived with a monster, just like I did. It makes sense why you understand me so well. I hate that that's why. But I'm also grateful. Because the darkness doesn't scare you. Because you lived in it, too."

Hell, she was right. Maybe that was why I felt such a kinship with Nova. Because we could face the darkness the way others couldn't. "Phoenix," I whispered.

The sound of her nickname swirled in the air between us. We were so close. My fingers ached to reach out, to skim across her cheek.

The door swung open, and Nova jumped back and away from me.

Wylder filled the doorway, his gaze pinging back and forth between us. "Sorry. I just wanted you to know he's gone. Got a photo so we can show it to the rest of the staff. Make sure he doesn't come back. I should've gotten his name—"

"Reese Gatlin." Nova's voice was stronger now, as if she'd shoved all the hurt and pain down, and her mask was back in place. I hated it.

"I'll add that to the info we already have," Wylder said.

Nova nodded. "I gotta get back out there."

She skirted around Wylder without a backward glance, and I felt some sort of invisible tug as she went, an urge to follow her. But I locked it down. Instead, I pulled out my phone and typed out a text.

> **Me:** *Need you to pull everything you can on a Reese Gatlin. Reporter. Wylder will send you his photo.*

It only took a second to get a reply.

> **Dex:** *Are YOU seriously asking me to do something illegal?*

I scowled at the screen.

> **Me:** *Are you going to help me or not?*
>
> **Dex:** *On it. This have something to do with Nova?*
>
> **Me:** *Yes.*

That was all I could give him. Because if I gave him more, the rage would take hold.

I shoved my phone into my pocket and looked up to find Wylder watching me. "Need you to send Dex that photo of the reporter."

"I can do that," he said slowly. "Since when do you activate Dex?"

He had a point. In the secret work we did in the shadows, I steered clear of anything that crossed a black-and-white line. If something strayed into less-than-legal territory, I wasn't part of it. Because I had more to lose than the rest of my brothers. I had a daughter who counted on me. I was her only parent, and I couldn't risk being a part of something that could create blowback on me—on her.

"I'm not breaking any laws. I'm just asking Dex to dig a little."

Wylder arched a brow. "You might not be breaking any laws, but you are bending them."

Which wasn't something I did. Ever. But for Nova? It felt like I'd do anything.

Chapter Ten

NOVA

I FELT MY PHONE BUZZ AS A BIG, FURRY BODY LEANED AGAINST me where I sat on the back deck. Yeti was aptly named, and it wasn't surprising that my best friend had named her dog after Bigfoot. I leaned right back against Yeti's strong form. She sighed, and I copied the sound.

Sometimes, at least these days, it felt like it was easier to be around animals than humans. And the nature all around us didn't hurt either. This was the perfect spot to take in the early morning sky painted with colors and the way it made the creek glow. It was almost…perfect.

I forced myself to glance down at my cell as I took a sip of coffee.

Kol: *How's today?*

Maybe the *no-human* rule wasn't entirely true. Kol got me. He understood. Even the way he phrased questions felt like less pressure. It wasn't *"How are you feeling?"* or *"Is everything okay?"* He left things more open-ended.

I lifted my phone, snapping a photo of me and the beast of a dog.

> **Me:** *I've got a damn good dog, damn good coffee, and a damn good sunrise.*

It was past sunrise now, but the sun still hovered low in the sky.

> **Kol:** *Sounds like a damn good day.*

> **Me:** *I think it's going to be. How about you?*

A second later, a photo appeared on my device. Skylar grinned back at the camera, flour smeared across her face and her rainbow apron.

> **Kol:** *We're making chocolate chip waffles.*

> **Me:** *I am very jealous.*

> **Kol:** *We'll make you some after you move in.*

A shiver of anticipation slid through me. I told myself it was nerves about my fresh start. But I couldn't help wondering if it was more about Kol.

The door opened behind me, but I didn't glance back. I hated that I hoped it wasn't Brae. I just wasn't ready to be cornered again. I wasn't ready for the analysis of how I was doing.

"Beautiful." The deep voice belonged to Dex, and relief flooded my system.

"It really is. You guys have a good spot."

Dex made a humming sound. "I'll miss it when our house is done."

He and Brae were building a new home on Twisted Oak Ranch property, but it would be several months before it was done.

"I don't know, your spot on the ranch is pretty epic."

"It is," Dex agreed. "But this is where I fell in love with Brae."

My heart squeezed as I finally looked up at the love of my best friend's life. He was still a little rumpled from sleep, and his tortoiseshell glasses were slightly askew, but I could see the love shining in his dark-hazel eyes. He was *gone* for my best friend. And God, she deserved that. More than anyone I knew.

I grinned up at him. "Who knew you were a romantic at heart?"

Dex chuckled. "Don't tell anyone. I like to keep it under wraps."

"Your secret's safe with me."

"Thank you." He studied me for a moment. "Kol asked me to look into the reporter."

I stiffened slightly, waiting for Dex to suggest I shouldn't be working because of this sort of thing. But he didn't.

"He never asks me to do that," Dex went on. "Never."

A buzz lit beneath my skin. "The reporter was pressing Kol, too. Wanted to interview him. He probably just wants to make sure Reese will steer clear of him and Skylar."

It made sense. Kol was incredibly protective of his little girl. And I understood why. Not only was she a special soul, but he was raising her completely on his own. Which was a different sort of pressure. Every decision rested squarely on his shoulders. I knew that Sky's mom wasn't in the picture. I just couldn't imagine why someone would ever give up those two.

Dex stared at me for a long moment. "I don't think that's why he asked."

My breath hitched, and I swallowed slowly. "I—"

Owen stumbled out the back door, still so tired, he looked a little drunk. He gazed up at Dex, his glasses also askew. "Pancakes?" he asked hopefully.

"Is it the weekend?" Dex shot back.

"Yes?" It came out as more of a question. Like Owen wasn't sure what day it was.

"It's the weekend, Bubs," I said with a laugh.

"Yes!" Owen shot his fist in the air and turned to me. "Will you help us make the pancakes, Supernova?"

My heart squeezed again. God, I'd missed this kid. It killed that I'd never get back the year I missed. But I would take advantage of what we had now.

I pushed to my feet. "Only if I can put chocolate chips *and* blueberries in mine."

Owen grinned. "You should add Oreos, too."

"Genius!" I said and followed him into the kitchen.

Brae guided her SUV through the outskirts of Starlight Grove. It wasn't an area I was familiar with, full of established neighborhoods with beautiful yards. I wondered if I could see myself in a house like that someday. It didn't seem quite right. Too many people, too close.

The thought was amusing, since I'd lived in a bustling city for almost a decade. But something had changed in me. And that shift craved wide-open spaces.

"So Cora invited you?" Brae asked, making another turn that took us out of the neighborhood we were in.

I nodded. "We had…a moment."

Brae's gaze flicked to me and then back to the road. "A moment."

"I needed to tell her it wasn't her fault."

Brae swallowed hard. "I can't imagine what she's going through."

"Me neither."

"And she's not talking to anyone. Not really. I think Wylder can occasionally get her to open up a little, but we're all…worried."

I studied my best friend. God, she had a lot on her shoulders right now. "You know it's not up to you to make sure everyone's okay, right? We have to take charge of our own lives."

Brae's lips pressed together—not in a frown or in frustration, but as if she were holding in her words until she was completely sure what she wanted to say. "We all need help sometimes. I learned that this past year: that it's okay to ask for help when we need it."

She pulled into a parking spot at a beautiful park. I was quiet for a moment before I replied. "I'll ask when I need it. I promise."

Brae stared at me, and I saw the hurt flash across her expression. Because, in her mind, I needed help now and wasn't asking. But she didn't understand that I had to stumble to find my way.

She blew out a breath and opened her door. "Okay."

Shit.

Just another moment to add to the tally of all the times I'd hurt Brae—the *last* person I ever wanted to harm. And that killed.

Adjusting my sunglasses, I shoved open my door and followed her toward a small pavilion of sorts with about a dozen or so people milling around. One of the picnic tables was full of food, snacks, and drinks. A couple of kids raced in circles as a woman with a smile and tanned skin, creased with age, looked on.

As she lifted her head, I saw her suck in a breath, her gaze locking onto me. But then her expression softened, and her eyes went misty. She shoved up from her chair and crossed toward us.

She pulled Brae in for a quick hug and then turned to me. "Nova?"

I nodded, a little uncomfortable that she knew who I was.

"I'm Alma. Been a member of this group for a long time. My daughter, Maya, she…"

Her voice trailed off, but I could've finished the sentence for her. Her daughter Maya was one of Travis's victims.

"I'm so sorry," I whispered.

"It's not for you to be sorry for," Alma said quickly. "I'm so glad to meet you. So glad you're here. That you got out."

My throat burned as I watched the kids who looked so much like Alma running and jumping and yelling. Kids I knew belonged to Maya, who would now grow up without their mom. But I was grateful they had a grandmother who had clearly stepped in. "Thank you," I rasped.

"Brae!" a woman called, a smile on her face. "It's so good to see you. It's been too long."

The woman wore cropped jeans and a pale-purple button-down shirt and had her blond hair pulled up in a casual twist with a clip. She looked to be in her late thirties with just a hint of some smile lines around her eyes. This had to be Holly.

Brae had told me bits and pieces about the Compass crew, and I'd met her friend, Aster, several times before. But I'd never met Holly.

"It has been too long," Brae agreed, giving her a quick hug. "Holly, this is Nova. Nova, this is the president of the Juniper County chapter of Compass, Holly."

The woman's eyes flared ever so slightly, but she covered it quickly. "Welcome, Nova. We're happy to have you."

"Thank you." I forced a smile. This might've been a mistake. Two people in, and I already felt like there was an ice pick chipping away behind my eyes.

But then I saw Cora. She stood a little off to the side, talking quietly with Aster. Her arms were curled around herself, her shoulders slightly slumped. I instantly knew why I had come.

"Excuse me," I mumbled. "I see someone I need to say hello to."

I crossed the grass, feeling eyes on me, but I shoved that knowledge down. Instead, I focused on Cora. She wore jeans that looked a little too baggy and a shirt she was drowning in. I wondered if she wasn't eating normally with all the stress. I wouldn't say a word about it, though. Because I knew exactly how that felt.

"Cora," I called as I walked up.

Her head jerked up, green eyes widening a fraction before a soft smile graced her face. "You came."

"I did." I scanned the group, each member looking away the second I caught them staring. Everyone except for one man. He had dark eyes and hair with a little silver at his temples. He might've been in his mid-forties or a touch older. He didn't stop staring in my direction.

A little chill went down my spine, but I forced my attention back to my small group. "Hi, Aster. It's good to see you again."

"You, too," she said with a genuine smile.

I really liked the woman. She had an ease to her. Nothing seemed to rile her. Maybe it was her skills as a therapist that kept her so even. She could deal with anything and everything, and she had more style in her pinky than I had in all of me.

Today, she had some of her pale-blond hair pulled back in a boho braid with the rest hanging in loose waves. She wore wide-legged jeans with a turquoise belt, and her artfully faded blouse was covered in tiny flowers. Cowboy boots I knew got some real use on her grandfather's ranch peeked out from under the hem of her jeans.

But the real showstopper was her eyes. The blue of her irises was so pale they almost looked translucent.

Aster held my gaze, not looking away like most did. "You look great, Nova."

I was sure I looked a hell of a lot better than when she'd first seen me, a week or two out of rehab and still jumping at every little sound and movement, not much more than skin and bones. Gaining the weight I so desperately needed had been a difficult task. When I was in the hospital and the rehab center, everything had been carefully monitored. If I'd eaten too much, too quickly, there could have been potentially deadly repercussions.

"Thanks. I'm feeling good," I told her honestly. I could feel myself getting stronger with my bike rides and swims. But I craved more. Things that reminded me I was alive. Maybe a self-defense course.

"Hey, Aster," Brae said as she walked up. "It's so good to see you." She pulled her friend into a quick hug. As she released her, Brae's gaze moved between the two of us. "You guys should talk. Aster might have some therapist recs you would like, Nova."

Everything in me hardened to stone. It felt like a slap—no, worse. Like the slice of a blade, cutting into all the progress I thought I'd made.

Aster sent Brae a gentle smile. "Nova knows I'm an open door, anytime she needs anything. But *she* needs to be the one who decides that."

Brae's cheeks flushed. "I just—"

"Nova, why don't you come with me?" Cora cut in. "I'll introduce you around."

"Thanks," I said quickly, heading toward the group of strangers, even though it was the last place I wanted to go. But I'd take gawking strangers over my best friend thinking I needed to head back to a shrink any day.

"She doesn't mean it in a bad way," Cora said softly.

"I know, it just..."

"Feels like someone cutting you down when you've just gotten your sea legs."

One corner of my mouth kicked up. "Exactly. You get it."

She let out a low whistle. "Brae and Holly are mama bears to the core. They want to fix and coddle and protect. But sometimes, what I need is space."

"God, do I feel that. I worry all the time that I'm going to bite Brae's head off in a way that does serious damage because I just need to…breathe."

"You're alive. You're breathing."

I heard Kol's voice in my head, my grounding stone.

"Get that space. Honestly, I lie if I have to." Cora let out a little laugh. "The other night, I told Holly I had to do an emergency deep-conditioning treatment on my hair and couldn't go to dinner." Her mouth curved wide. "Hair emergencies for the win."

"Your locks do look extra luscious today," I said with a laugh.

Cora flicked them over one shoulder. "Why, thank you."

I felt those eyes on me again. The kind that held a different sort of energy. I sought out the feeling and found the same dark-haired man staring at me. He was almost glaring but not quite.

"Who is that?" I asked, my voice dropping to a whisper.

Cora followed my line of sight. When she finally spoke, her voice went quiet. "Jack Hooper. His wife, Cynthia, was—"

"One of the victims," I finished for her so she wouldn't have to say the words.

Cora nodded. "He's mad. But not at you."

"At the universe."

"The universe and Trav. At first, I thought he would hate me, but he's been nothing but kind. Even brings me fresh-caught fish every few weeks because he knows Trav used to do that for me."

An ache settled in my chest. It felt like everyone in this small community had been marked by this thing. By Travis. If Dex hadn't already killed him, I'd be gunning for the job.

Cora's gaze flicked up to my face. "Can I ask you something? If it's too much, you can tell me to take a flying leap."

Tension curled around my muscles, but I managed to speak. Because I knew it would likely cost her to bring up whatever this was. "Sure. If it's something I don't want to answer, I'll tell you."

"Good." Cora said the word as if the syllable was an exhale. "Do you still not remember anything? I'm just…I'm trying to make sense of it." Tears swirled in her green eyes. "To me, he was wonderful. Always caring, *never* doing anything even close to violent. I'm just trying to understand who the other half of him was. *Why* he did it."

My heart broke for her. I couldn't imagine having someone I loved turn out to be the kind of monster Travis was. Kol's face flashed in my mind. The truth he'd bared to me. What he'd carried. It was so similar to Cora's yet so different.

"Nothing concrete," I whispered. "Just flashes now and then. But I'm honestly not sure if they're memories or something my mind conjured up because of the different things the doctors and law enforcement officers have told me. It's still mostly just blank."

Cora worried the corner of her lip. "I guess…that might be for the best."

I heard her unspoken words. *Even though I won't get answers.*

"If I do remember anything, I'll tell you." But that was a lie. Because not knowing might be better for Cora, too. Knowing the details of what her ex-fiancé had done would only give her nightmares.

"Thank you," she whispered.

A glint of something caught in the afternoon light. Sun on metal? Glass?

And then I saw him.

That same stupid mustard beanie. The blond beard. And a long-lens camera.

Reese, the reporter, was taking photos of me, and I could do nothing to stop it. I was in a public place. But something niggled at me.

How the hell did he know I would be here?

Chapter Eleven

KOL

"Quick, someone snap a pic of me for my profile," Maverick ordered, lifting the beam higher as he stood in the center of the garage apartment. "I look fuckin' ripped."

Wylder scoffed. "Is this for your desperation app?"

Mav glared at our eldest brother. "That's rude. There are plenty of people looking for lasting connections on there."

Dex let out a snicker. "The app is called Seven Minutes in Heaven."

Mav just shrugged. "Seven minutes to forever. Now, someone take the damn photo."

"I'll do it just to shut you up so we can get moving." I snapped a shot and then shoved my phone back into my pocket.

"Someone else," Maverick begged. "Kol is the worst with tech. He probably cut off my head or got an angle that gave me five chins. You'd think he was geriatric with his fumbling and bumbling."

I glared at Mav. "I might only be the second oldest, but I can still kick your ass."

Wylder pressed the nail gun to the beam in strategic places. "Remember when Kol lost his password keeper?"

Dex gave an exaggerated shiver. "Who keeps passwords written down in a notebook?"

"Not Kol anymore," Mav said with a laugh.

"I still haven't forgiven you," I clipped at Dex.

"Hey, you needed to learn a lesson," he defended. "That shit isn't safe."

"Oh, I did learn a lesson. I keep them locked in my safe now," I informed him.

Dex's jaw dropped. "You got a safe to *lock* away your passwords instead of just using the software I bought you?"

I shrugged. "My system works."

"Daddy!" Skylar called as she tromped up the stairs.

"In here, Little Princess," I called.

She appeared in all her badass princess glory. She wore sparkly, bright-pink tights with mud on the knees, combat boots, a sweatshirt that read *It Wasn't Me,* and a Nerf gun strapped to her front and fairy wings on her back. Skylar, through and through.

"Can Owen and I have an alpaca rodeo?" she asked nonchalantly as her bestie appeared at her back.

I arched a brow. "What does an alpaca rodeo entail?"

Sky shrugged slightly, making her fairy wings dance. "Like we could ride them and shoot at targets."

"And do jousting like in medieval times," Owen threw in.

"That sounds sick," Mav called. "I'm in."

I glared at him. "You are not in. No one is in. All of those activities sound like they'd put you at extreme risk. Plus, you can't ride an alpaca."

Skylar frowned. "But they like me. They almost never spit at me."

"I like it when they spit," Owen said with a grin.

I pinched the bridge of my nose, searching for something that might help me win this battle. My hand dropped. "It's not good for the alpacas. Their backs aren't made to hold a human's weight."

"It would hurt them?" Sky asked, instantly worried.

"It would."

"We can't do that," she said quickly.

"Naw, bruh, we can't," Owen grumbled. But then his face lit up. "What about on horseback?"

We only had six horses on the ranch, nothing like the spread Aster's family had next door. They not only had cattle but also a horse-breeding operation.

"O," Dex said. "You don't know how to ride."

"I could learn," Owen shot back.

Dex shook his head. "Not in a day. You want to learn? I'll get Aster to give you lessons. She's the best."

Mischief lit in Maverick's expression. "I can take him to lessons."

"Mav," Dex warned.

"What? The Ice Queen can't object to me dropping off my soon-to-be nephew at lessons," Maverick argued.

"No, but she can shoot you in the balls," Wylder said.

I had no idea what had happened between Mav and Aster. They'd been thick as thieves for years. She'd been the one person who seemed to be able to reach him after everything happened. But something changed at the end of high school. They went from the best of friends to enemies in a flash.

Skylar frowned. "Why would Uncle Mav bring balls to horseback riding lessons?"

I glared at Wylder. "Thanks for that."

"Hey, I didn't curse," Wylder shot back.

Skylar grinned, revealing another loose tooth. "My swear jar is so full, I'm gonna get the new supercharged Nerf gun in no time."

"Such great influences on my daughter," I grumbled.

"Hey," Maverick said, affronted. "I'm a *great* influence."

Dex just stared at our youngest brother. "You are the absolute worst influence in the history of influences."

"Uncle Mav's the best," Sky cut in. "He taught me how to jump off the hayloft."

The room went quiet.

"Maverick," I snarled.

Uncle Waylon broke into the room, breathing heavily. "These little whippersnappers are fast."

Skylar giggled. "Sorry, Grampa Way Way."

"What do you say we go look for Bigfoot?" he suggested to Skylar and Owen.

"Sick," Owen muttered. "Let's do it."

"Yeah!" Sky cheered.

"No firearms," I ordered.

Uncle Waylon looked affronted. "I would never harm a Bigfoot."

"Of course he wouldn't," Wylder muttered.

Dex struggled not to laugh. "Have fun, you crazy kids."

As they filed out of the room, I turned back to my brothers. "Come on. All we have left is the finish work." But that could be deceptive. It was important to get it right, so it could take forever. "I think we can get it done in another day or two tops."

Dex stared at me for a long moment. "Yeah, if we work around the clock."

Wylder's gaze changed, taking on that studious quality. "What's the rush, anyway?"

I shifted slightly, moving my weight from one foot to the other. I might as well let the cat out of the bag. "Nova's going to move in here."

Everything went dead quiet.

It was Mav who finally broke the silence. "Seriously?"

I gave a chin lift of assent. "Yeah. She needs her own space."

"Under your roof?" Wylder challenged.

I couldn't help but bristle at Wy's words. It was as if he was saying I was doing something wrong. "You have a problem with that?"

"I don't, but Orion might."

My back molars ground together. Our middle brother didn't want anyone but family on ranch land. It had taken him repeated dinners and Brae besting him in a hot-sauce-eating competition to get him to soften toward her. But he'd avoided Nova altogether. Every time she came for dinner, he ditched.

Maverick grinned and held up his phone. "Don't worry. I already texted him."

"You're a goddamned shit-stirrer," I growled.

Mav just shrugged. "Chill. You know you'll need to have it out with him eventually, and at least this will get him out of his hovel."

Orion's house was hardly a hovel. It was huge—which was ridiculous for a man who didn't let any of us inside. But since the incident with our father, Orion didn't like to feel fenced in.

"I needed some time to prepare," I shot back.

"Nothing's going to prepare you for Rion's wrath on this one," Wylder said. "You know that."

He had a point.

I heard an engine in the distance and knew it had to be our brother. Another handful of seconds passed, then a door slammed. I winced at the fury behind the sound. And it was only punctuated by heavy bootsteps on the stairs.

Orion filled the doorway. He had a good inch or two on the rest of us, his shoulders wider and his whole frame slightly more menacing. And the dark-hazel glare he cut my way told me he was not pleased with me.

He brought his pointer and middle fingers together with his thumb in a harsh movement. I knew the sign was ASL for *no*. And, of course, that was all Orion would say.

When he stopped talking after killing our father, it had been a slow retreat. At first, he would write, and then he learned to sign. But over time, he slowly communicated less and less. And when he did, he kept it as brief as possible.

I signed as I talked, a habit I'd picked up so Orion never felt like the outsider. "You don't get to just say *no*."

"No." Orion made the sign again.

"This isn't an autocracy," I shot back.

Orion's hands moved faster as he continued. *"I'm not having a stranger on this property. No one lives here but family."*

"She's not a stranger," I argued. But that wouldn't win Orion over. Because we all knew the truth: anyone could turn on you. So, in Orion's mind, the fewer people he let in, the better.

I tried a different tack as he glared at me. "She needs this." There was an almost pleading tone to my voice. "She said she can't breathe. She needs a safe place where she can start to stretch her wings a little more. She's not ready for an apartment in town. There are too many potential triggers."

Dex bristled beside me. Not in a way that said he was shocked, but that he was worried. Still, he didn't say a word.

A hint of indecision played out across Orion's expression, but he just shook his head. *"I'm sorry. No."*

"She told me she's scared." Guilt pricked at me for sharing something Nova had told me in confidence. But I needed him to see. To understand.

Orion scrubbed a hand over his face, but he wasn't saying anything now.

"Please, Rion. She needs this. And I think I do, too. I need to know she's safe and healing. What I saw when I found her…it still haunts me."

He stilled, his eyes locking with mine. *"She stays two hundred yards away from my house at all times."*

"She can do that."

Orion jerked his head in a nod. *"Fine."*

Relief swept through me. "Thank you." I winced, glancing around the room. "Can you keep this under wraps? You can share that Nova's living on the ranch but not over my garage. It's a gray area with me working the case."

Gray area was stretching it. If she found out, Sherri would reassign my ass so fast, my head would spin. And that was if she didn't suspend me.

Mav gaped at me. "When do you *ever* dabble in the gray?"

I met his stare head-on. "When it means doing the right thing."

"Fair point," he mumbled.

My gaze shifted to Dex. "Hold off on telling Brae. Nova wants to be the one to talk to her."

He studied me for a long moment. "I hope you know what you're doing."

Hell. I hoped I did, too.

Chapter Twelve

NOVA

THE WIND SWIRLED AROUND ME WITH A LITTLE MORE BITE than it normally had, and I was glad I'd worn a sweatshirt. But damn, it was beautiful here—the kind of beauty that reminded you of all the life you had left to live.

The sun made the dark green of the forest glow in a way that reminded me of Kol's eyes, all that green and gold. As I stood at the top of a steep drop-off, my fingers tightened around the handlebars. I watched two mountain bikers navigating a course that looked like a roller coaster through the wild woods. The one in a bright-orange shirt hit some sort of mound and went flying.

I wanted that. I *needed* it.

The article flashed in my mind. *Nova Monroe Seeks Solace with Fellow Victims.* Photos of me splashed across a stupid blog and the website for a paper out of Redding.

Energy hummed through me, though not the good kind. The

kind that made me feel like I wanted to claw my skin off. I'd gone cliff jumping right after seeing it, but it hadn't worked.

My face—still a little too pale. My cheeks—still a little too hollow. My eyes—still far too haunted.

It was as if the photo Reese Gatlin had snapped told the truth while I was living a lie. So when I went to jump off the cliff the way I always did, it didn't do the job like it normally would. There was no relief. No certainty that I was *alive*, that I was *breathing*.

I needed more.

The second figure, in a flame-printed shirt, coasted over a part of the trail that sent his bike practically sideways. I had no clue how he didn't fall straight on his head.

This was probably a mistake. Stupid. But I was desperate. And if I didn't get some sort of release, I wasn't sure I would make it through the day without breaking.

"Supernova?"

I jolted at the sound of my nickname, twisting on the bike that, while it could be considered fit for mountain trails, had seen far better days. As I turned, surprise flared as I took in Maverick. He was fully kitted out, looking like some ninja biker.

He wore an all-black material that skimmed over his form. Skulls decorated his gloves, and sunglasses in a metallic orange covered half his face.

He tipped those glasses up and took me in as if needing to make sure it was really me. "What are you doing out here?"

My shoulders instantly stiffened, as if I were about to be reported to the teacher. "I wanted to try mountain biking."

Mav's jaw slackened slightly. "You wanted to *try* mountain biking," he parroted.

"Yes. Is there something wrong with that?" I snapped.

"Not a damn thing. But you're sitting at the top of an advanced trail that's going to dump you on your ass for sure."

My chin jutted out in defiance, but I caught a rider out of the corner of my eye going through a harrowing series of obstacles, and that defiance slid out of me, leaving behind nothing but defeat—defeat and that anxious, muscle-twitching energy that needed an outlet. "I need *something.*"

Maverick frowned. "What do you mean?"

A wave of dizziness hit, telling me the anxiety was getting worse. "I need to breathe," I croaked.

It only took a second for understanding to dawn for Mav. "Follow me," he clipped.

He was already stepping down on one pedal, riding back toward the parking lot as I followed him. But instead of going there, he made a sharp left turn into some trees and onto another path. He stopped just shy of a different trail's start.

I hadn't seen this one right off, since it was protected by the trees. But it looked like one of those terrifying water slides that shot you straight down, then spat you out.

"This is called 'the Slingshot,'" Mav informed me.

"How is it better than the other one?" I choked out, my muscles still tight around my throat.

"This is a straight shot, and there's a long, flat tail at the end for you to slow. It'll give you the dose of adrenaline you need, but it's a hell of a lot safer than the Gauntlet because there's not as much to navigate."

I nodded slowly, adjusting my helmet. "What do I need to do?"

"Bent knees, bent elbows so you can adjust your weight forward or back. But mostly, you'll want to stay centered over your bike. Do *not* slam on your brakes. You'll go flying. Feathering touches to slow down. Take your time at the bottom. I'll follow behind you."

I played Maverick's instructions over and over in my head. Bent knees. Bent elbows. Centered weight. Feather the brakes.

I was sure Mav expected me to ask more, to see if it was okay to go. But I didn't. The anxiety was riding me too hard. So I simply shoved off.

It only took three pedal pumps to send me tipping over the top of the hill. For a second, I hung there, as if my body had no weight at all. And then, I flew.

The wind whipped against me as I hovered over the bike seat. It was like a harsh slap and a brutal wake-up call all at once. And it was everything.

The wind and the shock forced the air from my lungs. Forced me to breathe. But more, I *felt* my heartbeat. The rushing thrum of my pulse. And it all led to one simple piece of knowledge.

I was alive.

I held on to it with a vicious force. And suddenly, I could hear Kol's voice in my head again.

"You're alive. You're breathing."

I let it play over and over as I flew down the slope. It was beauty and force and living out loud.

Hitting the bottom of the incline, my bike shot out down the path, giving me a whole new understanding of why the trail was called the Slingshot. But it wasn't long before I started to slow. I feathered the brakes, just as Maverick had instructed, until I came to a stop.

And I was still breathing.

I pulled my bike over to the side, watching as Mav guided his bike far more smoothly than I had. He came to a stop in a move that sent dirt flying and grinned at me. "How'd it feel?"

"Amazing," I told him honestly.

"Hell yeah. Nothing like a little adrenaline dump to get the day started."

I studied the youngest Archer brother for a moment. "How'd you know?"

His dark brows furrowed. "What do you mean?"

"You knew this would help. How? Most people think it's weird." Okay, that wasn't exactly true. *Brae* thought it was weird. The little she knew. "Or unhealthy."

Mav shrugged, tipping his sunglasses up again. "Seems a hell of a lot healthier than medicating with drugs, alcohol, sex, or the million other things people reach for."

He had a point there.

"Sometimes, the world gets too loud," Mav said softly. "This helps. And it reminds me that I'm still here."

My mouth thinned—not in irritation but in understanding. This sort of thing called to us in similar ways. And I was grateful I had someone who didn't think I was a freak for needing this.

"Nova?" a voice called.

I turned to see a woman approaching the trail on horseback—a woman I recognized. Aster had her blond hair pulled back into a low bun and a flat-brimmed cowboy hat shielding her face from the sun.

"Hi," I called, surprise lighting the word.

She beamed at me. "I recognized the hair."

My long, nearly black hair was woven into a braid that went halfway down my back. "It's a giveaway." I climbed off my bike, leaning it against a tree and crossing to Aster and her horse. "And who's this sweet creature?"

"This is Daisy. And she loves to come watch the bikers."

She was beautiful, covered in a patchwork of large brown and white spots.

"Can I say hello?" I asked.

"She'd love that," Aster said with a smile.

"What about me, Ice Queen?" Mav cut in. "No hello?"

"Didn't notice you there, Satan. Maybe because you're in your home environment—the dirt," Aster shot back.

Maverick's lips twitched. "Come on, now. It's fun to get a little dirty once in a while. Live a little."

Aster's pale-blue eyes narrowed on him. "Our ideas of fun aren't the same."

My gaze ping-ponged between the two of them as I thought about stroking Daisy's cheek but decided against it. I'd never seen either of them this combative with *anyone*.

A hint of confusion lit in Maverick's eyes, but he covered it quickly. "That's a shame. Might be good for you to remove the stick from your ass every once in a while."

Aster gaped at him for a moment and then quickly shut her mouth, turning back to me. "Shoot me a text if you ever want to go riding. The horses can always use the exercise."

"I've never ridden before," I admitted. Growing up in coastal

Rhode Island with parents who were more focused on money for booze than food didn't exactly give me the opportunity for lessons.

"Not a problem," Aster assured me. "We've got plenty of good horses to learn from."

I studied the horse, a sense of peace gliding over me. "I'd love that."

"Good. I need to head back to the ranch, but we'll set it up." Aster's gaze flicked to Mav, her armor in place. "Satan."

"Ice Queen," he clipped.

Jesus.

Aster turned her horse and encouraged it into a faster gait, taking off for the forest beyond.

I turned back to Maverick. "What's the story between you two?"

Mav shrugged, shooting me a grin that was as fake as that orange cheese that shot out of a can. "Some people just hate me because I'm so damn attractive."

I stared back at him for a long moment. And for the briefest flash, I swore I saw sadness in those dark-hazel eyes.

"Come on, Supernova. You want your first real mountain biking lesson?" he asked.

I knew he was searching for a change of topic, but I gave it to him anyway. Because I knew what it was like to have things you didn't want to talk about. "Show me the ropes, trail king."

"Now *that's* the kind of respect I'm talking about."

I let out a laugh that sounded a little more like a snort. "You need help."

He waggled his eyebrows at me. "I could be into the nurse thing."

"I'm talking about the kind of help that reduces your ego."

Mav waved me off. "Naw, I'm perfect as is."

I just shook my head as I followed him toward the switchbacks that would lead us back up the mountainside.

We spent the next two hours covering the basics and doing some practice rides on the beginner paths. I even managed a ride down a trail that was rated a blue square, which meant it was more difficult, but Mav insisted I needed a little more practice before hitting a black diamond.

By the time we walked our bikes back to the parking lot, my whole body hurt. I might've pushed it a bit too much, but the relief that came from having tired muscles instead of anxious, twitchy ones was worth it.

"Thank you," I said, casting a glance Maverick's way. "You were probably coming to work out on that double black diamond trail, and you spent the day on the equivalent of a bunny slope."

"I don't mind," he assured me. "Honestly, it's good to go back to the basics once in a while. And I'm glad I could help." He opened his mouth to say something else, then stopped. Then started again. "I know you went through hell. If there's anything I can do to make things easier on you, that feels good."

Normally, I would have hated someone bringing that up. Especially now. But I found I didn't mind it as much here. Because Mav was talking about how this all made him feel. And I got that. What had happened to me, and to so many others, had marked a community—the people who knew the victims and the killer.

"I'm glad, then. And I will let you give me more death-defying lessons."

Mav barked out a laugh. "Just don't tell Brae. That little badass scares me."

One corner of my mouth kicked up. He was right to be scared.

My footsteps slowed as we approached Brae's SUV that she'd let me borrow for the day. There was an envelope on the windshield. One of those legal-sized ones. And there was no name on it. But as I took in the five or so other vehicles in the lot, I noticed that none of them had an envelope.

Before I could let anxiety grab hold again, I snatched it up and opened it. It wasn't sealed, but there were countless things inside. Newspaper clippings and blog printouts.

I started flipping through them, my anger mounting as I did.

Nova Monroe Missing for Nine Months.

Woman Disappears on a Hike with Friend. Police Have No Answers.

My stomach twisted at the next one.

House of Horrors Found in the Northern California Mountains. Woman Kept Chained.

A flash of something streaked across my mind. Memory or imagination, I wasn't sure. *I pulled at the chain in the wall as hard as I could. My fingers cramped, and I could tell that one of my nails had broken down the center, but I didn't care. I had to get out. Away. Then a deep laugh sounded. Through a speaker? "You'll never escape. You belong to me now."*

I blinked away the mental snapshots and the echo of the voice, but my hands trembled as I kept flipping through the articles and printouts. All covering my case, the other missing persons cases, Travis.

And finally, a piece of blank computer paper with block writing.

NEVER FORGET.

"Super—what the fuck?" Mav growled, peeking over my shoulder.

I tried to shove all the articles back into the envelope but failed. Instead, I scooped them into a pile and searched for my anger again. Because I knew exactly who'd done this. "It's nothing."

"That's not nothing," he argued.

"It's that goddamned reporter. He thinks I owe him something because he wrote a few articles and uses the word *thus*."

Maverick studied me for a long moment, not showing any signs of humor at my attempt at a joke. "You're probably right, but why don't you let me bag it just in case?"

I frowned. "Bag it?"

He beeped the locks on his SUV on the other side of the parking lot. "Put it in an evidence bag. That way, if anything else weird happens, we have it. Even if it is him, we should keep evidence in case you want to file a restraining order."

I frowned at him. "Why do you have evidence bags?"

Mav's gaze flicked to the side and then back to me. "You know, arson cases and stuff."

"Oh. Yeah, sure." It wasn't like I wanted to keep the stuff. And it did make sense that Mav would have things that allowed him to store evidence since he worked as both a smokejumper and a firefighter and medic for the Starlight Grove Fire Department.

He jogged over to his vehicle and then back, holding open a bag with *EVIDENCE* in big, black letters at the top. "Slide it all in here."

I dropped the envelope and stack of clippings in. "Hey, do me a favor and don't tell Brae about this. Dex either. Because he'll tell her, and she'll freak. I just can't…"

Maverick sent me a sympathetic smile. "I won't. I get it. Just do me a favor and keep an extra sharp eye out."

"Of course." But it was just a pretentious reporter or maybe a sick prank. It had to be.

Chapter Thirteen

KOL

"Who was in charge of snacks this week? Because this seriously sucks," Mav muttered as he took in the offerings of sodas, chips, and a hummus-and-veggie platter.

I scowled at my youngest brother as he pawed through the mini–chip bags. "Stop getting your germy paws all over everything. Did you even wash your hands when you got back from riding?"

"He certainly doesn't smell like he took a shower, that's for sure," Wylder said as he pulled back a chair at the massive conference table we had set up in one of the workshops on Twisted Oak Ranch.

Waylon had given us use of the space, allowing us to empty it of what had turned out to be a mix of old, rusting ranch equipment, clock parts, and a Bigfoot replica that would give me nightmares for the next year.

Before now, we hadn't really had an official meeting spot for the Hourglass Network. We usually met at Uncle Waylon's kitchen table or mine, sometimes even after hours at the Boot. But now that Dex was back in Starlight Grove, we needed this.

The Hourglass Network had started after the FBI arrested our second youngest brother for hacking into their files while trying to help a classmate look into their missing brother's case. Dex had taken working for the FBI in their cyber department over jail time, but he'd also realized just how many cases went without the proper support and resources.

We all knew better than most how easy it was for missing people to stay that way and for families to be haunted by the lack of answers. We wanted to help those who lived with the same. I wasn't an idiot. I knew this was some sort of atonement for crimes we weren't responsible for. But it helped all the same.

Only this one was a little more personal.

Maverick threw a Dorito at Wylder like a throwing star. "I smell like sunshine and wildflowers."

"If sunshine and wildflowers had BO," Wylder shot back.

"And ass sweat," Orion signed.

"All right, already," Dex cut in as he beamed whatever was on his computer to a projection screen at one end of the table. "Let's focus. I'm taking Brae and Owen to the diner for dinner in an hour."

"And Waylon's probably convincing Skylar that aliens are already among us. If she tells her teacher another abduction story, I'm pretty sure I'm getting a visit from the county," I muttered.

"Hey, they could be here," Mav said as he lowered himself into a chair.

I shook my head. "I need to limit her time with you, too."

"Rude," he clipped.

"Okay," Dex cut in again. "Kol, this is your show."

I opened the file in front of me. Dex might be high-tech, but I needed a pen and paper. I needed to be able to lay things out and move them around like pieces on a chessboard.

Flipping to a list, I looked up, signing as I spoke. "I found two more cases that might be Travis. While his victim profile varied, it's clear he had a favorite type."

"Women in their twenties with dark hair," Wylder supplied.

I nodded. "Exactly."

Wylder pulled out his phone—his preferred note-taking device. "I want to dig more into that. Who had a similar look in his life? His mother? An ex-girlfriend? A woman his father had an affair with?"

Maverick popped a chip into his mouth, speaking around bites. "He was with Cora forever. Did he even *have* a girlfriend before her?"

"Nothing serious," Dex supplied. "Not that I remember."

I leaned back in my chair. "We might want to talk to Cora—"

"No." Wylder spoke the single word with finality. "She's been through enough."

I studied my older brother for a moment. Wylder never lost his cool. Nothing made him panic. But when something tripped his trigger—usually something having to do with injustice or a wrong being perpetrated against someone he cared about—he went cold. Like now. Wylder's voice had dropped several degrees, icicles practically dripping from each syllable.

"Wy," I began.

"No. Not happening. If she tells me something useful, I'll share. But otherwise, it's a no-go zone."

"All right, then," Dex went on. "Kol, give us the two cases."

"Amber MacIntosh from Bainbridge Island, Washington. She was backpacking up the Pacific Crest Trail when she failed to check in at her expected point."

Mav frowned. "What makes you think it's Travis?"

"Her next checkpoint was Spruce Canyon. And a couple hiking in the opposite direction saw her about six miles south of Starlight Grove," I informed them.

Orion stood, rolling out a map I knew was his handiwork. Grabbing a pencil, he drew a circle, then signed, *"In Travis's hunting ground."*

It was a relief to see my brother speak, in his way. While he'd gone stonily silent for the majority of his life, he was still an active participant during these meetings. Maybe because the focus wasn't on him in any way.

"Exactly," I agree. "Second victim. Kimmy Oliver. A regular at the Well in Clover Creek. Never made it back to her apartment after walking home from the bar."

"Higher risk vic?" Dex asked.

I nodded. "Been known to abuse drugs. And a heavy drinker."

"Two very different types," Wylder surmised.

"But both with dark-brown or black hair. And both within Juniper County, which would give Travis access to their cases and their loved ones," I argued.

"They go on the list until we prove otherwise," Dex said. "I'll dig into their online histories. Mav and Orion, you handle the location profiles. Wy, you've got the psych bit." His gaze flicked to me. "Updates on the official end?"

I grimaced at the memory of my conversation with Sherri. "Pete is now working the case with me."

Maverick groaned. "That douchebag? Why?"

"Sherri thinks the caseload is too large," I grumbled.

"I mean, she's not wrong," Wylder said, concern flickering over his expression. "But let me guess, you assigned him work you've basically already done."

I grinned. "Gave him the five cases we already cleared."

Wylder just shook his head. "You said he's a good investigator."

"He is. But I don't trust anyone but us." And that was the honest truth.

We talked over a few more points, Dex assigning us all various tasks as different things arose, but it wasn't long before he was shutting his laptop and pushing back his chair. "I gotta go pick up Brae and Owen. Next week, same time."

Wylder shoved back next. "I gotta get to the bar."

Orion didn't say a word as he rose and headed for the door. That magical time when he communicated was over.

Wylder watched him go before glancing my way. "I'm worried about him."

My jaw worked back and forth. "Me, too. But I'm not sure anyone can reach him. We've all tried."

"Ever," Wylder said quietly.

Ever Devereux had been Orion's first love. His *only* love, given that he didn't interact with anyone but us now. Her parents had worked for our father, and they lived on the property while we were growing up. Their relationship was one of those you thought would stand the test of time, even with them being so young.

After Orion killed our father, though, he cut off all contact with Ever. He refused calls and letters, blocked her emails and social media accounts. And when she'd shown up here, he refused to see her.

But that didn't stop her. She still made trips out to Starlight Grove on the regular. And every time she got a break from serving communities in need of medical care with Medicine for Humanity, she came to the ranch and would simply stand outside Orion's house and wait, hoping he might see her.

He never did.

But she didn't stop coming.

I shook my head. "He's got to be willing to open the door. And I'm not sure that's ever going to happen."

Maverick crumpled his empty chip bag and tossed it in the trash. "We could hog-tie him and force him to listen to her."

Wylder sent Mav a quelling look. "That is definitely not the answer."

"We just keep thinking," I said.

Wylder nodded. "We do. All right, I'm out. See you guys later."

I gave him a salute as I gathered up my files. But Maverick lingered. Not moving closer but not heading for the door either. I lifted my gaze, trying to discern what might be on his mind. He looked…nervous.

"Why are you hovering?" I asked.

Mav's face twisted. "I don't hover. You make it sound like I'm a clingy boyfriend or something."

Which would be the ultimate insult for Mav. He never let himself care that much.

"There's something you don't want to tell me but know you need to say." My older-brother radar was pinging as I narrowed my eyes on him. "Did you get caught riding your dirt bike on national forest land again? I'm not fixing your ticket."

"I'm not trying to get you to fix a ticket," he grumbled as he lifted his backpack onto the conference table and pulled out an evidence bag.

I frowned as I caught glimpses of newspaper clippings through the plastic.

"Someone left this on Brae's SUV while Nova had it," Maverick went on. "She thinks it was that asshole reporter, but—"

I snatched the bag out of his hand. "Where." The single word wasn't a question; it was a demand.

"At the mountain biking trails off Spruce Canyon."

My gaze flicked to him. "And she called you?"

The sharp sting of that took me by surprise. I'd gotten used to being the one Nova turned to during the rare times she looked to others for support. And the idea of her reaching out to Mav for help instead of me had my stomach roiling.

Mav shook his head quickly. "I ran into her out there. She was about to get in way over her head on some trails, so I gave her a lesson instead."

That sick feeling eased, only to be replaced by a worry that rode me hard. The trails out at Spruce Canyon were like a maze of death-defying jumps and steep drop-offs. It would be really easy to get lost or hurt out there. Or worse.

My back molars ground together. "She shouldn't be out there alone."

"No shit, Sherlock," Mav clipped. "That's why I stayed with her."

I jerked my head in a nod as I studied the bag. I couldn't see all the articles the way they'd been shoved inside, but I saw enough. Articles about Nova. About other missing persons. I flipped it over, trying to see more, and my blood went cold.

The boxy, black lettering looked angry. *NEVER FORGET.*

What the hell did that mean?

At this moment, it didn't fucking matter. What mattered was that someone was clearly watching Nova. Following her. Taunting her.

I slammed the bag onto the table. "Help Waylon watch Sky. I've got dinner in the slow cooker at my house."

"I'm not your manny, you know," Mav yelled.

But I was already at the door and moving through it. Some phantom force buzzed in my ears, and memories battled to break through the bars I'd contained them behind.

Endless cop cars. Ambulances. A medical examiner van. All of them crowded around the driveway of the house, leading toward Dad's workshop.

A sick feeling spread through me as I slammed the brakes on the Range Rover. I shut off the engine and jumped out, only to come face-to-face with a police officer barely a handful of years older than me.

He put out a hand. "I'm sorry. You can't be here."

"I live here," I argued. "Where are my brothers?"

Something passed over the young officer's face. Pity. "The youngest is on the way to the hospital with Wylder and Dexter."

"Orion," I croaked. "Where's Orion?"

A muscle fluttered in the officer's cheek. "He's in custody."

All the blood drained from my body. "For what?"

"Murdering your father."

I shoved the memory down, putting it back into that box I never took out and never examined. Back into a place that held all the memories that came after: Maverick clinging to life in the hospital, Dex traumatized with nightmares, Wylder stealing whiskey from Dad's collection. Orion coming out of the police station and never speaking again.

I hadn't been there. Not when they needed me most. And I wasn't about to let that happen again.

My truck hit the turn onto Briarwood Lane so fast my tires spat gravel. Tenants' cars sat in front of cabins one and three. That was good. More people around meant less likelihood for someone to make a move on Nova.

Brae's SUV sat in front of cabin two, but I remembered that Dex was picking her and Owen up for dinner. Which meant Nova might be here alone. My gut twisted as I slammed on the brakes.

I was out of my truck and up the walkway in a matter of seconds.

My knuckles rapped on the door, and it took everything I had not to bang my fist against the wood.

No answer.

Anxiety clawed at me, and I knocked a little harder.

"I'm coming. Don't get your knickers in a twist," Nova grumbled from the other side of the door.

Relief swept through me at the sound of her voice and the cranky annoyance in it. The hint of fire.

The door swung open, and surprise lit Nova's features as she took me in. "Kol. What are you doing here?"

"I'm helping you pack."

Chapter Fourteen

NOVA

KOL HAD THAT AVENGING-ANGEL THING GOING FOR HIM again. Or maybe it was some sort of shadow demon. I was mostly into reading monster romance, but I dipped into fantasy every now and again. And in this moment, I fully believed Kol could command the shadows around him at will.

I shook my head as if trying to clear it. “Helping me pack?”

Kol shoved by me, careful not to make contact. “Yes.”

My brows pulled together. “I’m gonna need a little more to go on, Boss.”

He scowled in my direction. Those hazel eyes that were normally a mix of light and dark were now nearly black.

Shadow daddy, indeed.

“Mav showed me what was left on your car.”

My jaw went slack. “That little traitor.” I mentally began plotting my revenge, but first, I needed to deal with the alpha-male protector having a freak-out in the entryway. “It was that asshole reporter, that’s all. Or maybe some teen boy who thought it would be hilarious to spook the girl who was held captive for a year."

"Phoenix." The fury in Kol vibrated my nickname. "You need to take this shit seriously."

"That someone's an asshole? I'll always take that seriously. And I'll be happy to kick his ass if I see him again."

Kol's long, thick fingers fisted so tightly, his knuckles bleached white. "I mean it."

I saw it then. Something beneath the anger. Fear.

The annoyance burning through me was snuffed out in a single moment, transforming into empathy. I studied Kol, trying to put the pieces together. "This really freaked you out."

Kol's jaw worked back and forth. "I don't like that someone followed you there."

A shiver ran down my spine. Because I knew he was right. Reese had already proven he wasn't above tailing me. But I couldn't help wondering if he was tracking my movements some other way, too.

That, I wasn't exactly a fan of.

Kol tracked the shiver that spread through me in a wave. One hand unfurled, and for a moment, I thought he might touch me. Take my hand. Pull me into a hug. *Something.*

But then his arm dropped to his side. Disappointment and relief swept through me in equal measure.

Kol's eyes flashed, those specks of gold burning brighter. "I'm going to make sure you're safe."

A different sort of war waged in me then. Because as nice as it was to hear that, it wasn't what I wanted. "*I'm* going to make sure I'm safe." *That* was what I wanted more than anything. To protect myself. To know that I could defend myself if needed. That I could take care of myself.

Kol studied me for a long moment, taking in more than just my words. "Yes. You are."

I arched a brow in question.

"The first step is moving into the apartment at my house. The ranch is more protected than these cabins. It's the smart thing to do."

Annoyance lit again as I glared at him.

"Why are you scowling at me?" he asked.

"Because it's annoying when you're right," I clipped.

One corner of Kol's mouth kicked up, and it sent a different sort of shiver through me. The kind that spoke of an awareness I'd thought might be dead forever. Kol had certainly proven that wrong.

He started toward my bedroom. "Can you pack while annoyed?"

I had the urge to pinch his side. "*Yes.* But I'd watch your back because I am retaliatory."

"I'm pretty sure it's Mav who needs to watch his back," Kol shot back.

"It's both of you."

He stepped into my room, his gaze sweeping over the walls and items. I suddenly felt exposed. Brae had decorated it with everything from my old room in Oakland, but none of that felt like it fit anymore. It wasn't *wrong* exactly, but it wasn't me either.

Vintage-style posters dotted the walls, showing cities that had been on my bucket list to visit. Paris. Rome. Prague. London. Madrid. But even the colors didn't feel quite right anymore. The bold jewel tones, the purple and reddish bedding askew because I'd been reading on top of the covers…

Kol's eyes seemed to touch every item in the room. "Places you want to go?"

I stared at the city names. "Used to, anyway."

"Not anymore?" he probed gently.

"It doesn't call to me the way it used to." I shrugged, lacing my fingers in front of me. "I'd rather figure out how to plant roots in a way that feels authentic to me. Figure out who I am now, I guess."

Even giving him that made me feel vulnerable. But Kol simply nodded, moving deeper into the space. "Anything you want to leave behind, we can put into storage. You can take your time figuring out the stuff you want in your new place."

My heart contracted, and I wondered again if it was one of those palpitations the doctor had warned me about. "Thank you," I whispered.

Kol lifted his chin in assent as he crossed to my desk. He picked up a pad of sticky notes that read *I run on coffee and chaos.* His lips twitched. "What do we think? Does this fit the new life?"

A soft chuckle left my lips. "Definitely."

"Then we'll use these to mark everything we're taking. We'll load it all up and bring it over day after tomorrow."

"Okay." The word left my lips on an exhale.

"Posters?" Kol asked.

I shook my head.

"Desk?"

I studied it for a moment but couldn't really see it in what I wanted my new space to look like. "No."

Kol crossed the room. "Bedding?"

My nose scrunched.

"What?" he prodded.

"I just...even the colors don't feel right anymore," I tried to explain.

Kol looked at me, trying to read beneath my words. "What colors *do* feel right?"

"I'm not sure. Maybe tones that are a little more peaceful. I like the colors themselves; they just feel too loud."

He was quiet, seeming to mull that over. "Sometimes, when my surroundings get too loud, it's like I can't think. Can't function."

"Exactly," I agreed. And I couldn't help but wonder what tones filled Kol's house.

"Chair?" he asked, studying the overstuffed piece of furniture shoved into the far corner.

My stomach churned. The color was all wrong for me now: a deep burgundy. But I had so many beautiful memories from that chair. Feeding Owen. Reading him stories. Writing in my journal. Brae sitting in it while we had one of our heart-to-hearts.

"You could always put a slipcover on it. Or even different throw pillows would change the feel," Kol suggested.

My mouth curved into a real smile—the kind that so rarely found me these days. "Boss, are you a secret interior designer?"

He let out a huff. "I can watch HGTV with the best of 'em."

I laughed, and it relieved some of the building pressure. "I'm trusting your design eye and saying…keep."

Kol stuck one of the Post-its to it and then crossed to a small bookshelf stuffed with titles. He studied them, then picked up the paperback on my bed. I couldn't hide my giggle as he took in the cover with the purple man-monster with horns and wings in a clinch with the woman. "Interesting," he muttered.

"Aaaaaall of those are keeps."

Kol grinned as he put a sticky note on the bookshelf. "I like the definitiveness."

We kept working, deciding what to keep and what to toss or donate. Kol even found some boxes in the garage to start packing things up, and I found some tape in the kitchen junk drawer.

The sound of the dispenser as I sealed a box of mementos from a life that felt like a stranger's was like nails on a chalkboard.

"Jesus," Kol muttered.

I winced. "Sorry."

He studied me for a moment. "Think you can be ready by day after tomorrow?"

My brows flew up. "Seriously?"

"Just finishing up a couple of things, and it'll be ready."

"Okay." The word was an exhale, and I gripped the tape harder. "I'll be ready."

Kol opened his mouth to say something, but the sound of the door opening cut him off.

"Nova, we're home," Brae called.

Panic lit through me. I'd planned on talking to my best friend and presenting her with this *amazing* opportunity, hoping she'd understand why I needed to stretch my wings. But I'd dawdled. And during that dawdle, a grumbly mountain man had shown up at my door, demanding that I basically move now.

Which meant one thing: I was about to level an explosive device on my best friend's world. And that was seriously shitty.

"Supernova, I brought you boysenberry pie," Owen yelled as he ran into my bedroom holding a takeout container.

I beamed at him as I took the pie. "My favorite. Thanks, Bubs."

"Hey, Mr. Kol. What are you doing here?" he asked curiously.

Brae came up short in the doorway, Dex behind her. "Kol. Hi." There was confusion on her face and then concern. "Is everything okay? Did something happen?"

"Everything's fine," Kol said, his voice going a little bit flat.

"He's, um, just helping me pack," I said quietly.

Brae's eyes widened. "Pack?"

"I got an apartment." I forced my smile wide, hoping it would catch, and Brae would miraculously find the happy with me.

The confusion was back in her expression. "But you live here."

"Hey, O," Dex called. "How about thirty minutes of Switch before bed?"

Owen looked around the room. "Adult talk?"

"Super boring stuff," Dex assured him.

Owen sighed as only a nine-going-on-thirteen-year-old boy could. "You know I'm gonna find out eventually, bro."

Dex covered a laugh with a cough. "I'll make sure you're filled in by breakfast."

Owen headed out to the living room as Brae moved deeper into my room. Her brows pulled together in a combination of worry and annoyance. "Nova. It's too soon. You need support. People looking out for you."

"I'm not losing that," I said gently. "But I also need to start standing on my own two feet."

Dex moved in behind Brae, squeezing her shoulder in a show of support.

"But you aren't completely recovered. You have nightmares. What if you need something in the middle of the night?" Brae argued.

"Then she'll ask me," Kol cut in.

"She'll what?" Brae asked.

"Nova's moving into the apartment over my garage. Perfect blend of her own space but with people nearby if she needs them," Kol went on.

Brae's jaw went slack. She simply stared at Kol for a count of one, two, three, and then four. "But you don't like anyone."

He scowled at her. "I like lots of people."

Dex snorted. "*Real* convincing."

"You like your family and that's it," Brae argued. "You only started to tolerate me after I found Sky when she was missing."

When Owen and Skylar were at summer camp, the counselors had thought Sky had gone missing or had gotten lost in the woods. In reality, she'd been doling out some justice to a camp bully. But Brae and Yeti had been the ones to find her.

"That's not true," Kol muttered.

Dex grinned at his brother. "It's totally true."

"You don't even have an apartment over your garage," Brae pointed out.

Kol shifted from foot to foot.

"It's a new development," Dex explained.

"When did that project start?" Brae pressed.

Kol cleared his throat, not meeting anyone's gaze. "Almost three months ago."

Right after I got out of the rehabilitation unit and moved in with Brae and Dex. Right after I confessed that I felt like I couldn't breathe in my new living situation.

I stared out at the fast-descending twilight as I wrapped my arms around myself. Owen and Sky raced around Waylon Archer's backyard as a goat and an honest-to-goodness mini-Highland cow charged by them.

Their noise was a comfort. It helped when everything else felt like it didn't belong. Or maybe it was me *who didn't belong. Even my body didn't feel like mine anymore. Starved. Scarred. Terrified.*

I tried to breathe through it. To remind myself that I could breathe. Because I was still alive. I'd made it through. I should be grateful. Instead, I felt like I was drowning. Suffocating.

"See the fireflies?"

I jumped, startled, cursing myself at the reaction. But Kol didn't react.

He just stood there, watching the kids and the animals as a few glowing insects appeared. If I jumped around Brae, she rushed to apologize, to ask if I was okay. And worse, she looked like she was about to cry.

"We called them lightning bugs growing up." My voice still held a rasp from lack of use, and that didn't feel like me either.

"Apparently, they're starting to go extinct. We're lucky to see them at all around here."

I liked that Kol didn't hover. Didn't ask how I was. He asked about anything but things that had to do with my ordeal. Maybe because he'd gotten an up-close look at it.

"It is a beautiful place to live. I don't blame them for settling here."

"Is here where you still want to be?"

Kol didn't look at me as he asked the question. And I didn't feel pressure to answer, which was maybe what made me want to give him the truth. My truth.

"I love the air here. The land. The bigness of everything. Makes my problems feel small."

"Feels like there's a but in there somewhere."

He always saw beneath my words.

So I gave him my truth again. "Living in that cabin. The weight of those expectations. Even if she doesn't mean to have them, even if she's just happy I'm back…I feel like I can't breathe."

I pulled myself from the memory, staring first at Kol, wondering if he'd given me a place to go because I told him I needed it. But I'd have to deal with that possibility later. For now, I had to do something else. Something I'd been putting off. But if I wanted to step into my new life, I needed to be brave.

"Can I have a moment with Brae?" My voice didn't sound like mine as I asked the question. But it was time. And I had to try.

Kol and Dex shared a look, but Dex nodded. "Of course."

Kol studied me for a moment as if to make sure this was truly what I wanted. Then he, too, nodded—maybe a little more roughly than his brother, but the movement was similar.

My fingers started to tingle as the door closed behind the men, and I reminded myself to *breathe*.

"Nova, tell me what's going on." Brae's face was a mixture of emotions. Some tells I knew like the back of my hand. Others were new: tiny expressions she'd gained over the time I was gone. We were both different now, and maybe we had to get to know each other all over again.

I clasped my hands in front of me, trying to hold tight to the will to live. Not just simple existence but to live fully, freely. "I need…I need space to heal. I need to step out on my own. To have a little bit of independence."

"You'll be living with Kol." Hurt was the dominant emotion on Brae's face now, engulfing all the others. "How is that on your own?"

"It's my own apartment. My own entrance and exit. Space to… breathe." I wanted her to understand me, to see what I needed. We'd never struggled with that before. She'd *always* been the one who *got* me. And the fact that we were missing each other so much, misunderstanding each other, hurt way more than any of the physical scars I carried.

"You're saying I'm suffocating you," she said quietly.

"Brae…"

Her amber eyes started to glimmer, tears gathering there. "Do you blame me?"

Icy shock ripped through me. "What? What are you talking about?"

"It was my idea to go on the hike." Her voice cracked. "I'm the one who walked away from the trail to take one more damn wildflower picture. I left you alone."

Brae's tears came faster, sliding down her cheeks and falling to the floor. My heart cracked, shattering into millions of pieces that I knew I would never be able to reshape again.

"*None* of this is your fault. What happened to me is the responsibility of one person and one person only. And that's Travis Moore."

Something flickered in my memory—or my imagination. I was never sure. *A jerk of my hair, my head snapping back.* And then, it was gone.

I shook myself out of whatever it was, trying to focus on the here and now. On Brae. "You did *everything* for me, and it kills me that I can't just be magically *better* for you."

She jerked backward and then took a step forward as if she were going to touch me. God, I wanted that. I wanted to hug her, as I had so many times before. To feel that connection between us. She was my family. The only one I really had.

"I don't expect you to be better. But I want to make sure you're healing. And you won't...you don't talk to me. I don't know how to help." She shook out her hands as if trying to clear a muscle cramp. "I have been suffocating you. Thinking that if I just micromanage every tiny detail, I can fix it."

"B, it's not yours to fix. I'm the only one who can do that. And I need space to figure out how."

We were both quiet for a moment, and I realized that it was the most honest I'd been with her since I returned.

She let out a long breath. "I love you, Supernova."

I wanted to say those words back, but my throat closed around them. So I gave her another truth. "You've given me the biggest gifts of my life. And I know that it was you and Owen who kept me going down there. I may not exactly remember, but I *know* that. Because you always have. You're my family."

"Nova," she croaked.

"You *never* gave up on me. When the rest of the world did, you never stopped. You're the reason I'm still here." Her and Kol.

"Stop it," she rasped.

"It's the truth. I'll never be able to repay you."

Brae shook her head. "You already have. You helped me raise my son when I had *no one*. You gave him and me a family."

I shifted in place. "There was never any question in my mind. You two deserve the best."

Brae wiped at her eyes. "You know, you're an emotional bitch in another way. You just hide it better."

I burst out laughing, and God, it felt so good. Like breaking another set of chains.

Brae smiled at me. "Think you'd share that boysenberry pie with me?"

One corner of my mouth tugged up. "Only if we can add ice cream."

"Do I look like an idiot?"

I chuckled. "There might be whipped cream in the fridge, too."

"Now you're talking."

As we walked out of the room that had been mine for a time, I felt lighter. Everything wasn't magically better, but we were on our way to getting to know each other as we were now. And it was a gift in a way: getting to find friendship and sisterhood for a second time.

Chapter Fifteen

KOL

My eyes burned like I'd been standing in the middle of a forest fire all night. Or like they'd been dunked in paint stripper. I pinched the bridge of my nose as I stumbled down the stairs from the apartment and headed through the garage toward the kitchen. I'd grabbed a nap for all of forty-five minutes around three in the morning, but that was it. Today would be rough. But there was still so much to do.

Opening the door to the kitchen, I froze.

Oh hell.

I quickly checked my watch. It was only half past six. Skylar usually slept until after eight on the weekends. But here she was, in full princess-warrior glory, creating pure chaos in the middle of the kitchen.

She was in her princess nightgown with a camo hoodie over it and a Bigfoot apron on top. She was also mixing something in a bowl with a fervor I wasn't sure I'd ever seen before. And whatever it was had exploded *all* over the place.

"Little Princess?" I asked cautiously.

She whirled, some of the contents of the bowl slopping over the side. "Oh shoot." She grinned up at me. "Your surprise isn't done yet, Daddy."

I tried not to laugh. "And what surprise is that?"

"You were working lots and lots on Supernova's new home, so I'm making you a magic breakfast."

"Magic, huh?" I inquired.

Some of the *magic* was smeared across her face. "Yup. I'm not allowed to use the stove, oven, or microwave without supervision, so I was limited."

This time, I couldn't stop myself. I laughed. "Rules are a real buzzkill."

"You're telling me." She set the bowl on the counter. "But I made you a unicorn surprise."

My brow arched. "I really hope no unicorns were harmed in this process."

Skylar giggled. "Never. But all their colors are here. Look. Strawberries and raspberries. Blueberries and blackberries. Yogurt. Whipped cream. Rainbow sprinkles. Chocolate chips."

"You really went for it." I studied what looked like a stomachache in a bowl.

"Go big or go home. That's what Uncle Mav always says."

I leveled my eight-year-old with a hard stare. "In this house, we do *not* follow Uncle Mav's example."

That sent Sky into another fit of giggles. "He's naughty, but he's so much fun."

I let out a long sigh. "Should I be warning Roger that he's gonna have to lock you up before long?"

She beamed at me, making her hazel eyes—much lighter than mine—sparkle. "Oh, I'm never gonna get caught. I'm too good for that."

I barked out a laugh. "Good to know."

Skylar held out her mixing spoon to me. "Taste-test?"

I braced, knowing I'd have to fake the biggest smile for my girl. But I'd do it. Even if it tasted like liverwurst and sprinkles. "Let's see what we've got here."

Dipping the massive spoon into the concoction, I took a small taste. My brows rose, surprise lighting through me. "Little Princess, that is freaking fantastic."

It was like a berry sundae. And the sprinkles weren't half bad.

"I told you, Daddy. I know my stuff." She flounced over to the silverware drawer and pulled out two regular spoons. She handed me one and then dipped the second into the bowl. "Halfsies?"

"I don't know," I began. "I'm like four times your size, so four-fifths me, one-fifth you?"

My little girl leveled a glare at me that would make a biker cower. "Don't even think about it."

I grinned and scooped up another bite. "Have I told you lately that I love you?"

"Duh, only like all the time."

My grin only widened. "Okay, good." I studied Sky for a moment. "You have any more questions about Nova moving in?" We'd talked about it before bed last night, and she'd been stoked. But it sometimes took kids a little time to process change.

Skylar swallowed another huge bite. "You think she'll play dress-up and Nerf wars with me?"

Amusement swept through me—only the important things. "If you ask nicely, I bet she will."

"Good." Sky stared down at her breakfast creation for a moment. "How come she's moving out of Owen's house?"

Kids, man. Of course, she'd think of the cabin as Owen's.

I leaned back in my chair. "You know how when people grow up, they usually move out? Sometimes, they go to college and live in a dorm. Other times, they have roommates and then they live on their own."

Her face screwed up. "I never want to move out. Twisted Oak is the best. There's Tink and Pepper and the alpacas and all the Bigfoot."

God, I loved her. "Can't leave out the Bigfoot."

"Nope."

"Well, I'm glad you never want to leave. But I think Nova was ready to live a little more on her own but not totally alone yet."

Skylar was quiet again, mulling that over. Then her face brightened. "We're like her night-light!"

A foreign feeling invaded my chest—a unique blend of love, pride, and awe. "That is the perfect way to think of it."

Her little chest puffed up. "I can be a really good night-light. I know what it's like to be a little scared sometimes but wanna do it anyway. Like the rope swing at the lake. Sometimes, you just gotta know someone's at the bottom to catch you."

My throat constricted. "That's exactly right. And we're gonna be her safety net night-light."

Sky beamed. "I got it." She tapped her spoon against the bowl. "Think I can help you finish the apartment today? I want her to know I helped."

"I need my best helper if it's gonna get done." I held out a hand for a high five.

Skylar slapped my palm hard. "We're gonna make it the bestest ever!"

My chest tightened. There were times, like this one, when I knew this little girl had saved me. Stopped me from becoming a bitter recluse who couldn't see all the light out there in the world. She'd been *my* night-light. And now, we could give that to someone else.

Chapter Sixteen

NOVA

I watched as Wylder took off with the remaining couple of boxes. Everyone had pitched in. Kol and Sky had been the first to show up. She had been bouncing up and down with excitement about my moving into the space, while Kol looked like he hadn't slept a wink in the past thirty-six hours. I just hoped he wasn't having second thoughts about his new roomie.

A throat cleared, and I braced myself because I knew the owner. I slowly turned to face Brae, wondering exactly what I'd find.

"That's everything," she said with a slightly wobbly smile.

"I'm sorry," I whispered.

Brae's expression hardened. "Don't you dare. There's nothing to be sorry for. This is going to be good. First steps toward a new life. I'm just going to miss you."

I swallowed, my throat suddenly feeling as dry as a desert. "I'm nervous," I admitted. "And I'll miss you."

She was the best friend I could've ever hoped for. She'd uprooted her whole life for me, moving to a small town in the middle of nowhere to make sure people were still looking for me. She'd put herself in the crosshairs of a killer, hoping I *might* still be alive. And almost got herself killed because of it.

"Nova," Brae whispered hoarsely, reaching out to take my hand but then stopping herself. "I'm always going to be right here. Maybe I can have Dex make us a clubhouse or something at the new place. Nova and Brae only. No boys allowed."

I laughed, relishing the feel of the vibrations coursing through me. I'd laughed more with her in the past day and a half than I had since I returned. And that felt a lot like hope.

"Our new normal definitely deserves a clubhouse," I agreed. "And maybe bedazzled jackets."

Brae's eyes brightened. "Oh, I am in on the bedazzled jackets."

"Nothing can be too scary if bedazzled jackets are involved."

"Dang straight. Now, let's get you moved into your new apartment."

A smile tipped up the corners of my mouth. "Do you think you could take me to pick up my new car first?" I asked. Between what was left in my savings from when I went missing and a few weeks at the Boot, I was ready for the responsibility of a car payment. And that felt good, too.

Brae laughed and shook her head. "Man, you really don't mess around when it comes to fresh starts."

"No, I don't." And that also felt damn good.

I still felt a little rusty at the whole driving thing, and I was glad I had another month or so before I had to deal with any snow on the roads—something I had minimal experience with anyway. But the mechanic at Grit & Grove had assured me that the eight-year-old Subaru would handle the white stuff expertly.

I hoped so. Just like I hoped I could hold down my job at the Boot, because I now had a car payment on my shoulders, along with rent for my new apartment. I bit my lip as I followed Dex's 4Runner through the gate onto Twisted Oak Ranch. I hadn't actually discussed with Kol how much that rent would be.

I'm alive. I'm breathing.

The words swirled around and around in my head as I lowered my window to punctuate the point. I'd figure out rent and everything else. One step at a time.

The drive from the gate to Kol's house took almost ten minutes, but it made sense when the ranch was over a thousand acres. The vise around my lungs eased a little. A thousand acres. Endless space to breathe.

I followed Dex's SUV down bends and turns in the gravel road before Kol's house came into view. I spotted Wylder's truck, Mav's truck, and Waylon's supercharged golf cart/ATV hybrid with a Bigfoot painted on the hood. The last one had me smiling.

As I climbed out of my hatchback, I called out to Brae. "When are you going to get yourself a Bigfoot golf cart?"

She grinned back at me for what felt like the first time. "Oh, don't you worry. I've already put in my order with Waylon for when the house is done."

I chuckled. "Why am I not surprised?"

Dex slid an arm around Brae's shoulders. "Please, don't encourage this Bigfoot obsession."

Owen grinned at him. "You're gonna have to believe when Sky and I catch one on a trail cam."

"Yeah, he will," I agreed.

Owen bounced up and down. "I'm so glad you're moving to the ranch, Supernova. It's bussin', and we're gonna live here soon, too."

Brae had given me a list of Owen's newly acquired slang after I got out of the hospital, and I made the mental translation that *bussin'* meant really good or cool or something generally positive.

"I'm really excited, too. I want to make friends with the alpacas," I said.

"Supernova!" Skylar yelled, running around the side of the garage.

"We saw you out the windows! Your apartment's ready! You wanna see? Wanna right now?"

Sky looked like she was hopped up on 87 million grams of sugar as she bounded around the front yard.

I gave my sleeves a quick tug, making sure the scars on my wrists were covered. "I would *love* to see my new apartment."

"Come on," she yelled.

Wylder appeared by the entrance to the garage. "Mav brought her chocolate chip pancakes with whipped cream for breakfast. She's been running circles around us ever since."

"They were the freaking best!" Skylar shouted.

I couldn't hold in my laugh. "I hope Mav's on babysitting duty for the rest of the day."

Wylder's lips twitched. "Pretty sure Kol's gonna send her home with him tonight."

"Fitting."

We made our way through the garage and then up the stairs. The door was open, and I could smell the faint scent of finish or wood stain. But only a little before the pine from the wide-open windows took over.

As I stepped inside, I gasped. The space looked nothing like it had just over a week ago. Not only was everything finished, it looked like a literal dream.

In the far corner was a small kitchen complete with a 2/3 fridge, a smallish range, and plenty of storage. And I could see that the glass-fronted cabinets had been stocked with dishes and food. There was even a little coffee station with a machine and all the little supplies. And next to it sat a jar of my favorite wild berry Skittles.

I tried to swallow, to clear the burning in my throat. Because someone had to really pay attention to notice my affection for the candy. My gaze wanted to drift to the man in the corner, but I couldn't let it. Not yet.

My burgundy chair was in the other corner, and damn if Kol hadn't been right. Someone had put pale-pink pillows on it, along with a fuzzy cream blanket, and it softened the feel of it right up.

Next to the chair was a side table just large enough for a cup of coffee and a book. And the perch would give me a vantage point out over the forest at the front of the ranch. Absolutely perfect.

A small table for three sat in front of that window with a hand-painted vase filled with wildflowers—likely the last of the season.

"I made the vase and picked the flowers!" Sky cheered, bouncing up and down.

"It's perfect," I croaked.

And I didn't miss a small scattering of yoga gear between the chair and the table. A mat that looked like a watercolor painting, a block in the same design, a strap in soft purple, and a woven blanket that looked so soft my fingers ached to touch it.

On the wall next to the entrance were two doors. I wandered to one of them, peering inside to find a closet larger than I would've expected, with plenty of hanging space and a dresser along one wall. The next door was the bathroom. Everything had an antique feel, with a clawfoot tub and shower and a pedestal sink. There were built-in shelves, and everything was done in whites and soothing blues.

I swallowed hard as I stepped out and took in the bed. Someone had gotten me new bedding. It was in the color scheme I'd described to Kol just last night. It looked like a wildflower field of pale pinks, purples, blues, and greens. It was all the same colors but through a calming lens.

But the showstoppers were the bookshelves built around the bed. They were made of the most beautiful pale oak and had room for countless stories and knickknacks. It even had antique bronze reading lamps on either side that stuck out over the bed.

"When I saw your shelves the other night, I knew you needed these. The finish is still drying, so you'll need to wait a few days before putting anything on the shelves."

That voice. Low and quiet but somehow with a power that felt as if it vibrated through me. And my whole body recognized the tenor. Finally, my gaze lifted to the source of the sound, the feeling.

And there he was.

Kol stood in a far corner of the apartment, his gaze locked on me.

He wore a U.S. Forest Service tee in army green, the emblem over one side of his chest, with a worn flannel shirt over it, dark jeans flecked with paint here and there, and boots that had seen their share of the outdoors and hard work.

I wanted to throw myself at him.

I quickly shoved that urge down. "You…" My voice cracked on the word. "You did…all of this?"

The slightest hint of pink hit cheeks tanned from all his time outdoors. "Fresh starts."

"He did those damn shelves all by himself," Wylder cut in, looking my way and waiting for a reaction.

"Hey," Mav argued. "I helped with the finish."

Wylder rolled his eyes. "Do you want a medal?"

"I wouldn't mind a cupcake," he muttered.

Kol crossed the space and held out a key. It was new but looked antique in its shape, with knobby tines and the very top in the shape of an imperfect heart. "Your key." He swallowed. "There's a secondary lock and an alarm, but I thought you'd like the feel of this one."

I palmed the cool metal in my hand as unshed tears stung the backs of my eyes. I hadn't cried since the hospital. I'd fought to keep any tears at bay, unsure if I'd be able to stop them if I ever got started. "I can't believe you did this for me."

Kol shoved his hands into his pockets. "It's nothing."

I stared into those hypnotizing hazel eyes. "It's everything."

Chapter Seventeen

KOL

In true Archer-family fashion, chaos reigned as Nova's unpacking turned into a family barbeque. We'd migrated from the apartment to the back deck, where Waylon was manning the grill in his Carhartt overalls with a tiny Bigfoot stitched on the bib.

"Order up: One alien burger for Mav, one Bigfoot special for Brae," he called with a grin.

"You can't just call it a cheeseburger and a hamburger with grilled chilis?" I complained.

Waylon arched a brow in my direction. "Now where's the fun in that?"

Skylar let out a squeal of delight as Nova raced after her, wearing a set of Sky's fairy wings, a sparkly feather boa, and carrying a Nerf gun.

"Down with all alien invaders!" Nova cried out as she sent an array of foam darts in Sky's and Owen's direction.

Owen acted out an elaborate dying scene after being hit, while Sky claimed that she was magically healed by her alien powers.

"I think she's the happiest with them."

My gaze flicked down to the new voice beside me. Brae watched Nova dart toward Tink the mini-Highland cow and Pepper the goat, both of whom were also adorned in fairy wings. There was a longing in Brae's gaze, as if she wanted to take part so badly but wasn't sure she fit.

"Kids accept you as you are. There's no need to put on any pretenses. You can just be," I said quietly.

Brae nodded, still watching the scene play out in front of her. "I've been putting pressure on her and didn't even realize it." She sighed. "Or maybe I did. I just thought I was right. Actually, I was so damn wrong."

I shifted uncomfortably. I wasn't good at this sort of thing. Feelings and emotional processing. That was Wylder's arena.

But the hurt in Brae's eyes had me wanting to try to help. "Now you know. And you can just be her friend."

Brae's gaze flicked up to me. "Just be her friend."

"I think that's what she needs the most." I was trying to remember that myself. Nova needed friends and support. And I needed to keep her firmly in that *friend* category.

But I couldn't stop myself from thinking about her, feeling pulled in her direction, hungry for every smile or spark of mischief in her eyes. My gaze found her in every room. And sometimes, I swore I smelled the scent of sunbaked cherries long after I'd left her presence. I knew none of that was good, but I kept walking closer to the open flame anyway.

"Order up: I've got two alien burgers," Waylon called.

Sky ran for the back deck. "Me, Grampa Way Way! Me!"

As she hit the steps, I bent, lifting my girl into the air as she shrieked and laughed. I wasn't sure how many more years I'd be able to do this or how long she'd let me. So I soaked up every delighted moment.

"Daddy!"

I chuckled. "The alien is in flight. Coming in for a landing."

"And for fuel," she said, giggling as I swooped her toward the grill.

As I lowered her, I felt eyes on me—on us. I sought out the source. And there was Nova, wearing the ridiculous outfit and standing between a goat and a cow. But it wasn't all that that knocked me sideways. It was the look of longing on her face.

She sent me a half smile that didn't quite reach her eyes as she started for the steps. "Waylon, can fairy warrior princesses get alien burgers?"

He chuckled, sending her a wink. "Got some extra fairy magic for you on this one, warrior princess."

"No hot sauce," I warned, my voice going hard.

Nova sent me a pointed look. "Maybe I want hot sauce."

"You hate hot sauce," I shot back. But it was more than that. It was the fact that her whole system was still recovering from starvation. And things like hot sauce should be avoided at all costs.

She let out a huff of annoyance. "Fine. But you still don't need to be so bossy, Boss."

My lips twitched. "What if I add a please?"

"Better," Nova grumbled as she headed for the grill.

"I know what my girl likes," Waylon mumbled as he lifted some thin onion rings from a fryer he'd insisted he *needed* to bring over.

The words *my girl* sent a wash of annoyance through me. Which was ridiculous. Uncle Waylon was old enough to be Nova's grandfather. But when her eyes lit and she did a little jump-cheer, a new wave of jealousy shot through me. That wasn't me. I hadn't been jealous about a woman…ever.

I hadn't dated seriously since high school and that fateful day when everything fell apart. I had the occasional fling when it suited, if our particular interests aligned, but I was always honest about what I was looking for. After Sky's mom? There'd been nothing at all. Because I hadn't been able to trust a soul enough to let my guard down.

"Onion crisps." Nova grinned. "My favorite."

"Welcome home, warrior princess," he said with a grin as he handed her a plate.

The rest of us got our burgers and headed for the massive outdoor table I had on the deck that spanned the length of my house. I'd been determined to find a table big enough to fit our entire family because I wanted Skylar to be surrounded by people who loved her.

I never wanted her to feel like she didn't have a whole slew of people in her corner, even though her mom had chosen not to be in her life.

And she had more than her fair share of people who loved and adored her. Now, she even had a new soon-to-be cousin in Owen. And all of those people didn't just show up for her; they showed up for Nova, too. Everyone had joined in to help today—everyone but Orion.

I'd hoped he'd come around on Nova after our talk in the apartment. Apparently, not standing in her way did not equate to welcoming her into the fold.

Mav pushed back from the table, arguing with Wylder over who got the last root beer. Dex scooped some pasta salad and potatoes onto Owen's plate as Brae looked on with a tender expression. Waylon got himself his own double cheeseburger as Sky took the seat next to Owen.

There were two chairs left: one next to Mav and one next to Nova. I knew I should've taken the one on my brother's right. I needed to be careful not to let myself get too close.

I didn't.

I let embers spark to flame and pulled out the chair next to Nova. She grinned up at me as she popped a potato into her mouth. "I adore your family."

Warmth spread through my gut, and I tapped one of her fairy wings. It was the closest I'd come to touching her since the day I found her. "I like your wings."

Mav's chair grated against the deck as he sat back down. "I can't believe you took the last root beer."

"You snooze, you lose," Wylder shot back.

Maverick bit into his burger. He chewed once, twice, and then his eyes went wide as his face turned bright red. He shoved his chair back, sending it toppling backward as he spat his bite into a napkin.

"What the hell did you put in that, Waylon?" he demanded as he choked and coughed.

Nova gave a little finger wave as she smiled sweetly at my youngest brother. "That was me. Just a little reminder that payback's a… female dog."

I tried to cover my laugh with a cough. I guessed Nova wasn't a fan of Mav going behind her back and telling me about the newspaper clippings.

Mav's gaze shot to me. "This is *not* funny." He kept sticking his tongue out as if access to the fall air would help him. "I think my taste buds burned off."

Owen's face scrunched. "Why would payback be a female dog?" He shrugged. "I guess Yeti is a trickster. She stole my bacon the other day."

Waylon thumped a hand on Mav's shoulder. "It's good for you. Puts hair on the ole chest."

"I'm good with the hair I have already." Maverick reached for Wylder's soda, starting to chug.

"Hey," Wy protested.

"Desperate times," Mav said with a pant.

Dex grinned at Nova. "What'd you put on there?"

Nova flipped her nearly black locks over one shoulder. "One of the hot sauces from Brae's collection." She bent, pulling it from her bag. "Death by Chili."

Maverick's jaw dropped. "That has Carolina Reaper peppers in it. That's the second-hottest pepper in the world. You could've killed me." He looked longingly at his plate. "And you ruined my burger."

Dex snickered. "On the upside, you won the hot sauce competition for the day."

He glared at Nova. "You'd better make me a trophy, and it'd better be bedazzled."

"Ooooooh, I'll help," Sky offered.

My phone dinged, and I pulled it from my pocket. God, I hoped it wasn't Pete. He'd been incessant with his texts about the case, bragging about findings one moment, making giant leaps the next. By the time we finished with this one, it would be a miracle if we didn't come to blows. But it wasn't Pete.

Orion: *Left something on the front porch.*

I frowned at my screen.

Me: *It better not be an exploding food dye water balloon. Or a bag of goat shit on fire.*

Orion simply replied with a middle finger emoji.

I pushed back from the table and made my way through the house. As I stepped onto the porch, I saw it. A platter of chocolate fudge cupcakes. I grinned.

Orion might not be ready for family gatherings with Nova, but this was his version of a welcome.

I bent and picked up the platter, heading back for the group.

"Whatcha got there?" Waylon asked.

"Orion dropped off some cupcakes." I set them in front of Nova. "I think they're for you."

She gaped at the perfectly frosted cakes. "Me?"

"Did he get those from a bakery? They look amazing," Brae added.

Wylder's mouth curved. "He made them."

"Wait, wait, wait," Brae said. "Orion. Scowls at every outsider. Refuses to let anyone on his property. Booby-traps his house. He's a *baker*?"

Dex grinned. "A hell of a good one, too."

Nova scooped up a cupcake and dipped her finger into the icing. Her lips closed around the digit, and she moaned.

Fuck.

My dick twitched, straining against my zipper. Those were not sounds I needed in my head.

Nova's eyes sparked silver as they opened. "That is the best chocolate icing I've ever tasted."

Me, too. And I hadn't had a bite.

Chapter Eighteen

NOVA

Closing the door to my apartment, I leaned against it. Every part of me was exhausted, from the tips of my toes to the ends of my hair.

Today had been amazing, but it had also been a lot. A lot of people. Activity. Emotions. And if there was one thing I was never particularly good at, it was feelings. It even made me twitchy when Brae told me she loved me.

I was sure I had my super-stable childhood to thank for that one. Memories of my mother's voice flickered in the back of my mind.

"Stop your whining. No one cares."

"Enough with the crying already. No one likes a baby."

"Do you think I give a shit how you feel?"

Shoving off the wood, I tried to clear my mind, but it was hard when I was reminded how good family could be. My father had mostly been negligent, absent, and uncaring. But my mother? She lived with unquenchable anger in her. And I was the most frequent recipient of it.

But not anymore. Anger didn't live here. I flipped the lock on my door and turned to take in the apartment. *My* apartment. It was the first time I'd ever had my own space. I could do whatever I wanted to decorate it and wouldn't have to ask a soul. There would be no yelling or cruel voices. There would only be peace, safety, and freedom here.

Moving deeper into the space, I caught sight of a bag on the bed. It was pale purple with tissue paper and a note sticking out of it. I plucked the card from the bag.

To help you make yourself safe. Welcome home. – K

I traced that K with my eyes, memorizing the lines of it. I had the bizarre urge to hug the card to my chest, but I refrained.

Pulling out the tissue paper, I peered inside and frowned. I tugged out the first item that looked like an adorably angry key ring. It looked like a pink kitten, but the ears were sharp points, and you could put your fingers through the eye holes.

Next, there was a tiny bottle of pepper spray. A purple Taser. A silver whistle. And a package that read *Emergency Alert Button.*

Kol had given me an arsenal. So I would feel safe. Not because someone else made me safe but because he'd empowered me to give it to myself. And that meant more than he would ever know.

Fingers wrapped around my throat, digging in and cutting off my air supply. I kicked against the thin mattress, trying to claw at the arms pinning me, strangling me. But it was no use. It was as if the man didn't feel an ounce of pain. It was almost as if he liked *it.*

"I'm the one who decides if you live or die. I'm the one who lets you breathe or not. Me. No one else even cares about you. I'm all you have now."

My eyes flew open as I thrashed in the bedding. A soft glow came from the bathroom and the moon through the window. It was just enough light to see my surroundings, but it took a few jerky inhales for me to remember where I was.

The new apartment.

I tried to even out my breaths.

"You're alive. You're breathing."

I replayed Kol's words in my mind, using them to paint over the ugly ones from the man. From Travis. But was it Travis? I wasn't sure.

"Memory or imagination?" I whispered into the dark.

Throwing the blankets off, I crossed to my closet. I dug through an open box until I found a sweatshirt that read *Namaste in Bed*. It was from my past life. It didn't really feel like it fit me anymore. I had certainly abandoned my yoga practice, and sleep was hardly my friend.

Pulling the sweatshirt on, I headed for the stairs. Once I reached the bottom, I took the back door out onto the deck. The moment my bare feet hit the wood planks, panic gripped me.

Darkness. So much of it, I worried it would swallow me whole. That I would get lost in it and no one would find me this time.

"You're alive. You're breathing."

I forced myself to stare it down, the darkness. I had to make peace with it because I'd never escape it altogether.

I kept breathing as I walked deeper into the shadows, across the deck, and to the wide steps that surrounded it. I lowered myself to the middle stair and let the cold seep through my sleep shorts.

And then, I stared into the dark.

I made myself study it. And as I took it in, a little of the panic eased. Because it wasn't just endless blackness—it was an infinite array of grays. Darker spots and lighter ones, kind of like Kol's eyes. That eased the panic even more.

The back door opened. There was no squeak of hinges, but I could hear the lock unlatch and the knob turn. I didn't look back because I knew who it was.

Because he always came. My trauma calling to his, maybe.

Kol lowered himself to the step next to me. Leaving about a foot between us. Gray sweats and a worn the Boot tee clung to his form, making me want to curl into him. The fabric of the T-shirt was nearly see-through in places.

I swallowed hard and stared back out at the shadows in front of me as he stared into the darkness, too.

I wasn't sure how much time passed. Five minutes? Fifteen? But he finally spoke. "Hard to sleep in a new place?"

"I have nightmares," I admitted. It wasn't something I shared. Brae and Dex knew because I screamed sometimes. Thankfully, Owen slept with a sound machine that seemed to block out everything.

Kol's large form stiffened, his fingers tightening around the wooden step. And then I felt his gaze on me, the telltale gentle roughness of it. "Memories?"

Of course, he would ask the most important question.

"I'm not sure," I told him honestly. "Could be. But it could also be my mind making things up from the information I've been given."

It wasn't much…as if my body were a patchwork of pieces of evidence. I hadn't been raped. I'd almost cried when the kind doctor told me that. As if that would've been the thing to break me after I'd endured so much.

The marks on my wrists and ankles told them I'd been shackled. The damage to my eyes and my vitamin D deficiency told them I'd been kept in the dark. The two healed scars on my torso showed I'd been stabbed at some point early on in my captivity. My weight said I'd been starved. And the scarring inside my throat and the bruising outside it revealed that I'd been repeatedly strangled.

That was all I knew for sure—those snippets and the fact that Travis Moore had been my monster. In my dreams, I could hear his voice, clear as day, the weirdly calm fury. But I could never see his face. It was as if my mind had blocked it out. Blurred all his features into something that made no sense at all.

"I have them, too. Nightmares," Kol offered.

I stilled. I'd expected him to push, to demand every detail in the event that it could help him with the case. I knew he was still working it. One of the officers from the State Police had told me Kol would be in charge of it. And given our proximity, I'd thought he would level me with countless questions. But he hadn't. Instead, he'd given me a gift—the gift of knowing I wasn't alone in what I was going through.

"What are they about?" I asked, even though I had no right.

Kol stared straight ahead, studying the dark horizon he likely knew by heart. "My brothers mostly. A different outcome of the day Orion killed our father."

I sucked in an audible breath. Everything about the surly middle brother suddenly made more sense.

"He saved them, Mav and Dex. They'd gone exploring in the one place they weren't allowed. Hadn't even realized what they'd found. Trophies of all the women Edmond had killed. But he knew. Almost killed Maverick because of it. It was touch and go for a bit. But Orion shot Edmond. Killed him on the spot."

"I'm so sorry he had to do that." Because it didn't matter that he'd done the right thing, Orion still carried the weight of ending someone who was a part of him in so many ways.

"In my nightmares, Orion doesn't save them. I come home, and they're all dead. And then Edmond kills me." Kol's voice was devoid of all emotion, as if he were reading off numbers for a math problem.

But the dream? It told me so much about the man who was still largely a mystery. He blamed himself. For not being there. For not being the one to end their father.

"What happened wasn't your fault," I said softly.

"No, it wasn't."

"But that doesn't change how you feel."

Kol's gaze flicked to me through the darkness. "No. It doesn't."

"I guess we're both survivors in a way."

Kol gave the slightest shake of his head. "You're so much stronger than me, Phoenix."

"We're both strong," I argued. "But we both carry a weight. The cost of making it to the other side of a nightmare."

Kol's fingers flexed, straightening as if he might reach out, might touch me. But then he tightened them around the step again.

Disappointment flooded my system. I thought I'd kept it from my face, but Kol's brow furrowed. "What?"

I swallowed against the dryness in my throat. "No one touches me anymore."

"They don't touch you anymore…" he parroted.

"Everyone stops themselves because I freaked out in the hospital.

And what's worse? I don't know if I'd do it again. Even now. So I'm too scared to ask." Each confession tumbled out, one after the other, not making complete sense.

But Kol still understood me, as if we shared a language—one created the day he found me. "Do you want me to touch you?"

His voice was quiet grit. The same potent combination as the rest of him.

My eyes filled with unshed tears. I managed a jerky nod that wasn't all that convincing.

"But you're scared," Kol surmised, filling in the silence.

I managed that same robotic nod, not trusting my voice.

"That you'll scream again?"

Of course he knew about the scream. My cheeks heated as I nodded again.

Kol twisted on the step. "Sky sleeps like the dead. Mav blasted an air horn outside her room to wake her up for breakfast once, and she didn't even stir. It's okay if you scream."

That same bobblehead nod was back.

Kol stared at me, not moving. "Tell me what you need."

There was a command in those words. A certainty that told me he would not move from that spot if I didn't use my voice.

I tried to swallow, but my tongue got stuck to the roof of my mouth. Loosening my jaw, I tried again. The movement was clumsy and almost painful, but I managed it.

"A hug," I croaked. "I need a hug."

Chapter Nineteen

KOL

"I NEED A HUG."

Fucking hell. Those four words killed me. Sliced me right to the quick.

A hug. How had everyone around Nova been so blind to the fact that she wanted human connection but was too scared to ask for it? How could *I* have been so blind?

I stared at her for a beat of *one, two, three*. I memorized her raven hair in the moonlight. The way her pale skin seemed to glow. The curve of her lips, pink as the lupines that grew deep in the forest.

Doubt flashed in those gray eyes, and Nova started to retreat. I moved then. Not waiting. I didn't often hug people other than Skylar. And she was a tiny ball of energy that hurled herself at me most of the time.

This was so damn different.

My hand slid across her back, feeling her shoulder blades through her worn, bright-purple sweatshirt. My arm curved around Nova as I pulled her to me and waited.

There was no scream. Only a scent that took me out at the knees. Nova smelled like sunbaked cherries and the barest hint of vanilla.

Her heart hammered—I could feel it through the wall of her chest—and then she let out a sort of animalistic sound. A keening. Her hand fisted in my tee, and then she was climbing.

Nova hoisted herself into my lap as if she was meant to be there. But she never let go of my shirt, her fingers clutching. So damn strong. She curled into me, forming a tight ball.

And I did the only thing I could do: I held on.

I covered her body with mine in a silent promise to be her shield or her comfort anytime she needed it. It was such a simple request: A hug.

Contact. Connection. The knowledge that someone else was there.

Nova pressed harder against me, those delicate fingers pulling at my shirt even more. My chin rested atop her head, and I just kept holding on. I could feel her heart against my chest, the intense, fluttering beats. It was erratic at first, and then it started to slow.

I was drowning in sunbaked cherries and vanilla, but it would be the best way to go.

"I'm not screaming." Nova's voice cut through the night air and the quiet stillness all around us.

"You're not screaming."

She sighed, her body relaxing even more into me. "This is nice."

My mouth curved. "It is." And not just for Nova. For me, too. "It's been a long time since I've gotten to hug someone like this." This might have actually been a first.

Nova's head tipped back, the moon making her eyes glow silver. "Really?"

"Not really in the market for someone in my life in that way." And it wasn't because I didn't want it. It was because I knew I'd never be able to trust in the way you really needed for a relationship to work.

A tiny frown pulled at her beautiful, lupine lips. "You don't have to answer if you don't want to, but where is Skylar's mom?"

The barest bit of tension stiffened my muscles. In response, Nova started rubbing those fingers that had a hold of my shirt in tiny circles. The minuscule gesture eased something within me, allowing me to speak.

"It wasn't a relationship, exactly. We met at a bar a couple of towns over. I'd gone there to hang out with a friend from college who was in town. Kendra and I probably saw each other a handful of times. It wasn't serious, but it was…nice."

It wasn't a deep connection, but it was comfort. "We would talk, but not usually about anything especially deep. Work. Our families, a little bit. What we wanted from life. Then, one day, she stopped returning my calls or texts. Just…gone."

It was Nova's turn to stiffen, and I knew why.

"Not that kind of gone," I assured her. "But that's where my head was at, too. I went to the diner where she worked, and she told me to take a hint. Said she wasn't interested."

Nova's mouth thinned to a hard line. "She could grow up and say that. Not make you worry."

"I told her no problem. Promised I wouldn't bother her again."

Nova shifted. "Why don't I have a good feeling?"

Because she was smart. That was why. "A little over nine months later, she showed up on my doorstep, a baby in her arms. Told me it was mine, and she didn't want anything to do with me or the baby. Someone had told her about my father."

Nova sucked in a sharp breath, fingers fisting tightly in my shirt again.

"She didn't want anything to do with someone who had *'psychopath DNA'* running in their veins. And that's what she thought of me and Sky. She hadn't even named her. The birth certificate said Baby Girl Keller."

"Kol," Nova whispered.

"I tried giving her time. Thought for sure she'd come around. That maybe it was the shock of the pregnancy and birth, hormones, just…

everything. But she never did. Not six months in, or after a year, or two. She wanted nothing to do with her daughter. I should've told her about who my father was. I just—"

"You don't owe anyone that." Nova's voice was pure steel. "Not one damn person. That is deeply personal, and it doesn't sound like you two were serious."

"No, but—"

"But nothing," she snapped, her silver eyes searching mine. "Is that why you told me? Because you thought I'd freak out and want nothing to do with you?"

That stiffness returned to my muscles. "You deserved to know whose house you were moving into."

"I did know. The man who saved me when I'd all but given up. The man who gave me back my fight when I couldn't find it. The man who *found* me. The man who hugged me when no one else would."

Fuck me.

My hand lifted, ghosting over the side of her face. "Phoenix, I'll hug you anytime you want."

Her whole face softened, and more than that, it lit with a glow. "You're an amazing man, Kol. And Skylar is pure magic. Everyone who comes into your orbit is better for it. If your ex couldn't see that, then it's her damn loss."

And for the first time, the burn of everything that had happened didn't hurt quite so much. And Nova? She was pure magic, too.

Chapter Twenty

KOL

"I'M TELLING YOU, I THINK THIS CASE IS CONNECTED," PETE argued.

I sighed, pinching the bridge of my nose as I sat at the conference table. There wasn't enough coffee in the world to deal with him today. "It doesn't track."

"Because she has blond hair?" Pete snapped. "Travis didn't have a consistent victim profile."

That much was true. Even if his largest victim pool consisted of women in their twenties with dark hair, he also targeted men, older women, and all different ethnicities.

"You're right," I began, hoping that might appease Pete's ego. "But there is a strong geographic profile."

Pete scoffed. "That geographic profiling stuff is a bunch of bullshit. It hasn't even been proven to work."

My back molars ground together. I'd have liked to tell him that my brothers and I had used it on countless cases, and it had been a game changer. It had led to us discovering linked cases, even identifying the area where an unsub lived or worked—information that Dex then anonymously dropped into an investigating officer's email inbox.

But no one knew about our little side project. And that was how it needed to stay.

"Call it whatever you want, but you know good and well that Travis only kidnapped victims from a circle of towns and counties where he could insert himself in the cases. You've seen the profile. He needed to be a part of the case."

"Profiling," Pete huffed. "It's a pseudoscience at best."

He'd better not say that to the people who spent countless years training and honing their skills. And I'd seen profiling lead to numerous breakthroughs. Not to mention all the stories Dex had shared from his time supporting the Behavioral Analysis Unit at the FBI.

"Fine," I clipped. "Don't call it profiling. Just call it halfway decent investigative work and look at the damn commonalities."

Pete opened his mouth, most likely to spew more bullshit, but my phone rang, cutting him off.

Roger's name flashed on the screen. I swiped the cell off the table and answered quickly. "Archer."

"Hey, man. I caught a case that has my spidey-senses tingling."

Everything in me went on alert. "What is it?"

"Twenty-three-year-old woman with dark-brown hair went missing from a campsite near Three Creeks Canyon Trail. Her boyfriend said she went off to pee and never came back."

Everything in me stilled. Three Creeks Canyon Trail was where Brae and Nova had been hiking when Nova was taken. "It's probably a coincidence."

"Probably," Roger agreed. "Still wouldn't mind your eyes."

"I'm on my way. Which campsite?"

"Aspen Falls."

"Got it." I stood from my chair, ending the call.

"What is it?" Pete demanded.

Damn it all to hell. If he hadn't heard the call, I never would've taken him with me, but now there was no avoiding it. "Missing woman, Aspen Falls off Three Creeks Canyon Trail."

Pete's eyes lit with excitement. "Seriously?"

My gaze narrowed on him. He sounded like a kid who'd just been told dinner was ice cream sundaes. "Take your own vehicle. I have stuff to do after."

I stalked out of the conference room but didn't miss Pete's muttered "asshole" as I walked out.

I might be an asshole, but it was a hell of a lot better than being an opportunistic bloodsucker.

My truck hugged the curve of the gravel road as I made my way deeper into the wilderness. Fall in Starlight Grove was the time of year I loved most. The golden glow of aspen leaves turning. The crisp bite to the air.

But today, everything seemed sharper. More shadowy. As I pulled into the small parking lot at the campsite, I saw a host of vehicles. It looked like the local search and rescue team was assembling at one end. There were several Juniper County Sheriff's Department vehicles as well, along with two Juniper County Crime Lab SUVs. Roger wasn't messing around, and I was relieved to see it.

Pete was already parked, having passed me on the two-lane road leading to the campsite—as if it were some sort of competition. He could have at it. All I cared about was finding the missing woman.

I pulled into a spot at the very end of a row, hoping I wouldn't get boxed in if additional vehicles showed up. I climbed out of my truck and grabbed my pack from the back of the cab, just in case. You never knew when you might need to pivot to a search.

My pack was always ready to go. Water. Energy bars and trail mix. First-aid kit. Emergency blanket. Sat phone. Bear spray. But my weapon never left my hip.

Slinging the pack over my shoulder, I headed toward the sound of voices. I found Roger and a deputy talking to a distraught man who looked to be in his mid-twenties. He ran a hand through his hair, leaving canyons behind. "It's like she just vanished. How does that happen?"

"Try to breathe," Roger told him. "We're doing everything we can to find her."

The female deputy next to him lifted her phone a little higher. "Can you walk us through your trip one more time?"

Roger turned and headed in my direction, looking tired as hell. "Hey, man. Thanks for coming."

"Tell us what happened," Pete demanded as he stepped up to our huddle.

Roger's gaze flicked to the man before he turned back to me. "They woke up around seven this morning. No one else had been at the site."

"It's a little late in the year for camping," I surmised.

Roger nodded. "Fuckin' cold at night. But Heidi, our missing person, went off to relieve her bladder and never came back."

"How's the boyfriend look?" It was always the first question that needed an answer.

Roger scrubbed a hand over his face. "Doesn't read as guilty, and he has no record. But you never know."

Pete scowled at both of us. "Shouldn't search and rescue have started already?"

Roger sent him a look that said he thought Pete was an idiot. "Takes time to assemble a team, divide quadrants. They need to prep for a safe search so we don't end up with more casualties."

I crossed to the boyfriend, Roger and Pete following behind. "Do you remember which direction Heidi walked in?"

The man with the red-rimmed eyes just pointed toward the forest. "That way."

I started walking, Pete hot on my heels.

"What are you doing?" Pete asked.

"Tracking, hopefully." Something I liked to do *alone*. "Why don't you listen in on the boyfriend's interview?"

"So you can cut me out of the good stuff?"

"No," I ground out. "So we can cover all our bases."

Pete didn't move for a moment.

I didn't want to have to pull rank—it was an asshole move—but I did it anyway. "I'm the senior officer, and I'm asking you to listen in on the boyfriend's interview in case this is related to the case we're working."

It was likely a coincidence, as I'd told Roger. But it could be someone *inspired* by Travis's heinous crimes.

Pete glared at me, his eyes flashing in anger before he stalked back to the boyfriend.

Roger let out a low whistle as he approached. "Looks like that's been a laugh a minute."

"Don't even get me started," I grumbled.

A throat cleared. "Excuse me, Special Agent Archer? Would you mind if I followed behind you? I promise not to get in your way. I just want to be ready to collect any evidence we might need."

The woman who walked toward us was tall and willowy. Her light-brown hair was streaked with blond and pulled back into a ponytail. She looked to be in her early to mid-twenties and peered up at me nervously through black-framed glasses. She had interesting eyes behind those frames, a light hazel, but one eye had a lot more brown, almost making it look as if her eyes were two different colors.

"Livie, you don't gotta call him Special Agent," Roger grumbled.

"It's respectful," the woman hissed.

"You can call me Kol," I said, holding out a hand.

She blushed. "I'm Olivia Bishop, crime scene investigator and lab tech. But most people call me Livie."

It was rare for someone to be both an investigator and a tech, but with how rural our community was, a handful of folks in the crime lab did double duty.

"It's nice to meet you, Livie. As long as you're quiet and stay behind me, you're welcome."

Roger rolled his eyes. "Kol's gotta do his psychic mind meld with the land."

I flipped him off. "You're the one who called me in, remember?"

"Yeah, yeah, get going," Roger mumbled. "I'll stay behind you, too."

I started moving in the direction the boyfriend had pointed. Scanning the surrounding forest and brush, I saw a little unofficial trail our vic would have likely taken. "What was she wearing?"

Roger pulled out his phone. "Sweats. Green top, blue bottoms."

Sweatpants and sweatshirts didn't lose strands as often as other kinds of material did, but it might still give us something.

"Was she wearing a shirt under the sweatshirt?" Livie asked.

Roger frowned. "Yeah. A plaid pajama top. Red, black, and pink."

Livie made a note on her phone. "That might shed more easily than the sweats."

I sent her a grudging nod of respect and refocused on the work at hand. Stepping onto the trail, I crouched low and scanned everything in front of me. The morning sun broke through the trees, casting a patchwork of light and shadow on the underbrush.

One of the patches of light illuminated some brambles, and on one of them, I caught sight of some long, brown strands of hair. I pushed to my feet and strode ahead. Pointing to the branch, I turned to Livie. "Bag and tag? Could be hers."

Livie jerked her head in a nod, lifting a camera from around her neck to take a couple of shots before pulling gloves and an evidence bag from her pack.

I kept on going, surveying the path in bits and pieces. We repeated the process when I found a red and pink thread, another strand of hair, and a few footprints in the deeper dirt.

Livie crouched to snap a shot of the latest footprints. As she straightened, she stumbled slightly. I reached out to steady her, and her cheeks flushed. "Sorry."

"Don't worry about it. This trail is uneven."

She bobbed her head in a nod. "Yeah."

I moved deeper down the trail, seeing a spot where a few branches had been broken when someone stepped off the path. There was a cluster of trees that would've made the perfect makeshift restroom.

And then I saw it.

All-terrain vehicle tracks. My blood went cold. "Rog," I said, my voice low.

"What?" He was by my side in a second.

"Look." I lifted a hand toward the tracks.

He let loose a stream of curses.

Travis had used an ATV to kidnap a number of his victims. He'd incapacitated them and then tied them to the back of his four-wheeler.

"Copycat?" Rog asked.

I hoped like hell it was. But one thing swirled in my mind. After Dex shot Travis, and he fell into the river?

No one had ever found his body.

Chapter Twenty-One

NOVA

Stepping out of my Subaru, I closed the door and tipped my face up to the sun. It was one of those magical fall days, when even though the temperatures had dropped, the sun took the edge off. I felt…lighter.

And when I closed my eyes, I swore I could still feel Kol's arms around me, his big body almost cocooning me. Those rough fingers ghosting over my jawline.

"Whatcha thinkin' about so hard over there?"

The familiar voice had my eyes flying open and my hand fisting around the adorable angry cat key chain Kol had given me. Reese Gatlin stood about twenty feet away with a grin on his face.

Anger surged as I reminded myself to breathe. The back door of the Boot was only ten feet away or so. If I screamed, someone would come running.

"Wylder's going to have you arrested for trespassing," I warned the reporter.

Reese simply grinned at me. "I'm on the art gallery's property, actually. So I think I'm safe."

I muttered a curse as I saw that he was, in fact, right. "What do you want?"

He held up both hands in surrender. "I'm not trying to make your life harder. I'm really not. I was over the moon when they found you alive. With all the time I spent covering your case…I feel like I know you."

"You don't," I snapped. I thought about asking him about the news clippings, but something told me he'd get a charge out of my discomfort. Better to make him think it hadn't bothered me at all.

He lifted one shoulder and then dropped it. "I bet I know more than you think. I know that you come from a tough family situation. Mom has been arrested for public intoxication five times. Dad lost his license after a second charge of drunk driving. Brother in prison for armed robbery."

My fingers curled tighter around the angry cat key chain. It wasn't as if people hadn't dug up those details before; it was just that they weren't usually hurled at me in person.

"You worked hard to get yourself out of that situation," Reese went on. "Worked hard to break the cycle."

I bit the inside of my cheek so hard I tasted blood. Because he wasn't wrong. I'd known from an early age that I didn't want to be anything like my parents. Didn't want anything to do with the stuff they drank that burned when you smelled it. I didn't want to fight and throw things like they did. I didn't want to have kids and then ignore everything about them.

"Let me tell the real story," Reese cajoled. "Beginning to end. In your voice."

"Not interested," I clipped and stalked toward the back door of the Boot, making sure to keep the reporter in my periphery.

"Come on, Nova," Reese called. "I'm gonna tell it with or without you. Don't you want to have some control?"

Damn him to hell. Of course I wanted some control. That was the thing I'd clung to my whole life. A safety blanket—one that had been ripped out from under me and torn to shreds when Travis took me. Because I realized I'd never had any control to begin with. No one did.

I punched in the code on the Boot's back door and yanked it open, stalking inside. The moment it snicked closed behind me, I stopped. I took a second to breathe because I knew if Brae or Wylder saw me now, they'd know that something was up.

In and out. Nice and steady.

Reese could write whatever the hell he wanted to write. He could make a stupid documentary. It wouldn't be my voice, my story. Because that would always belong to me.

The reminder helped. With a long exhale, I started down the hall toward the voices. We had about fifteen minutes until opening, so the music was still turned down low.

"I'm telling you," Piper said with a sigh, "he is the absolute dreamiest. And a true gentleman. He opened doors, paid for dinner, walked me to my porch, and only kissed my *cheek*."

"What's going on?" I asked as I took in the crowd around the bar.

Cora and Brae were refilling salt and pepper shakers while Fiona was working on the ketchup. Aidan frowned as he sliced lemon wedges, and Piper was pink-cheeked and practically vibrating.

Brae grinned at me. "Piper's met herself a real live cowboy."

"A *bull* rider," Piper amended.

I let out a low whistle as I stuck my bag into the cabinet where we housed our belongings for our shifts. "This is big news."

"You know," Aidan cut in, "I rode a bull once."

Fiona arched a brow. "The only bull you know is bull hockey."

"Hey," he shot back, offended. "It might've been mechanical, but I set a record for that bar over in Clover Creek."

Brae let out a soft snicker, and Cora just shook her head and moved on to the next pepper shaker.

"It counts," Aidan pressed.

Piper reached across the bar and patted his arm. "Keep telling yourself that." She did a little spin away from the bar. "I'm telling you guys. I think this is it. *Love*."

Fiona's lips curved. "Ah, to be young."

Cora's gaze lifted, a cross between pain and worry in her eyes. "Just be careful. You don't know a lot about him yet."

An invisible fist ground against my sternum. She'd learned that you never really knew anyone in the most brutal of ways.

Piper stilled, her face falling. "Of course. I'm taking it slow."

"Good." Cora wiped her hands on a bar towel. "I'll get the front doors open. It's almost time."

"I'll help," I offered quickly, meeting her on the other side of the bar as she headed toward the entrance.

I didn't say anything as I fell into step beside her. But Cora's gaze flicked to me for the briefest of moments. "I'm fine."

"It would be okay if you weren't." I realized I was the biggest fraud, walking around telling everyone I was okay when I was far from it but encouraging Cora to be honest about her feelings. "But I also get that it doesn't always feel safe to let anyone else in on that. Find someone. Just one person you can let in. It helps."

Cora's gaze flicked to the back hallway and held as Wylder appeared, his dark hair a little rumpled, and his scruff a little longer. Then her focus flicked back to me. "You find someone you can be honest with?"

I thought about it for a long moment. "I have. And I think it's starting to set me free."

Cora let out a long breath as she flipped the locks. "I'm gonna find that one day. Freedom."

I wanted to reach out and squeeze her shoulder or her arm. But I wasn't quite brave enough. Not yet. "I know you will."

We got to work on the trickle of customers who were there right at opening and wrapped up refilling all the condiments and restocking the bar. As I finished with the limes, I glanced at Wylder.

"Need something?" he asked, not looking up from his phone. If there wasn't a customer in front of him, his gaze was on that screen. But he didn't look like he was playing a game or scrolling social media. It *looked* like he was reading something. Or maybe he was a crossword puzzle aficionado.

"I have a question."

He straightened, his gaze swinging to me as he locked his phone and shoved it into his back pocket. "I may have an answer."

"How would you feel about training me behind the bar? I could be a backup bartender when things get busy."

His dark brows rose. "You wanna tend bar?"

I shrugged. "I'd like to learn. Maybe I'll hate it, but it seems kind of fun."

Wylder's lips twitched. "It can be. It's a hell of a lot to memorize."

"I can make flashcards."

A low chuckle left him. "All right, then. You can start with beers. Once I see you're not pouring drafts that are half foam, we can move on to simple drinks. But why don't you stay behind the bar with me for the first few hours today? You can handle food and beer as you watch and learn."

I did a little half jump. "Thank you."

Wylder shook his head but did it with a smile. "You might regret this when I'm asking you to pull the night shift for me."

"We'll just have to see about that." I dumped the lime wedges into the container and then turned toward the bar. I nearly stumbled back a step as I took in the man opposite me.

Jack.

I remembered his name from the Compass meeting I'd attended, but it was the dark shadows playing across his features that I'd truly memorized.

Clearing my throat, I forced a smile as I grabbed a menu and deposited it on the bar top. "Hey there. Can I get you something to drink while you're looking at the menu?"

"Coke." His voice sounded just a little rusty. "Please," he added.

"Coming right up." I used the ice scoop to fill a glass and then reached for the soda gun. "Straw?"

Jack shook his head.

"Here you go. Do you know what you'd like to eat?"

He studied me for a long moment. "I saw the news article."

Everything in me went rigid.

"That reporter bothering you?" he growled.

The tension running through me eased. Jack might be a little scowly, but he was just checking on me.

That knowledge had a smile coming more easily to my lips. "He's nothing I can't handle."

Jack studied me for a long moment before giving me a slight nod. "You let me know if you want me to handle him instead."

There was an edge to Jack's voice that worried me. Not because it was directed at me, but because I could tell it came from pain. I understood it. Losing your wife to a serial killer—someone you knew—was bound to mess with your head. But I worried that he was so on edge, he might do something he regretted.

"Thanks for the offer," I said softly. "You just make sure you're taking care of yourself, okay?"

Jack didn't answer for a moment, then moved his head in a small, jerky nod. "Can I get the fried chicken wrap with sweet potato fries?"

"You bet." I scrawled the items on my pad and placed the paper on the order wheel. "Order in."

"Thanks, honey," Fiona called with a smile.

As I turned back around, I caught sight of movement. The bar was getting more crowded, but it didn't matter; my whole body was attuned to the man crossing the space. Kol wore those olive-green tactical pants he often donned for fieldwork and boots that had seen their share of miles. His tan Forest Service tee skimmed over his broad shoulders and muscular chest.

Everything about him was like a finely tuned weapon. My gaze went up, up, up, until it collided with hazel eyes, darker than usual, the demons swirling.

My stomach twisted. Something was wrong. I was already moving to the end of the bar, and Kol met me there. "What's wrong?" My voice came out a little choked.

Pain flickered over Kol's eyes as if he didn't want to say what he was about to. "A woman went missing from a campsite by Three Creeks Canyon Trail."

The world fell away. There was no din of conversation, no country rock wafting from the speakers, no clatter of dishes. And only specific words punched through.

Woman.

Missing.

Three Creeks Canyon Trail.

A woman like me. Vanished. And all I could wonder was if she had been taken. If, even now, there was still a monster haunting those woods—or worse, if they were walking among us.

Chapter Twenty-Two

KOL

IT WAS THE LAST THING I WANTED TO TELL HER. I WANTED to soothe all of Nova's fears, not add to them. But I also didn't trust gossip and small towns. It wouldn't take long for word to spread, and I didn't want her blindsided by some Nosy Nelly.

A slight tremble took root in Nova's hands, her fingers fluttering. I moved in closer, shielding her body with mine and weaving my fingers through hers. She instantly gripped my hand with a ferocity that reminded me just how strong she was.

"I'm alive. I'm breathing." The words were barely a whisper, the slightest sound hovering in the air between her and me.

Shock ripped through me, shredding my goddamned chest. My words. The ones I'd given her as I begged her to stay. She was repeating them as if they were a mantra. "You are," I rasped. "And you're perfectly safe."

Nova's gaze snapped to my face. "I'm safe."

"That's right. You make yourself safe." And I'd give her every damn weapon in my arsenal to ensure that. "You want me to take you home?"

That was damn well what I *wanted* to do. Get her back to the apartment. Hold her like I had last night.

Nova let out a long breath, those pink-lupine lips parting as she did. "No. I want to finish my shift."

Somehow, I knew that would be the answer. "All right. I'm gonna stay."

"Kol—"

"I missed lunch. Need to eat something."

One corner of Nova's mouth kicked up, even as it wavered a little. "Food, I can get ya, Boss."

"Good." The word sounded more like a grunt than anything else—my annoyance that I had to let her go bleeding through. With one final squeeze, I released my grip on her fingers.

When I turned, it was to find Jack Hooper with his eyes locked on us—not in a jealous way, but a curious one. As if he were trying to figure out exactly what was going on between the two of us.

I wished like hell I had the answer to that.

I slid onto the stool next to him.

"Everything okay?" he asked.

I could lie, but he'd know the truth in less than twenty-four hours. "Missing woman at Aspen Falls campsite."

Jack stiffened. "That's near Three Creeks Canyon Trail."

"It is." I answered Jack but didn't take my eyes off Nova as she moved, grabbing a menu and handing it to me.

"Coke or root beer?" she asked.

It did something to me that she knew those were my two choices of drink outside of the times I opted for a beer at the end of the day. "Root beer. Wylder's got the good stuff here."

Nova's lips twitched. "You got it, Boss."

As if I'd beckoned my brother, he made his way down to my spot as Nova got my drink. "Gonna have to get you a frequent flyer membership."

I simply grunted in response.

Wylder stared at me for a long moment. "What's going on?"

It was Jack who answered, tension bleeding into his words. "Missing woman near Three Creeks."

Wylder's gaze went hard, assessing, that coldness that rarely found him taking over. "You're sure?"

"Sure," I said quietly. "Not here. Later."

Instantly reading me, Wylder's focus flicked to Nova. "Later."

Jack wanted to know more, but I artfully dodged his questions as I ate a turkey club that I barely tasted. When he left, I breathed a little easier but was still on alert. I watched every customer who came to the bar, each person who stared at Nova for too long.

And that was a task because some knew her story and watched her because they were curious. Others watched her simply because she was stunning. Those acres of raven hair swished around her as she moved like a goddamned ballerina. Her dark jeans hugged every curve I shouldn't be studying like they were the key to acing my next exam. She wore a flannel shirt over a Boot tee that stopped right at her waistband, except when she reached for something, a tiny sliver of skin showed—skin I wanted to trace with my tongue.

Fuck.

A hand landed on my shoulder. "Look what the cat dragged in," Brae said with a grin.

"Hey," I greeted, trying to force my version of a smile.

"I'm about to clock out. I have an errand to run before I pick up Owen. You need me to get Sky?" she asked.

I checked my watch, doing the mental math on how much time I had. I could make it work. "I'm all good, but thanks."

"All right. Enjoy those fries." She gave the rest of the crew a wave as she headed out.

I knew she'd know about the missing woman soon enough, but I'd let Dex tell her. It would bring things back for Brae—memories of her best friend disappearing practically in front of her eyes—and she'd need him.

"Done?" Nova asked, cutting into my thoughts.

I nodded. "Thanks."

She cleared my plate and then refilled my soda.

"Hey, will you do me a favor?" I asked.

A puzzled look spread across her face. "Sure."

"Come pick up Sky with me." The words were out before I could stop them. But I realized I didn't think I could leave her. Not with all the worry bearing down on me.

Understanding swept into her eyes. "I really am okay, Kol."

Her saying my name…it was just one syllable, but it echoed in my mind forever. "I know you are. But maybe I'm not."

It took a lot for me to admit weakness, that maybe I needed something. But that was all it took for Nova to accept.

She leaned across the bar, that sunbaked-cherry scent invading my space. "I have one condition," Nova purred.

I arched a brow in question.

"We get pie after pickup," she told me very seriously.

A soft chuckle left my lips. "I think we can make that happen."

Sky bounced up and down in her booster seat as we drove away from the Grove Griddle toward home. "Chocolate cream pie and boysenberry and peanut butter pie and lemon meringue?"

Nova twisted in her seat to grin at my daughter. "I have pie-decision paralysis. I can't choose."

Sky giggled. "I like not choosing. Then I get everything I want."

I grunted at that. Between the two of them, I'd been helpless to protest, despite the threat of sugar coma, or worse, a sugar high.

"Daddy usually only has us split one," Skylar explained.

Nova let out a huff as I turned onto the ranch road. "Amateur."

"I'll be looking to you at midnight when this one is hopped up on sugar and refuses to sleep," I said as I hit the remote for the gate.

"If I can have leftover pie for breakfast, then I'll sleep," Sky offered.

Nova shot her hand in the air in some sort of victory celebration. "Dang straight."

Skylar copied her move. As Nova pulled her hand back, she

hurried to cover the scars on her wrist. The action had me clenching my jaw. I hated that Nova felt she needed to hide them. That she even had them in the first place.

"Let's have a picnic on the back deck," Sky singsonged. "We can put out a blanket, and Tink and Pepper can come."

"They're gonna try to eat your pie," I pointed out.

"They can have one bite each," she acquiesced.

Nova's mouth curved. "Can mini-Highland cows and goats eat pie?"

"Goats eat *anything*," I grumbled. "And so does Tink. Just no chocolate."

"She's a growing girl, that's why," Skylar said sagely.

The moment I pulled up to the house, Nova and Skylar were out of the truck. I watched in fascination as they raced inside to create a picnic fit for a fairy warrior princess. And Nova was all in.

While I looked on from the deck, they grabbed a quilt and spread it out. Then they brought out dishes, including wineglasses that hadn't been used in years. They pulled out all sorts of items from Sky's dress-up trunk, and Nova ran to get the flowers Skylar had picked for her from her room. In a matter of fifteen minutes, the feast was laid out on the deck, and Pepper and Tink were already meandering over from one of their various pastures. Sky, of course, let them out to join the party.

I swallowed hard as I took in Nova and Skylar, wearing tiaras and boas and toasting with wineglasses filled with milk. Sky hadn't ever had this before. Not really. My brothers and I would play make-believe with her anytime she wanted, but having a woman along for the ride, someone who knew how to create the perfect picnic? It was different.

Doing my best to shove down those feelings of failure, I lowered myself to the quilt. "Thank you for doing this," I whispered to Nova as Sky chattered to Tink and Pepper.

Nova beamed at me. "Are you kidding? Dream ending to a day that could've been hard."

"I'm glad," I said hoarsely.

She leaned forward and rested a tiara atop my head. "But you need to be dressed to come to this party."

Her hands lingered there for a moment, fingers in my hair, her face so close to mine. I swore I could feel her mouth on mine, even though it was inches away. Some part of me knew what it would be like to feel her tongue stroking in, twisting with mine. The only thing I didn't know was what she'd taste like. Lemon from the pie she'd just bit into? Cherries and vanilla like that scent that haunted me? Or something uniquely Nova?

Her breath caught as we froze, so damn close. I wanted to erase the distance. To know it all with a certainty that would never leave me.

Pepper let out a loud bleat that had Nova stumbling back to sitting. She let out a laugh, her cheeks flushing the most stunning shade of pink. "Pep, you scared me."

Sky giggled, rubbing the goat's head. "She wants more pie."

I muttered a curse under my breath, forcing my gaze away from Nova—from the only place my eyes wanted to be. I needed an ice-cold shower. And I had a feeling I'd be needing them daily for the foreseeable future.

Chapter Twenty-Three

NOVA

I STARED UP AT THE CEILING, THROUGH THE SKYLIGHT KOL had cut into the roof so I could always see the sky. It was as if he'd somehow known I would need it after having been robbed of it for so long. But right now, it wasn't enough. Not even as the first hints of daylight crept across the space.

Everything in me was twitchy. My skin felt tight. My body was hot. And it was more than anxiety pumping through my system. It was Kol.

"I need to get laid," I muttered, throwing off my covers.

I needed that connection, that heat. The feeling of being spent that only came from losing yourself in another person. I'd always chosen my partners carefully. It wasn't always because I was in love. But there was always a deep respect.

I didn't know how I was supposed to find that now, when my head was a supremely messed-up place and the only person I'd managed physical touch with was my landlord/the special agent of my kidnapping case. But I needed to make it happen. Because I'd dreamed about a man's forearms last night.

Forearms.

Maybe it was because I'd watched said forearms flex as he ate pie and then chased his daughter around, throwing her in the air. And God, there'd been something about that, too. The fact that he was giving Skylar the kind of childhood I'd only ever dreamed of.

"Stop it." I hissed out the words in warning as I crossed to the closet and pulled on some workout leggings and a tank. I needed to burn out whatever was eating at me. Because Kol was a no-go for so many reasons. Our lives were too intertwined, and I was sure his higher-ups wouldn't love our involvement. To say it was complicated would be a huge understatement.

I glanced at the yoga mat in the corner but knew that wouldn't do. I needed cliff jumping, but I was a good ten miles from my usual spot. My muscles twitched with the need to move, invisible claws shredding my insides.

The world swirled around me as a wave of dizziness hit, but I fought it off and slipped my feet into some sneakers. I grabbed my keys with the adorable angry cat key chain and the mini pepper spray. The moment my feet hit the gravel, I started running. The cold air swirled around me, telling me I should've grabbed a sweatshirt, but I couldn't go back now. The anxiety might win if I did. So I kept on running.

I'd never been a runner in my past life. The idea of embarking on anything other than a walk for *fun* was beyond me. But the second my muscles started to burn, I knew this was exactly what I needed.

I followed the road as far as it went, passing alpacas and goats and even some yaks. The sun crested over the horizon, bathing the land around me in a peachy-pink glow. Even though my lungs ached, I felt more at peace than I had since Kol had held me.

Pushing my legs harder, my chest heaved. I climbed the hill in my path, forcing myself to maintain my pace. But by the time I got to the top, my legs nearly gave out. I bent over, barely able to take in the house that had come into view.

Large and rambling, constructed from wood so dark I wasn't sure if it was black or brown. And the siding itself looked rough, as if aged by wind and weather. The image before me blurred, and I bent over, trying to catch my breath.

I sucked in air, but the inhale was painful, as if the breath itself were composed of shards of ice.

The sound of a screen door slapping against the frame had me straightening, my vision still a little blurry. A hulking form I didn't recognize stalked down the steps of the front porch, and I stumbled back a step.

Panic swirled, my breaths coming faster as another wave of dizziness hit.

The moment the man recognized the move, the fear behind it, he stilled. Frozen as if some magic ice machine had zapped him.

It was just enough for me to put the pieces together. Dark hair. The same hazel eyes as the other Archer brothers. But his were just a little darker than the rest.

Orion.

It had to be.

I struggled for composure. To get my body to believe I wasn't in any danger. But it wasn't quite past the whole flight-fight-or-freeze thing. And apparently, it had chosen freeze.

Orion lifted a hand, holding up one finger as if telling me to wait.

I winced as he turned and headed back into the house because I had a feeling he might be texting Kol. The last thing I wanted was for my landlord to know that I'd had a freak-out—I didn't want *anyone* to know but especially not him.

A second later, Orion reemerged with something in his hands—a bottle with orange liquid. He stopped a good twenty feet from me and tossed the bottle.

I somehow managed to catch it, despite my lack of experience in team sports of any kind. It took me a second to recognize the Gatorade label.

Orion sighed and made a drinking motion as if annoyed that I was a moron.

Cracking the seal, I took a sip and then a longer drink. The sweetness played over my tongue as the liquid coursed through my system. In a matter of seconds, I'd downed half the bottle.

Orion nodded as if satisfied.

"Thank you," I croaked.

He simply pointed in the direction I'd come from and glared.

I guessed we weren't at bestie status quite yet.

Nodding, I started walking back but turned. "Sorry about infringing on your home. I didn't know this was where you lived." Kol had mentioned that I needed to steer clear, but I'd never gone this deep onto ranch land before.

Something passed over Orion's expression, but it was gone so fast I couldn't identify it. And he didn't respond in any way.

I watched him for one more moment and then turned back in the direction of Kol's house. I was sure Orion was watching to make sure I really left, and I didn't blame him. Sipping the Gatorade as I went, I finally took stock of how far I'd run. Several miles, at least.

My muscles would hate me later today. Especially since I had to work a full shift. *Shit.*

Still, I took my time getting back. I tried to soak in every bit of the beauty surrounding me. The fall sun was different than it was in the summer, more golden somehow. And it painted everything in different hues.

As Kol's house came into view, I saw someone step out onto the back deck. I instantly knew it was him, even before I could clearly see his features or clothing. It was as if my whole body could recognize him, even in the dark.

He didn't move as I got closer and closer. There was no silent judgment like I received from Brae when I returned from my "swims," but there was concern.

I crossed the back lawn and climbed the steps with trembling legs.

"Tell me you took your phone," he said, his voice low.

I pulled it from the pocket of my leggings. "Right here, Boss." I held up my key ring. "Along with adorable angry cat and Mr. Pepper Spray."

Kol's brow quirked—not quite a smile, but like he was fighting one off. "Adorable angry cat?"

I flipped to the key chain. "Come on, you can't tell me that's not the perfect name for this."

"Let's focus on the fact that it could take someone's eye out."

"Hence the angry," I said exasperatedly.

Kol just shook his head, his gaze sweeping over my form, catching in different places. My face. My neck. Where my tank rode up just a fraction. He cleared his throat. "Couldn't sleep?"

I shrugged. "Sleep rarely comes easy. But that's okay."

"So you went running."

I nodded.

Kol was quiet for a long moment. "Can we do something?"

My mind did not go to G-rated places at the question. I shoved the images down. *Damn, those slutty forearms.* "Depends, Boss. If the *something* is eating pancakes, I'm in. If it's hike Mount Kilimanjaro, I'm afraid I'm going to have to pass. I'm out of shape."

His lips twitched as he pulled his phone from his pocket. Opening an app, he showed it to me: Find My Phone. "Can we share locations?"

My throat went dry. There was something about him not just asking for my location but also sharing his. As if the request for safety and security went both ways.

But it was more. There were times when the darkness still swirled around me, when I worried I'd get lost again. That I'd disappear, and no one would be able to find me. But now, Kol would know. He'd be able to find me wherever I was.

I swallowed hard. "You know what this will mean, don't you?"

Kol simply stared back at me, waiting.

"I'll know every time you're near the Grove Griddle, and I'm gonna make you bring me home pie."

One corner of his mouth kicked up. "I think you have an addiction."

"And no interest in a cure," I shot back.

"Supernova!" Skylar called from the open door. "Come have breakfast with us."

I hesitated for a moment, but Kol cut into the silence. "Yeah, Supernova. Have breakfast with us."

My gaze flicked down to my wrists. "Just let me grab my sweatshirt and I'll be back."

I jogged for the back door to the garage and my apartment. Opening it, I took the steps two at a time, even though my legs were mad about it. As I reached the top, my phone flashed. A text.

> **Brae:** *I just wanted to give you a heads-up so you're not blindsided at work.*

There was a link with an article. It was a step in the right direction that Brae was trying to equip me instead of protect me, but the headline still took me out at the knees.

A Legacy of Horror: The Real Nova Monroe Story by Reese Gatlin.

Suddenly, I wasn't hungry for breakfast at all.

Chapter Twenty-Four

KOL

Something was off with Nova. I wasn't sure if something had happened in the five minutes it had taken for her to grab a sweatshirt or if I'd missed something earlier. It could've been the missing woman. That would definitely do it. But something was scratching at the back of my brain, telling me that wasn't it.

"Thank you so much for the most *amazing* breakfast, Sky," Nova said with that smile that looked real but wasn't.

Skylar executed a spin and then a bow. "Anytime, milady."

Nova's gaze flicked to me. "I'm just going to shower and change real fast. Are you sure you're okay with dropping me at my car?"

"Of course," I said, frowning.

"I got the dishes, Daddy!" Skylar hurried to grab one from the table. Helping with the meal process and the chores afterward had become her thing lately.

"You don't have to, you know," Nova said softly. "Brae can give me a ride."

My frown deepened. "You don't want me to drive you?"

"You're all scowly." She reached up, her thumb rubbing at the spot where I could now feel my brow furrowing.

"I don't like it when you fake smile."

Nova's eyes widened, and her hand dropped away. I instantly missed the contact, the point of connection, the heat. Now, it was Nova's turn to frown. "How do you always know?"

I shrugged, but I knew the truth. Because I'd made a study of Nova Monroe. All her smiles and frowns. Her tells and covers. Every mask she donned to face the day.

But the most beautiful sight I ever saw was when Nova was real. I lived for those moments.

She sighed and pulled out her phone, showing me an article by that asshole Reese. A slew of curses slid free, making Nova chuckle. "Pretty sure that qualifies for the swear jar."

"Only if Sky heard," I shot back. My gaze lifted to Nova's face. "I'm so sorry."

She stared at the screen. "Feels like someone stripped me naked in front of the whole world."

I wanted to kill the reporter for that. Taking choice and autonomy from someone who'd already had it stripped away in the worst way imaginable? It was lower than low.

"I'm gonna get Dex on it. See what he can do," I ground out.

"You don't have to. It's not the first article. It won't be the last."

I reached out and took her hand, squeezing. "You're gonna make it through."

Those gray eyes flashed silver. "Damn straight, I will. And I'm going to find someone to hex Reese Gatlin with a limp dick for the rest of his life."

I barked out a laugh. It was the last sound I'd expected to make when I was this angry. "That's one way to deal with it."

Nova was constantly a surprise. How she dealt with things. How she rose from a knockout punch every damn time. Everything about her wove a spell around me. Which was exactly why I let go of her hand.

"I'd better get that shower," Nova said, her voice just a little hoarse.

"Yeah." Mine was pure sandpapered grit. As she headed for her apartment, I could still feel her hand in mine. My skin buzzed and burned as if it refused to forget.

"All the dishes are in the washer," Skylar said, landing in front of me with a jump. "I rinsed *really* good."

I stared down at my girl. Today, she wore pink camo pants and a sweatshirt that read *Feeling Cute, Might Cause Some Chaos Later*. That one had to have come from Mav.

Hoisting Sky into the air, I hugged her tight. "You know you're the awesomest helper, right?"

"Duh, Daddy."

I chuckled. "I'm glad you're secure in your awesomeness."

She stared down at me, her hazel eyes nearly identical to mine. "Can I ask you a question?"

I instantly braced. There had been some awkward ones over the years. The highlights included:

"Why don't I have a penis?"

"Where do babies come from?"

"What does asshole mean?"

That last one was Mav's fault.

I set Skylar in our conversation spot on the counter. It put her closer to my level without us sitting on the couch and making things feel formal. "Sock it to me, Little Princess."

I really hoped we were still too early for the birds and bees. The baby discussion was bad enough. And while I had a book on my nightstand about girls going through puberty to prepare for that talk, I thought eight was a little young for questions about her period.

Skylar stared up at me. "What happened to Nova's arms?"

I braced for a whole other reason. It made sense that Sky had noticed. Kids were far too perceptive, and they registered differences because they wanted to understand them. But I didn't have the first clue how to explain this to an eight-year-old.

"She doesn't like those marks," Sky said softly. "She's always pulling at her sleeves and checking that they're covered."

My gut twisted because Skylar wasn't wrong. "Sometimes, it's hard to have things that make us different."

Sky nodded. "Owen didn't like his glasses because not a lot of kids have them. But now he loves them because Uncle Dex got him the perfect pair."

My mouth curved at that. "It can take a little time to figure out, but what makes us different is also our superpower. Though sometimes, we can't see that those differences make us beautiful."

She was quiet for a long moment, as if mulling something over. She looked so much older, and it was a punch to the gut. "Owen said she was gone for a long time. Is it like…is it how it was with my mom?"

Every muscle inside me twisted so hard, it was a miracle my bones didn't crack. Skylar almost never asked about her mother anymore. There had been questions when she started school, around Mother's Day, or when they did projects about family, but I couldn't remember one time she'd asked about Kendra in the last year.

I'd always tried to be honest and protective when it came to the topic. But trying to figure out how to ease the blow of her mom leaving was like walking through a minefield. "Did Owen telling you that make you have questions about your mom?" I asked gently.

Skylar shrugged in a way I knew meant yes.

I took my girl's hands, so tiny in mine. "You are the most amazing kid on the planet. I don't know how I got so lucky to have you as mine."

"Daaaaaaad."

"It's true," I said.

Sky bit her lip, a little uncertainty in her gaze. "Then how come she didn't want me?"

God, I wanted to kill Kendra in that moment. Even knowing it was better that she'd simply left. The pain she'd caused ate at me. Even more so because I worried it was my fault.

"She wasn't ready to be a mom," I told Skylar. "But she knew I would love you. That I would *love* being your dad. So she gave me the best gift I've ever been given. You."

Sky thought about that for a moment. "I am pretty great."

I laughed, scooping her up into my arms again. "The absolute greatest."

Skylar slapped her hands on my cheeks like she had when she was little, rubbing her tiny palms on my scruff. "I'm gonna make something for Supernova."

The way kids' minds worked was a trip. "I think she'll love whatever it is. Your vase is her favorite."

Sky's smile widened. "I like her."

"Me, too," I admitted. Only I was starting to think *like* didn't come close to encompassing how I felt about Nova. And that was dangerous.

I scowled at the road as Pete kept futzing with my radio. He changed the station thirty seconds into every song when he realized he didn't actually like it. Then changed it back again.

"Pick a station and keep it there," I clipped.

"Touchy, touchy," Pete sniped. "You'd think I'd get a thank-you for filing the majority of the paperwork from yesterday while you took off early."

My fingers tightened on the wheel. "I didn't take off early. I went to talk to a victim."

He bristled. "And you didn't take me?"

I wouldn't take him anywhere if I had a choice. Today, he'd caught me heading out to meet Roger to interview Heidi's family, and there'd been no shrugging him off.

"You weren't needed," I ground out.

Pete's glare bored into the side of my head. "It was Nova Monroe, wasn't it?"

It didn't take a genius to figure that out. She was Travis's only living victim, at least to our knowledge. And the only other case I had on my desk right now was out-of-season poaching in a section of national forest land.

"Yes." That was all he was getting from me.

Pete muttered something under his breath, but I just turned up the radio, letting the sounds of Credence Clearwater Revival drown out any attempts at conversation until I pulled up in front of Heidi's parents' house in Clover Creek.

Only about twenty minutes from Starlight Grove, Clover Creek was slightly larger but was still rife with that small-town feel. The house looked straight out of textbook Americana—white with black shutters, a wraparound porch complete with a swing, and immaculately mowed grass with a tire swing hanging from a tree in the front.

Shutting off the engine, I climbed out of my truck. Pete was already hurrying to the door as if it were some sort of race. It wasn't. And the longer he was on the job, he'd start to realize that.

The door swung open, and Roger frowned at Pete but then nodded in greeting. "Pete."

Pete only scowled at the acting sheriff. "Where's the family?"

That had Roger bristling. "You're here as a courtesy. That campsite's on state land, and since the state police are drowning in cases at the moment, they gave jurisdiction to us. You're not point on this."

"Maybe I'll get Sherri to request jurisdiction," Pete shot back.

"Enough," I clipped, my voice low as I stepped onto the front porch. "This isn't about you. This is about showing respect for the people who are hurting in there and doing everything we can to find their daughter."

Roger cracked his neck. "You're right."

A muscle in Pete's cheek fluttered, but he said nothing, just stepped inside.

"That went well," I muttered.

Roger clapped me on the shoulder. "You're doing everything you can."

I wasn't so sure about that. I also wasn't sure what would break through when it came to Pete. But he hadn't been faced with true loss. His caseload had mostly consisted of poachers, illegal grow sites for marijuana, and a couple of arson investigations. He'd had one accidental death—a rock climber. But he hadn't been the one to notify the family.

Maybe time with this family would change things for Pete.

As I moved inside, I could feel the grief. The air was thick and stale with it. The lights were dim, whether from its residents just forgetting to turn some of them on or not being able to deal with the brightness, I wasn't sure.

A woman and a man who appeared to be in their fifties sat on a couch with a delicate floral pattern. The woman gripped the man's hand with such ferocity that her already pale skin was white around her knuckles. Another man, who looked to be in his late twenties, paced behind them.

The moment I stepped into the living room, his gaze cut to me. His green eyes blazed with anger. "Let me guess. You're here to ask the most stupid-ass questions when you could be out there looking for my sister."

"Dustin," the woman warned, but her voice held no heat, only a tremor of emotion.

"This is Special Agent Archer and Special Agent Simpson," Roger said, introducing us. "They work as investigators with the Forest Service. They will be coordinating their officers to aid in the search."

I didn't miss that he'd left out what case we thought this might be related to. That was smart. These people didn't need that swirling in their heads.

"This is Cal and Sarah Ingram, Heidi's parents. And her brother, Dustin," Roger went on.

Dustin glared at us. "If you're aiding in the search, why the hell aren't you out there?"

I lowered myself onto one of the floral chairs opposite the couch. The back was unbearably straight, but I wanted to be on the parents' level, not looming over them.

"I will be out there. But we need information from you to make sure we're looking in the right places," I assured them.

We'd followed the ATV tracks to a parking area a few miles away from the abduction site yesterday. It looked like whoever had taken Heidi had used the all-terrain vehicle to take her to a larger vehicle. Roger had pulled camera footage from the road, but the techs were still going through it.

Sarah gripped her husband's hand even harder. "We'll tell you anything you want to know."

I nodded. "In these cases, the first thing we have to do is clear the last person to see the victim. So I have to ask: Were there any issues between Heidi and Garret?"

Cal's jaw tightened, a muscle flickering there at the mention of Heidi's boyfriend. "She never should've gotten involved with him. A goddamned hippie. Only works to pay for camping gear and gas to get to the national parks. Doesn't save or plan. Life just passes him by."

"Our Heidi is a hard worker. A nurse at the hospital," Sarah explained. "They just didn't seem like a match."

Dustin scrubbed a hand over his face. "There was no tension between them. An occasional fight, sure, but he'd never hurt her. He's a freaking vegan because he doesn't want cows harmed in the milking process."

I was pretty sure there were still vegan murderers out there, but I got what Dustin meant. And Garret hadn't raised any flags for me as a likely culprit. His distress at the campsite had seemed genuine, and we had the ATV tracks.

"Was anyone else giving Heidi trouble or unwanted attention?" I asked.

Sarah shook her head. "No. Not that she told us."

"Heidi would've told Mom," Dustin said quietly. "They're tight."

I didn't miss how they all spoke of Heidi in the present tense, their hope for her bleeding through.

"Please," Sarah said, her voice breaking. "Find our daughter. She's…she's everything to us."

She broke down then, sobbing into her husband's shoulder as he held her, his own tears flowing silently down his cheeks.

My jaw clenched, teeth grinding reflexively. How many times had my own father put families through this? Living in the hell of unknowns until they got the worst possible news: that their daughter or sister or friend had been brutally killed, tortured by a monster.

Swallowing hard, my gaze swept over the Ingrams. "We'll do whatever we can to find Heidi. I promise."

I didn't wait for a reply. They didn't owe us one. I simply pushed to my feet and started for the door. The moment I stepped outside, I sucked in air. Fresh. The scent of pine clinging to it. No grief here, no choking staleness.

"We should tell them we think it's connected to the Travis Moore case," Pete complained, stepping out the door behind me as Roger followed.

My gaze cut to him. Apparently, grief and pain didn't reach Pete, either. "For what purpose?" I demanded. "To torture them further? Did you see them in there? They're falling apart. Their worst nightmares are coming true. And you want to add to that?"

Pete flushed. "I just thought they deserved the truth."

"They do," I ground out. "But that isn't the truth. It's conjecture."

Pete snapped his mouth closed, his gaze dropping to the ground.

Roger cleared his throat as he rocked back on his heels. "Livie's trying to fast-track the evidence, but you know how the crime lab is."

"Understaffed and overworked," I muttered.

"Understatement of the century," Roger agreed. "She did find a fiber that didn't look like it matched anything Heidi was wearing. Green. Not sure what that will get us unless it miraculously has DNA, but she'll do her best."

I nodded.

Roger was quiet for a moment, but I could tell he had something else to say. So I waited.

He cleared his throat again. "We need to talk to Nova again—"

"No." The single word whipped out.

"We need to see if she remembers anything new," Roger protested.

"No." It was all I could say. I wasn't putting her through that again.

"What if it saves this woman? Someone who could still be alive—just like Nova was," Roger pressed.

I stared back at him. He knew the right buttons to push. "Fuck you," I muttered, though without heat.

"You know we have to do it," he said quietly. "It can be just you and me."

"I'm working this case, too," Pete spat.

If he thought he was getting within a mile of Nova, he was dead wrong. My gaze met his, and I knew he read the coldness in it when he took a step back.

"You will ask Nova nothing. You will not be present at any questioning. You will not go around me to do it on your own. You have shown zero empathy for victims and their families."

Fire blazed in Pete's eyes. "You seem pretty damn protective of her. You think Sherri needs to know about that?"

The muscle along my jaw fluttered wildly. "You didn't see her. You weren't the one who found her, so close to death you could feel it in the goddamned air. You weren't the one who kept her alive. Who breathed for her when she couldn't do it on her own. So, yeah, I'm fuckin' protective. Because she shouldn't have to live through even one more ounce of pain in this life."

A hint of doubt flickered in Pete's expression, and I thought I might've broken through, but then he doubled down. "Sounds like you're a little too personally involved, Kol. Might be time for a reassignment."

It took everything in me not to punch him. The only thing that held me back was the fact that doing it would get me suspended. But if they found out just how close I'd gotten to Nova? They'd fire me for sure.

Chapter Twenty-Five

NOVA

I ROLLED MY YOGA MAT OUT AS THE MORNING SUN CASCADED over the wide-planked wood floors of my apartment. It was time to try. To see if I could reclaim a small part of who I used to be.

Staring at the beautiful mat Kol had gotten for me, I stepped onto it. I pressed my feet into the foam and spread my toes out, gently stretching them. It felt…good.

Elongating my spine, I straightened into mountain pose. I stood tall, feeling the energy coursing through me. I stretched my neck taller and *breathed*.

The twitchiness started almost immediately—that need to move. To run. To hurl myself from a cliff into ice-cold water. Anything but *feel*.

A wave of dizziness spread through me, and I moved into downward dog. The stretch helped for a moment, but then I was battling snapshots. Memories? Nightmares? I didn't know.

Hands tightening around my neck.

"No one's looking for you, Nova. I'm all you have."

I couldn't suck in air. My lungs burned.

I shot to standing, shaking out my arms and legs. "It's not real. You're alive. You're breathing. You're not forgotten."

Unshed tears sprang to my eyes at those last words, and I quickly swiped them away. My phone dinged, and I crossed to my bed where I'd left it, grateful for any distraction from the dumpster fire that was currently engulfing me.

Kol: *This is Sky*

She sent a dozen emojis ranging from butterfly wings to a tiara to a sword, making me grin.

Kol: *Come to breakfast*

Kol: *Dad says yes*

Kol: *I have a thing for you*

I couldn't help but chuckle.

Me: *On my way.*

I needed to pay them back for all these meals. Maybe I could make dinner. I used to do that a lot, trying out different dishes and cuisines. That could be the thing I reclaimed from my old life. Especially since it seemed yoga wouldn't be it.

I quickly rolled up my mat, stowed it, and headed for the door. I stopped at the last second and cursed. Moving to my closet, I grabbed a sweatshirt to cover my arms.

As I pulled it over my head, I made my way down the stairs and into the kitchen. It was so different from the one I'd grown up in. Homey with a four-seater table and Bigfoot salt and pepper shakers. Sky's art was all over the fridge. And it was clean. Not an exacting sort of spotlessness, but certainly not messy. There were no rotting-food smells like I'd grown up with. No insects or mice. I shoved the memories down. "I heard there was breakfast."

Kol looked up from his spot at the stove, those damn forearms on display as he flipped—yes, *flipped*—an omelet. "Just need to know what you like in your omelet."

Skylar ran over to me, holding a hand behind her back. "I made you something."

I crouched low so we were at eye level with each other. "You're really spoiling me, Sky."

She just grinned, then started to look a little nervous. She took a deep breath and shoved a pile of beaded bracelets in my direction. "I know you don't like your wrist marks."

I sucked in a sharp inhale and struggled not to tug my sleeves down.

"Dad says that what makes us different makes us beautiful," Skylar went on, and I struggled not to look at Kol. "And I think you're super beautiful. But until you're ready to show them, I made you these."

My eyes burned. I hadn't cried once since leaving the hospital, but this sweet girl was threatening to be the thing that cracked my iron fortress walls. I studied the bracelets made of sparkly beads in every color under the sun. "Sky," I whispered.

She looked so damn uncertain. I wanted to hug her, but I didn't trust myself quite yet.

"This is the best gift anyone has ever given me," I croaked.

Skylar's hazel eyes lit with sheer joy. "Really?"

"Really." I pulled up one sleeve and slid about six bracelets on. They didn't cover the scars completely, but they disguised them. People would be looking at the colorful creations and not my mottled skin.

"They look so pretty on you," Sky encouraged.

I slid the other half on my left wrist. "And they will look good with everything."

"That's why I picked every color," Sky said sagely.

"You are the smartest."

"I got a one hundred percent on my spelling test yesterday."

I chuckled as I straightened. "Why am I not surprised?"

As I turned, my gaze collided with Kol's. He studied my face, clearly checking for signs of distress, as if not sure how the gift would go over.

I moved in a little closer, playing with fire as that scent of pine, cedar, and fresh air swirled around me. "You have an incredible daughter."

A little of his tension eased. "I'm pretty partial to her." He glanced at his daughter. "Think I could get some of those bracelets, too, Little Princess?"

She beamed. "I'll make you some with all the colors, too."

His lips twitched. "My favorite."

Now that I was closer to Kol, I could see the circles beneath his eyes. "Is everything okay?"

He sighed. "Late night. Case."

A shiver ran through me. It shamed me to admit that I'd tried to shove the missing woman from my mind. I hated myself for it. She was a human being. Someone who might be facing what I already had. "Anything?"

Kol shook his head. "Roger wants to talk to you again."

Alarm shot through me, but the moment it did, Kol's fingers wove through mine and squeezed. "I'll be with you."

I swallowed the panic. If I could help in some way, I needed to. "Okay. When?"

"How about after your shift?" Kol suggested. "Roger is running down a few things this morning."

I nodded as relief washed through me. I didn't want to do it before work. If it messed with my head, I'd be a wreck while trying to serve. But this way, it would be hanging over my head all day. Still, it was better than the alternative.

"Okay," Kol began. "Why don't we do it here? No prying eyes or ears. Brae can take Sky for a few hours if I ask."

Here felt safe. Because Kol had made it that way. "Okay."

"You're stronger than you know." He gave my hand one last squeeze and then released me.

I missed the contact instantly. But I'd also memorized the feel of it. The rough calluses on Kol's palm and fingers. The story of him. The pressure and heat. His safety and assurance. And I'd carry it all with me, even when I didn't have him.

"Date number two, and I'm halfway gone," Piper said dreamily as she flounced behind the bar to tuck her purse away. She was early for the evening shift, but maybe she just needed some time to talk about the new love of her life.

I focused on the drink in front of me. Wylder had moved me up from beers and sodas to simple mixed drinks. But given that I'd broken two glasses and spilled an entire beer today, that might've been a bad idea.

"He took me on a picnic to this beautiful waterfall. A *picnic*!" she squealed. "Who does that these days? Usually, it's all Netflix and chill."

Cora cast a worried look in Piper's direction, then quashed it. "Two Cokes and an Aspen Pale Ale."

The moment I finished with the vodka soda, I moved on to Cora's drinks. "Why don't you invite him in here one of these days so we can all get a look at him?" I suggested.

Piper grinned at me. "He's out of town for a rodeo the next couple of days, but then I will."

I sent Cora a quick look and knew we were both thinking the same thing: We'd suss him out. And if he wasn't on the up and up, I had the adorable angry-cat knuckles to scare the piss out of him.

Piper looked between us. "Oh no you don't. There will be no threatening of any kind."

Aidan chuckled as he walked up, putting her in a headlock and executing a noogie. "What good are honorary big brothers and sisters if we can't threaten your boyfriends?"

Piper ducked out of his hold. "You're the worst."

"I think you mean the best," Aidan singsonged.

I chuckled as I deposited the final drink on Cora's tray. "Here you go, madam."

She gave a faux curtsy in response. "Thank you, madam."

Just as she headed to a table, I spotted Aster and Holly making their way toward the bar. Aster beamed. "We heard there was a new bartender in town."

"I wouldn't go that far. I'm only allowed to serve beer, wine, and simple mixed drinks. And I still have to measure out the shots."

"Everyone starts somewhere," Wylder called from the other end of the bar.

"He's right," Aster agreed, sliding onto a stool as she tucked a strand of hair behind her ear.

Holly followed suit but looked a little uncertain, as if she'd never sat at a bar before. The confused look on her face had me fighting a giggle. "What can I get you guys?"

"I'll just do an Arnold Palmer and a basket of sweet potato fries. What about you, Holls?" Aster asked.

"Oh." Holly looked at the beer menu and wrinkled her nose. "How about a club soda with lime?"

"Lucky for you, I've got those covered." I sent the fries order to Fee in the kitchen and quickly got the girls' drinks.

As I slid them across the bar top, Holly leaned in and lowered her voice. "Are you doing okay? With the missing camper and everything?"

Aster's mouth thinned, and I knew instantly that she had wanted this *check on Nova* mission to be a bit more discreet. I tried to shove down the tiny flicker of annoyance I felt at Holly's question and take it for what it was: concern.

"I'm okay. Really." Even if Reese had written an article for the Redding paper that asked if a new monster was residing in the Starlight Grove woods.

Holly's lips pursed. "You can be honest with us."

"Or," Aster cut in, "you can *not* talk about it at all."

"I just hope they find her," I said, wiping down the bar.

"If you need anything, just shout," Aster said. "Even if it's just a movie night where we watch completely unrealistic rom-coms and drown ourselves in candy."

"Now that…I'm in for," I said with a grin.

Something about Aster put me at ease. Maybe it was something that had been trained into her as a therapist or perhaps it was because she was so good with animals. Whatever it was, she had a way about her.

"You're off," Wylder called from the other end of the bar.

I looked up and realized it was already fifteen past four. Brae had left an hour ago to pick up Owen and Sky, and now there was nothing between me and my chat with Roger and Kol.

"Thanks," I muttered, reaching for my bag in the cabinet. "I'll see you tomorrow." I glanced at Holly and Aster. "Next time, come in for actual drinks and give me a challenge."

Aster laughed. "Assignment accepted."

Holly's smile was more strained. "Take care, okay?"

"Will do." Swinging my purse over my shoulder, I headed for the parking lot.

The temperatures had definitely dropped in the past few days, and I wished for a sweater. But thanks to Sky, today had been the first day since my return that I'd worn short sleeves. And God, that had felt like reclaiming a little freedom.

I crossed the parking lot to my forest-green Subaru and was about to climb in when something stopped me. It was a glimmer. Metal in the sunlight.

Frowning, I moved around so I could see the windshield. Everything in me froze. Resting on the glass was a silver necklace with a turquoise gemstone. Only the stone was crusted with what looked like blood. And below the necklace was a note.

My heart hammered against my ribs, and blood roared in my ears. Boxy, black lettering. An angry bend to each one.

IT'S NOT OVER.

Chapter Twenty-Six

KOL

I looked over the map as I did my best to tune out Pete. He was droning on about some case he'd worked before. A story where he played the hero and everyone else was the fool. But I couldn't help wondering if he had that backward.

The standard-issue map had nothing on the creations Orion made. His were works of art, drawn exactly to the specifications we needed. Not this one. Just a run-of-the-mill map.

Still, I did my best to mentally cross off possibilities. I'd personally overseen an additional search of Travis's old property. With no next of kin, it would revert to the state, and who knew what they would do with it. Regardless, there'd been no signs of inhabitance there. No copycat serial killer in the making, using it to stow this latest victim. And there'd been no jump scare revealing that Travis was still alive and back in his favorite hunting ground.

So we were back at square one, surveying the campsite where Heidi had been taken. And I hated that with a fucking passion.

But there was only so much we could do. The camera feeds hadn't turned up much. Two were down for maintenance—some issue with the solar power that kept them running. And all the vehicles on the road from the others had checked out.

Only two had been towing trailers large enough to house an ATV, and we'd been able to clear both parties. But someone didn't just disappear into the ether. Whoever it was had gone *somewhere.*

My phone rang, cutting into my thoughts. *Roger* flashed across the screen. I swiped it off the table but not before Pete saw.

He was like a dog salivating before dinner, on instant alert.

"Archer," I answered.

"Need you to go to the Boot." Roger's voice was calm—too calm. But I could hear him moving. A door opening, the beep of vehicle locks.

Everything in me stilled. The kind of lack of movement that was deadly. But it didn't stop the panic from raging within me. "What?" I clipped.

"Someone left something on Nova's car. A note. And a bloody necklace."

The words were like a series of electric shocks. I had no awareness of moving, but I was suddenly running. I could hear Pete behind me, demanding to know where I was going.

I didn't give a damn. I could only think about Nova. The woman who'd already endured so much was now being hunted again.

It took two tries for me to start my damn truck, my foot slipping from the brake as I pushed the start button. But I finally got there.

As I flipped on my lights, I didn't miss Pete pulling out right behind me. *Asshole.* The last thing I wanted was for him to be around Nova, trying to get a high from her pain—an eerie echo of Travis.

I made the twenty-minute drive in twelve, rolling through stop signs and running red lights. I knew Nova parked in the back lot, but I also knew that it would likely be littered with emergency response vehicles. There were already some on the street. Just like there were countless lookie-loos hanging around.

That fact only made me curse as I pulled into a spot half a block down from the Boot. Then I was running again. There was a closed sign on the bar door, and as I passed, I tried to force myself to slow to a jog and hide exactly what I was feeling.

I rounded the building to see half a dozen sheriff's vehicles and a crime scene van. My gaze tracked over the lot, searching for only one person. It took me mere seconds, but they felt like an eternity.

Nova stood staring at nothing, her arms curled around herself. There were people around her: Wylder, Cora, Fee, a couple of deputies. But no one touched her. No one even got close.

She looked so damn alone.

I kept up my jog, cutting through the people milling around. Wylder's gaze cut to me as I approached, but he didn't say a word. I moved into Nova's space, crouching slightly to make sure I was in her line of sight.

She didn't react. It was as if she didn't recognize that I was there at all.

"Phoenix," I whispered, so softly only she would be able to hear.

Nothing.

I skimmed my knuckles against the back of her hand, careful to shield the movement with my body. Nova jolted slightly, blinking a few times.

"There she is," I whispered.

She blinked again. "Hey, Boss."

"Hey." I didn't ask if she was okay. It would be the most moronic of questions. She was about as far from *okay* as you could get. "Anything hurt?"

Those pink-lupine lips pursed, but she shook her head.

"That's good," I said quietly. "What do you need?"

It killed me not to hold her. Not to pull her into my goddamned arms and try to shield her from all of this. But I couldn't.

Nova's slender throat worked as she tried to swallow. "I need you to find out who the hell is doing this," she croaked.

Footsteps pounded behind me. "What the fuck happened?" Pete snarled. "You leave me in the dust with no explanation. You'd better believe I'm gonna tell Sherri about that shit. Tell me what the hell is going on."

I whirled on Pete, letting the fury blaze through me, knowing he could see all of it. "Get the fuck back. You wanna know what's going on? You talk to a goddamned deputy. But right now, you show a little respect. Decorum. Not that you've done that a day in your life."

His jaw went slack, but he quickly snapped it shut, rage burning through his brown eyes. Still, he stalked away and over to the obvious crime scene. I could see the woman I'd met at the campsite, Livie, working the scene. She marked a couple of spots around Nova's car and was currently dusting the hood and window for fingerprints.

My back molars ground together, a spark of pain shooting through my jaw. I forced myself to turn back around.

Wylder's impassive stare greeted me. "Well, that's one way to deal with it."

Fiona started clapping. "I think it was just the right way. Pete's always been a d-bag."

Cora's gaze flicked to Nova, worry creasing her brow. "Do you want to go inside?"

Nova shook her head, sending those long tendrils of hair swirling around her. "No. I want to stay here."

I wanted to take her home. I wanted her safe. I could get Wylder to do that, but sending her with my brother felt like ripping off a limb.

A throat cleared, and I glanced over to see Roger.

"Can I get a minute, Kol?"

My gaze returned to Nova, searching.

"Go," she said softly. "I've been through way worse than this."

That fact killed something in me. Still, I listened and stepped aside with Roger.

He didn't start speaking until we were out of earshot of everyone—not just Nova, but his people, too. "At first glance, the necklace looks like the one Heidi Ingram wore every day."

I let a slew of curses fly at that. "Keep going."

"Note, written in boxy black lettering, said, 'It's not over.'"

All the blood drained from my head as I struggled for composure. There were only two options now. Copycat or Travis wasn't as dead as we all thought. Both made bile churn in my gut. But something else flagged in my memory. "It's not the first note."

Roger's spine snapped straight. "What are you talking about?"

"Someone left news articles and a note on Nova's car when she was mountain biking with Mav. She thought it was the reporter in town, but Mav wasn't so sure, so he bagged it."

"Gonna need that for processing," Roger gritted out, his annoyance clear.

"I'll get it to you."

"What did the note say?"

"'Never forget.'"

It was Roger's turn to curse. "This isn't fuckin' good."

"No, it's not." My gaze moved over the crowd in the parking lot: the people working, the onlookers. I tried to take stock of any faces that shouldn't be there, but there were too many. "Ask Livie to take some shots of the crowd. Just in case."

"You're thinking copycat," Roger surmised.

I scrubbed a hand over my stubble. "I'd take that over Travis still being alive. Wouldn't you?"

Something streaked across Roger's expression. Pain? Guilt? I wasn't sure. But having your best friend turn out to be a serial killer had to mess with your head. Probably in a similar way to finding out your father was one.

"Something else," Roger said, his voice tight.

"What?"

"You gotta watch your back with Pete and play that more careful. He was over there cursing your name and all but plotting his revenge." Roger's gaze locked with mine. "Said you're too close to the vic and he could get you fired for it."

Fire and ice battled in my veins, but I locked everything down—something I was so damn good at. I pulled on a mask of nothingness and shoved away everything I was feeling. I knew I'd been reckless, letting my protectiveness of Nova show, letting myself get too close to her. But I would get fired before I let him anywhere near her.

Chapter Twenty-Seven

NOVA

A SHIVER RACED THROUGH ME AS I WATCHED THE DIFFERENT law enforcement officers working the scene. The air had gotten chillier over the past hour. Or maybe it was just the fact that Kol hadn't looked at me once. I told myself it was because he was working and focused, but something niggled. As if things had shifted between us.

I'd gotten spoiled, I realized. So used to him always being 100 percent attuned to me. And now that the connection was gone, everything felt colder. But it was more than just me feeling cold.

I also felt so damn alone.

"I think I need to go home," Cora said next to me.

Her voice was so soft I barely heard it. But as I turned, I realized I wasn't the only one affected by all of this. Cora's skin was just a bit pale, and she held her hands together so tightly that her knuckles were free of color.

Just thinking the word *knuckles* had heat blooming across the back of my hand, where Kol had skimmed his fingers over my skin.

I shoved that thought down. "I'm sorry. You didn't have to stay."

Cora shook her head quickly. "I wanted to. I just…I think I hit my limit."

I nodded. I understood it so well. We had the kind of messed-up bond that no one wanted to share. But here we were. And I was glad that neither of us was in it alone.

Wylder looked back and forth between us, indecision playing out over his face. Finally, his focus stilled on Cora. "Want me to walk with you?"

"You don't have to. I—"

"There are a lot of people out there," Wylder said softly.

God, he was such a good guy. Always looking out for those around him.

Cora glanced at the crowd of onlookers we could glimpse only part of at the end of the driveway between the Boot and the building next door. "Sure. That'd be good."

Wylder's gaze flicked to me. "You'll be okay right here?"

It was part question, part assurance. "I'm good."

Those two words were such a lie, it was almost comical. But I said them with enough confidence that Wylder nodded.

As he and Cora started down the driveway, I let out a sigh of relief. It was better this way—to be alone, the way I almost always felt. It was like I no longer had to pretend.

Fiona had taken off thirty minutes ago, needing to get to the grocery store before it closed. The deputies and other personnel gave me a wide berth, only glancing at me occasionally. Except for one.

He wore a Forest Service polo shirt, and when his brown eyes cut in my direction, there was anger there. It didn't make sense, but I felt it nonetheless.

"Are you ready to go home?"

I jumped at the deep, familiar voice. I hadn't heard Kol approach, but here he was. Only it wasn't the Kol of my memories. This one wore a mask so impenetrable I wasn't sure a missile could pierce it.

But I didn't have the energy to try. Everything hurt. And the pain vibrated, giving me that familiar twitchy feeling. I needed to run, to hurl myself off a cliff, to fly down the side of a mountain. To breathe.

And I couldn't. Not right now.

"Let's go." My words were strangled, as if a python had my vocal cords in its grip.

There was something in Kol's hazel eyes. A flicker. But I didn't care. He'd already shut me out.

And I didn't care why. I needed to be alone anyway. Alone was safe.

No one could hurt me there.

It was a lesson I should've learned by now. From my parents. My brother. Travis.

So now, I wrapped *alone* around me like a blanket and held on tight.

"I'm parked on the street. That okay?" Kol's voice was tight, but his eyes had already moved from my face.

"It's fine."

He jerked his head in a nod and started walking.

I chose to follow him. Not at his side but in his wake. At first, I stared at his back. But that was too hard.

I knew what it was to have those arms wrapped around me, those shoulders cocooning me. My gaze dropped to his feet. The heels of his scuffed hiking boots that he always wore beneath those tactical pants.

There was some brand name etched into the backs of those boots, but it was so worn I couldn't make it out. Still, I made that my mission, studying the half letters until Kol slowed and opened his passenger door.

I could feel eyes on me as I climbed in. They scraped against me like brambles and claws. They tugged and pulled like they wanted to rip me apart.

A wave of dizziness hit me as I settled against the seat and struggled to get my seat belt into place. I still hadn't secured it by the time Kol climbed in.

"Do you want me to—?"

"I've got it," I clipped.

Hot tears pressed against the backs of my eyes, but I shoved them down, locked it all away. Alone. I needed to be alone.

Finally, the buckle clicked. I sat back against the seat, staring straight ahead and letting my eyes go unfocused as Kol reversed out of the spot. Only my blurry vision wasn't helping now. Not one damn bit.

The dizziness was still there, and my muscles felt like they were on fire. I needed to move. To explode. To do something. Anything.

I struggled to keep a hold on it all as Kol drove out of town. He turned onto a back road and, a moment later, I recognized something familiar.

"Pull over," I rasped.

"What?"

"Pull over."

"We're not back at the ranch."

"PULL OVER!" I screamed the words so loudly I was sure Kol thought I was losing it—and maybe I was.

But he pulled his truck to the side of the gravel road. I flung open the door and leapt out, running toward familiar scenery.

I heard a curse behind me but ignored it and pushed on. My lungs burned as I hit the path I'd memorized over the past several months. It took me about five minutes to reach the cliff. But the moment it came into view, I started peeling off my clothes.

My shirt fluttered to the ground as the cold air wrapped around me.

"What the hell are you doing?" Kol barked.

I ignored him as I reached the edge. I toed off one shoe and then the other. My fingers dropped to the button on my jeans.

"Nova," Kol said, his voice strained.

Not Phoenix. For whatever reason, I wasn't Phoenix to him anymore.

That hurt more than I wanted to admit. But it didn't matter. I would take care of myself.

"I'm alive." My body shook as I whispered the words. "I'm alive." My jeans fell to the dirt. "I'm alive." I stepped out of them.

"Stop." There was panicked command in Kol's voice. "What are you doing?"

Something about the panic broke through, enough for me to look at him. When I did, I saw the fear there. Maybe he thought I was trying to end my life. I wasn't. I was doing the opposite.

"I come here when it gets to be too much," I explained. "It helps."

Angry little furrows appeared between Kol's dark brows. "You come here *alone*? And you... *cliff jump*?"

Apparently, what I said didn't help. My anger surged then. "I take care of me."

"Not damn well, apparently," Kol snarled. "You could hurt yourself or a hell of a lot worse."

I took a step toward the cliff's edge. "It makes me feel alive."

Kol's hand shot out. "Don't."

"I have to," I whispered.

He was already toeing off a boot. "You jump, I jump."

That was ridiculous. He could supervise me from up here if he really wanted to. I took another step.

Kol tore off his tee. As it fluttered to the ground, I saw golden skin, muscle that rippled in a way that came from real use, not the gym. I saw a dusting of dark hair over a broad chest and two pieces of ink. Neither was overly large. On his left rib cage was a feather with *Skylar* etched in delicate script. On his right was a phoenix. Smoke and ash flew around it, and his brothers' names were on different feathers. All four.

My gaze snapped to his face in question.

"We all have one. All of my brothers."

It meant something, Kol calling me a name that was interwoven into the fabric of who he was. But it didn't matter because that had been stolen from me, too.

I took another step backward. I needed to be away from him. I needed my alone time. I needed to breathe.

"Nova," he warned, shucking his pants, leaving him in only black boxer briefs.

I ignored him. And I jumped. But in my wake, I heard *"Phoenix"* on the air around me.

Chapter Twenty-Eight

NOVA

THE AIR CAUGHT ME LIKE IT ALWAYS DID. THE SHARP BITE from the cold soothed me like a warm blanket. But I understood it. Because everything seemed to be opposite for me these days. Nothing made sense the way it used to.

The sting of the air had nothing on the slap of the ice-cold water. In the days or weeks since I'd last jumped, it had changed, shifted into a shocking temperature that stole my breath instead of giving it back.

But still, I trusted it. I shot downward, nearing the bottom of the lake, then tipped my head back. I could see the sky peeking through the inky blue-green water. The streaks of the setting sun painted it in different designs and colors than it did in the morning hours.

And then something pierced the surface. The splash created bigger ripples than mine ever did. But then again, Kol's body was far broader than mine could ever hope to be.

I watched as the water moved and danced. Then my lungs began to burn, a reminder that I hadn't yet started swimming for the surface. My feet kicked on instinct, and my thigh muscles began to ache slightly. But not as much as they had in the past.

I held on to that sign of growing strength. Gripped it with all I had.

My head broke the surface, and I sucked in air.

"You're alive. You're breathing."

I ached to hear Kol repeat those words. Sometimes, I felt like they were still clear as day in my mind, while at others, it was as if they'd gone fuzzy—the way my eyes struggled after living in the dark for so long.

My chest heaved as my breathing regulated. Jumping was like a factory reset. And I was so damn grateful for it.

Kol treaded water a good ten feet away from me, not looking grateful at all. He looked pissed as hell. But he didn't say a word.

His anger was both a wound and a balm. The hurt because he'd never been mad at me before, at least, not in any real way. And a comfort because he trusted that I was strong enough to handle that anger.

"This is how you deal with things?"

The low, rumbling timbre of Kol's voice skated over my skin as the cold of the water started to set in. "Yes."

It was as simple as that. He could judge me if he wanted, but I wouldn't let it hurt.

"Alone?" he pressed.

"Yes."

"Fucking reckless," he growled.

"Maybe," I hedged.

"Definitely," he shot back.

Fire ignited, and I knew the gray of my irises had bled to silver, the way they always did when my emotions were heightened. "Any more reckless than letting a panic attack catch hold, seize me into passing out or freaking out or something so much worse?" I demanded.

He snapped his mouth closed.

"That's what I thought," I muttered. "I deal how I deal. It's *my* choice. Not anyone else's."

Something I didn't expect flashed in Kol's eyes. Hurt. "You could talk to *me*."

I stayed silent for a moment, my hands swirling through the icy water, relishing the feel of it as I picked my words carefully. "Talk to you when you won't even look at me? I felt it, you shutting me out. Maybe it was because you were working, but I get the feeling you want to make that shut-out permanent."

A part of me wondered if I was crazy—that mean word thoughtless people hurled my way. But maybe it was true. Maybe I'd imagined him pushing me away.

"Nova," he rasped, but made no claim that I was wrong.

Water had soaked Kol's hair, and tiny droplets streaked his face. He was so damn beautiful.

"You *were* shutting me out."

More pain in those hazel eyes. "I had to."

"Why?" That might've been my bravest act—asking for a reason that might ruin me.

"I'm already walking a tightrope that could get me fired, bending rules the me from a few months ago never would have."

I swallowed hard, trying to loosen the muscles tightening around my throat. I swam closer. One stroke. Two. Until I was so close I could've reached out and touched him.

I imagined what it would be like to trace one of those beads of water down the side of his face to that iron-sharp jaw, then his neck with the pulsing line of tension, and across one of those broad shoulders. And lower.

For the first time in what felt like forever, I *wanted*.

It both terrified and relieved me in the same breath. I was so damn scared to let myself be that vulnerable again. So damn happy that I could even want it.

"What if you just…took yourself off my case? No more conflict of interest."

A war of emotions played over Kol's face. "You want me off your case?"

I could see now that that would be the ultimate insult to someone like Kol—me not finding him capable. "No, I just mean…it would be easier."

A divot appeared in the corner of his jaw. "I don't trust anyone else to do what needs to be done."

A different sort of warmth spread through me, fighting off the cold of the water. Kol didn't trust anyone to do as good a job as he would. Because I mattered to him.

My gaze tracked over his face, landing on his mouth. I traced the line and shape the way I'd traced his fingers once. I memorized their story as I tried to imagine what they'd feel like pressed against mine, humming over my skin and running down the column of my throat. Across the line of my collarbone. Lower.

The ice-cold water pushed me closer to Kol. So close the lake wasn't as frigid as it had been. Because I could feel Kol's heat, from his words and from his body.

"I believe in you," I whispered.

Pain streaked across his face, as if that knowledge hurt because so few had shared the sentiment.

My fingers reached out, ghosting over his brow. "But you're more to me than solving this case, than tying up loose ends. You give me so much more than that every single day. And maybe it makes me greedy, but I want more."

"You think I don't want every moment I can get with you?" Kol croaked. "It's never enough."

I stared at him, the water holding me there, on that precipice. But Kol was right: I was reckless, and he made me remember I was alive.

I closed the distance, brushing my lips across his, featherlight. And for a moment, I thought he wouldn't answer my kiss. I began to pull back, but Kol surged forward. His fingers slid into my hair as his mouth took mine.

There was no hesitation now. No uncertainty. Kol was a man starved, and I wanted to give him every last part of me.

My body buzzed, my skin hummed, and as I pressed myself harder against Kol, he tore his mouth from mine. In a flash, his hand was gone from my hair, and he was swimming backward, creating distance.

"Nova."

My name on his lips was a curse, an oath, and a vow.

My gaze shot to Kol's.

"Don't."

God, it was unfair. For both of us. But he was the one who'd kept bringing us closer. If he knew those blurred lines would never be crossed, he shouldn't have danced so close in the first place.

"Don't look at me like that." Kol's voice gentled. "It's not because I don't want to. Trust me. If I could, I'd rip those goddamned heart panties clean off you. I'd take your mouth all over again as I sank into you so that I could feel your moans everywhere."

Heat spread through me as my nipples pebbled and my core tightened. And then that different heat spread, the kind that came from anger because Kol was hiding behind his job and his badge and his certainty that no one could work this case as well as he could. But I knew the truth: He was scared.

Well, so was I. But I was still *living*. I wasn't sure Kol was.

I met his dark stare dead-on. "Well, since you won't, I guess you'll just have to watch those *wet* heart panties march right up the side of that cliff, Boss. Good thing you're basically in an ice bath already."

Chapter Twenty-Nine

KOL

TWO WEEKS. FOURTEEN DAYS OF BLUE-BALLED HELL. THREE hundred and thirty-six hours of missing her. Twenty thousand, one hundred and sixty minutes of feeling like I was living with a ghost.

I caught glimpses of her: playing in the yard with Skylar, Tink, and Pepper; coming with our big group to trick-or-treat on Halloween. She'd even slipped an invitation under my door for Sky, asking her to a tea party at her apartment and telling Sky to wear her very best princess dress.

Nova was making sure my daughter didn't feel her absence, even when I was consumed by it.

But the worst? Her scent. I'd catch it on the air sometimes. Sunbaked cherries and vanilla. Sometimes, I was sure it was her. Others, I was certain it was my imagination because she'd been gone for hours.

Nova had done her interview with Roger alone. I'd gotten a call from him, asking me what the hell was up. I'd dodged and weaved.

And then I'd done what I always did: I threw myself into work. Usually, I had a minimum of two cases. One for the Forest Service and another for the Hourglass Network with my brothers. It just so happened that they were currently one and the same, and Nova was at the center of both.

So my escape was also my torment.

Fitting.

I forced my focus back to my damn paperwork instead of the back windows of my house. I could've told myself I was simply watching the animals roam in the fields beyond, but I knew that was a lie. I was an addict jonesing for a tiny hit of all that was Nova. Even a hint of that cherry-vanilla scent.

It didn't come.

At least I could be thankful that there'd been no more incidents since the necklace and note. But there were also no leads. Livie had sent the same report to Roger and me. No fingerprints on the news articles, notes, or the necklace. The paper the notes had been written on was standard computer paper and impossible to track.

The blood had been a match for Heidi Ingram. I'd gone with Roger the day he'd had to tell her family. It wrecked us both.

But there wasn't a damn thing leading us to who this monster was.

I'd gone with Roger to question Reese Gatlin because the reporter's arrival had been a little too convenient for me. But we'd gotten nothing. He, on the other hand, had gotten another byline with a long-lens photo of Nova, arms wrapped around herself at the crime scene, looking so damn alone.

Because I'd left her that way.

A knock sounded on the front door, and I felt a twisting sensation in my chest. Like my heart was doing goddamned acrobatics. It didn't leap, though. It was steady, predictable. Only got out of rhythm when I worried about Skylar or my brothers.

So whatever this was, I wasn't down with it. I grimaced as I got to my feet and made my way to the front door. Opening it, I couldn't deny the wave of disappointment I felt as Waylon filled the front porch, his Irish Wolfhound, Lucy, at his side.

He frowned as he took me in. "Somebody steal Christmas?"

My scowl only deepened. "Did you need something?"

"Was coming to ask if you and Sky wanted to come up to the house for boysenberry pie tonight."

It wasn't his fault, but those words were a knife to the gut. Images of the picnic on the back deck filled my mind. The pie taste test. The way Nova made every damn thing better.

Waylon's frown only deepened. "Why do you look like I just offered you arsenic?"

"Skylar's at a sleepover at Owen's. I think they're working on decimating their collection of Halloween candy," I answered. "I'm just trying to catch up on work."

His fingers hooked into the straps of his overalls as he rocked back on his heels. "I'm seein' we have bigger problems than pie."

"Way—"

He held up a hand to cut me off. "Don't." Those dark-brown eyes focused on me in a way that shut me up. Waylon rarely got serious, but I could tell he was about to. "I know you were nearly grown when you came to live here."

My gut tightened as flashes of memory caught in my mind. Getting off the plane and then having to make the hour-and-a-half drive to the ranch. Mav still recovering from his injuries. Dex having a nightmare as he dozed in the van. Orion shoved into the back corner, not talking to anyone or touching them. Wylder trying to hide how much it all affected him.

And God, I'd felt like I didn't have a right to be affected by it. Because I hadn't been there. Not when they needed me.

"So I may not have a right to say any of this," Waylon went on.

I flashed back to the here and now. "You have a right to say *anything*. You've been more father to me than anyone. You gave us back a sense of family."

Waylon's eyes misted at that. "Best thing you could ever tell me."

"It's the simple truth."

"The truth is rarely simple." Waylon's gaze leveled on me again.

"But I'm gonna give it to you now anyway. You're lettin' your life pass you by."

I jerked as if those words were bullets.

"You take care of Sky, make sure she has everything she needs, but you don't take care of *you*. All you do is work. Throw yourself into it like some sort of atonement. The rare extra time you have is spent with the Hourglass Network. Same thing. There's no time for you to live."

"Waylon, I—"

"Give me a minute," he said, cutting me off. "I see the connection you got with that girl." His eyes flicked to the apartment above my garage. "I see what you did for her. What you keep doing for her. Don't miss out on something beautiful because you think you don't deserve it."

Fucking hell.

My jaw worked back and forth as I stayed silent, trying to process what he'd just said. "You some Bigfoot-hunting, cuckoo-clock-making, alpaca-wrangling therapist?"

Waylon barked out a laugh. "You know it." He tapped the little embroidered Bigfoot on his overalls as if to punctuate the point.

"I can't go there," I said quietly. "For many reasons."

He scowled. "Give me the number one."

"It could get me *fired*. How about that?" I challenged.

Waylon pinned me with a hard stare. "And you're telling me you couldn't have a heart-to-heart with Sherri and step aside? Sure, she might give you a slap on the wrist, but I highly doubt she'd fire you."

It was my turn to scowl. It was a refrain so similar to Nova's that it made my gut churn. But there was something else, too. A fear I hadn't given voice to, not once.

"It's wrong." The words were out before I could stop them. I hadn't realized I even felt that way until the feeling slipped free.

"Why the hell would you think that?"

"I saved her. I kept her alive. It gives it sort of…I dunno, a power imbalance. Maybe she's just grateful I saved her."

Waylon stared at me for a long moment. "Boy, did someone hit you with the stupid stick this morning?"

"Excuse me?"

"You heard me. That girl up there." He gestured to the apartment with a jabbing motion. "She may have been through hell, but she's sharp as a tack. She's also working through it. I've seen her put just about every one of you in your place when you need it, and yet you think she'd show interest in you just because she thought it was the sort of gratitude she owed?"

"I don't know. I just—"

"It's called flowers or cookies or a homemade pie. That's a thank-you. Not looking at you like you're the only thing she's ever wanted."

Everything in me tightened, muscle winding tight around bone. "You think she looks at me like that?"

Waylon barked out a laugh, then shook his head. "The stupid stick *definitely* got you this morning."

I glared at him. "You're not helping."

"I could hit you upside the head and see if that shakes anything loose," he offered.

I opened my mouth to shoot something back when I saw a pickup heading our way. It wasn't one of ours, but it only took a matter of seconds for me to recognize it as Aster's. Maybe she was coming over to have a girls' night with Nova. Movies and face masks or some sort of thing.

But as the woman who'd been haunting my every waking thought rounded the garage, I knew I was wrong.

Fucking hell.

Nova's nearly midnight hair cascaded down her back in loose waves. She wore a navy dress made out of some sort of silky material that skimmed over her delicate curves in a way that had me knocked stupid. The only part that wasn't silky was a panel of lace that formed the straps and ghosted over her cleavage.

But it was the boots that nearly sent me over the edge. They were a variety of blue tones that hit at mid-calf, with silver stars stitched into them. All I could think about was Nova in nothing but those damn boots.

Waylon elbowed me hard in the stomach. "You look like you want to break something."

I did. I wanted to break any man who had the privilege of looking at Nova. Including me.

"Where are you going?" The words came out more harshly than intended, making Nova jump.

She quickly recovered, masking anything she might've been feeling. "There's a band at the Boot. We're going to dance."

A million different curses flew through my head. "You can't."

I knew it was the wrong thing to say the moment it left my mouth.

Nova arched a brow as one graceful hand came to her hip. "Oh, I can't?" The move only accentuated everything about what she was wearing and the beauty that was the lines of her body. It was also then that I realized she was wearing the bracelets Skylar had made her.

"It's not safe," I choked out.

Nova rolled her eyes. "I'm going with Aster, and we're using the buddy system. Wylder and Aidan are working. I'm not going to be stupid."

"I didn't say you were stupid—"

"Good, then we agree. See you around, Kol." She sent a soft smile in Waylon's direction. "Don't get into too much trouble, Way Way."

He only chuckled and waved. Then Nova hopped into Aster's truck, and they were off before I could say another word.

"You really fucked that one up good," Waylon muttered. "Stupid stick is alive and well."

I glared at him before turning on my heel and heading back into the house. "I need to go change."

"You might want to practice your groveling on the drive into town," he called after me.

Goddamn it, he was right.

Chapter Thirty

NOVA

I LACED MY FINGERS IN FRONT OF ME AS THE MUSICIANS onstage played a cover of a Steve Miller Band song. They were good. *Really* good. But I wasn't sure I could exactly enjoy it.

I hadn't been around this many people since…I didn't know when. I tried to think back, through the patchy memories of my time in captivity, to before and the woman I barely knew anymore. I'd liked music and dancing.

Brae hadn't been able to go out often because of Owen, but I would occasionally go see some live music with friends from the yoga studio or the coffee shop. I tried to remember the last concert I'd been to.

Memories came in flashes. A jam band on the water. The smell of the sea and a hint of pot in the air. So much laughter. I wanted that again. To let loose.

"You say the word. Anytime," Aster offered, moving toward my side.

We'd found a corner where I wouldn't get bumped, but there were so many people that I wasn't sure it would last. I swallowed hard. I didn't know how I'd do if anyone but Kol touched me.

"I'm good," I said with a solidness to my words. I didn't try to fake a smile, not with Aster. She saw too much. "I want to try. If I don't stretch myself now and then, I won't ever move past where I am right now."

Aster sent me a soft smile full of reassurance. "The only thing we can do. Gentle challenges on the days we feel up for them."

"I like thinking of it that way—gentle challenges."

Her fingers wrapped around her club soda and lime, showing off her pale-purple nail polish. "Me, too."

"So," I asked, moving into new, *normal* territory. "Any of these fools tearing up the floor exes?"

Aster choked on a laugh, patting her chest. "Warn a girl before you ask things like that."

I grinned, but her reaction had me curious. Aster was stunningly beautiful, with pale-blond hair and the lightest blue eyes I'd ever seen in real life. It was clear that fashion was a form of expression for her. Even now, everything she wore read *artful ease*.

Wide-leg, dark jeans were cinched with a chestnut-colored belt featuring an ornate—yet aged—golden buckle, paired with a tucked-in, sleeveless white top. Peeking out from under the flared legs of her pants were red boots, the one piece of flashy flair she wore. And around her neck were several delicate gold chains.

I had a feeling that the majority of the men in this place would be happy to take Aster to dinner and do a heck of a lot more than that. But she seemed shocked that I thought she'd dated anyone.

My gaze swept over her face, trying to pull the pieces together. "Dating not your thing?"

She searched the crowd as if in answer. "It's not that. I just…my family's a mess. I'm not sure I'd want to bring anyone into that."

I frowned. "I thought you and your grandfather were close."

Aster lived on his ranch. And I got the sense from Brae and the Archers that she was pretty intricately involved with the operations over there when she wasn't working at her psychology practice.

Aster's whole face lightened. "He is the best. Very much not a mess. Everyone else…not so much."

"I know a little something about messy families."

She arched a brow in question and invitation. This was friendship. A give and take. Opening up.

My fingers tightened around each other as if that would help. "My parents are alcoholics. Have been for as long as I can remember. I've got an older brother, Benji. He looked out for me until he was about twelve and I was ten. Then he got mixed up with a bad crowd. He's doing time for armed robbery now."

Aster looked at me for a long moment. "That's hard."

I liked that she didn't say she was sorry. This was somehow more real.

I shrugged. "I had Brae. She and I got through what we did because we had each other. Everyone has their stuff. You just have to find someone to lean on to help you through."

For the briefest of moments, I saw genuine grief on Aster's face. The deep, raw, brutal kind. But then she covered it like a master artist, layering a new painting over an old one. "We do all have our stuff. My parents think children are pawns. My sister rarely thinks about how her actions will impact anyone but her, not even her son."

"Eli, right? The one who comes out to stay with you in the summers?" I asked. Brae had told me about him. He was a couple of years older than Owen, but they'd hung out on Aster's ranch a couple of times.

A real smile stretched across Aster's face now. "He is the best kid ever. And amazing with animals. Says he wants to be a vet or a horse trainer. And he could do it. There's a tenderness to his spirit. I just hope it doesn't get stomped out by the rest of our family."

That was a hell of a load to carry, worrying about a nephew you only got to see for a couple of months out of the year. And feeling like you didn't fit in with your own family. I couldn't imagine how I'd feel if Benji had a son or daughter.

"Well, well, well, if it isn't two of the most beautiful ladies in Starlight Grove," a familiar voice greeted.

I looked up to see Maverick grinning at us with what looked like a whiskey in his hand.

"Hey, Mav," I greeted. "You look very handsome as well."

He gave a slight bow, his worn Starlight Grove Fire Department tee looking more like a vintage band shirt. "Why thank you."

Aster's expression had gone perfectly blank as she took a sip of her club soda.

"Not going to say hello, Ice Queen?" Maverick challenged, nothing but mischief in his eyes.

"Hello, Satan," she said in a deadpan voice.

My gaze ping-ponged between the two of them.

Mav gave an exaggerated shiver. "Nothing like frostbitten greetings to keep a fella warm. I can see why your dance card is so full."

A scowl tipped Aster's lips. "I don't see the usual gaggle of women you're leading on. Or did you leave them crying in the bathroom?"

A hint of annoyance flickered over Maverick's expression. "Free as a bird over here." His gaze flicked to a redhead who was making her way to the bar. "But that might be about to change."

He strode away and followed in the woman's wake, leaning in and clearly offering to buy her a drink.

Aster let out a derisive sound. "Disgusting."

I turned away from the bar and back to her. "What is the deal between you two? I asked Mav the day we ran into you on the trails, and he dodged my question."

"I bet he did," she mumbled.

"So?" I pressed.

Aster let out a breath that sounded like it carried the weight of the world. "It's a long story. But I guess what it comes down to is that we weren't as good of friends as I thought. Or maybe he wasn't who I thought he was. And that's on me as much as him."

She glanced over my shoulder toward the bar, and pain flickered over her face before she could hide it.

Brae had shared that the two had been friends growing up, after the Archer brothers moved to Starlight Grove, but I was starting to wonder if there'd been something more than friendship between them.

I opened my mouth to ask something else when a man in a cowboy hat and boots stepped up to our huddle. His gaze roamed over me, not in a lascivious way but in an appreciative one. He gave a little dip of his head that would've made me giggle if my palms hadn't already been sweating.

"Ma'am. Would you do me the honor of letting me buy you a drink?" he asked.

My mouth opened and closed as a wave of dizziness hit—the telltale sign that panic was setting in. I thought for sure I might have to run for the door when a low, gravelly voice cut in. One I knew all too well. One I played over and over in my mind in moments of panic.

"She already has one."

Kol.

Chapter Thirty-One

KOL

I KNEW THE MAN ASKING TO BUY NOVA A DRINK. STEVE. HE had a ranch a few miles outside of town. It had been passed down through his family for generations. Single. Never married. Solid family. No skeletons in the closet.

He was exactly the kind of man Nova deserved. He'd come into whatever they'd have with no baggage.

Yet, here I was, squashing that opportunity like a bug.

I slid the purplish bubbly drink into Nova's hand. "Marionberry lime seltzer, right?"

Those gray eyes flared in surprise. "How'd you know?"

"You said it was your favorite when you did the local beer taste test." It wasn't a beer, but some of the local breweries had gotten into hard seltzers as well, and this had been Nova's favorite.

"Thank you." Her words weren't whispered, but they weren't exactly loud either. She took a long drink.

"Sorry about that, Kol. Didn't mean to overstep," Steve said, then dipped his hat to Nova. "Have a good night, ma'am."

Nova took another drink. "I don't think I've ever been called ma'am in my life."

Aster chuckled, but her gaze moved between the two of us. Curious. "Better get used to it around here."

Nova pulled the straw from between her lips. "Thank you. On both fronts. I don't know if I'm ready for…that."

Everything in me seized. Because one day she would be ready. Especially if I didn't pull my head out of my ass. "No problem."

Aster toyed with the straw in her own drink, a smile spreading over her face. "You know, Kol, I don't think I've ever *once* seen you at the Boot on a music night."

I scowled at her. "I like music."

Nova's lips twitched. "Boss, you do *not* like music."

My scowl swiveled to her. "I do, too."

She looked like she was fighting a laugh now, her mouth thinning as her eyes danced. "You like quiet. Open spaces. No one around except for your daughter. Maybe occasionally your brothers and Waylon."

She knew me too well.

"I like when you're around." The words were out before I could stop them. Waylon had said the truth was rarely simple, but this one was. Everything was better when Nova was around.

Her jaw went the slightest bit slack, loosening the hold she had on her smile.

Aster sucked in an audible breath. "I need a refill on this club soda. Be back." With that, she hurried away.

Nova stared up at me, those gray eyes searching. "That's not fair."

"Probably not," I admitted.

I wanted to touch her so damn badly. I wanted to pull her into my arms and know what it was like to dance with her. Because while I might not like music and unnecessary noise, I more than liked Nova. My brain and my mouth danced around a word I only used with a handful of people.

"What are you doing here?" Nova asked, pulling a little of her shield up.

"Waylon said I got hit with the stupid stick."

Those beautiful lips twitched again. "I need to tell that man just how smart he is."

I grimaced. "He doesn't need anything else going to his head."

"Gonna make him a Bigfoot cake."

"Please, don't encourage that."

"Maybe I can figure out how to knit and make him a Bigfoot blanket. There's that craft store, the Yarn Barn. I bet they can teach me."

"Phoenix," I warned.

Pain flashed across her features, and I couldn't figure out why. But then I realized. I'd made an effort not to call her that. Not since the crime scene when Pete had all but threatened my job.

The urge to pull her to me was almost too much. I did a quick sweep of the bar and cursed. Too many eyes. I spotted Roger in the corner, chatting up a pretty brunette. A few other deputies. A woman I recognized as a local Forest Service agent. And then there was Pete—at the end of the bar, staring straight at me.

Fucking hell.

"I'm sorry," I whispered, dropping my voice low.

Nova's gray eyes flashed silver. "I don't want your apologies. You can't have it both ways, Kol."

My jaw worked back and forth because I knew she was right. But she was also wrong. "I'm not trying to push you away."

She arched a brow at that.

"Okay, I was. Because the truth is, you scare the hell out of me, Phoenix. I haven't let myself reach for something I want in a long time—maybe not since my brothers and I found out who our dad really was."

A fissure appeared in Nova's mask, the slightest slip as her empathy broke through.

"I think a part of me thought—still thinks—I don't deserve it."

"Kol," she whispered.

I took one step and then another, catching the slightest hint of her scent. "But I can't stop myself from wanting you. Can't stop myself from dreaming about you. You haunt me. Awake. Asleep. No matter what I do."

Nova frowned. "That doesn't exactly sound like a compliment."

"Does it look like I'm trying to get exorcised?"

One corner of her mouth kicked up.

"I'd take your ghost over anyone else. Even just the memory of how it felt to hold you." My knuckles skimmed the back of her hand. Just the barest graze. "How you smell—like sunbaked cherries and vanilla. Sometimes, I think you spray it into the air vents."

"Kol."

My ribs constricted around my lungs, but I continued my confession. I couldn't stop now. Moreover, I didn't want to. I'd gotten a taste of living without her, and I hated it with every fiber of my being. "You make everything you touch better."

Some unnamed emotion streaked across her face. "It doesn't feel like that. Not lately."

I hooked my pointer finger around hers. "You make me better. My life. My world."

Nova's hand trembled in mine. "What do you want?"

"Come home with me." It was both a question and a plea. A reckless leap and a spark in a desert-dry forest. But I didn't give a damn. All I could do was wait to see if she'd meet me in the potential ruin.

Chapter Thirty-Two

NOVA

I TRIED TO FOCUS ON THE BAND. WHAT SONG WERE THEY playing? I couldn't make it out over the blood roaring in my ears.

"Come home with me."

It was what I wanted. But now that it was being offered, I was terrified.

Something shifted in Kol's expression, and a new fear lit inside me, one where he would take back his words, his offer. He didn't. He met me in the mess, like always.

"Home can mean whatever you want, Phoenix. It can mean sitting on the back deck and talking till sunrise. It can mean me holding you like before and nothing else. It can mean whatever you want it to mean."

This man. He wrecked me. In the best possible way.

"Okay," I rasped.

His finger contracted around mine and then released. "Gonna be a little tricky getting out of here."

My brows pulled together in confusion. "Why?"

"Well, lots of folks who might say something that could get me fired are in this bar right now."

My stomach twisted. "Where's your truck?"

He frowned. "On the street a block south."

"I'm not built with an internal compass like you."

His lips kicked up in the barest smile. "Toward the Yarn Barn."

"Thank you." I took one more sip of my drink and set it on a vacated table. "Meet me there in five."

"You're not walking alone—"

"No, I'm not. Aster is going to walk with me."

Kol still looked a little unsure but finally nodded.

"Go talk to someone else."

The scowl that erupted on Kol's face had me biting back a laugh.

"I don't like talking to people," he grumbled.

"Buck up, Boss. You gotta take one for the team." And with that, I turned to find Aster.

She was at the bar, obviously trying to avoid the advances of a slightly inebriated man who was talking about the intricacies of pig farming.

"Aster, I need you. Girl emergency." I looked at the drunk man. "Sorry. Cramps. You know, that time of the month."

He looked absolutely horrified, like he hadn't just been talking about pig shit. "You…go." But he scampered before we had a chance to move a muscle.

Aster turned to me in awe. "How did you do that?"

"Periods are the secret weapon against douchebags."

"How can I ever repay you?" She gave a bow with her arms out like she was worshipping me.

"Can you walk me somewhere really quick and keep it between us?"

Aster looked confused, then something clicked. A mischievous smile spread over her face. "Where to, my hero?"

"Just down the block."

She nodded, and we made our way out of the bar. It was a bit of a challenge with all the people, but I managed not to get bumped or jostled. The moment we stepped outside, I sucked in fresh, clean air. "You know, I'm not sure crowded bars are my thing anymore."

Aster sent me a little nod. "I might be heading into my grandma era because what sounds really nice right about now is a hot bath and a good book."

"Preach."

She eyed me. "Why do I have a feeling that's not what you're going home to?"

I rolled my lips over my teeth.

"You don't have to tell me. Just be careful. You've been through a lot, and that dance might take a little time to ease back into."

"You're a good friend," I whispered.

"I'm here for whatever you need," Aster assured me.

We passed Aster's truck. Kol's was only a few down, and as we walked up, he came running from the other direction.

"What are you doing? You were supposed to talk to people for five minutes," I demanded.

He shrugged. "Talked to Wylder in front of my douchebag coworker. Told him I was heading home to help Waylon with some alpacas that got out. Left through the back door—"

"And ran around the block," Aster cut in.

Kol sent her a glare, but it softened slightly. "Thanks for walking her."

She saluted. "Anytime."

"You want us to drop you back at the front door?" he asked.

She shook her head. "I'm going home, and my truck's right there." She pointed. "I'll see you guys later."

Kol watched as Aster made her way to her vehicle and climbed in, but he didn't move until she was backing up and on her way. A gentleman. His gaze flicked to me. "Ready?"

I squeezed my fingers together. "Ready."

He helped me into the truck, then got inside himself. I tried not to think about the fact that the last time we'd been in this vehicle had been a breaking of sorts. Letting out a long breath, I reframed it. Not a breaking, a break*through*. Because it had led us to the honesty of tonight.

The darkness wove in around us as we drove. Starlight Grove

wasn't one for many streetlights outside of downtown. You could see it as ominous, where the monsters hid, or you could see it as breathtaking, where the stars shone.

In reality, it was both. But without the dark, you couldn't see those stars. And I didn't want to live without them. Which meant one thing. I had to face my monsters—the real ones and the ones I'd created.

Kol hit the button on a remote, and the gate to Twisted Oak Ranch swung open. A wave of nerves hit me as we drove over the cattle guard. And then I felt something else…anticipation, the good kind.

Neither of us said a word as Kol guided his truck toward the house we now both called home. I tugged my lip between my teeth, a cascade of doubts tumbling over me. What if I messed this up and Kol didn't want me to live here anymore? What if I freaked out in the middle of sex? What if I couldn't feel any of it anymore?

Kol slowed to a stop in his garage and turned off the engine. I was out before he could say anything, trying to buy myself more time to escape all the doubts. I rounded the front of the truck and slid into the house.

The lights were out, and it was quiet, which had me frowning. I turned at the sound of Kol's footsteps. "Where's Sky?"

"Sleepover with Owen." He stopped a few steps from me, giving me plenty of space.

He looked so damn good in a flannel shirt I wanted to skim my cheek across it to feel the softness, dark jeans that hugged his thick thighs, and boots that had seen their share of work.

"Phoenix."

My gaze lifted. The nickname carried a sting because I'd missed it so damn much. Only two weeks without it, yet hearing it again made me feel like I could breathe.

Kol ran his dark gaze over my face, reading every curve and line. "You can go up to your apartment right now or at any time, right?"

I nodded like one of those bobblehead dolls.

"You're in control." A muscle fluttered along his jaw as he spoke the words.

I couldn't tell what that tension was about. My discomfort? His dislike of someone else holding the reins?

"Talk to me." Kol's eyes bore into me, pleading.

"What if I mess it up?" I croaked.

Kol took a step closer. "Yes?"

It took me a second to realize what he was asking. To approach. If it was okay for him to be in my space. "Yes."

He took another two steps, and his hand lifted, just shy of my face. "Yes?"

I swallowed hard. "Yes."

Kol's knuckles skimmed my cheek. "Impossible for you to mess anything up. Because whatever we share, it's going to be you and me."

My eyes stung, and my throat tightened, but I kept breathing. "Okay."

"Tell me what you want next."

I could feel the restraint pulsing through Kol. The strength it took for him not to dominate the situation. And something about that eased my nerves slightly.

"I want to see your bedroom," I whispered.

One corner of his mouth kicked up. "Why do I suddenly feel like I'm a freshman in high school?"

A soft laugh bubbled out of me, easing the tension a little more. "Height of hormones and breaking all the rules."

Those knuckles slid over my jaw and down my neck. "I'm down for some dry humping."

My lips twitched. "Lead the way, Boss."

Kol's eyes flashed, that mix of dark and light. He took my hand and led the way up the stairs. I'd been up here to play with Skylar but never to Kol's bedroom. He turned right and headed to the opposite end of the hallway from Sky's room.

I tried to focus on the details. The rugs with their intricate patterns that lined the deep reddish-brown floors. The detailed woodwork. The clock I knew must have been a gift from Waylon.

At the end of the hall was an open door. As we stepped inside, I could see that everything was shades of gray. The bedding, the bed frame, the dresser. Hanging over it was a stunning, black-and-white photo of Mount Lupine. It looked staggering. Intimidating.

But then I caught a flash of color. A drawing that had been framed and set on the dresser. Flowers in every color under the sun. Ones I knew had to be drawn by Skylar.

Because she softened him. Maybe even saved him. When he was pushing everyone away, she wouldn't let him.

"I love this." My fingers ghosted over the frame.

"Saving it for when the artist hits it big. Going to sell it for millions."

My gaze flicked up to Kol. "You wouldn't sell for a billion."

His mouth curved. "Truth."

My heart fluttered as if it had grown wings and they beat against my rib cage. "It's the only color."

Kol shrugged. "Easier this way."

Because everything fit. Nothing broke the confines he put it into. Nothing was hard to categorize.

"What's next?" Kol asked gently.

My tongue darted out to wet my suddenly dry lips, and Kol tracked the movement. Because that was what he was good at. Finding people with the barest of hints. It made me wonder what else he could track over my body.

"I want to feel again. To *really* feel. I spend every day shoving it all down, locking it away. And when it bubbles over, I run, jump, or I—"

"Hurl yourself off a cliff?"

"Or that," I muttered. "I want to choose feeling for once. I just…I don't know if I can handle it."

Kol took a step toward me. "Yes?"

I nodded.

"Words or nothing, Phoenix."

"Yes." The single syllable was an exhale.

Kol crossed the distance between us. "This might be hard, but I need you to tell me what the triggers might be. If there are things that won't feel good. If we talk about them now, the rest might go easier. But you also need to know that anytime you say stop, this stops. Okay?"

I started to nod but then remembered the rule. "Okay."

"That's my girl," Kol whispered, running his knuckles over my cheek. "Think you can tell me?"

"My neck." The words erupted from me almost harshly, as if I didn't get them out right now, I'd explode.

"Your neck," he echoed.

"Feeling like hands could be around my neck. Or someone being on top of me."

Kol's throat worked as he struggled to swallow, and the battle for restraint vibrated through him. "Because he strangled you."

"I think so," I whispered. "I have flashes."

Kol jerked his head in a nod. "But he didn't..." I was sure he'd know this from my file. The police reports. But I was also sure that some victims lied because they felt shame that wasn't theirs to carry.

"No. He didn't hurt me like that."

Air left Kol in a whoosh. But he still struggled to even his breathing. "I have an idea. But if it doesn't sound good to you, just tell me."

My brows pulled together as Kol moved away from me and toward a closed door. I felt the loss of him instantly. That heat that always emanated from him. The knowledge that around Kol, I'd never be cold.

He opened the door to a walk-in closet and scanned a row of shelves above where the clothes hung. His gaze stopped on a box. It looked like it was made of black fabric. Stretching up, he tugged it down and then crossed to a wooden bench at the foot of his bed.

Setting the box down, Kol pulled off the lid. Curiosity had me moving closer. As I did, Kol lifted something.

Black rope.

My breath hitched, anxiety sweeping through me as I remembered a flash. A shackle digging into my ankle, tearing at the skin. I breathed through it. Because this wasn't a metal shackle. This was rope. Rope that was black and looked incredibly smooth.

Kol's gaze locked with mine. "I want you to tie me up."

Chapter Thirty-Three

NOVA

My mouth went dry as my breath caught in my throat. "You want me to tie *you* up?"

Kol nodded. "You need to be in control. To know that I *can't* do anything you don't want me to do."

Everything around me swirled just a little too fast. As if I were suddenly able to feel the earth's gravitational rotation. But as it all moved, some pieces started to come together.

"Do you do that a lot? Get tied up?" That curiosity was back, but this time with some heat. The kind that settled low in my belly and spread out slowly. The image of Kol tied up would now be haunting my dreams in the best possible way.

He barked out a laugh. "No. Never."

The corners of my mouth pulled down, but realization dawned. "You like to tie up your partner."

Kol let out a long breath. "I'm not normal, Nova. What happened with my father, it ripped any sense of trust away. And sex? It requires trust. I could give it in some ways, but I still needed…"

"Control," I filled in for him.

He scrubbed a hand over his stubbled cheek. "Maybe I can give you the thing that worked for me."

A buzz lit beneath my skin, and I pressed my thighs together, trying to alleviate the pressure building there.

Kol didn't miss the movement. "Phoenix," he choked out.

I moved closer, my fingers running over the loop of rope. I'd been right. It felt like it was silk woven together. "It's so soft."

"The goal isn't pain. That's not something I'm into." His voice had dropped the barest amount, as if another layer of sandpaper coated it now. "It's about control. Choice. Trust."

My gaze lifted to Kol's face. He watched me intently. His focus split between my fingers and my eyes. My heart tripped as another discovery hit me. "This will cost you. Giving me control instead of the other way around."

Two tiny divots hollowed out Kol's jaw. "You need it more right now."

"Kol."

"And I want to give it to you."

Everything hurt. What Kol was gifting me…

"Okay," I whispered.

His knuckles skimmed across my cheek again. "Think you'll be able to talk me through how you're feeling as we go? If anything's approaching too much or you want to stop?"

I didn't look away as I answered him. "You've always been the one I could tell anything to."

The hard lines of Kol's face softened. "Trusting that. Trusting you."

And God, I knew what that meant for Kol. Something he never gave anyone but his family. And he was giving it to me.

Kol dropped the rope onto the bed, and his fingers moved to the top button on his flannel.

"Can I?" The words were out before I could stop them, bolder than maybe I felt in the moment, but I went with it anyway.

Kol didn't say a word, but his hands dropped to his sides. I moved in instantly, my fingers trembling slightly as I unfastened the top button. A dusting of dark hair peeked out from beneath the fabric. It teased my fingers as I moved to the next button.

Each unfastening revealed a little more. Golden skin and muscle that wasn't overly manufactured but real. Those dips and ridges came from working a ranch, spending time in the field for work, and building me an apartment.

The shirt fell completely open, and I couldn't help but run my fingers over Kol's chest, down to the ridges of his abdominals. His ink. He let out a humming growl, his hands fisting at his sides.

And I knew then just how much it was costing him not to touch me.

But I could give him that. Maybe not in the throes of sex, but I could give him this.

I turned, my back to his front, and swept my hair to the side. "Can you get my zipper?"

Air left Kol on a sharp exhale, one so strong I could feel his breath against the nape of my neck. It sent sparks of awareness skating over my skin.

Kol's knuckles slid along my spine before his hand rose again. The feel of bone against bone had vibrations cascading over me in the most delicious way. My breath caught as Kol's fingers gripped my zipper.

"Yes?" he asked, stilling.

"Yes."

Kol pulled the zipper down, the action so painfully slow I could feel the unfastening of every metal tooth and tine, like tiny bombs detonating against my skin. My mouth went dry, and my breath caught.

His hand stilled where the zipper ended, just at the top of my tailbone. The tipping point. I dipped my shoulders, and the dress fell.

The cool air hit my suddenly bare body, nothing but the delicate lace of a thong standing between Kol and me.

He let out an audible hiss.

Kicking off my boots, I turned to face the man who'd been my safe space since the moment I met him.

Kol devoured me with his eyes. Every flicker and spark spoke of hunger and want. And it made me feel powerful for the first time in a long time.

"Most beautiful sight I've ever seen. You're like the moon starting to rise in twilight. You fucking glow, Phoenix. Maybe because you're made of embers."

And I felt it. That beauty. Even as my finger traced one of the scars along my ribs.

Kol didn't miss the movement. "Warrior marks. You made it through the battle to the other side."

And I felt that, too. Powerful. Strong. I took a step closer. "Touch me, Kol."

Sparks of light swirled in those dark eyes. "You're sure?"

"I'll tell you if it's too much." But right now, it felt like I might combust if I didn't know what it was like to have his hands on me.

Kol lifted his hands slowly, giving me every chance to tell him that I'd changed my mind. But I hadn't. He palmed my breasts, and I arched into him, relishing the pressure, the feel of his rough skin against my smoothness.

Calloused thumbs circled my nipples, calling them forward. They tightened, right along with my core. Everything in me ached for Kol.

I let out a soft moan.

Kol's gaze snapped to my face. "More?"

"More," I breathed.

His head dipped as he crouched slightly. One hand fell away from my breast, and his lips closed around its peak. Then he groaned. He sucked gently, making my body bow. I pressed harder against him as his knuckles skimmed the apex of my thighs.

I let out a strangled sound, and Kol froze.

"More." The single word was both a plea and a command.

And Kol obeyed.

He stroked me through the lace of my thong, and I moved against him, needing more. His fingers stilled as they pulled the lace to the side, his mouth losing its hold on my nipple. "Yes?"

"Please." I wasn't above begging.

Those thick fingers slid under the fabric, through my slick, wet heat.

I gripped Kol's shoulders, my fingers digging in.

"Give me one right here," he rasped against my breast. "Let me know what you sound like when you shatter."

My breaths came in short pants, not because of panic but because I was already so damn close. Two of Kol's fingers teased my entrance, circling, stretching. As they slid in, his thumb found my clit.

I could barely stay upright. My head dropped back, and I pressed my lips together to stifle my noises.

"I want to hear you, baby. Don't steal those sounds from me."

Moving slightly, I straightened, breathing through the war of sensations coursing through me. And then I let go. I let my body move with Kol's. I soaked up every feeling. And I let him hear it all.

A tremble lit in my legs, spreading through me as Kol's fingers moved in and out of me. With every thrust, they circled and stretched. My body quaked as his thumb stroked my clit.

A fresh wave of heat and tension sparked beneath my skin. That thumb circled, edging closer before sweeping up and tipping me past the point of ignition. Flames licked over my skin as a sound left my mouth that wasn't entirely human. And then his name—part breath, part plea, and everything I wanted.

Kol stroked me through wave after wave, and as I came back to myself, I found him watching me through hooded eyes. "That's my girl." He pulled his fingers from my body and sucked them clean, never once taking his eyes from me. "That's my fucking girl."

A different sort of heat coursed through me. "More."

It was both a request and a command. But Kol didn't wait for another. His fingers tangled in the band of my lacy thong, stilling for a moment until I gave him the word he was waiting for.

"Yes," I breathed.

He tugged the lace down, staring at the apex of my thighs. "Fucking heaven."

I swallowed hard as he straightened, kicking off one boot and then the other as he dropped his flannel to the floor. I studied him, the way those two tattoos rippled across his rib cage as he moved.

Kol's fingers came to the button on his jeans, his eyes colliding with mine. "Yes?"

My mouth curved. "Hell yes."

His beautiful lips twitched, and then he was shoving his jeans down in one rough motion, those black boxer briefs with them.

I couldn't help but stare, almost slack-jawed, at the man in front of me. His broad shoulders and thick thighs spoke of power. The gold sparking in his hazel eyes said things like hunger and need. And I wanted to experience it all. Kol wrapped his fingers around his cock, stroking once, twice, a drop of precum sliding from his tip. Then he cursed.

"What?" I asked, panicked.

"Condoms. I don't have any. It's, uh, been quite a while for me," he mumbled.

Relief swept through me. "I got a complete workup in the hospital, and I ended up getting on the pill to regulate my cycle last month."

Kol nodded slowly. "Had a physical last year, all good. But we don't have to—"

"I want to. If you do."

Air hissed between Kol's teeth. "I want. But this is a lot. It's more than—"

"I know. I want to…" I swallowed. "I want to try." I wanted to reclaim this piece of normalcy, and I wanted it with Kol. He was the one who'd helped me find trust when I thought I'd lost it, helped me hold tight to life when that grip felt tenuous at best. I wanted this with him, too.

He moved then, grabbing the rope from the bed. I saw then that there were two lengths, and I watched in fascination as he expertly executed a sort of cuff on each wrist.

"These are half hitches. They won't tighten if I pull on them, but they will keep me in place," Kol explained as he climbed onto the bed.

Everything about him was hard lines and smooth planes. Defined muscles I wanted to memorize with my fingertips.

Kol quickly tied the ropes to one of the wooden slats in the headboard. "You'll have access to the end that unties these, but once I lie down, I won't. You'll have all the power. All the control."

His voice tightened as he spoke. And I could feel his own sort of panic setting in.

I moved closer, getting onto the bed with him. My hand skated over his face, and I relished the prickle of his scruff against my palm. "You don't have to—"

Kol took my mouth, his tongue stroking in. Not forceful, but not gentle, either. Meeting me where we were. "I want to," he rasped against my mouth.

And then he dropped to the mattress.

Suddenly, I was the taller one, the one kneeling over him. Looking down at Kol and all his beauty and power. And it had wetness gathering between my legs.

Kol's mouth curved. "You like me being at your mercy."

I grinned as I climbed between his legs. "I think I do."

I wrapped my fingers around Kol's length, stroking. His back arched, and he let out a moan. But that wasn't enough for me.

I leaned forward, closed my lips over his tip, and slid down, taking Kol into my mouth. My cheeks hollowed out as my ass lifted into the air.

"Fuck," Kol growled.

I worked him with my mouth and hand, every second, every sound making me feel more powerful.

"Gotta stop," Kol begged. "I won't last."

My tongue flicked over his tip one last time as I straightened, power and heat surging through me all at once.

He shook his head as he took me in. "I think you're part demon. My little demon."

A smile stretched across my face as I straddled Kol. "I'm taking that as a compliment."

"You should."

I planted my hands on his chest as I hovered over him, feeling his muscles tense beneath me. This time, it was my turn to ask. "Yes?"

"Fuck yes," Kol rumbled.

I guided his tip to my entrance, already feeling the stretch.

"Breathe with me," Kol instructed. "It's just you and me."

My eyes found his, and they didn't leave as I slowly sank down onto him. My mouth fluttered open as I took in the stretch, pausing halfway and trying to adjust.

"We can stop anytime," Kol gritted out.

I knew how much that cost him, too. But Kol always gave me everything without me having to say a word.

That was him, but so was this stretch, this pressure. This power. And I wanted all the pieces of Kol.

I slid down farther, taking all of him. He let out a groan that reverberated through me in the best possible way. The vibrations made me clench around Kol, and that had him letting out a curse.

"My little demon," he swore.

I rocked against him, investigating the movement, seeing how it felt, what it did to me. And for the first time in my life, I felt free to do exactly that: find what felt good to *me*.

Rising up, I lowered again, not losing Kol's eyes. I could've watched the way the light and dark danced across those irises forever. And as I moved again, I realized they also told me what he liked.

My back arched as I took him deeper, faster.

"So goddamned beautiful," Kol rasped. "Taking me. Owning me. All that control."

His words sent a ripple of sparks sliding through me, my core tightening around him in a pulsing wave.

Kol gritted his teeth. "Trying to last, but you're killing me."

I could feel that restraint wavering in him, and I knew we didn't have long. But I wanted to see it snap. I found my clit and circled the bundle of nerves.

"Fucking gorgeous," Kol swore as his hips arched into me, his wrists pulling at the bindings for leverage.

My walls fluttered around him, just shy of that tipping point, as I struggled for breath. Each inhale and exhale was a short pant of need, want—desperation.

"Let me see you fly, Phoenix," Kol whispered.

I swiped my finger across my clit as I took Kol impossibly deeper, and that combination was all it took. I came in a wave of darkness and light, just like Kol's eyes. Sparks danced across my vision as he thrust up, hitting a spot that had me closing around him in a vise grip.

Kol gripped the ropes, his teeth clenched as he came. Thrusting through wave after wave as our bodies battled. Shadows gathered at the edges of my vision as I rode out everything he gave me.

My lungs burned, my thighs ached, and as the last pulsing wave swept through me, I collapsed on top of Kol.

My chest heaved, and Kol's heart beat against my cheek. But some part of my brain remembered the ropes. I reached up and pulled the end that would release them.

Kol's arms came around me instantly, holding me to him. "Never knew it could be like that," he whispered.

"Me neither," I croaked.

And it felt miraculous and terrifying all at the same time.

Chapter Thirty-Four

KOL

I WOKE UP WRAPPED AROUND NOVA, DROWNING IN CHERRY and vanilla—the best way to start the day. But I wasn't just spooning her. I'd somehow curled my entire body around hers. She was tucked almost into a ball, and I was her armor.

A part of me wished it could always be this way: me standing between Nova and the world. Only I knew that wasn't what she wanted.

Still, I'd soak it in for now. I'd let myself revel in every single second.

My mouth curved against her hair as I realized my hand had slipped beneath the T-shirt of mine she was wearing and was cupping her breast. Apparently, I was even a horny bastard in my sleep.

Nova let out a soft moan, arching into me.

"You make sounds like that, and my dick is going to take them as an invitation."

"Is that a bad thing?" she mumbled.

"Baby, you've gotta be sore."

"Maybe," she admitted, a slight pout to her tone.

A chuckle slid out of me, easier than maybe ever before. She made it easier: the smiles, the laughs. "How about we make breakfast instead?"

"I like breakfast," Nova mumbled, still half-asleep.

She flipped onto her back, and I lifted onto one arm, needing to see her better. That long, raven hair spilled out in waves around her as she studied my face.

"How does the rest of you feel?" I asked quietly.

Nova's mouth curved, those plush lips still a little swollen from last night. "I feel good. You?"

"Better than I have in years," I admitted, spilling secrets I should've held tight.

Light sparked in those gray eyes as she lifted her hand, tracing the faint indentations on my wrists still left behind from last night. "Thank you. For giving me that."

My body tightened, my dick springing to life. Never in a million years did I think I'd be able to hand over the reins—the control—to someone else. But for Nova, I could. Because she needed it.

I brushed my knuckles over her cheekbone. "I think it was good for me, too—an exercise in letting go."

"My favorite kind of exercise," Nova said, grinning.

"My little demon."

She tossed the covers off, sending me a wink as she rose. "Come on. I need a shower."

Nova had music on, and for the first time in a long time, it didn't bother me. It was an oldies station that played a mix of songs I didn't care about one way or the other. But what I *did* care about was the way Nova's hips swept back and forth as she moved across the kitchen.

She wore a pale-purple workout set: leggings and some sort of top that stopped just above her belly button, exposing a strip of creamy skin I had a burning desire to lick. She'd thrown on my flannel shirt from last night for warmth, and her wearing something of mine had sent a surprising reaction coursing through me.

Chest-beating pride. Completely ridiculous. It wasn't like Nova wearing my shirt was some kind of trophy. But it felt like a claiming. Me of her. And her right back.

I liked it. Way too much.

A knock sounded on the front door, and I frowned. I wasn't expecting anyone, and I didn't need to leave to pick up Skylar for another hour.

Pushing off the counter where I'd been watching Nova assemble breakfast, I headed for the door. I opened it, and Skylar instantly leapt into my arms.

"We had the best slumber party ever!" she yelled. "We had a pizza-making competition and then ice cream sundaes, and we made a fort in the living room to watch a movie. We got to stay up an hour past bedtime."

I shifted her onto my hip, my gaze flicking to Waylon, who had obviously picked her up. "Sounds pretty awesome, Little Princess."

Waylon's eyebrows waggled. "Thought you might like to sleep in this morning."

"Hi, guys," Nova greeted, walking up behind me, a huge smile on her face. There were no nerves there, only easy acceptance of my family's presence. And I loved that, too. "You want breakfast? I made breakfast potato pie."

"I love pie," Sky offered helpfully.

"I could eat," Waylon agreed.

And it was as easy as that. They set the kitchen table while I pulled out drinks, and Nova plated her breakfast creation.

"You got any hot sauce around here?" Waylon asked.

I rolled my eyes. "You give each of us a set of hot sauces for Christmas every year so you're never without."

He grinned as he rested a hand on his rounded belly. "Always be prepared."

One corner of Nova's mouth kicked up as she lowered herself into an empty chair. "Were you a Boy Scout?"

Waylon frowned. "It was the Bigfooters' motto first."

"Bigfooters?" Nova asked, trying to fight off a laugh.

I slid the hot sauces in front of Waylon. "Do not get him started."

"The Bigfooters have been around for centuries," Skylar mumbled around a bite of the egg-and-potato dish. "I'm a junior Bigfooter."

"One of the best I've ever seen," Waylon praised.

Nova lifted her glass of orange juice. "And what is a Bigfooter?"

"Those who revere and respect Bigfoot," Waylon said proudly.

Nova mulled that over for a moment. "I want to go with you when you go Bigfoot hunting next time."

"Yes!" Sky cheered. "But we need to work on your outfit. You need some camo. And Grampa Way Way says they don't mind a little glitter, so you can still sparkle."

Nova's mouth curved as she beamed at my daughter. "You always have all the best info. How'd you get so smart?"

Skylar practically glowed under Nova's praise. "I just like to learn a lot of things."

"Me, too," Nova agreed.

My hand slid over her thigh, and Nova's gaze swung to me. There was warmth there. Acceptance. She fit. At this table. Next to me. Next to Sky.

But I couldn't help the frisson of fear that swept through me at that. Because life could change in a split second. Someone could get stolen away. Someone could betray you.

Skylar began chatting about a project from school that had Nova rapt, but I could feel Waylon's eyes on me. Worried eyes.

I tried to stay in the present moment as we finished breakfast and started cleaning up. A phone rang, and Nova swiped up her cell from the counter. "Hey."

A pause, then Nova glanced at the clock on the wall. "Yup. I'm ready."

A muffled response on the other end. "See you in a sec."

"Brae?" I asked. It seemed like the two were doing better, now that they weren't living under the same roof.

Nova shook her head. "Mav. We're going mountain biking."

A foreign feeling slid through me. It took a second for me to recognize it as jealousy. Of my own damn brother. But hot on its heels was worry, then crippling fear.

"You sure that's a good idea?" I asked.

It was the wrong thing to say.

Nova bristled. "Why wouldn't it be?"

I sent Skylar a quick glance, but she was already slipping out the back door to see Tink and Pepper, who'd appeared on the back deck, missing their girl.

"Are you forgetting the note that got left on your car? The necklace?" I left out the blood part, but my words packed a punch just the same.

Nova's face paled, but she recovered quickly. "I'll never forget. But that doesn't mean I'll let myself live like I'm still in captivity. I'm out, Kol. I'm free. I can't stop living because there are bad people in the world."

"I'm not saying you shouldn't live. I'm just saying that maybe you shouldn't be taking off with Mav to take on whatever hairbrained scheme he's come up with. Are you really so desperate for an adrenaline high?"

Nova's gray eyes flashed—not with the kind of heat from last night but from anger. "You know it's about more than that."

And with that, she took off out the front door, the wood slamming in her wake.

Waylon let out a low whistle. "Well, you fucked that one up good and proper."

I glared back at my great-uncle, but I really wanted to kick myself. Because he was exactly right.

Chapter Thirty-Five

NOVA

"YOU GONNA TELL ME WHY YOU'RE GLARING THROUGH THE windshield like you suddenly got laser beam eyes and want to fry everyone in your path?" Maverick asked cheerily.

I let out a very unladylike grunt. "You gonna tell me what happened between you and Aster?"

Silence suddenly reigned in his SUV.

I sighed. "Sorry. Low blow."

"Naw," Mav said easily. "The Ice Queen just can't handle how much she wants my body. Makes her cranky around me."

Despite the levity, I could hear the tension wrapped around Mav's words.

My gaze flicked over to him as he navigated the gravel road, his fingers gripping the wheel like a lifeline. Whatever had happened between the two of them had marked him. No... *both* of them.

"Your brother let his overprotective gene override his brain,"

I said, giving Maverick the answer he'd been looking for from the beginning.

"Which one?"

"Which one do you think?"

Mav sighed. "Kol."

I kicked my sneakered feet up onto the dash. "I love that you got it in one guess."

"Well, that particular brother has the protective thing going in spades. If it helps, it only shows up for the people he cares about. Took Brae a few weeks to sneak under his defenses, but you had her beat."

A little voice of doubt told me it was simply because Kol had been the one to find me. A more taunting voice told me that was the *only* reason he cared.

"I need to be able to really live," I said softly. "Otherwise, what's the point?"

Maverick was quiet for a long moment. When he finally spoke, his voice was different than I'd ever heard it before. More serious. "Sometimes, you have to press the boundaries to know for sure you're still breathing."

My gaze flicked to him again. He stared straight ahead at the road and the forest beyond before turning into a parking lot. And then I remembered what Kol had shared with me. That Mav had been the one their father had almost killed.

It had to be a whole other sort of head trip, your father being the architect of your nightmares. At least my monster was a stranger.

Mav pulled into a parking spot. There were four other vehicles in the lot, but the time it had taken for us to get here told me this spot was more off the beaten path than the first place I'd tried.

"All right," Mav began as he pulled our bikes off his rack. "The trickiest part of this trail is the beginning. I'll lead so you can watch how I handle the drops and turns. But I want to map out the path with you. It's a loop, but there are plenty of turnoffs that you don't want to take."

I nodded, following him over to a massive map printed on a

wooden sign. He was right about all the different options for trails. It looked like a huge maze of paths.

"Basically, always stay on the center trail, and you'll be good," Mav explained, his finger tracing over the Meadow Peak Trail. It had a blue square for its difficulty delineation, meaning it was one step up from easy. "I'll be within sight of you at all times, except for a few hairpin turns and drops. But just for a minute."

"Got it."

"Okay, not to court comparison to my overprotective oaf of a brother, but can we do an in-case-of-emergency check?"

I made a face at Mav that only made him laugh.

"I'm taking that as a yes. Water?"

I pointed to the bottle affixed to my bike.

"First-aid kit?"

"Thanks to your Boy Scout self." Mav had given me a little one that attached to my handlebar.

"And you've got your phone?"

I nodded, patting the pocket on my leggings.

"Good," Mav went on. "I would say you're ready."

I grinned back at him. "Let's do this."

He just shook his head. "I think you might give me a run for my money as the adrenaline junkie of the group."

If he saw my cliff-jumping escapades, he'd know how true that was.

We donned our protective gear and moved to the start of the trail. It was one that split into three and would continue to divide as we went. The forest consumed it on every side, and the sun through the trees cast the area in an array of colors that reminded me how lucky I was to still be here, to be experiencing all life had to offer.

Maverick came to a stop at the top of the hill and looked over his shoulder, doing a silent check-in. I gave him a nod, and he tipped his bike over the edge.

My body was already humming, desperate for the release that would shove the anxiety and fear down. Because it had been ramping up again since my heated words with Kol this morning. As if he hadn't worn me out last night, leaving me completely sated and spent.

Shoving down the concern that none of my escapes were helping like they used to, I straddled my bike and focused on Mav. The last thing I needed was to be distracted and end up with a broken clavicle or a dislocated shoulder.

Maverick was clearly an expert. His bike hugged each curve and bend in the trail. His body preemptively adjusted to what lay ahead.

I tried to take mental notes of how he handled each obstacle—leaning in and out of turns, staying light in his seat, accelerating and braking.

When Mav reached the bottom of the trail, he took the center path and disappeared into the trees. My turn. The buzz beneath my skin intensified, my body, mind, and spirit desperate for the high I knew this would bring.

Shoving off, I stood, balancing on the pedals as the bike tipped over the edge. The drop felt like heaven. Wind whipped against my face as I charged down the mountainside.

I tapped my brakes lightly, even though it was the last thing I wanted to do. It decreased my speed just enough for me to make it through the turn without taking a spill. As I straightened from the curve, the path dipped, launching me into a jump.

Leaning forward, I braced for impact by keeping my knees bent and absorbing the contact with my whole body. A whoop left my lips as I crested a hill and dipped into the next curve.

It was everything I needed. The ever-changing landscape forced me to stay in the present, not letting my mind get caught up in the past or mired in the future. There was only the now.

Mav and I found our cadence as we traversed the forest paths. We saw the occasional biker or hiker, even a couple of folks with dogs. Everyone was enjoying the heart of fall before winter descended, and snow was a very real possibility.

While I loved that they were all living, too, my favorite moments were the times when it was just me, the bike, and nature all around. My breathing sounded loud in my ears, punctuating the fact that I *was* still living. I lost myself in it. The blur of the trees as I raced past, the feel of the wind sharp against my face, my muscles pushing me as fast as I could go.

I wound my way through the trails until my lungs ached and my thighs trembled. As I slowed my bike, I frowned. This didn't look like anything I'd seen on the map. The Meadow Peak Trail was framed by a babbling brook and the meadow it was named for. I couldn't remember the last time I'd seen either.

All I saw now were trees—taller and thicker than how they'd started out, no meadow or creek peeking through the branches. Anxiety swept through me, but I bit down on the inside of my cheek, staving it off. Mav had made sure I had my emergency supplies for a reason. I guided my bike off the trail, in case another biker came tearing through, and pulled out my phone. I unlocked it and hit Maverick's contact.

Nothing.

No ringing. No beeping. No nothing.

I looked at my phone screen. No bars. Then half a bar. Then none again.

A wave of dizziness slid over me, and I forced myself to climb off my bike.

"You're fine, Nova. You're perfectly safe." But I could hear the tension in my voice, the tendrils of panic weaving through my words.

"No one even misses you. They're not even looking. They don't care at all."

Travis's words swirled in my mind. The cruel twist of his mouth. His hands tightening around my throat.

I couldn't breathe.

"You're alive. You're breathing."

I tried to fight off Travis's words with Kol's. I desperately attempted to hold on to that safe space in my mind as I struggled back up the trail the way I had come. I'd find my way back. I wouldn't be lost.

"No one even knows you're gone."

It was Travis's voice but new words. Cruel and taunting syllables that had to be a figment of my imagination. Still, I couldn't get them to stop.

"They're happy you're gone."

"Life would be so much easier without all the trouble you cause."

The words were a mix of Travis's and my mother's now—the twisted cruelty they both loved so much.

"Gone is exactly where we want you to be—us and everyone else."

Chapter Thirty-Six

KOL

A BIRD CALLED OVERHEAD. I TIPPED MY HEAD BACK, TAKING in its tiny body and the flash of red feathers on its head. The ruby-crowned kinglet was likely on its way south as colder weather approached.

It instinctively knew how to care for itself, what it needed to survive. And I guessed I did, too.

As I walked through the forest, I let the sounds of nature soothe my ravaged edges. Every part of me felt out of sorts. And Waylon had seen it written all over my face.

He'd offered to take Sky for the day, bringing her along for ranch chores and rewarding her with a trip to the Grove Griddle afterward. And the fact that he'd needed to offer it just made me feel like more of a failure.

But my head could be a dark place even on good days. And everything with Nova had thrown me out of balance. Yet I couldn't help wondering if that was something I needed.

I stared down at my phone. Three calls and four texts. All unanswered.

> **Me:** *I'm sorry. I was an overprotective prick.*
>
> **Me:** *I get that you need to live your life.*
>
> **Me:** *Just let me know you're okay.*
>
> **Me:** *I'll be buying the Grove Griddle out of pie as part of my apology world tour.*

Not a damn hint of a response. Not even those three little dots appearing and disappearing.

Scowling, I dropped the phone to my side and kept walking.

The forest had been my refuge since I'd come to live with Waylon. It offered the quiet, where I could be myself. Where I could feel whatever was raging through me without having to expose my brothers to it—brothers who had been through so much more than I had.

So often, I felt like I didn't have a right to those feelings. But in the wilderness, I didn't have to hide any of it. I could simply be.

But the ease and comfort I usually found within nature didn't come today.

I felt twitchy, on edge. Letting a curse slip free, I lifted my phone again. This time, I hit Maverick's number. I didn't care that it would give away more than I wanted it to. I just needed to know that Nova was okay.

Mav answered on the second ring, a little out of breath. "Yo."

"What are you, a nineties rapper?" I grumbled as I turned back toward my truck that was parked about a quarter of a mile away, back on a Forest Service road.

"What do you want, Kol?"

"Where are you?" I clipped. I was over trying to soothe my raw edges with nature and peace. I needed Nova.

"Uhhhhh…I was mountain biking with Supernova, but…"

"Don't call her Supernova," I clipped. Then something hit me. "What do you mean *but*?"

"I, um…I can't find her."

I stilled in the middle of the forest, and I swore birds scattered overhead as if they could feel the fear and fury pulsing through me. "What. Do. You. Mean. You. Can't. Find. Her?"

My rage swept through each word, the anger a living, breathing thing.

"She was right behind me. I kept checking. And then she was just gone. I've been calling, but she's not answering. I think she lost service. So I'm riding the trail back, looking for her. She probably just got a flat—"

"How long?" I demanded, my ears starting to ring.

"Ten minutes. Fifteen, tops."

"Send me your location now. Then call Dex and Wylder," I snarled. "And get Orion on a fucking map."

I didn't wait for an answer. I hung up. Pulling up the Find My Phone app, I held my breath. *Phoenix. No location found.*

The fear had a hold now. I picked up to a full run, hitting my truck in a matter of minutes. There was only one problem. I was a good twenty minutes from where Maverick and Nova had been riding.

A million different scenarios played out in my mind. Some, innocent missteps. Others, devastating, violent tragedies. But the longer the possibilities swirled in my head, the darker and more twisted they got.

Looking at my GPS and seeing Mav's location, I did a mental calculation. There was a Forest Service road off the country road that led to the trailhead. If I took that, it should get me to Mav quicker. And I hoped like hell, to Nova.

Jerking the wheel to the right, I took the pothole-riddled road until Mav's GPS marker was parallel with my location. I quickly pulled off to the side of the road and jumped out. In a matter of seconds, I had my emergency pack slung over my shoulder and was jogging in the direction of Maverick's location.

It only took me about fifteen minutes to get there. But that still meant Nova had likely been missing for at least half an hour. In the best case, she'd been alone in the woods during that time—in the worst case…in the hands of a monster.

Familiar voices cut through the trees. Brae was yelling at Maverick. "What the hell were you thinking?" she shouted. "You should've been with her every second."

"Hellion," Dex said quietly.

"She's right," I growled, making my way into the clearing. "She was with *you*, on *your* watch."

Guilt flashed across his face. "You can't exactly ride side by side on these trails."

"But you can be in each other's line of sight," I snapped. "How long was it before you saw she wasn't behind you? Or were you too caught up in looking for your next adrenaline high?"

"Kol." It was Wylder's turn for a gentle warning. But I didn't give a damn.

Only I'd crossed a line for Mav, who was now in full pissed-off glory. "She said you were being an overprotective prick. No wonder she wanted to get away from you."

I moved so fast, no one had a prayer of stopping me. My fist struck out, right into Maverick's jaw. It snapped his head back, causing him to stumble.

Brae gasped, but Wylder and Dex cursed, already moving in. Dex went to restrain Mav, stopping him from retaliating, while Wylder shoved me back.

I tried to dodge him, but he just gripped my shirt. "Pull yourself together. Only one thing's important right now, and that's Nova."

He was right, goddamn it. I jerked my phone out of my pocket, ignoring Mav's curses. Nova's location hadn't popped up on the ride here, and as I looked now, I saw there was still nothing.

I started walking anyway, following the trail they'd clearly been on and hoping I'd see a sign.

"Do you see something?" Brae asked, worry in her voice. "Should Dex and I get Yeti? If she can catch a trail, she might be able to help."

Brae's massive beast was a damn good search dog, but Nova had likely been flying over this terrain, making it a hell of a lot harder to follow a scent trail. But I couldn't tell Brae that. I couldn't say anything at all.

I had to completely clear my head. Focus.

Dex whispered something I couldn't make out to Brae, and they fell into formation several feet behind me. Everything got quieter as my gaze scanned on a swivel. One side of the path, my phone, the other side. The same staccato rhythm.

Until a new dot appeared on my device.

Phoenix.

Her location was active.

I didn't think. I simply ran.

Chapter Thirty-Seven

NOVA

I SPUN AROUND, BRAMBLES TEARING AT THE SKIN ON MY ARMS as the voices got louder, angrier. Taunting laughter as the forest closed in around me.

"Lost forever."

And then it wasn't just the trees. I could feel walls closing in. I was back there. In the dark. Nothing but the dark. The shackle digging into my ankle. My neck aching. My throat raw.

"No one cares. No one will miss you."

Pressure built behind my eyes, burning. The memory of that door in the ceiling opening. The sunlight flickering in. Hurting my eyes. The sound of thumping footsteps on metal stairs.

"Go ahead and scream. No one will hear."

And I had screamed. I remembered now. I'd screamed and screamed and screamed. Until my throat was raw. Until…another memory slammed into me.

The man lunged forward, gripping me by the throat. "I'm the one in control. I decide if you live or die. I decide if you breathe."

My air supply cut off, and panic shot through me like an electric shock. I clawed at his arms, desperate for just a tiny respite, enough for the smallest breath. It didn't come.

I raked my nails against the man's forearms, but he only laughed. A sick sort of sound. As if he liked the pain.

His head tipped back as he cackled, and I could make out his features then, the light from the door illuminating him. He was letting me see him. Brown hair with hints of red. Green eyes. But there was a deadness to them. And the fact that he didn't care that I saw only meant one thing…

I was going to die.

Those hands tightened their grip as he brought his face closer to mine. "No one cares about you but me. No one's looking for you. Everyone is grateful you're gone."

And then the darkness closed in around me.

I blinked against the too-bright sun, as if remembering the dark made the light hurt more. A wave of dizziness hit me, and I pressed a palm against a tree, trying to steady myself. Memories of Kol teaching me to let the tree calm me flooded my mind.

The way he'd stepped in when I needed him, just like always. How he'd slipped off his boots right there behind the bar, not caring if someone found it odd—not if what he was doing was helping me. And he stood with me, making the panic subside.

Tears stung my eyes. All I wanted was him. My safe place.

But I'd driven him away. I wouldn't blame him for not looking. Not after I yelled at him and took off. It was so stupid. Pushing him away because…what? He cared?

"No one will ever find you. You're mine now."

I stumbled, trying to keep myself upright. Blood stained the knees of my leggings, and there was a tear down the shin of one of them.

"Nova!"

Everything in me stilled as I whirled around. It sounded like Kol. Tears stung my eyes, spilling over for the first time in forever. I wanted him so badly, my mind was conjuring his voice. Just like it always did. But I'd driven that voice away.

The world in front of me blurred, nothing but light and shapes and colors.

I stumbled again, not able to discern what was in front of me. It was like I was losing my vision all over again. Terror dug its icy claws deep into me.

And then someone was there. Someone taking my arms.

I screamed, fighting the figure as another wave of dizziness hit. I wouldn't let him take me, not again.

"It's me, Phoenix. It's Kol."

I kept right on fighting. "It's not. It's not you. I drove you away."

"Fuck," the voice muttered.

Something about the curse seemed familiar. It was my mind playing tricks on me. Not Kol. Not my safe space.

"It's me. Phoenix. Please, hear me." He moved in closer, his voice getting stronger. "Feel me." Knuckles slid across my cheek, but I batted them away, unsure if it was the enemy or Kol. "Trust me."

It was the desperation in the voice that made me pause, going still just long enough for rough hands to cup my cheeks. "I'm lost," I croaked.

"No, you're not. You're found," the voice rasped. "I'll always find you, remember? I'll always come for you."

I blinked through the blur of tears and light, trying to see the person in front of me. Dark hair and scruff. Hazel eyes, both light and dark, swirling. "Kol?"

"That's right. I'm right here, baby. I've got you."

I collapsed against him, and he hauled me into his arms as he lowered himself to the forest floor, cradling me. His heart hammered against my cheek as I curled into a ball, wanting nothing more than to disappear into him.

"Did he just call her baby?" a new voice asked. Some part of my brain recognized it as Maverick's, but I couldn't get myself to look.

I shoved myself deeper into Kol's hold as he rocked me. He held me to him as if he could shield me from every ounce of pain. From every stare and question. From everything that had happened in the past and might happen in the future.

"He's touching her," Brae said almost reverently. "How is he touching her?"

Kol only continued to rock me. My hands fisted in his shirts. One grabbed onto the worn cotton of a tee. The other wrapped around soft flannel. That one reminded me of last night. Of everything we'd shared. I rubbed my cheek against it, trying to escape into that memory.

"What the hell is happening?" Brae demanded. "What's going on?"

"Breathe, Hellion," Dex said quietly. "I think you know."

I could just make out the people surrounding us, even if I didn't want to see.

"I knew this was coming," Wylder said quietly. His words were free of judgment, but I thought I heard concern there.

Maverick let out a grunt. "Of course, you did. Psychic mind games."

"Enough." Kol's voice cracked out over my head. "None of that matters right now. What matters is Nova. I need to get her back to my truck and home."

"Maybe we should take her to the hospital," Brae said softly.

My hands jerked, tightening around Kol's shirts as if someone might rip me away at any moment. "No," I croaked. "No hospitals."

"No hospitals," Kol echoed, trying to calm me. "I'm gonna take care of you. Okay, Phoenix? I've got you."

And for the first time since I'd been taken, I believed.

Chapter Thirty-Eight

KOL

I KEPT LOOKING OVER AT NOVA AS I DROVE, AS IF SHE MIGHT suddenly vanish right in front of my eyes. I wanted to touch her. To comfort her. But she was covered in scratches and had some nasty gashes on her knees. I didn't want to hurt her in an attempt to help.

But she found me instead.

Even as she stared out at the road in front of us almost vacantly, she reached out to me. Her hand searched for mine, and I met her in the middle, weaving my fingers through hers and bringing them to rest on my thigh.

God, I was worried about her. I didn't have the first clue what had happened in those woods, if something had broken in her more deeply than what I could fix.

My hand spasmed around Nova's instinctively, as if holding her more tightly was some magical cure. Only I knew it wouldn't be. I'd seen that firsthand with Brae. Clinging more tightly had only hurt.

I focused on my breathing as my house came into view. Nova didn't even seem to register it. My gaze flicked to the rearview mirror, and I saw a trail of vehicles behind me: Mav's. Wylder's. Dex's. My brothers wanted to help, but part of me just wanted them to go.

But I had no choice. They were here, and that's how it was going to be.

Shutting off the engine, I turned to Nova. "I'm gonna come around and get you, okay?" I didn't want her jumping down and hurting herself.

Nova's hand only gripped mine harder. "Don't go."

Those words broke something in me. But they had nothing on her next ones.

"Don't leave me. Everybody leaves me."

Fucking hell.

I pressed my lips gently to her temple. "You're stuck with me, Phoenix. Not letting go."

I shoved my door open, unfastened my seat belt and then Nova's, then carefully extricated her. "Think you can lean over the console so I can take you with me?"

She moved instantly. Complete trust. And that slayed something in me.

Trying to mitigate the awkward angles, I pulled her over and into the driver's seat, then lifted her into my arms. As I did, more doors slammed.

Nova curled into me, burying her face in the crook of my neck as if she didn't want to see anyone.

"What can I do?" Maverick asked softly. I could hear the guilt in his words, like I could see the bruise already darkening his jawbone.

My own guilt swirled. "You can get me the first-aid kit. I'm going to take her to my room," I said quietly.

"She'll need a change of clothes. I'll get them," Brae said as she walked up, her voice tight. Her expression battled between anger and worry. And I understood both. I couldn't blame her for either.

Wylder moved into the open door of my truck, swiping up my keys. "I'll get the door."

And that was the thing—even when it felt like they were invading my space, my brothers were always there. Showing up for me.

Wylder watched me as I carried Nova up the stairs. "Ever's in town. Want me to have her give Nova a once-over?"

I stilled for a moment. I hadn't known that our childhood friend, Orion's first love—his *only love* as far as I knew—was in town. She might be taking a break from working as a doctor for Medicine for Humanity, but I wasn't above asking her to put that hat back on for Nova.

"Call her," I said, my voice low.

"Someone might want to warn the god of the brood," Mav singsonged.

"Just sent him a text," Dex cut in as I carried Nova inside.

We'd made it clear to Orion that just because he'd cut Ever out of his life, that didn't mean we would. She'd grown up with us. Her family had worked and lived on the property we'd grown up on… until it all fell apart.

But for the first time in a long time, I didn't give a damn if Ever being here tripped his triggers. Nova needed a doctor, and Ever was one of the few I trusted.

Nova held tightly to me as I climbed the stairs. Her strength was a reassurance, but the fact that she was clinging so hard worried the hell out of me.

Navigating the doorway, I crossed to my bed and lowered her to the mattress. She stayed sitting, but her eyes were too unfocused. She'd lost my flannel I'd seen her leave in somewhere along the way and wore only the soft purple workout gear from earlier. Angry scratches dotted her arms and chest, and her knees and one shin were bloody.

Just the sight of it had anger rushing to the surface. Anger at Mav, at everything Nova had been through, at myself.

Footsteps sounded. "Here's the kit," Maverick said softly, lowering it to the floor next to me. "I'm sorry—"

"Not now," I gritted out. "I know you are. Just…not now."

"Yeah. Okay."

He slid from the room as new footsteps sounded.

"I got some loose sweats and a T-shirt," Brae began, stepping inside. "Why don't you let me help her get changed and—?"

"I've got it."

I could practically feel Brae bristle, but she battled it back. "Supernova, you okay with Kol? You need me to stay?"

"Good—with—Kol." Nova's voice sounded rusty, raw, but it still cut through the room like a blade.

"Okay, babycakes. But I'm here if you need me. I'll just be downstairs."

When the door shut behind Brae, I breathed a little deeper. I gently brushed my knuckles over Nova's cheekbone, and she leaned into the touch. "Okay, Phoenix. We're going to do this together. You want anything to stop, you just say the word, all right?"

She nodded, her eyes focusing on me a little more.

"I think we need these leggings off, but I'm gonna get you a pair of shorts to wear while I clean you up. Okay?"

Another nod.

I pushed to my feet, grateful she didn't panic about me leaving her again. I moved to my dresser and pulled out the oldest pair of shorts with a drawstring I had, hoping they'd be slightly smaller.

I knew she'd still swim in them—as I crossed back to her, she looked so damn tiny sitting on the edge of my bed. So vulnerable.

And I had the sudden, visceral urge to kill every person who'd ever hurt her.

It took everything in me to relax my grip on the shorts and ease my expression. I dropped to my knees on the floor in front of Nova, carefully unlacing one shoe and slipping it off. Then the other.

I looked up at her and found her watching me. "Do you think you can stand?"

Her hands found my shoulders, using them for balance and leverage. Then, she stood.

My fingers hooked in the band of her leggings, careful not to get her underwear, too. "Okay?"

"Okay," she rasped.

I pulled the leggings down as gently as possible, but Nova still winced when I got to her scraped knees. "I'm sorry," I whispered.

"It's all right."

"It's not," I ground out, pulling one foot out and then the other.

"I've been through worse. I'll make it through this, too."

That didn't make me feel any better. But there was nothing I could do but take care of her right now. I helped her into the shorts, having to double knot the drawstring to get them to stay in place. Nova's hands gripped my shoulders as she sat back down on the bed.

"I just need to wash my hands." I bolted for the bathroom. The second I caught my reflection in the mirror, I cursed. Wild-eyed and pale, I looked like some sort of cornered animal.

Turning the water as cold as it would go, I splashed some onto my face, as if that would miraculously bring me back from the edge. It didn't.

Instead, I focused on meticulously washing my hands. Drying them. Pulling on that familiar mask that disguised anything I might be feeling.

I went back into the bedroom and knelt in front of Nova again. I felt her eyes on me, watching, but I couldn't make eye contact. I couldn't handle seeing the pain there.

Swallowing hard, I donned gloves and poured some hydrogen peroxide onto a cotton ball. "This might sting a little."

"That's okay."

No, it fucking wasn't. But I did it anyway because I had to.

Nova jumped just a little as I cleaned one knee. I bit the inside of my lip so hard I tasted blood, then moved to her other knee and down to her shin.

Afterward, I cleaned the scratches on her arms and then her chest. I was obsessive, searching for anywhere that might've been affected. Then I forced myself to look at her face.

"Does it hurt anywhere else?"

Nova stared at me, searching. "I'm sorry."

I recoiled as if she'd struck me. "What do you have to be sorry about?"

"I shouldn't have bitten your head off this morning. I shouldn't have taken off without talking things out."

"You don't have to apologize." I struggled to keep my voice even.

"I do."

"I shouldn't have tried to keep you from doing the things that are helping. I just want you to be safe."

One corner of her mouth kicked up the barest amount. "Well, you were right. The only monster was me. And I still managed to do some serious damage."

I scowled at her. "You're the farthest thing from a monster."

"I thought I was your little demon," Nova challenged.

Relief spread through me at seeing some of her fire returning, but I still struggled with Nova thinking of herself as anything monstrous. My knuckles grazed her cheek. "You're perfect."

"No one's perfect, Kol."

"You're perfectly imperfect. Because all those things you see as failures only make you more beautiful."

Her gray eyes shone in the light streaming in from the window. "Boss…"

I brushed my lips against hers, featherlight. "I'm with you. Whatever you need."

A knock sounded on the door. "It's Ever," I told her quietly.

Nova stiffened.

I brushed a hand over her hair. "It's okay. It's the childhood friend I told you about. She's a doctor."

The pieces started to slide into place. "Orion's Ever?"

Any remaining fear was replaced by instant fascination.

"That one." I studied her for a moment. "Okay to let her in?"

Nova nodded quickly.

I pushed to my feet, snapping off my gloves and opening the door. Ever stood there, wearing jeans, combat boots, and a worn T-shirt with a logo that looked to be in some foreign language. It might've been for a beer company.

Her hair hung down around her shoulders, and countless

necklaces looped over her tee. There was nothing but concern in her features. "Hey, Kol."

"Thanks for coming." I pulled her into a quick hug, having to bend over to do so.

"Of course. Introduce me."

I released her and turned back to Nova. There was zero jealousy on her face, only curiosity.

"Nova, this is my friend, Ever, a.k.a. doctor extraordinaire. Ever, this is Nova." I didn't know how to introduce her. As my friend? My girlfriend? Neither seemed appropriate. And introducing her as my everything felt more than a little over the top.

"It's lovely to meet you, Nova," Ever said with an easy smile. "Can I take a look at your injuries?"

She struck the perfect balance, I realized. Gentle but not placating. Down-to-business but not harsh in any way.

"Sure," Nova said, that rasp still clinging to her voice. "Kol cleaned them. The scrapes."

Ever arched a brow in my direction. "If I remember correctly, when I was eight and you were twelve, you told me to rub dirt on my skinned knee because it *helped*."

I winced. "Sorry about that. But you'll be happy to know my medical skills have improved since then."

"Glad to hear it." Ever crouched, pawing through my first-aid supplies. "Impressive kit, too."

She grabbed a pair of gloves and then looked around the room. Snagging a stool from the corner that was mainly used as a clothes catcher, she carried it over and sat. As she pulled on the gloves, she started asking questions.

"Did you fall?"

Nova shook her head, her cheeks pinking slightly. "I don't...I don't think so. I just got turned around and confused and panicked."

"Happens to the best of us," Ever said easily. "Follow my finger with your eyes." Ever moved her gloved pointer up and down, then from side to side in an H motion. "Does anything hurt more than the sting of these scratches?"

"No. I just feel a little tired," Nova admitted.

"I bet," Ever replied. "Mav never knows when to call it quits on his adventures."

"I think I might've been a bit of a buzzkill for him today," Nova mumbled.

I glared at the floor at that.

"Mav could use a little calming, buzzkill force in his life." Ever glanced up at me. "Got a penlight? I just want to double-check something."

I jerked my head in a nod, moving to a box atop my dresser that held all sorts of random things. A Swiss Army knife. Assorted change and pens. Chapstick. A couple of pretty rocks Skylar had found and given to me. A mini flashlight.

I handed the last item to Ever just as she instructed Nova to turn her head from side to side.

"Thanks." She took the light and flashed it over each of Nova's eyes. Nova instantly winced. "Does that hurt?"

"A little. I, um..."

"She's got a sensitivity to light," I explained.

Ever looked up at me, confused.

"You probably know already. I was kidnapped. He, um, kept me in the dark most of the time," Nova said quietly. "For a year."

Fury like I'd never seen on Ever's face before erupted, but she quickly covered it—swallowed it down and snuffed it out. "That makes sense, then. I'm not seeing any signs of a concussion, but if you get dizzy or get a bad headache, can't remember simple information, feel nauseous or throw up, I want you to go to the emergency room."

Nova tugged her bottom lip between her teeth.

"Are you already experiencing any of that?" Ever asked.

"When I get anxious, I can get dizzy. Happens off and on," Nova explained.

Ever nodded and leaned forward, her elbows on her knees. "It can be a symptom of a panic attack. Less common than shortness of breath, but more common than people know. Do you experience anything else?"

Nova's gaze flicked to me and then back to Ever. "Sometimes, I have shortness of breath. But more often, I feel like…like I'm crawling out of my skin."

My gut twisted. Just one more scar Travis had left her with.

"Another symptom for sure. But the good news is, there are lots of things out there that help. You just have to find the thing that's right for you," Ever encouraged.

Nova's eyes took on a bit more fire. "I hate therapy."

Ever barked out a laugh. "I mean, I sometimes hate it, too. My therapist can be a real bitch when she's right."

Nova's mouth curved. "You go to therapy?"

"Honestly, I think we'd all be better, happier humans if we did. But you've got to find the right match. It's kind of like dating in that way."

Nova let out a breath. "I'll think about it."

But I knew it would be hard, facing the things she'd gone through… It might be more than she could take right now. But if she didn't find someone to talk to, I worried what might happen.

"Tree Man, do me a favor and make Nova a snack while I bandage these scrapes. She needs some water and maybe some juice, too," Ever called over her shoulder.

I scowled at her. "I hate that nickname."

"Do you or do you not love trees?" Ever pressed.

"He does," Nova answered for me.

"You're both horrible," I grumbled.

Ever snapped her fingers twice. "Snacks, Tree Man."

Nova pressed her lips together to keep from laughing.

"You okay up here?" I asked.

She nodded. "I'm good. I'm gonna get all the dirt on you from Ever."

Ever let out that raspy laugh that she'd had since she was a kid. "We'll start with the time he let me dress him up and marry him off to one of my dolls."

"I'm leaving," I called, heading for the door.

"Good, we don't need you," Ever shot back.

I slipped through the door, then waited, just in case Nova couldn't handle being alone with someone she didn't know. But instead of any sounds of distress, her laughter cut through the door. It swirled through the air and coated my skin.

I wanted that laughter to be enough. I wanted to believe it fixed everything. But I worried it couldn't. Not even close.

Chapter Thirty-Nine

NOVA

Ever's fingers worked deftly yet gently as she applied an antibiotic ointment to my worst cuts. But after Kol had cleaned them, it was really only the ones on my knees that still needed attention.

"I'm putting some waterproof bandages on these so you can shower tonight if you want," she informed me.

My nose wrinkled. "Given that I was biking for a couple of hours, I will definitely need one of those."

"Try working in the blazing sun in a place where air-conditioning doesn't exist," she said with a half smile.

"That's gotta be rough."

"It is at times. But the highs outweigh the lows, ten to one. I just miss seeing my niece and nephew as often as I'd like."

Just her saying that sent a pang through me at the reminder of how much of Owen's life I'd missed. "That would be hard for sure."

"Thank God for video chatting, or I'd be lost." Ever covered the final cut. "You know...I don't think I've ever seen Kol quite that protective over anyone but Skylar or his brothers."

My stomach flipped. "Oh."

A laugh bubbled out of Ever, throaty and free of any inhibition. "Yeah."

"He saved me." I said it simply, but it had Ever straightening and leaning back on her stool as she studied me. I saw the flicker of concern there and pressed on. "I don't mean the fact that he was the one who found me. Who kept me alive. I mean, he *saved* me. He let me feel whatever I was feeling and didn't blink. Not even when it was scary."

Her expression softened. "He gave you a safe place to land."

I nodded. "He made it safe for me to tell him things I couldn't tell anyone else."

Ever's blue-green eyes glistened. "That's a gift."

A pang lit along my sternum, and I saw grief living in those eyes. "Orion?" I asked, unable to stop myself.

Her mouth curved into a sad smile. "It's always Orion. Hard to let go of someone who was such a fundamental part of your life for so long. Especially when you know they're hurting. Or maybe I'm just a glutton for punishment."

I had so many questions, and most of them were none of my business. But I thought something was interesting: Ever traveled the world for her work, never staying in one place for too long, never having a real *home* to return to; it was almost like she was keeping herself from putting down roots.

"I can't imagine."

Ever shrugged. "We've all got our things to carry. Sometimes, I think it's good to remember that. It keeps us human."

"Holding on to our humanity is the most important thing. Even when it hurts," I whispered. Because when you didn't, you had the potential to become what Travis had been—uncaring about anything others were feeling and only looking to feed his own twisted needs and evil pleasures.

"Even when it hurts," Ever echoed. She snapped off her gloves and pushed to her feet. "I know we don't really know each other, but if there's anything I can do to help, call." She pulled a card out of her pocket. "I might be in weird time zones, but I'll always get back to you as soon as I can."

I frowned down at the card. "When do you leave?"

I liked Ever. She struck that balance between kindness and take-no-shit I admired.

One corner of her mouth lifted. "Tomorrow morning. Gotta leave for the airport at three thirty."

I winced. "That's brutal."

"Eh, I'm used to it. I don't usually work in places with major airports. It's typically pretty remote."

"Where are you working now?"

"Haiti." Ever tossed her gloves into the wastepaper basket Kol had brought over, then tied off the bag. "But I'm heading to Brazil next, a small village in the mountains, to help establish a new clinic. Never been before."

"Never in one place for too long," I said, seeing that my earlier estimation just might be right on the money.

She sent me a knowing smile. "Sometimes, it's easier that way."

"Never slow down long enough to risk staying put?"

Another of those raspy laughs left her. Ever was stunning. Those hypnotic, blue-green eyes and the badass air of her fashion choices. The fact that she was smart as hell and kind to boot. It all meant she likely had more than her share of interest when it came to romantic partners.

"You don't pull any punches, do you?" Ever asked.

I shrugged. "I mean, if you leave tomorrow, how else am I going to find out everything I need to know?"

She grinned at me. "Now, *that* I can help you with." She picked up her phone and began scrolling. "I keep an album for blackmail purposes. I present you with Kol's superhero phase."

Ever handed me the device. I stared at the image for one, two, three, and then burst out laughing. "Oh, I'm framing this one. Maybe having it painted. An oil painting of a masked, caped, tighty-whitied Kol in all his glory."

As I quickly sent the image to my phone, I shook my head. Tiny Kol was adorable, and he would absolutely *hate* anyone seeing this. It was perfect.

"Please do it, and film his reaction," Ever said, chuckling.

"You got it."

She started for the door. "You're right."

"About?" I asked. But I already knew.

"Never staying somewhere for too long. It's hard to think about building a life with someone when you already know what it's like to have that ripped away."

It was straight-to-the-heart honesty. It shouldn't have surprised me—Ever was clearly honest and got right to the heart of things—but it somehow still did. And, at the same time, it cut me to the core.

The loss she'd experienced and the fact that she was still going… and more than that, making the world a better place—it made me want to find a purpose for my pain. It also made me realize I shouldn't take a single second with Kol for granted.

As Ever slipped out of the room, Brae appeared with a snack plate and some juice. "Is it okay if I come in?" she asked cautiously.

A hint of nerves bubbled up from somewhere deep. Things had been better between us since we had our heart-to-heart, but I worried my freak-out would send us hurtling backward. That Brae would insist I move back in with her, or worse, go to some hospital or rehab.

"Of course." I wove my fingers together and then unlaced them, repeating the movements over and over until Brae settled next to me on the bed, the plate of assorted snacks between us.

She was quiet for a long moment. "You know, when you go for the surprise factor, you really go for it. *Kol?* Grunty mountain man, *I speak only to trees and my daughter* Kol? Damn, girl."

A laugh bubbled out of me and, with it, relief. "It's a recent development. But he certainly packs a punch."

One corner of her mouth kicked up. "I can only imagine." Her nose scrunched. "Actually, that's weird. He's almost my brother-in-law. I take it back."

"You're not actually blood-related. You can still appreciate his hotness."

"Do *not* tell Dex that. He already gets annoyed that Mav calls me Little Badass."

That had me snickering. "Why am I not surprised?"

We were both quiet again for a moment. Brae toyed with the friendship bracelet I'd given her years ago—the one she'd never stopped wearing. "Scared the hell out of me when Maverick said you were missing." Her breath hitched. "I'm terrified of losing you again."

"Brae…"

"Only I can't put that on you. Because I know it will just suffocate you all over again. But I feel it, and I think that's where all the overprotectiveness and controlling stuff comes from. I can't stand the thought of losing you. Not again."

I put myself in her shoes. Maybe for the first time. I'd gotten glimmers before, but now I really let myself feel it. "I'm so sorry you went through that," I croaked. "I'd do anything to change it."

Her eyes glittered with unshed tears. "I'm so sorry *you* went through that. And I'd do anything to change it."

And that was the crux of it. We'd both been irrevocably changed by what had happened, just marked in different ways. We had our own healing journeys to go on, but we could also help each other.

I wanted to grab Brae's hand, to squeeze it the way I had countless times before. But I wasn't quite brave enough. Not yet. But maybe soon. "I'm so grateful you're my bestest bestie."

She sent me a wobbly smile as she fished something out of her pocket. "I'm so grateful you're mine. Think we could make that official?"

I frowned. "If you want to do some blood-brothers pact, you know that's not for me."

She laughed. "No slicing palms required." She held out a friendship bracelet. "I know Sky made you some bracelets, but I thought I could, too. It could"—she swallowed—"it could replace the one you lost."

Brae meant the one that had been found in the graves of Travis's other victims. The item that had convinced everyone but Kol that I was gone.

This was like a new beginning. A fresh start. But also, a reclaiming. "I'd love that," I whispered.

My hand trembled as I held it out, but Brae was careful not to touch me as she tied the yarn bracelet around my wrist.

I stared down at the colorful string. "It's perfect. Thank you. For everything."

Brae met my gaze and didn't look away. "Thank *you*."

Every part of the moment felt like a step toward healing—for both of us.

Chapter Forty

KOL

I STOOD ON THE BACK DECK, WATCHING AS A FULLY KITTED-out Skylar and Owen played some battle game where Tink and Pepper were their fellow soldiers. Sky had put fairy wings and a superhero mask on the mini-Highland cow and somehow affixed a tiara to the goat's head and a cape to her back.

Skylar herself wore a feather boa, a cape, and goggles, and she carried a Nerf gun. Owen had a mask beneath his glasses, a crown, another cape, and a Nerf gun. The image of it was completely ridiculous and the only thing that might be comforting in the moment.

Their innocence amid all the pain that circled our family…we had to hold on to it. Make the world a better place for them.

But all I could think about was Nova. Up in my room. Ever tending to her wounds. I was scared as hell for her on every level. Her heart, her mind, her soul. And that didn't touch her physical safety. Because we still hadn't found Heidi Ingram or who'd left her bloody necklace on Nova's car.

I forced myself to let out a breath, nice and slow. I needed to get myself together before I went back up there. When I reached the kitchen, Brae had already been hard at work making Nova a snack while Waylon was preparing a pot of chili and biscuits for everyone.

Family showed up. At least, the one we'd managed to cobble together. And they all loved Nova. Wanted to be there for her.

"Do you want to punch me again?"

I glanced over at Maverick as he moved in beside me, hands in his pockets. I winced. The bruise looked worse already. "I'm sorry. I shouldn't have hit you."

Violence wasn't something I reached for unless it was unavoidable. And I sure as hell didn't use it on my brothers outside of our version of shit-talking.

"I deserved it." Mav's focus lifted to my bedroom window.

My jaw worked back and forth. It was both Mav's fault *and* it wasn't. And I didn't know how to put that into words.

"She's more fragile than I realized," he went on softly. "I should've seen it, but I didn't. Regardless, I should've been more careful, especially given everything that's going on."

The reminder of the missing woman and the notes churned in my gut, but I wouldn't pile on more when Mav already knew he'd messed up. "Nova covers well," I said. "But we can't forget what she's been through."

He nodded slowly. "You two…"

The words hung in the air.

"I care about her." God, those words felt like a lie. Because some part of me had fallen for Nova the moment I saw her fighting to stay when it would've been so easy to give up. And that falling had only dug itself deeper and deeper the more I got to know her.

Wylder appeared on my other side, moving silently but clearly having taken in the exchange between Mav and me. He studied me for a long moment. It was the kind of assessment that had me squirming.

"Just say whatever you're thinking," I grumbled.

"Are you sure it's smart? You two have a trauma bond. If it's that and nothing more, it could cause a lot of damage. To her"—his gaze flicked to Skylar, who was rolling in the grass with Tink—"and to you."

My back teeth ground together until my jaw ached. "First, when Nova cut me off, she still saw Sky all the time. She'd never bail on my kid because this wasn't working between the two of us."

Wylder opened his mouth to argue, but I kept right on going.

"Second, it may have been trauma that brought us together, but that's not what binds us. It's how she battled her way out of the ashes. It's the way she *lives,* how she gives me quiet and acceptance to be whoever I am and share whatever I need to. And maybe our wounds make us understand each other better than anyone else, but that doesn't mean this is some toxic connection."

"I never said that," Wylder argued.

Frustration and something just a bit greater than annoyance flitted through me. "Didn't you? And like you're one to talk. I see the way you look at Cora, how you're the one picking up the pieces for her."

Wylder's mouth slammed shut.

It was a low blow. I shouldn't have gone there. I scrubbed both my hands over my face. "I'm sorry."

God, I was fucking up left and right today.

"Let's all take a breath," Mav said. "And be honest. None of us enters into relationships from a perfectly emotionally healthy place."

"Or at all," Dex said, moving into our group and slapping Mav on the shoulder.

He glared at Dex. "You know what I mean. Healing is a journey. The best we can hope for is to find someone who's willing to go on it with us."

The back door shut. "Maverick Archer, have you become a wise sage?"

I turned at the sound of Ever's voice, anxiety washing through me. Where was Nova? Was she alone? Was she okay? Did I need to go up there?

"You should know by now that I'm the genius of this bunch," Mav shot back with a grin.

Ever sent me a reassuring smile. "Brae's with her. She's good. They're eating, and Nova's getting ready to come downstairs."

"She should rest—"

Ever cut me off. "She should do what feels right to her."

I let out a huff of air. "Damn you for always being right."

Ever's lips twitched. "That's what I like to hear." Her gaze swept over my brothers. "I'll also say, we had a good talk. Encouraging her to find some therapy or a therapist that works for her would be good. But don't push it. That'll do more harm than good."

Ever turned to me, her expression softening. But there was something beneath it. Pain or even longing. "I'll also say, she's with you for the right reasons. Because you give her a safe space to express herself, not because she feels she owes you anything."

I fought the urge to send Wylder a pointed look.

"But this won't be easy," Ever went on. "She's going through a lot."

"I know that," I gritted out.

Dex cleared his throat. "And not to be a Debbie Downer, but what about your job? They aren't going to like this. Is that why you've been keeping it a secret?"

My gut churned because it was more than them not liking it. Sherri would fire my ass—or maybe just suspend me if I was lucky. It was as if two parts of me were locked in battle. One that needed control and justice, and didn't trust anyone else to get it. And one that simply needed Nova.

"If we close the case quickly, it won't be an issue," I gritted out.

"Because we're so close to that," Wylder muttered.

This time, I did glare at him. "Then maybe we should be a little more focused, a bit more dedicated. Because I'm not the only one who cares about this outcome."

Dex held up a hand. "We all care."

Ever looked back and forth between us, a hint of confusion on her face. And that's when I realized my mistake. She didn't know about the Hourglass Network. She didn't know that we secretly helped to find missing people whose families had nowhere else to turn. And by connecting my brothers to the case, I'd almost blown that cover sky-high.

I pressed the heels of my palms against my eyes, trying to beat back the headache and pressure building from all my screwups.

Ever glanced around the back deck, but she let it go. Instead, she simply said, "I'm going to go try to see him."

That stopped us all. Because we knew who *him* was. Just like we knew that Orion would never see her.

But it didn't stop her from trying. She'd stand outside his door and wait. Sometimes, just thirty minutes. Other times, she'd wait hours. She'd tried every method under the sun.

She'd held up signs, knowing the security cameras would pick up the words. She'd blared music he hated, music he loved. She'd tried just talking at the cameras. She'd tried silence.

Nothing ever moved him.

And the longer it went on, the harder it was for all of us to take.

I needed to talk to Orion. Because I thought if he saw her just once, if he gave her the closure she deserved, maybe Ever could move on.

"Come back for dinner," I said gruffly. "Waylon's making chili and biscuits."

One of Ever's brows arched at that. "One, two, or three pepper?"

My mouth twitched. "Just one. Nova's stomach is still tender."

"That's okay, I'll bring my own hot sauce to spice things up," she said.

Dex chuckled. "It's no wonder you're Waylon's favorite."

Mav looked thoughtful. "I wonder who would win in a hot-sauce off: Little Badass or Ever?"

"Stop calling my fiancée Little Badass," Dex growled.

"I'm not calling her *Hot* Little Badass anymore. What more do you want from me?" Mav argued.

Dex dove for Maverick, taking him down to the grass for a noogie. The kids and animals instantly joined in on the fun, but Ever moved closer to me, squeezing my hand and then letting it go.

"You're good for her. And she's good for you. You make each other better. More yourselves. And there's no greater gift than that."

With those words, she slipped off the side of the deck and headed for her rental car. But the words stayed with me, and I'd hold tight to the hope in them. Just as long as nothing else blew up in my face.

Chapter Forty-One

NOVA

Hot water streamed down from the showerhead, easing my aching muscles. It had stung the scrapes and cuts at first, but now it just felt damn good. I rolled my shoulders back as I rinsed the last of the conditioner from my hair, reveling in the feeling after the longest day known to man.

I almost felt back to normal. The word had my face screwing up. *Normal.* I wasn't sure I'd ever been there or ever *would* be. But I didn't know if I wanted to be.

At least I was feeling less out of my body. For that time in the forest, the time after, it was almost as if I were hovering over myself and taking everything in from above.

The memories that had surfaced flared again. Snippets of Travis's voice. Glimpses of his twisted face. The feeling of hands around my neck.

And more was coming. Other things were swirling now. Memories of the dark. Of trying to grasp the concept of the passing days and weeks. Wondering if it was Thanksgiving, Christmas, or my birthday. Trying to picture Brae and Owen in my mind but starting to lose their images.

Tears stung the backs of my eyes. I didn't force them down this time. I breathed through them as I shut off the water.

"You're alive. You're breathing."

The words and voice were my comforts. I held on to them now but tried not to shove down the memories, either. Some part of me knew it would be a healthier path through if I could hold both at the same time.

Stepping out of the shower, I wrapped two towels around myself. Kol had given them to me, along with a hairdryer he used for Sky. The towels were soft and plush—nothing like what I remembered of my single towel in the cell. That had been rough, small. And I'd always been so scared to shower that I'd only done it when I started to smell.

"You're alive. You're breathing."

I moved to dry my hair, studying the incredibly long strands in the mirror. I hadn't cut it in almost a year and a half. Not in the time I was in the dark, and not after, when I couldn't handle being touched. Maybe now.

A surge of something hit me. Bravery.

Tightening the towel around my body, I opened the bathroom door. I expected the bedroom to be empty, but instead, I found Kol sitting on the edge of the bed in worn sweats and a tee emblazoned with the emblem for Wylder's bar. He looked tired.

But the moment I stepped out, his eyes were on me. Searching. Seeking. He didn't ask anything. Instead, he simply said, "Sky's asleep."

My mouth curved the slightest bit. "She raced Owen for hours. I'm not surprised." I was quiet for a moment. I shouldn't ask him for yet another thing, but I couldn't stop myself. "Can you do something for me?"

Kol instantly straightened. "Anything."

The answer came so quickly, it was a balm, easing my nerves a fraction. "Will you cut my hair?"

He blinked back at me. "Cut your hair…"

I nodded. "It's too long. I just…I haven't been able to because I didn't want to risk a freak-out. But now—"

Kol stood. "I can cut your hair, Phoenix."

"Thank you." He always understood. He could fill in the blanks when I didn't have the exact words.

He grimaced slightly as he crossed to a box on his dresser. "This might not be a salon-style job."

"Doesn't have to be."

Kol opened the box and pulled out two pairs of scissors. "I've got these from making a costume for Skylar for Halloween last year. I feel like fabric scissors would be best."

I gaped at him. "You *made* Sky's Halloween costume?"

His mouth curved the barest amount. "Don't give me too much credit. She was a princess superhero. I just had to make the cape because she had everything else."

"I'm still impressed."

Kol grunted. Still not liking any compliments, he handed me the scissors. "Take these. I'll get the stool."

We filed into the bathroom, and I lowered myself to the wooden seat. I could just see myself in the large mirror.

Kol gathered my wet hair in his hands, the sensation sending beautiful chills skating over my skin. "How short?"

I studied myself in the mirror. How short would the new me want it to be? A bob? Just a few inches? I kept looking until I felt the answer. I wanted to be able to pull it back in a braid or up in a ponytail, but I wanted the weight gone. I wanted to feel…free.

"Here." I gestured to just below my shoulders. "Right here."

Kol met my gaze in the mirror. "You're sure?"

I didn't look away from those light and dark eyes. "I'm sure."

He nodded. "I'm going to get some of the length off first, and then I'll make it even shorter."

"Good plan," I said, a little breathless, nerves and excitement stirring in equal measure.

Kol kept a hold of my hair in one hand but leaned down and

pressed a kiss to the top of my head. "You're the strongest person I know."

Unshed tears stung my eyes, and I didn't battle them back. I just let them hang.

Kol lifted the large pair of scissors. He placed them just above where my hair was gathered in his fist and waited, his eyes asking silently for one more confirmation.

"Do it," I whispered.

He began to cut through my strands bit by bit. And as he did, my tears started to fall. Silent grief for all the hair carried. Silent relief for beginning to let it go.

"I'm remembering," I told him quietly.

Hair fell to the floor as Kol stilled, his eyes jerking to mine in the mirror.

"Keep going," I croaked.

He forced his eyes back to the task, kept cutting.

"I remember being alone in the dark. I remember wondering if I would die there in that hole."

Kol sucked in a sharp breath but didn't stop his work.

"I remember the shackle biting into my skin. And I remember the light was worse than the dark because it meant *he* was coming."

Energy, a battle for restraint, hummed through Kol, making the scissors almost vibrate.

"I remember shaking so hard my teeth chattered. The taunting words he spat at me. His hands closing around my throat."

Kol's fingers were gentle now. So opposite of the man in my memories, my nightmares. He lifted a piece of hair, trimming even as I knew I was breaking his heart. But he was doing it for me.

"I couldn't breathe. And I thought for sure that would be it. But it wasn't. He just wanted to see how close he could take me without the game coming to an end."

More pieces of hair fluttered to the floor. Bit by bit. More of the weight leaving me.

"But that wasn't the worst." I swallowed hard. "He told me that no one cared. That no one was looking. That everyone was glad I was gone. That he was the only one I had."

Kol's eyes blazed with gold fire as they met mine in the mirror. "I cared. I was looking. I didn't even know you yet, but I was looking. And now? I'd find you anywhere you went, Phoenix. Because you carry me with you. You always will."

Tears tracked down my face. "I know. I don't feel alone. Not anymore."

"You're killing me," he rasped.

"We're almost done," I promised.

Kol jerked his head in a nod and kept cutting, more hair falling to the floor.

"When you found me…" My throat constricted as I tried to let go of my greatest shame. "I didn't want to go on. I didn't want to fight."

"Nova," he croaked, unshed tears glistening in his beautiful eyes.

"But you lent me your strength when mine was burned out. You gave me what I needed to push on when I couldn't take another step. And you remind me every day what it is to fight."

Tears slid down Kol's cheeks as the scissors made one final cut. He set them on the counter with a clank, his hands moving to my shoulders. "Greatest honor of my life, holding you here when you needed it."

I felt those words even as I saw him through the mirror. As I saw myself as the person I was now, freer and stronger. I didn't look away from the mirror as I spoke the words that had always terrified me. Until now. "I love you."

Kol stilled, both the dark and the light blazing in his eyes now.

It didn't matter if he said it back or not. It wasn't about that. This was about me giving something to Kol. Telling him exactly what he'd done for me and who he was to me. And the only word for that was love.

He moved in a flash, turning me and lifting me onto the counter. "Tell me again."

My mouth curved as I wrapped my legs around him. "I love you."

Kol took my mouth then—a long, hungry kiss. His tongue slid across mine as if he were trying to drink the echo of the words.

He pulled back ever so slightly, his lips brushing against mine and then staying right there. "Tell me again so I can feel it here."

"I love you." Each word stroked my lips against his. Each syllable burned into his mouth.

"I love you with all I have. It might not be perfect or everything you deserve, but you have all of me."

My nose stung as I breathed through a fresh wave of tears. "Perfectly imperfect, remember?"

"I remember."

My fingers sank into his hair. "Boss?"

"Yeah, Phoenix?"

"Take me to bed."

"Now who's bossy?" he asked, smiling against my lips.

I nipped his bottom lip. "Sometimes, it's good to be the boss."

Chapter Forty-Two

NOVA

There was no hesitation in Kol. He lifted me as if I weighed nothing, my legs hooked around his hips as he carried me over the scattering of hair on the tile floor. I felt like I weighed no more than that snow on the air I thought I'd seen when he found me.

Because I was starting to let it all go. Let it all out. And that was the path to freedom.

Kol sifted a hand into my hair as he took my mouth, that powerful tongue sliding against mine. As he pulled back, his eyes were pure fire. "I like this." His fingers tightened in my hair.

I grinned back. "Me, too. Makes me feel free."

"Like you were always meant to be."

My smile softened. "You showed me how."

Kol slowed his steps as we reached the bed. He lowered me, my feet finding the floor as if there was no rush and he was determined to take his time. I could feel *everything*. The way the soft towel brushed my skin. The hard planes of his body. The ridge growing in those sweatpants.

"Time to feel that freedom. Time to fly," he rasped. His finger came to the knot in my towel, light sparking in his dark-hazel depths. "Yes?"

"Yes," I breathed.

With one flick of his fingers, my towel dropped. Kol took a step back, as if he were examining a work of art in a museum. Only it wasn't analysis I saw in his eyes. It was pure, blistering heat. "So damn beautiful."

And he made me feel it. There was no want or need to cover my scars or hide my insecurities. Not the marks from the shackles or the reminder of the stab wound on my torso. They only felt like reminders of everything I'd overcome to get to this place. To Kol. To freedom.

The man in front of me took one step and sank to his knees as if he were ready to worship me. And maybe he was, in a way.

His hands skimmed up my calves, the touch featherlight, then twisted around and slid up my thighs. "I'll never forget this sight, you in the moonlight. Skin glowing like the damn stars themselves."

Kol's hands stopped just shy of where I wanted them the most. "Yes?"

"Please." There was a begging note in my voice, but I didn't give a damn.

One corner of his mouth kicked up. "Nothing makes me harder than hearing you beg. Than hearing you say *yes*. Say *please*. Say *more*."

"Yes. Please. More." My words vibrated with all the need curling inside me.

"My little demon." Kol's thumb slid along my slit, and I couldn't help my sharp intake of breath. "Tell me, do you want my mouth on you?"

My legs trembled in response, giving me away. "Your tongue, your fingers, your cock."

"My greedy girl." But he didn't begrudge my selfishness. His thumb parted me as his tongue flicked out, circling my clit.

I couldn't help the gasp that left me, didn't care that it gave me away, because I could feel whatever I needed, whatever I wanted. With Kol, I could feel it all.

He slid two fingers inside me and circled. My back arched, my body leaning into his, seeking more. His tongue moved in some sort of nonsensical figure eight over that bundle of nerves as his fingers stroked in and out.

My legs trembled again, and I wasn't sure I could stay upright if this continued, but Kol read that, too. One arm came under my ass, holding me to him, telling me he'd never let me fall.

His fingers thrust deeper, and as they curled, he hit a spot that sent light sparking over my vision. My mouth fell open as my breaths came in quick pants. Sharp, staccato beats only punctuated by flutters of convulsions through my core.

My fingers dug into Kol's shoulders, biting into the skin. "Not going to last."

He only hummed against my clit, then sucked lightly on that bundle of nerves. The gentle pressure was all it took. I cried out as the first orgasm hit me hard and fast. My walls clamped down on Kol's fingers as I struggled not to collapse.

Kol simply held me to him, his fingers moving through the pulses as his tongue circled that tiny bead, drawing out every last ounce of feeling I had in me. Just when I didn't think I could take anymore, Kol slowed his ministrations, easing back and gazing up at me, even as his fingers were still inside me.

"Flying yet, Phoenix?"

"Flying free," I whispered.

"More?" he asked, a wolfish grin on his face.

It called on one of my own as I looked down at him. "If I'm your demon, you're my devil."

That grin only widened. "Seems only fair." He slowly pulled his fingers from me, licking them clean. "Tell me what you want, little demon."

"You. Filling me. Stretching me. Taking me."

Those dark eyes flashed. "I'll get the rope."

Kol started to stand, but I gripped his shoulders. "No. No rope."

A hint of uncertainty swept over his face. "Are you sure?"

I nodded. "I'm sure. I want to feel that freedom with you. For both of us."

Kol slowly got to his feet, his hand skating across my jaw and then into my hair. "If something feels like it's too much, you have to tell me. Promise me."

"I promise," I whispered against his mouth.

He kissed me, quick and deep, and then took a step back. A wave of cold hit me, but it was soon replaced by a wash of heat. Because Kol reached behind his head and pulled off his tee in one swift motion.

All that golden skin on display. All those dents and curves of his beautiful body. The tattoos that told the story of his life.

Then his fingers were in the band of his sweats, shucking them down thick thighs and kicking them across the floor. I swallowed hard, taking him in. All of him. He was pure power, which only made his restraint more beautiful.

Kol stayed exactly where he was, muscles rippling with that restraint. "Yes?"

"Yes. Please. More."

A flash of gold fire, and then Kol was striding toward me. One hand slid into my hair as the other went around my waist. He twisted us as we fell to the mattress, my body atop his. He hauled us up the bed so he was nestled in the pillows, my newly shortened hair falling around us like a curtain.

"Take what you need," he growled.

My hands landed on his chest as I lifted myself. "What we both need."

One hand reached lower, curling around Kol. My fingers tightened ever so slightly, and he let out an almost pained hiss. I relished the power, the feel of him. The way he hardened further in my hand. How he thickened. But more than anything, I savored that I could make him *feel*.

"You always give me what I need," Kol growled.

We gave it to each other—a give and take, a steady presence.

I guided him to my entrance, slowly sinking down, feeling all of him. Kol let out a guttural groan as I seated him fully inside me.

"Everything. This is everything," he whispered.

One of my hands found his, using it for leverage and balance. His other hand found my breast, palming, thumb circling the nipple as I rocked against him.

Tiny barbs of sensation embedded themselves under my skin, pleasure with the barest flickers of pain. And that was life at its core: pleasure and pain. But if you focused on the good, the beauty, you realized it was only deepened because of the hard and the painful.

My body moved more, gliding up and then down, reveling in the feel of all that was Kol. He was careful with me. Thoughtful to keep his hand away from anywhere near my neck, but I wasn't afraid—and I wanted more.

"Flip us," I begged between panted breaths.

Kol stilled for only a moment. "You're sure?"

"Yes. Please. More."

I spoke the words that were a stroke to his senses, and Kol gave me exactly what I needed. He flipped us but moved his hands to mine. He pinned them above my head, not in a show of force but as a message that we were together. That he would follow wherever I wanted to go. And I knew I would give him the same.

Kol pulled out and then slid back in, the friction everything I'd been needing. My legs hooked around him, digging into the muscular divots in his ass. My body encouraged him as he moved, rising up to meet him, spurring him on.

We met each other in the fading twilight, the way we always had from that very first moment.

"With me," Kol rasped.

"With you."

His body arched, driving him deeper inside me as he released. And I could feel it all as my walls tumbled down. Nothing kept us apart now. Everything had been laid bare.

I knew nothing would be the same, but I also knew we'd find something new, something better. Together.

Chapter Forty-Three

KOL

"I WANT DOUBLE STRAWBERRIES AND MAYBE SOME CHOCOLATE chips." Skylar sent me a look that was a cross between hopeful and sly.

"Why do I feel like you're turning this breakfast granola bowl into an ice cream sundae?" I leaned against the counter, giving my daughter an over-the-top, eye-narrowing stare.

She let out a giggle. My favorite one, the laugh that said nothing weighed on her shoulders and the world was her oyster. "Because I'm smart."

"That you are, Little Princess. That you are."

There was nothing like the normalcy of a kid trying to get away with everything they could to bring comfort after a tumultuous twenty-four hours. My gaze lifted to the ceiling as if on instinct, seeking out Nova. I'd left her sleeping hard when it was time to get Sky up. But she'd needed it.

Grabbing the chocolate chips from the pantry, I sprinkled a few on Skylar's granola. A chuckle left me as she started dancing in her chair, raising her hands over her head, spoon in hand.

"Granola sundae for breakfast," she singsonged.

"We're having sundaes for breakfast, and nobody told me?" Nova asked as she moved into the kitchen.

I did a full head-to-toe sweep, surveying everything about her. She wore jeans and boots, with a figure-hugging tank peeking out from beneath a flannel. *My* flannel. God, I loved that she kept wearing my clothes.

Skylar's eyes went wide. "Your hair, Supernova!"

A hint of nerves made its way into Nova's expression. She did a twirl. "What do you think?"

"I think you look beeeeeeeeautiful and sassy," Sky said definitively. "And like you should have a granola sundae with me."

Nova laughed. "Just what I was going for. And I'm always down for a sundae of any sort."

I'd told Sky that Nova was going to sleep over because she had taken a fall off her bike and shouldn't be alone. Sky had simply said, *"She should sleep over every night. Everything's better when she's here."*

Some parents would take that as a failing, but for the first time in forever, I hadn't. I'd taken it for what it was: the simple truth. Nova did make everything better.

"How are you feeling?" I asked, moving into her space and stroking a hand down her back.

Nova's mouth curved as she looked up at me. "Good. Better than I have in a while."

And I understood that. She'd released some of what she'd been holding inside. It wasn't some magic bullet, but it helped.

Nova tugged on the corner of my shirt, moving us toward the makeshift granola bowl stand and away from Sky's keen ears. She'd picked up the book her class was reading, thoroughly enthralled in that and her granola sundae.

I studied Nova's face, her body. She twisted the corner of the flannel she wore between her fingers. "I called Aster this morning."

I waited for more.

Nova let out a breath that trembled as she exhaled—not fear exactly but nerves with an edge. "She's going to help me find a therapist. One I feel safe with. I need…I can't keep pushing all of this down. It's tearing me apart from the inside."

Relief washed through me, but something else was hot on its heels. Pride. My knuckles skimmed across Nova's cheek before I tangled my fingers in her hair. "That's my girl. So goddamn brave."

"Hold that praise until I actually make it to the office."

One corner of my mouth kicked up. "You'll make it."

She nodded, inhaling deeply. "I will. I'll make it. I'm going to head over to Aster's ranch this morning to talk to her. She had an idea about a type of therapy I might like, and she said she wanted to show me."

"I'm really glad you have her."

"Me, too," Nova whispered. "Thanks for walking with me through the darkness. For being the light when I need it."

My fingers twisted in her hair. "You're the same for me. And I think that's what it's all about. Being the light for each other when we've lost it. Life will never be perfect, but we can be here to remind each other that it's still beautiful."

Nova's eyes glistened. "I love you."

"I love you, too," I rasped. The words came so easily. The only one it had come easily with before Nova was Skylar. Even with my brothers and Waylon, it was a struggle to get them out. But with Nova? It was as easy as breathing.

"Are you guys going to kiss now?"

At the sound of Skylar's voice, Nova and I startled apart, as if we were two teenagers caught making out.

Shit. Apparently, she had been paying more attention than I thought. Sky had never seen me with a woman in a romantic situation before. Hell, it was only since Dex started helping Brae that she'd seen me with any women at all. And I wasn't sure how she'd react to the possibility of a woman entering my life as more than a friend.

I turned, studying my daughter. "What did you say?"

She looked supremely annoyed. "The prince is supposed to kiss the princess now, Daddy. I thought you paid better attention during movie night."

I practically gaped at my adorable daughter. It seemed she had no issue with someone becoming more than a friend to me. She was just annoyed at how slowly I was taking it.

Nova let out a soft snicker. "Yeah, Boss. I thought you paid better attention."

I sent the love of my goddamned life a scowl and crossed the distance to her in one long stride. I slid one arm around her waist while my other hand went to the back of her head to dip her. My mouth met Nova's as I tried to prove a point, but the second I tasted her, I lost all sense.

Mint from her toothpaste still clung to her, but there was something else. Something undeniably Nova. And I drank it in.

Skylar let out a hoot and a cheer as she danced around us.

When I straightened, I met Nova's dazed look. "How's that for paying attention?"

Nova sent me a slightly drunk smile. "A for effort, Boss."

Skylar's chattering had slowed as we got closer to school. I knew my kid, and I knew she was puzzling through something in her mind. Sometimes, the topics were heavy, like her mom. Other times, it was as simple as wondering why goats liked to headbutt each other. I always just waited.

I never wanted to rush Sky the way my father had rushed me when I was growing up. Even in the time before we found out the kind of monster he was, he was always busy, in a hurry. Important business meetings for his import/export business, calls, and things that didn't involve listening to us kids. But maybe what he was really doing was hurrying off to kill another woman with brown hair and green eyes.

"Daddy?"

"Yeah, Little Princess?" I asked, my gaze flicking to her through the rearview mirror as I turned on my blinker.

"Are you and Supernova boyfriend and girlfriend?"

My gut tightened. "I guess that's what you'd call it."

Just her asking had uncertainty filling me. Not about Nova and me—that felt rock-solid. But about the need to hide what we were. I couldn't ask Sky to do that. And I shouldn't have been asking Nova either.

I closed my eyes for the barest of seconds as I pulled to a stop in the drop-off line. Another time for me to cede control. Another stretch of what I could handle. I needed to hand off Travis's case to someone else.

Because knowing that I would handle it the best wasn't enough for me to make my family keep secrets. And it didn't mean I'd stop working it. Not really. Not when my brothers and I could keep investigating from the shadows.

Skylar's legs bounced against her booster seat. "What happens if you guys get married?"

A zing of energy zapped through me. Apprehension, nerves, fear, and…want. I wanted that. I never thought it would be in the cards for me, but I wanted Nova to be a part of our family in every way.

I put my truck in park and twisted around. "What do you mean?"

Sky's legs bounced faster now. "Like, would she maybe…be my mom?"

I saw it then, the hope burning brightly in Skylar's hazel eyes. She wanted that. Just like I did.

I reached out and took Skylar's tiny hand in mine. "Little Princess, it's usually a long wait before people get married. It takes time to get to know each other and make sure it's a good fit."

Sky glared at me. "Nova fits with us."

I had to fight a laugh because I agreed. "I think so, too. But we're still gonna take our time. I can tell you one thing I know for certain, though."

"What?" Skylar asked, annoyance still in her voice.

"She loves you with her whole heart."

A small smile tugged at Sky's lips. "I know she does. She plays with me, and she listens and always has the best voices when we play princess warrior battle games."

"It's the voices that are the most important, huh?" I asked, still fighting a laugh.

Skylar shook her head. "It's most important that I can be me with her. And she thinks I'm awesome."

God, I loved Nova. I loved my kid. I loved the way they loved each other. I was becoming a sentimental sap, and I didn't give a damn. "That is the most important."

"Daddy?"

"Yeah?"

"You gotta pull up. Everyone's waiting."

This time, I did bark out a laugh. It looked like our emo moment was over. Kids, man.

I helped Skylar out of the truck, making sure she had her backpack and lunch. But before I could even tell her I loved her, she was running toward Owen, who was waiting at the school doors. I was grateful she felt so confident. No fear. No worries. It was everything I'd ever wanted for her.

My phone rang, and I answered it as I climbed back behind the wheel. "Archer."

"It's Roger."

The tone of his voice had my blood running cold. "What is it?"

"Heidi Ingram. We found her."

Chapter Forty-Four

NOVA

Taking a deep breath, I looked around Moonridge Meadow Ranch. Aster's family's spread was absolutely breathtaking and an operation far greater than Waylon's smaller setup. But it had its own special energy.

I couldn't quite define it. A peacefulness that came from wide-open spaces surrounded by forests, maybe. The rolling hills where horses and cattle grazed. It calmed the soul.

The air was different, too. Pine with a crisp bite, thanks to the change in the weather, and the scent of horses. A couple of years ago, I wouldn't have thought I'd have liked that. But I found it oddly comforting. Earthy. Grounding.

"Nova," a familiar voice called.

I turned to see Aster striding toward me. She wore that same cowboy hat with the flat brim and colorful ribbon at the base.

"This is quite the operation," I said, gesturing to the massive horse barn, complete with stunning architectural finishes like exposed beams and expert arches. It even had chandeliers.

Her mouth curved, making those pale-blue eyes twinkle. "Granddad always says the horses deserve somewhere pretty to lay their heads."

"I can't argue with you there."

Aster's gaze roamed over my face, settling on my eyes. "How are you feeling?"

"I'm okay, really."

She arched a brow.

I couldn't help the laugh that escaped me. "All right. Normally, when I say that, it's a big fat lie. But right now, it's the truth. I'm okay. Some things are amazing. Other things are really freaking hard. But it's all sort of evening out, making me feel like I can make it through."

"You will," Aster vowed. "And it's good to mark the amazing stuff. Helps us walk through the rest."

"I'm starting to see that."

She glanced toward what looked like some sort of ring where half a dozen horses were tied to the inside of the fence at different intervals. "I'm glad you wanted to come early. I think you might like this."

Nerves bubbled up from somewhere deep, but I kept breathing.

"My friend and colleague, Marly, works in a special discipline called equine therapy. She actually trained me in it," Aster began.

She inclined her head toward a woman in a curved cowboy hat with wild gray hair that hung around her. She moved with some combination of confidence and gentleness that spoke to me.

"Therapy with horses?" I asked.

"That's it. Sometimes, having your focus on something other than simply sitting and talking helps the process. And honestly, I think horses have a healing magic of their own, something no human can bring to the table."

That was something I valued about Aster—that she talked to me about the process. Explained what would happen. During my therapy experience in the past, it felt like the doctor was constantly trying to trick me into opening up. Aster made me feel like maybe I could be on the same team as a therapist.

"Think maybe you'd like to meet Marly and take part today? It'll give you a feel for things, see if this modality might be right for you," Aster suggested.

Those nerves amplified. "I can't do just one with you?" The idea of opening up to someone new had my stomach cramping.

Aster's expression was full of understanding. "We're friends, Nova. At least, I hope we are. And that means I can't be your therapist. But I will always be your friend. I'll listen, and I'll be here. I'll help you find someone who is the exact right fit to walk you through this on the therapeutic side."

"Okay," I rasped. "Thank you."

"I'm with you all the way. Whatever you need."

And that was a comfort. Because I believed her.

The woman with the gray hair and smile lines around her eyes approached.

"Marly, this is my friend Nova. Nova, this is my friend, Marly."

The older woman smiled, and it came easily, just as I'd expected it would. Nothing about it was forced or too big. "It's nice to meet you, Nova. Aster said you might want to join our group today."

I swallowed hard. "Nice to meet you, too. I think I'd like to…try."

"That's all any of us can do," Marly said sagely.

I kept breathing. "They're beautiful," I admitted, taking in the six horses. There were a variety of colors. I recognized the brown and white patchwork one that Aster had been riding the day Maverick and I had run into her on the trail. There was a black horse with a white stripe down its nose. A brown one with a little white patch between its eyes. A reddish-brown one. Another that looked like the horse equivalent of a blonde. And the one standing farthest away was a deep gray, kind of like my eyes but with a freckled swath over its rump.

"Is there one calling to you?" Marly asked.

My gaze flicked to her. "Calling to me?"

She shrugged easily. "You might think I'm a little woo-woo, and that's okay, but I think there's something spiritual between horses and people. Maybe horses and everything around them. When we open ourselves to it, it creates a connection that can heal."

I took a deep breath. I remembered feeling that way from yoga. Before. Before everything fell apart. But even then, I didn't let it in deep. Maybe because I was already carrying so many wounds. I'd basically raised myself, my parents not giving a damn and making it clear. I'd been on my own at such a young age, and it was terrifying.

But now, it was time. To dig deep. To heal the things that were harming me so I didn't bring them into this new chance at life.

I stared at the horses, letting my gaze hover over each one and opening myself to whatever I might feel. My gaze kept landing on the gray the longest. Something about the horse tugged at me.

"The gray one," I croaked.

Aster smiled, genuine pleasure moving across her face. "Twilight. That's her name. She's an Appaloosa mare. And she's a tough judge of character."

A chuckle left my lips. "Of course, I'd choose the picky bitch. It's only fitting."

"Takes one to know one," Aster teased as Marly chuckled.

"You know it." But a hint of excitement filled me.

"Hey," a deep voice greeted.

Something about it was familiar, and I turned to see Jack, the man from the Compass meeting—the one who'd lost his wife to Travis's reign of terror.

I forced a smile, even though it wavered. "Hi, Jack."

His gaze stayed on my face as he frowned slightly. "You okay?" When I didn't answer right away, he went on. "Was at the Boot when Wylder got the call that you were missing."

Great. I couldn't wait for my coworkers' reactions about that. "Just a little mountain biking mishap. My sense of direction isn't so great."

"You need to be careful," he said, making an effort to gentle his voice. "With everything going on..."

I did *not* need that reminder, but I knew it came from a place of care, so I simply nodded. "I will. I think I'm going to stay off the mountain biking trails for a while."

"Smart," he said gruffly.

"Okay," Marly cut in. "I think it's about time."

A wave of excitement and nerves swept through me, but it was a lot better than the dread I'd felt before my past therapy appointments. I followed Marly toward the ring, but Jack stuck close, as if he were keeping an eye on me.

Shit.

I could only imagine what I represented to him, someone who had made it out of the torture his wife hadn't. Me getting lost probably stirred all that up.

We headed toward a group of three other people who'd clustered near the ring. I didn't recognize any of them. There was a man who looked to be in his sixties, with gray hair and a mustache. A woman in her fifties, with brown hair swept up into a ponytail. And finally, a younger woman, probably about my age, with hair that was a mix of light brown and blond.

"Hello, everyone," Marly greeted. "I'd like you to meet Nova. She's joining us today."

There was a smattering of hellos.

"Nova, you obviously already know Jack. This is Eddie, Gena, and Livie." Marly introduced the group in age order, from the oldest to the youngest.

"Nice to meet you." I gripped my hands in front of me to keep them from trembling.

The youngest woman, Livie, sent me a kind smile, and something about her was familiar. "First time doing equine therapy?"

I nodded. "That obvious?"

"I recognize the nerves. It's pretty amazing, and that's coming from someone who was terrified of horses before this."

Marly laughed. "And look at you now. You even went on a trail ride with Aster last week."

Livie flicked her hair over her shoulder in a dramatic move meant for humor. "I think I've earned the cowboy hat I have my eye on at that secondhand shop in town."

"Girl, snap it up," Gena said, her brown eyes sparkling.

A low ringing sound cut into the conversation, and Livie pulled out her phone, frowning. "Olivia Bishop," she answered. Her frown only deepened. "I'll be there in about fifteen."

"Work?" Marly inquired sympathetically.

"Always," Livie grumbled. "I'll be back next week." She glanced at me. "Nice to meet you, Nova."

As she headed to her car, I wondered if she was an on-call doctor or a nurse or something else.

"All right," Marly said. "Let's begin. I'll assign your horses."

I made my way into the ring and toward Twilight, getting close but not within kicking or biting range. I could hear Aster giving the rest of the group instructions, but I couldn't take my eyes off the mare.

She was beautiful, but her eyes were haunted in a way I recognized. Like I saw in the mirror every single morning.

Marly moved in next to me. "First time around horses?"

"I think I did a pony ride when I was nine," I admitted. "The handlers led us around a ring at a carnival." One Brae's parents had taken me to—never mine.

"You can take your time," Marly assured me. "There's no rush. This is all about discovery—of her and of you. There's no wrong lesson. But caring for her will teach you things about how you care for yourself and how others have cared for you throughout your life."

My lips pressed together, but I nodded.

"Twilight is the best of them. She came to Aster through a rescue organization," Marly went on.

My focus switched from the horse to Marly, because I'd been right about those haunted eyes.

"An abuse situation. Aster said it took her a good long while to start to trust, and they're still finding their way." Marly moved toward the horse. She stroked the mare's neck and dropped her forehead to Twilight's. "But she's getting there. Aren't you, girl?"

The horse blew out a breath between her lips.

"That's right." Marly scratched under her chin. "The main things when starting out are: no quick movements and keep your palm flat when you come up to her mouth." Marly demonstrated, the mare lipping at her open palm. "She wants a treat."

"I would, too."

"Want to try giving her a pet?"

I did, but anxiety stirred, that familiar buzz lighting in my muscles along with the urge to bolt.

"There's no rush," Marly encouraged.

"I want to," I croaked, taking a step closer.

Marly shifted so she was standing by the horse's neck. "I'm right here. Why don't you start out by letting her scent you? Hold out your hand like I did."

Painfully slowly, I stretched out a hand. There was no missing that it shook, but I kept it out anyway.

Twilight sniffed twice, then lipped my hand. Her whiskers tickled my palm, and I let out the last sound I expected—a laugh.

Marly placed a hand on the mare's neck. "You can stroke her cheek or her face, scratch between her ears. She likes that."

I lifted my hand slowly, gently setting it against her cheek. The horse moved closer, startling me back a step. My throat burned.

"Talk me through what happened just then."

"She moved too fast and…"

"And?" Marly pressed.

"I thought she was going to bite me." The burn in my throat spread behind my eyes. "I thought she was going to bite me because I'm always waiting for the bite. The slap. The hurt. The pain."

It was what I'd known for so long. Way before Travis. He'd only cemented the fear.

"But not everyone or everything will bite. Not everyone or everything will hurt," Marly said softly.

"No. They won't." Kol didn't. Neither did Brae. Or Owen. Or Skylar. Or the whole new world I was building.

"So," Marly continued, "we're cautious, but we let people show us who they are. We don't rush it. But we don't assume, either."

I took a step back toward Twilight. "Sorry, girl," I whispered.

"Sometimes, I think the worst." I slowly lifted my hand again and stroked her cheek.

The horse stretched out her neck and pulled part of my jacket between her lips.

A giggle left me. "There aren't any carrots in there."

She blew out a breath through her nose as she released my coat.

Gathering my bravery, I raised my other hand, ghosting it over her forehead. Twilight pressed into my touch, a silent request for more. So I gave it to her. Stroke after stroke until we found our rhythm.

"It's quite a give and take," Marly whispered. "We just have to be still enough to see the signs."

My chest ached, but it was the beautiful kind. If this gorgeous creature had found a way to trust again, maybe I could, too.

Chapter Forty-Five

KOL

I GROUND MY BACK TEETH TOGETHER, STRUGGLING FOR composure. I knew the only tell was a slight fluttering in my cheek or the divot formed by the strain in my jaw. We all had our coping mechanisms. I was pretty sure mine would end in me needing half a dozen root canals before I retired.

But I needed to bite down or I'd lose it completely. Because the woman who lay sprawled in the middle of the campsite she'd disappeared from had so much life left to live. Instead, she was here. Far too pale for any chance at that life, her body riddled with too many stab wounds to count and bruises ringing her neck.

Heidi Ingram.

There was no question it was her. You could barely make out the color of her eyes now that they had clouded over, but there was no denying the dark-brown hair. The slope of her nose.

"Identity confirmation," Livie said, looking up from the tablet, where she'd just scanned in a print from the dead woman's finger.

"Fucking hell," Roger swore, dragging a hand through his disheveled hair. "How long?"

That second question was directed at the medical examiner, a man in his late forties, who had been with the county for years. Dr. Dominguez looked up from where the temperature gauge was still getting a reading from Heidi's body. "I won't know for sure until I've done my complete exam."

He was always thorough. The best we had.

"Ballpark it if you can, Doc," Roger pressed.

Dominguez frowned.

"Jesus," Pete muttered next to me. "We're just looking for something so we get on this asshole's trail. We're not asking you to testify."

Pete just had to be a prick about it.

Dominguez ignored the asshole next to me and looked at Roger. "I think a safe window would be sometime between midnight and four this morning. She hasn't been dead that long."

Somehow, that made it worse, when you knew you were close yet way too fucking late.

Quiet reigned over us. Because we all felt that weight of the near miss.

Roger laced his hands behind his head, straining. "Okay, we've got a window. Livie, anything?"

The forensic tech had obviously been called in while off-duty. She wore civilian clothes instead of her usual uniform, and her mouth was pressed into a hard line. "We need to print the body. I'll work the scene, but so far—wait." She moved, crouching low. "Dr. Dominguez, can you roll her, just a bit?"

"Crime scene photos are done?" the ME asked.

"Yes," she assured him.

Dr. Dominguez lifted Heidi's body ever so slightly. There was something beneath her, and Livie's sharp eyes had spotted it. A piece of paper.

Livie quickly took a couple of photos before picking up the paper with gloved hands. We all moved in around her, trying to see.

The page was smudged with dirt and smeared with blood in places, but none of that meant we couldn't read the message.

IT'S NOT OVER. IT'LL NEVER BE OVER.

Every part of me ran cold. The letters were less controlled now. More chaotic. Angry slashes of black against the dirty white paper. Another sign of escalation, like all the rest.

Livie moved, taking another photo and then placing the sheet into an evidence bag.

Pete's eye lit up, almost like a kid at Christmas. "This is it. We've got another serial."

"We've got one fuckin' case," Roger snarled. "And stop acting like you just won the lotto. A woman's dead."

Pete's mouth snapped shut, but anger swept across his expression. He glared at Roger before stomping off to talk to a deputy.

Roger watched him go, shaking his head. "What the hell is wrong with him?"

I didn't look at Pete. He was the last person I wanted to see at the moment. "He's never experienced real loss or even the threat of it."

A look of confusion overtook Roger's face.

"When you don't know what loss truly feels like or how it invades every part of your life, it's not real. It's like a TV show or a movie. For him, it's exciting."

"Well, he's a world-class prick."

I scrubbed a hand over my face. "I don't disagree there. And at some point, karma's gonna kick his ass. It has to."

"I'll just be holding my breath until then," Roger muttered.

We both watched as Dr. Dominguez and his assistant prepped Heidi Ingram for transport. The weight of that hung heavy in the air for both of us. Especially the fact that Roger would have to go to the family after this and tell them that their only daughter would never be coming home.

"Fuck," he swore.

I clapped a hand on his shoulder, squeezing before I released. "Want to run it through?"

"Yes."

The single word was clipped and angry, but I knew the anger wasn't directed at me.

"Most likely scenario is we've got a copycat, someone obsessed with the original case. I think we need to talk to Reese Gatlin again." That reporter had always seemed like a supreme asshole. Only time would tell if he was an asshole with darker tendencies.

"Or it could be someone who had those dormant urges and seeing what Travis did woke them up. Inspired them," Roger suggested.

He had a point. If someone had the desire to kill but hadn't acted on it yet, seeing someone else do it could've kicked them off.

"There's one other possibility we're not talking about." My voice was low because I didn't want to say it. Didn't want to even think it. And neither did Roger.

Roger scrubbed a hand over his face. "We never found his body."

The last thing I wanted to think was that Travis was alive, that he had somehow survived the shooting and the fall and was still out there…hunting.

Tension wove its way through my body, knitting my ribs so tight it was hard to breathe. I reached for my phone on instinct, typing out a text.

Me: *Keep an eye on Nova. She goes nowhere alone.*

My brother's response was almost instant.

Wylder: *What happened?*

I shouldn't tell him. It was against protocol. But apparently, I was breaking all the rules these days.

Me: *We found Heidi Ingram.*

Wylder: *fuck*

That pretty much summed it up.

Wylder: *I'll keep eyes on her. You coming in?*

Me: *After I finish up at the scene.*

Wylder: *Be careful.*

Me: *Always am.*

I shoved my phone back into my pocket.

"Nova?" Roger asked knowingly.

Fucking hell. I needed to work on my poker face.

"I wanted Wylder to keep a close eye on her. Gonna have to figure out a system so she's not alone."

Roger studied me for a long moment as if peeling back the layers of my mask. He was usually lighthearted and carefree, on the Mav side of the aisle in terms of living life. But it disguised deep waters. Roger knew how to analyze people when he wanted to. And he was damn smart.

"It serious?"

I exhaled, the air hissing through my teeth. "I love her."

He whistled. "That complicates things."

"Gonna talk to Sherri today. I have to pass the case off."

Roger's brows pulled together in a supremely pissed-off look. "Do not leave me with that prick."

"She won't reassign it just to Pete. There has to be a more senior agent involved."

"If I wasn't so goddamned happy for you, I'd be seriously ticked."

I let out a low chuckle. "Happy to know you care."

One corner of Roger's mouth kicked up. "Been wondering about those bracelets you've been wearing. Thought maybe you just had a thing for pink and purple glitter."

I scowled at my friend as my fingers went instinctively to my wrist, to the bracelets that Sky had made in that time when Nova had been keeping her distance. They'd started to feel like a touchstone, something that made me feel close to her even when we were apart. And not just that. They felt like a way to honor our bond. "If you're not down to rock pink and purple glitter, you're missing out."

He let out a low chuckle. "I'll keep that in mind." The humor on his face dropped away. "Take care of her. She's been through a lot."

"Nova's stronger than anyone knows. But I'm also going to have her back, no matter what." Just saying the words made me twitchy. I wanted to get to Nova. To feel her against me. To be sure she was okay.

But I also had to tell her that another woman was dead. And that the monster of her nightmares might still be here in the waking world.

Chapter Forty-Six

NOVA

I FELT...LIGHTER. MAYBE IT WAS THE COMBINATION OF sunshine, fresh air, and letting go. Maybe it was the magic of horses, just like Aster had said. But for the first time in a while, I was hopeful that I could find the healing I needed.

Crossing the bar floor, I grabbed the watering can we stashed behind the hostess stand. Wylder changed out the planters he kept out front depending on the season, and we were in the fall mums era. And while the weather had gotten colder, they still needed water now and then.

"Where are you going?" Cora asked, her gaze flicking back to the bar, where Wylder was talking to a distributor.

I frowned at her, holding up the watering can. "To tap dance on the moon. I'm going to water the mums."

Cora sent another look in Wylder's direction. I saw it then... nerves. Her fingers fluttered at her sides, and her gaze was jumpy. "I'll come with you."

"Are you okay?" I asked gently.

"What?" Her gaze snapped back to me. "Oh yeah, I'm fine. I just thought fresh air might be good."

"All right..." I started for the front door. Maybe she needed to talk, away from prying eyes and ears.

Cora held the door for me but scanned the sidewalk and street. I wasn't sure what she was expecting to find, but everything looked... normal. Fall was certainly quieter in Starlight Grove—not as many tourists and no packed streets—but that didn't mean it was dead. People milled around, going about their usual business.

I saw the two women who'd been nosy on my first day at the Boot coming out of the Yarn Barn. Waylon's friend Blaze stepped out of the Cozy Cup, wearing rainbow-heart sunglasses and holding a to-go bag. More faces I didn't recognize milled around. It was just...normal. And God, I needed that.

Going to the first planter made from a water trough, I gave the blooms a healthy drink. As I moved along, my gaze flicked to Cora, who was still on alert. "Can I ask you something?"

She startled. "Me?"

I nodded.

"Sure."

I shifted to refill the can from a small hidden tap. "Are you still going to therapy?"

Cora stared at me for a second. "That wasn't what I was expecting you to ask."

My mouth curved. "What did you think I was going to ask?"

"Oh, I don't know. Where I got this fabulous shirt?"

She gestured to her Boot T-shirt.

I chuckled before starting in on the other planter. "I just...I did a workshop with Aster's friend Marly this morning."

"Equine therapy?"

"Yeah. And it was...surprising. I always hated going to see the doctor at the hospital. It felt so invasive. Like he was trying to break into my mind."

The corners of Cora's mouth pulled down in a frown. "I'm sorry it felt like that."

I shook my head. "It's okay. I know he was trying to help. It's just…we didn't fit. But I think this, the horse therapy, might help. I think I'm finally ready."

Cora tugged her lip between her teeth before speaking. "I stopped going."

"To therapy?"

"Yeah. I just…" Her eyes began to glisten with unshed tears. "I can't keep talking about him. It's too hard. I know everyone thinks I should hate him, but I can't."

Empathy washed through me, and I set the watering can down to cross to Cora. I reached out and took her hands, squeezing. "You loved him for half your life. Of course, you can't. Those feelings don't just magically disappear overnight."

Cora sniffed, trying to pull her emotions back. "I just…I miss him. I'm so mad at him, but I miss him. The *him* that was just for me."

I gave her hands another squeeze. "Also normal. It's going to take time to reconcile all the things Travis was."

"I guess you're right…" Cora's eyes shot to mine. "Wait, you're touching me."

I hadn't even realized I was doing it. It was just instinct. Wanting to comfort a friend who was hurting. "I guess I am," I said with a small smile.

"Big step," Cora whispered.

I swallowed hard. "I'm starting to remember some things. And as hard as it is, I think it's helping."

Cora's eyes went wide, and she opened her mouth to say something, but a voice interrupted.

"Now isn't this sweet?" Reese said as he strode up. "My readers will love knowing how you two have bonded."

Cora instantly tugged her hands from mine, whirling around, her green eyes blazing with pure fire. "Get the hell away from here. Away from us."

One corner of Reese's mouth tugged up. "I'm just trying to tell the truth, and this sidewalk is public property, so I'm well within my rights."

"You're not telling the truth. You're profiting off people's pain. And if the universe has any justice, you'll know exactly how it feels to lose everything," Cora snarled.

"Come on," I said, my voice low. "He wants a reaction. He's trying to provoke us into saying something." But I let my mask slip. I let all the rage and hurt show because Reese Gatlin should have to see what he was stirring up.

I thought I saw a quick intake of breath as I tugged Cora toward the entrance of the Boot, but Reese quickly covered it and doubled down. "I heard they found a body at Aspen Falls near Three Creeks Canyon Trail. Heard it was a woman, too. Any comment about a new monster out there?"

All the blood drained from my body. Dizziness crashed over me in waves, but I still managed to get myself and Cora inside. I threw the lock on the door on instinct.

Wylder was already striding across the space. "What happened? What's wrong?"

It was Cora who spoke, her voice shaking as she did. "They found a body. A woman. Near Three Creeks."

Wylder moved then, wrapping an arm around Cora's shoulders. I saw the war on her face, not wanting to give in to the comfort but needing it so desperately. Finally, she turned into him, pressing her face to his shoulder.

Wylder's gaze cut to me. "Kol's on his way."

That's when I understood. Wylder had already known. I wasn't sure what he'd told Cora—maybe just to stick together because something was up—but that's why she'd come outside with me. Because she was a good friend. And it had gotten her emotionally annihilated.

The dizziness ebbed as pure fury took its place. When would enough be enough? I'd already been kidnapped, held captive, tortured, and tormented. But still, the universe demanded more. And the fact that Reese Gatlin was helping it along only pissed me off more.

A shadowy figure appeared in the far hallway, and I braced. If it was Reese, I was going to knee him in the junk so hard it burst his goddamned balls.

But it wasn't Reese.

It was my avenging angel. And I saw the same pissed-off fury on his face that I felt on mine. Kol scanned the sight in front of him. Wylder and Cora. Me. That fury went even more on alert. "What. Happened?"

"Reese," I gritted out.

"He told them," Wylder explained.

Kol swore, his gaze finding mine. "I wanted you to hear it from me."

I understood that, but the weight shouldn't have had to fall on his shoulders alone. Always the one to level me with a gut punch. "I'm glad it wasn't you," I said softly.

A look of hurt flashed on Kol's face, but it quickly transformed into one of understanding. "Phoenix."

I went to him then. His arms opened, and I fell against him. Those strong arms wrapped around me, and I knew the feeling of safety I only got with Kol. I trusted that I'd feel that safety all the time one day. That someday, I wouldn't just feel free with Kol but everywhere and always.

His lips ghosted over my temple. "We're going to figure this out."

"I know." Because there was no other way. "I'm going to keep fighting."

"That's my girl," Kol whispered. "But we need to take some precautions."

"Okay. But I'm not letting another monster win." And that meant I would keep living. I was going to keep working. I was going to keep going to therapy. I was going to play princess warrior battle with Sky. I was going to game with Owen. I was going to have family dinners with the Archers.

Kol shifted, peering down at me. "Never alone, okay? Someone drives you to and from work. You're not at the house alone. We're careful."

My brows pulled together. "You think whoever this is will come after me?" A shiver skated down my spine.

"You already got the necklace, the notes."

That was a long way from trying to kill me. "What aren't you telling me?"

Kol's thumb stroked across my cheekbone. "A couple of possibilities. Copycat or someone inspired by the things Travis did."

"Or?" I pressed, sensing there was more to the story.

Kol's gaze flicked to where Cora and Wylder stood. Cora had pulled out of Wylder's hold. Her arms were curled around herself now, as if she was trying to be her own comfort. I could see the battle in Wylder's eyes. He wanted to go to her so badly, but he knew it had to be her choice.

Kol turned back to me, searching. "We never found Travis's body."

A jolt of lightning speared through me. Pain and panic. *"No one's looking for you. No one cares."* All that darkness.

Dizziness swept over me, but I fought it off. I fought it off, and I found Kol's eyes. My light and dark. My safe place. "It could be him." I said the words Kol wouldn't.

I felt the battle for restraint surging in him, his struggle to keep his hold on me gentle. "I don't know," he growled. "But no one is going to hurt you, Phoenix. Never again."

Chapter Forty-Seven

KOL

I watched as they played: Skylar, Owen, Brae, and Nova. Their outfits were completely ridiculous, a mix of superhero fare, combat gear, princess costumes, and what I was pretty sure was a milking bucket for one of the goats that was currently being used as a helmet. Nova had even added a full ballgown to her repertoire.

But seeing them like this? It helped. It also made the idea of a monster hunting and killing women seem impossible. How could there be that kind of evil when there was this kind of light?

"I want to ask how you're doing, but I know that's a completely ridiculous question," Dex said from his spot next to me on the deck steps, where he was sipping one of those energy drinks that likely corroded his insides.

Usually, on a day like today, where we could enjoy the last bit of fall warmth, we'd crack a beer. Not today. Neither of us. Because we needed to be on alert from now until this thing was over. Nothing would be consumed that could dull our senses.

"I love her," I rasped. "I love her, and I don't know how to keep her safe. That absolutely kills me."

"We keep her safe together," Dex vowed. And he'd already lived up to that promise. He'd spent the last two hours beefing up my security system and checking everything that was already in place.

"Thank you. For doing this. For being here."

Dex clamped a hand on my shoulder and squeezed. "You did the same for me. You walked with me in the darkness and helped me find the other side."

"I'll do it anytime you need me."

"I know. And we're damn lucky that we have that from all our brothers."

Dex was right. Even though we each had different strengths and capacities, we all showed up. Even Orion.

As if I'd conjured him by thinking his name, our most surly brother rounded the house, carrying something.

"Is that a cake dish?" Dex asked, struggling to keep the laughter from his tone.

"Pretty sure it is," I muttered.

"And he's bringing it in person. One might almost think he *likes* Nova."

Orion set it on the corner of the deck, beginning to sign. *"For Nova. I'm working on a new map. Trying to find where he was keeping Heidi."*

"Thank you," I said, making the sign with it.

Orion's gaze, the one just a few shades darker than the rest of ours, surveyed the chaos on the back lawn. He watched as the kids screamed and howled with laughter, as Brae dove for Owen and tickled his sides.

"I got you," Nova yelled, lifting Sky into the air and then landing her on the dog pile of Owen and Brae.

"Death by squish," Owen called, adding in some truly gruesome sound effects.

I thought I saw a hint of a smile on Orion's face. Only for a moment. And then it was back to stoic nothingness. He turned back to me, lifting his hands again. *"Watch her back. She's good for you."*

"Jesus," Dex muttered, signing as he spoke. "That might as well be Rion giving you the family heirloom ring."

We all made an effort to sign. Anything to make Orion feel less different, less *other*.

Orion flipped him off, and it only made Dex laugh.

"Mr. Orion! Mr. Orion!" Owen called as he ran over. "I'm learning to talk with my hands. Look!" He raised his hands, moving through signs a little clumsily as he spoke. "Hi. I like your maps. And your cake." The signing stopped as he took in the plate. "Dude, another chocolate? That's bussin'."

Orion frowned.

"He means it's awesome," Dex translated.

Orion stared at Owen for a moment and then just nodded before turning to go.

Owen grinned. "I got a nod. That means he likes me."

I couldn't help it. I laughed. "You know him well."

Nova crossed to me, sliding into my lap and wrapping her arms around my neck. "I don't know, Orion made me cupcakes, so I think I'm his favorite."

"He made you this full cake, too," Dex added.

She grinned. "Total favorite status."

"I could make you cake," I said, suddenly defensive.

Nova pressed her lips together to keep from laughing. "You could, but have you?"

"Brutal," Dex said with a grin.

An alert sounded on my phone, and I swiped it off the deck, opening the camera app for the gate.

"Sherri?" Nova asked as if she could feel my tension.

"Yeah." I hit the *open* button so my boss could get onto ranch property.

Nova pulled back, searching my face. "You're sure about this?"

I stared up at her. "I'm sure. I don't want to have to hide this. I don't want our beginning to be full of lies."

"I love you," she whispered.

"I love you, too."

"Kiss! Kiss! Kiss!" Sky chanted.

Nova grinned, lowering her face to mine.

I kissed her, not letting it get too deep but taking my time, letting her taste soothe me.

"Siiiiiiiiick," Owen moaned. "And not a good sick, Mr. Kol."

Nova grinned against my mouth. "We win. We grossed the tiny human out."

I chuckled. "No better victory."

A door slammed, and Nova straightened, pushing off my lap. "How about afternoon ice cream sundaes?"

The roar of cheers from the two kids and Dex was deafening as they raced into the house with Nova. Brae just shook her head, but as she walked up the steps to follow them inside, her hand dropped to my shoulder.

I looked up at her in question.

"Thank you," she whispered.

My brows pulled together. "For what?"

"For taking care of my best friend, my sister. For loving her. For making her happy."

My throat constricted. "She does the same for me."

"That's how it should be. But it isn't always. I love that you two found the good."

It was the seal of approval from the only family Nova really had. And it meant something.

"Gonna ask her to marry me. When she's ready, I'm gonna ask her."

Brae's mouth curved. "You asking for my permission?"

"Not permission, but a blessing would be nice."

"You've got it, Kol. I don't think anyone has ever seen her more. Not even me. And that's a gift, too."

I swallowed against the lump in my throat. "It is."

Brae's hand left my shoulder just as Sherri rounded the house. My boss scanned the landscape in front of us. "Forgot how beautiful it is out here."

"Not a bad place to sit, that's for sure," I said.

She settled next to me on the steps, still looking out at the horizon. "Please tell me you aren't quitting."

"I'm not quitting."

"Thank fuck," she muttered.

"You know me better than that. This job is in my bones."

Sherri turned, taking me in. "What is it, then? You don't usually call me out here for clandestine meetings."

"Didn't want to leave Nova," I admitted.

She stiffened. "Kol…"

"That's why I called the meeting. I need you to reassign Nova's case to another senior officer."

Sherri's jaw went slack. And I understood why. In my fifteen years with the Forest Service, I'd never once asked for a case to be reassigned.

"I fell in love with her."

"Well, shit," Sherri said, letting out a sigh. "I knew there might be a personal connection, but I didn't go to love. Kol, I don't think I've ever even known you to go on a date."

I barked out a laugh. "I don't think I have since high school."

"Jesus, go big or go home, huh?"

"I guess so."

Sherri drummed her fingers against her knees. "You're the best I've got."

"That means something coming from an investigator I admire so much."

She sent me a perturbed look. "Don't think that gets you out of me being pissed at you."

I held up both hands. "Never."

"How's Pete doing on the case?"

I stayed silent.

"Damn it, Kol. All my other senior officers have other big cases."

"Pete's not ready. Maybe he will be one day. Maybe he won't. But he needs a senior agent who's going to respect the case as more than some exciting new adventure."

"Bloodthirsty," Sherri mumbled.

"That would be accurate."

She sighed again. "Can you give me a few more days to shuffle some things? Just make sure you have a second with you on all investigative stuff. Just in case anyone ever calls anything into question. These two cases are at the very least tied together."

I knew what she meant. I needed to have someone who could back me should this ever go to trial. Because someone was still out there hurting women. Killing them. "Not a problem. Roger's got his department running better now, and he's been on top of the Heidi Ingram case."

"Good," Sherri said. "We may even be able to let them take over as local primary on Travis Moore with us as support."

"That works for me."

Roger was a good investigator and an even better man. He'd take the case seriously and put in his best work.

Sherri leaned back on her palms. "In love, huh?"

I chuckled. "I'm afraid so."

She whistled. "Last thing I was expecting."

"You and me both."

Her lips twitched. "When do I get to meet her?"

"How about now?" I asked. "We're having afternoon ice cream sundaes."

Sherri straightened. "I like ice cream."

I grinned, pushing to my feet and offering her a hand. "Let's do this."

As we walked into the chaos of the kitchen, with its mess of chocolate sauce, sprinkles, and whipped cream, I took it all in and really let it land. This was what life was about. Finding happiness amid the heartache and holding tight.

But as I let that land, fear made a home in my chest, too. Because when you had this much good, you had so much more to lose.

Chapter Forty-Eight

NOVA

"Supernova, can we eat outside together, just you and me?"

Skylar asked the question the second my foot hit the bottom stair. I froze. Was I in trouble? She bounced up and down on the balls of her feet. She seemed…excited. So that had to mean no trouble, right?

"I'd love to eat with you." I glanced into the kitchen, where Kol was pouring a cup of coffee. "But don't you think we should ask your dad, too? He might feel left out."

Sky shook her head. "We need girl time. He gets it."

I struggled not to laugh. Wise beyond her years. "Well, I think we'll also need blankets. It's cold outside."

It had been a week since Heidi Ingram had been found, and the temperature had dropped significantly since then. It had also been a week since I'd had my breakthrough. And I hadn't fallen back on my promise.

I'd seen my new therapist almost every single day. Marly Cooper wasn't anything like I'd expected. She always came to our sessions in jeans, work boots, and a barn jacket. And she never pushed. While she had a take-no-shit attitude, she was as gentle as could be with the horses and with me.

It wasn't a magic bullet, but more was coming back to me. I wouldn't lie, the remembering hurt. Even the patchwork of tiny flickers was agonizing. But I knew it was the path through. It didn't matter that each session zapped every last ounce of energy I had. It was worth it.

"I got those, too. Come ooooooon, Supernova. We've got granola sundaes, too," she urged.

"Well, I can never say no to you and sundaes."

That had her beaming and rushing for the back door. I followed but paused by Kol as he handed me a cup of coffee and brushed a kiss to my temple.

"Tell me the truth, Boss. Am I about to get grounded?" I asked.

He chuckled. "I think she just wants some time for the two of you. I've been cramping her style lately."

I gave him a quick kiss and grinned. "I like being the favorite."

"Hey," he protested.

But I just grabbed the two blankets and hurried outside with my coffee. Skylar was already settling in on the back steps. I wrapped a blanket around her and then sat down next to her, our display of breakfast sundaes between us.

"These look delicious," I said, picking mine up.

"Don't worry. I gave you extra chocolate chips."

"I knew I liked you."

She giggled and then went quiet, staring out at the rolling fields. I gave her time, sensing there was something she wanted to broach. While I waited, I took in the scene in front of us. Everything about it was stunning: the golden, rolling hills of fall, the alpacas and horses in the distance…

I could imagine watching all four seasons from this exact spot. Each one would have its own unique beauty.

"You love me for real, right?" Sky asked softly.

My gaze cut to her in an instant. "For the realest. You and Owen are the two coolest kids I know. Sky, you're kind and funny. You make every single day an adventure. You see the people around you and make them feel special. There's not one thing about you that I don't love."

Breath left her in a whoosh. "That's what I thought."

Everything inside me warmed. But still, something niggled. "Is there a reason you wanted to make sure?"

Skylar worried her bottom lip. "My mom didn't love me. And I just wanted to make sure, in case you and Daddy ever get married, that you'll love me. I was sure you did, and then I just…I…"

"A little voice made you wonder?" I asked gently.

She nodded. "It's silly. You show me all the time."

God, I wanted to get this right. It was one of those moments that mattered. And I wanted to show up for Skylar in exactly the right way. In the way that my mom never had.

"Sky, can I tell you something?"

"Anything."

I took a deep breath, hoping Kol would understand why I shared, hoping that it was the right thing to do. "My mom didn't love me. At least, I didn't feel it. She didn't take care of me or show up how I needed her to or any of that. And sometimes, it makes it hard for me to say those words. Because I get scared."

Skylar's eyes, so similar to Kol's, went wide. "*You* get scared? But you're so brave."

"Just because you're brave doesn't mean you're not scared."

She thought about that for a moment. "I guess that's true." Her gaze met mine. "I'm sorry your mom wasn't the best, too."

"You know what I realized?"

"What?"

"She gave me what she could. And I bet your mom did, too. In fact, she did the best thing ever. She gave you to your dad, who loves you so much, I can see it every time he looks at you."

Sky's lower lip trembled just a little. "You see it?"

My heart cracked. "I do."

"What does it look like?"

"It looks like a million sparkles all around the two of you."

"I like sparkles," Skylar said quietly.

"Me, too."

She was quiet again for a moment, seeming to puzzle through something else. "You know, I think I'm glad she left."

"How come?" I asked, trying not to show any judgment about how Sky was feeling.

"Because she left room for you."

It took everything in me not to let my tears flow. But I battled them back. "Sky?"

"Yeah?"

"Can I hug you now?"

She didn't wait to answer. She didn't even answer with words. She just threw herself at me. And that hug was *everything*.

"You know," I began, leaning forward and resting my elbows on the SUV's console as I looked between Brae and Dex. "I could really get used to this chauffeur service. Door to door. No money wasted on gas. Yeti snuggles."

The massive dog yipped as if to agree with me.

Dex chuckled as he pulled to a stop outside the Boot. "Happy to be of service."

"I think I'm going to get you a chauffeur's cap and have Sky help me bedazzle it," I went on, sending Brae into a fit of giggles.

A surly glare hit me in the rearview mirror, all amusement vanishing. "Don't even think about it."

"Come on. It's gonna be a vibe," I argued.

"Yeah, Buttercup," Brae cajoled. "I think you're gonna look real cute in pink sparkles."

"You two together are dangerous," Dex muttered.

I grinned at my bestie. Things had been really good between us. We'd even had a girls' night, where we'd had a few glasses of wine and tipsily drawn plans for a she shed between Kol's property and Dex's. But more than that, we were finding our rhythm again.

"Don't mess with double trouble," Brae said, grinning at her fiancé.

A smile tugged at my lips in answer. "He's just lucky he didn't get the Brady Silverton treatment."

"I'm scared to ask," Dex muttered.

"We let the air out of his tires the same day we broke into the boys' gym after football practice and stole all his clothes," Brae explained.

Dex gaped at his soon-to-be wife.

A laugh bubbled out of me. "We left him a princess shirt and a Speedo to change into. We aren't monsters."

Brae couldn't hold back her laughter any longer. "But we did take photos and videos while he was waiting for Triple A."

I wiped a finger under my eye to clear the tears spilling over. "The mechanic who showed up was so confused."

"Honestly, he's the one I felt bad for," Brae said.

I nodded. "But you know what? That douche canoe never messed with us again."

Dex just shook his head. "You two truly scare me."

"Good," I said, opening the back door as I saw Wylder step out.

We'd landed on a system of sorts. Kol dropped me off with Dex and Brae after we took Skylar to school. They took me to and from therapy and then to work, where Wylder always met us outside. I did not step outside once during my shift, and then Kol would come pick me up and take me home with Sky.

I wasn't alone for a single second. I wouldn't lie; it was suffocating. But I also wasn't an idiot. It was needed until they found this monster.

A shiver raced through me, even though the sun was out. Because I couldn't help but wonder if it really was Travis. Was he still playing his torturous games?

Rolling back my shoulders, I smiled as I crossed to Wylder. Travis, or whoever this was, didn't get to win. They didn't get to steal my life when so much had already been taken from me.

"Morning," I greeted.

Wylder studied me for a moment. "You seem good."

As I looked back at the eldest Archer, I couldn't say the same about him. His eyes housed dark circles beneath them, and they were bloodshot. I frowned. "Are you okay?"

He scrubbed a hand over his face. "Haven't been sleeping all that much."

I knew why. All the Archer brothers had been working on this case, trying to pull together the pieces to figure out who the hell this was and where they might be hiding. Kol had finally shared what they did in the shadows, helping missing persons get the justice they deserved. And I was so damn proud of him—of all the Archers.

"Thank you," I whispered. "It means more than I can say."

Wylder's expression gentled. "I want to help. I just wish I were contributing more."

His gaze traveled back inside, and I saw it land on Cora, who was already at work refilling saltshakers. It wasn't just me that Wylder wanted to help. It was her.

"We're going to get him," I vowed.

Wylder turned back to me. "We are."

"Morning, boss man," Brae greeted as she walked up to our mini-huddle.

"Morning. You two want to tackle the condiment refills?" he asked.

"We've got it," I said.

"Just make sure you don't cross them," Dex called through the open window. "I just learned how vicious they can be."

Wylder looked confused, but Brae and I just laughed as we made our way into the bar. We waved at Cora, who answered in kind, but she, too, looked like she hadn't been getting a whole lot of sleep. I needed to get her alone so I could really check on her.

I followed Brae toward the stockroom so we could get the jumbo tubs of ketchup and mustard. She held the door open for me, and I slipped inside, flipping on the overhead lights.

"How was Marly today?" Brae asked.

She was careful not to inquire when Dex was around, because she knew it was usually a bit of a tender topic for me. But when I started sharing a little more, she'd gotten more comfortable asking.

"Good, hard, exhausting, hopeful," I told her honestly.

One corner of Brae's mouth tugged up. "Sounds like you've covered all your bases."

I stilled, my hand resting on one of the many shelves packed with bar-and-grill supplies. A wave of nerves took flight in my stomach, but I reminded myself that their presence only meant this mattered. And my conversation with Sky that morning reminded me to be brave.

"I love you." The words were barely audible yet like the boom of an explosion all at once.

Brae's jaw dropped. "You don't say the L-word."

I let out a shaky laugh. "I'm trying to get better at it. And I've always felt it. You have to know that. You're my sister in every way that matters."

Tears gathered in Brae's eyes. "I love you so much, Supernova. I'm so in awe of who you are, and I'm so sorry you've gone through what you have."

"I'm not." It was a simple but powerful truth.

Brae studied me, confusion swirling. "You're not…"

"Don't get me wrong. That pain will always live in me. But the beauty that came afterward? This life I get to live now? You, Owen, and the Archers—Kol?" My tears crested over, tracking down my cheeks. "It's everything. And it's a gift that I can feel all the more deeply because of what I went through."

"Nova," Brae croaked.

I moved then, pulling her into a hug and holding on tight.

She only cried harder. "You're hugging me."

"It's been too long."

"It has."

The door opened. "Hey, do you guys—oh shit. I'm sorry, I—"

We turned, still hugging, to see Cora, frozen in the doorway.

I just beamed a watery smile at her. "We're hugging out the bad. You want in?"

"I, uh…"

"Come on," Brae encouraged.

We opened our arms to Cora, who looked comically unsure as she slowly walked toward us. The moment she was within reach, we pulled her in and began a sort of rocking dance, which only made us all laugh.

A throat clearing startled us apart. Wylder stood there, and I expected a smile or at least an amused look on his face. There wasn't one. Instead, his expression was completely blank. "Have any of you talked to Piper since yesterday?"

Dread bloomed in my gut. "No." My voice sounded removed from my body as Cora and Brae shook their heads.

Wylder's skin paled even further. "She's an hour late, and she's not picking up her phone."

Chapter Forty-Nine

KOL

The Boot was devoid of its usual din of patrons. No clatter of dishes or calls of "order up." Because, yet again, the bar was closed to those looking for lunch. Instead, a handful of law enforcement had taken up residence and would likely remain for at least the next hour or so. And I was sure when Wylder reopened, every nosy Nellie in town would be darkening the Boot's door.

I moved in next to Nova, curving my hand around hers and squeezing. "You hanging in there?"

She let out a long breath, but it didn't tremble or struggle. It was as if she was centering herself. "I'm hanging in. Just worried about Piper."

I was, too. More than worried. Just like I was fucking terrified for Nova. Because I'd realized something. Heidi Ingram had long, dark hair and fair skin. Piper Richardson had long, dark hair and fair skin. And they both resembled Nova.

Someone was playing copycat. Or someone was trying to replace her.

I felt eyes on me. On us. And my gaze moved on instinct. I found Pete's surly gaze focused on Nova and me.

He'd thought he had a trump card, something he could hold over my head to get me suspended or fired. I hadn't actually thought he'd try to use it, but he had. He'd gone to Sherri to report me for misconduct. Apparently, he'd said I was *"fucking a witness."* To which, Sherri had responded, *"Two grown adults typically have intercourse when they're dating, Pete."*

She'd let him know that I'd already reported the relationship and that she was in the process of reassigning the case. For a moment, he'd thought he would get everything he wanted. But he'd had to come to terms with disappointment when he learned that Sherri was reassigning the case to Gretchen Harrison when she returned from maternity leave on Monday.

I was thrilled because Gretchen was a hell of an agent, and she wouldn't let Pete take an inch. In the meantime, I'd simply have to put up with the douche's petulant stares.

"Who shoved a stick up that one's ass?" Fiona asked as she sidled up to us.

Nova stifled a chuckle. "He really doesn't like Kol."

Fiona raised a brow at that. "Want me to give him a coffee with some hot sauce mixed in? I call it the Archer special."

My lips twitched as I patted her shoulder. "You're a good egg, Fee."

She beamed back at me. "High praise coming from you. But I see this one"—she nodded at Nova—"has you coming out of your strong-and-silent phase."

Nova grinned up at me. "See, Boss? I'm a good influence."

I scowled at both of them. "Don't ruin my rep."

Fiona laughed as Nova just shook her head.

Sometimes, people didn't understand that laughter was needed even more during times of turmoil. Some thought it was inappropriate. But in reality, it was a release.

Movement caught my eye—Roger striding through the front door.

"I'll be back," I said before crossing to him.

Pete instantly did the same, and I had to bite back a snarl.

I didn't have to ask; Roger instantly began speaking. "There's no sign that Piper made it home last night. Still lives at home with her mom, and her mother never got a call. Bed wasn't slept in. Car is missing. I've got a BOLO out on that."

I nodded, even as my gut soured. "Went through Wylder's security footage. His cameras show most of the parking lot. You see her get in her car and pull out, but that's the end of it. No one was lingering back there. No one followed her."

"Fuck," Roger muttered, dragging a hand through his hair.

I understood the sentiment. Other than a new boyfriend the deputies were trying to track down, there were no leads. It was as if Piper and her vehicle had been abducted by aliens.

"We need to be looking around Three Creeks Canyon Trail," Pete interjected. "Could already be a body out there."

That same anger I'd felt before at his bloodthirstiness swelled. It was almost as if he *wanted* to find a body and not a living victim.

"You keep wishing her dead, and you and me are gonna have problems," Roger snarled.

Pete opened his mouth, likely to say something that would get him punched, but I held up a hand to stop him. "It's not a bad idea to take a look out there. Pete, why don't you take two officers and comb the area? Let us know if you see signs of anything."

He eyed me suspiciously. "You don't want to tell me I'm a moron, too?"

"You're not a moron, so not sure why I'd say that. You *are* an asshole, though."

Pete's cheeks reddened. "I can't wait until your ass is fired," he said, stalking off.

"Well, that day isn't today," I called after him.

Roger watched me for a moment. "You think she's dead?"

"No." I scrubbed a hand over my stubble. "Whoever this is, they kept Heidi alive for a period. I think if we can find Piper in the next forty-eight hours, we'll find her alive. But if Pete wants to search that trail, good on him. He'll be out of our hair, and maybe he'll find this asshole's hunting ground."

Roger was quiet for a moment, and then he began shaking his head. "You're diabolical. You know that, right?"

I shrugged. "Only to assholes."

"Come on," Roger muttered. "Let's see if anyone got anything good on their canvasses. I'm asking stores to pull their footage from last night. Maybe someone at least got the direction Piper was traveling in or caught someone following her."

It was a long shot, but you never knew. So we made the rounds. We talked to officers who'd spoken with various shop owners and citizens. When I glanced at my brother, worry set in.

I stepped away from the Starlight Grove officer, who looked barely out of high school, and crossed to Wylder. He stood behind the bar, gaze unfocused, fingers curved around the counter.

"Hey," I said softly. "This isn't on you."

"My employee."

"Who I saw you watch get into her car. Just like you watched Cora and Aidan."

Wylder blew out a harsh breath. "I should've had her text me when she got home. Then we would've known twelve hours earlier."

"Wy," I said quietly.

"I didn't do enough," he ground out.

"That's bullshit—and the past talking."

I knew my eldest brother carried scars similar to mine, yet his were somehow worse. Because while he blamed himself for not being there when our brothers needed him, he'd also seen it all unfold in real time.

He'd gone into our father's workshop just in time to see our dad stab Maverick. In time to see Orion grab the gun. In time to see our father go down.

He saw all the hellish aftermath as emergency services arrived. And he was the one who kept Mav alive.

"Sometimes, the past is the greatest truth-teller," Wylder whispered.

"And sometimes, it's a dirty liar. Don't let him win. Not now,"

I ground out. Wylder had worked so hard to get himself together. He'd battled back from a war with alcohol, built an incredibly successful business, become a mentor in the program that had helped him beat his addiction, and he was the best brother anyone could ask for.

But maybe all of that was just hiding a different sort of war inside him—one he hadn't dealt with fully.

Radios crackled, instantly putting everyone in the room on alert. Roger lifted his to his ear, his face going hard. When the muffled voice stopped, he straightened. "They found Piper's car. And there's blood."

Chapter Fifty

NOVA

THE CHANGING OF THE SEASONS MEANT THE SUN WAS leaving us early. And today, that felt fitting. The growing darkness crept around Kol and me as we sat on the back deck.

It had become our spot, the place we'd go when we simply needed to be. Or we needed to process.

We both probably needed more than a little of both tonight. But as twilight gathered, I held on to the moon rising with it. It might not have been a full one, but even the tiny sliver in the sky gave off a glow. And the building darkness only made the moon shine brighter.

A beacon of hope.

Hope we desperately needed. Hope I wanted for Piper. Hope I wanted for us all.

I'd gone with Dex and Brae to pick up the kids for a sleepover at their cabin while Kol had spent the rest of the day at the overlook where Piper's car had been found. It was obvious someone had met her there, hurt her there, taken her from that spot. Roger and his team were looking into Piper's new boyfriend, but none of us had a name for him.

But all of us were terrified for Piper—Aidan, Fiona, Wylder, Brae. Maybe Cora most of all. She'd looked sick when I left and the Boot reopened for patrons. I'd asked if she'd come over after her shift, but I wasn't sure she'd actually show. Then again, we all had to deal in our ways, and I wouldn't push her.

Kol was certain that whoever had taken Piper was the same person who had taken Heidi. He just had no answers about *who* that was.

And that destroyed him.

I looked over at the man beside me and really took him in. The rising moon battling against the twilight cast him in shadow and light, just like the gold and green in his eyes. Both were like the man himself. He was darkness and light, and the combination was beautiful.

I moved then, unable to hold myself back. Climbing into Kol's lap as he sat on the top step, I wrapped myself around him, my legs encircling his waist as my arms went around his neck. Suddenly, we were face-to-face.

Brushing the hair out of his eyes, I studied his beautiful features. "I love you," I whispered.

"I know."

That knowledge was a gift. That he was so sure of my love for him. "Tell me what I can do."

Kol exhaled, the air whistling between his teeth. "I should be the one comforting you."

"What makes you think you aren't?"

"I'm not good at it. Out of practice."

I couldn't help it; I laughed. It was the last sound I expected to come out of me after everything we'd been through today, but it also felt damn good.

Kol glared up at me.

"I'm sorry." I let my hands sift through his hair again. "But that's one of the most asinine things I've ever heard."

The glare deepened. "It's not nice to call people asinine."

"What you *said* was asinine," I corrected. "Kol, you are the most caring, comforting person I've ever known. And it comes from your soul. You may not give it to many, but you give it to the people who are important."

His glare ebbed, transforming into curiosity. "Do I really give you what you need?"

My heart broke. For the boy who, at just seventeen, had watched his family shatter. For the one who'd had the rug pulled out from under him when he realized who his father truly was. For the man who'd had every lie reinforced when a woman couldn't see who he and his daughter really were.

He'd had every confirmation that he wasn't enough. That everything about him was wrong, bad, and freakish. And it killed me that those doubts still lived inside him.

I stared into those dark-hazel eyes and let all my walls down. I let him see it all. "Kol, you helped me live. And I don't mean you kept me breathing when I couldn't carry on. You taught me how to find life again, how not to run away from it but *live* it. You gave me beauty and fun and a family. You let me show you who I really was when I felt like everything inside of me was ugly."

A fierceness spread over Kol's expression. "All of you is beautiful," he rasped. "Your hope and your fear. Your joy and your pain. Because all of it is *you*."

"There is nothing more comforting than knowing, down to your bones, that you are loved for exactly who you are. That is the most precious gift I'll ever be given."

Kol searched my face. "I love you."

"I know," I said, my mouth curving.

"Stop stealing my lines."

"They're good." I brushed my lips across his and then straightened. A buzz lit in my muscles, not one of anxiety but those butterfly wings I'd felt before I told Brae I loved her. Anticipation and some nerves, but all of it meant I was alive. And because of that, I wanted to truly *live.* Not in fear but in freedom. "I want to try something."

Kol's dark brows pulled together in question. "Okay. You going to tell me what?"

"I want you to tie me up."

Chapter Fifty-One

NOVA

The show of emotions that played across Kol's face was more than a little satisfying. Shock, then a hint of concern, then hope, then pure blistering heat. "Phoenix," he growled.

I knew what would come next. Telling me now wasn't the time. And I understood the concern. Everything swirling around us had stirred up my trauma. However, that was also why now was the exact right time.

"Trust me," I whispered. "Trust me to know what I want. What I need."

"Explain it to me."

I could feel that same battling restraint in Kol's muscles—one of the things I loved most about him. That he worked so hard to contain a strength that could easily overpower most people. That he cared enough to make sure he never got too rough.

My thumb tracked beneath his bottom lip, tracing the shape. "I need to let go. To know I'm not in control and am still okay. I want to reclaim what it means to be bound. And know that it will never be a bad thing for me again."

Kol studied me, taking in everything I said and turning it over.

"And I want to give this to you."

"Nova, you already give me everything."

"You like it? Tying someone up?"

His gaze shifted to the side, and I had my answer.

"Let me give this to you," I pressed. "Let me give it to me. Let me give it to *us*."

That dark-hazel gaze was back on my face, searching again. "You have to promise to tell me if anything is too much."

"I'll never lie to you." The words slipped from my mouth effortlessly. Because I never had. Kol made it so easy for me to share my truth with him because he accepted me just as I was.

He shoved to his feet in answer, grabbing my ass as he took me with him. He strode toward the back door like a man on a mission. The moment we were inside, he flipped the lock and set the alarm. He carried me as if it took no effort at all, taking the steps two at a time and making me giggle.

"You think you can offer me everything, and I'm not gonna be in a fuckin' hurry?" Kol asked.

I grinned against the side of his face. "I think I like you in a hurry."

His only answer was a rumbling growl as he strode into his bedroom—a room that was becoming ours. He slowly lowered me to the floor, and the friction of the movement sent sparks dancing across my skin.

Kol stared down at me for a moment and then ghosted his knuckles against my cheekbone. "You're sure?"

"I'm sure." That buzz in my muscles intensified. It was a different sort of high than throwing myself off a cliff or hurtling down a mountain on a bike. There would always be something about those things that called to me, but this? This was better. It was *more*.

Kol waited for a moment, checking to see if I would change my mind. When I didn't, he gave me a single nod and turned, padding barefoot toward his closet.

There was something so damn sexy about him in low-slung jeans, a tee, and a flannel, the clothes he often opted for once we were home for the day. But I loved that the flannel still allowed me to see those broad shoulders bunch and strain as he reached for the cloth box.

I never would've thought that something as simple as that could make me shiver in anticipation. But it did.

Kol set the box on the bench at the foot of his bed with a soft thud. Logically, I knew the sound wasn't loud, but to me, it resembled a cannon shot.

Calloused fingers lifted the lid and pulled out the rope. It was coiled perfectly, the end wrapped around the loop in several passes. It was then that I realized that Kol had carefully and methodically tucked the rope away after the night I'd tied him to the bed. Like there was a reverence to it.

Kol set the rope on the bench and crossed to me in two long strides. I wasn't sure what I expected, but this wasn't it. He gently lifted my hand, tapping the bracelets and hair tie on my wrist. "May I?"

Such a proper question from a man who was about to defile me in the best ways. "Yes."

His gaze sparked and swirled as it tracked over me. Who would've thought such a simple word would be the thing that heated Kol's blood?

He carefully removed the bracelets from one wrist and then the other. Crossing to the dresser, he set them down with the same reverence he'd treated the rope, but he kept one item in his hand.

Moving back to me, Kol's hands lifted to my hair. He gathered up the now-shorter strands and coiled them like he had the rope. With the hair tie, he knotted it in place and stepped back.

"Still sure?" he asked.

"Yes," I said, giving him that word again.

His thumb tracked across his lower lip. "Will you strip for me, Phoenix?"

My heart tripped and stuttered, but I didn't give him words this time. I gave him actions. I kicked out of one slipper and then the other, my hands reaching for the hem of my sweatshirt and tee and beginning to pull them up.

"Slow." There was a bite to the command, a deep need.

My hands answered the order, my fingers taking their time as my knuckles skimmed over my flesh. I could feel the raised skin of the two scars along my torso from wounds I didn't remember getting, but I felt no hesitation in exposing them to Kol, no inhibition.

I lifted the clothes up and over, dropping them to the floor. And when my eyes found Kol again, his gaze was burning.

"No bra?" he rasped.

My nipples pebbled in response. "I was home for the night."

His expression gentled on the word *home*. "I'll have to remember that."

My mouth curved as my fingers hooked in the waistband of my sweats and underwear.

"Eyes on me," Kol commanded. "Don't want to lose my silver."

I bent, feeling the stretch, versions of which I'd practiced endlessly in my years of yoga. I didn't lose Kol's green-and-gold stare as my skin heated. As my sweats dropped, I kicked everything to the side.

Kol's lips parted as he reached for the rope. "A goddamned vision in the moonlight."

That glow from the crescent moon was stronger now that twilight was dipping into darkness. I could feel it on my skin, the darkness and the light.

Kol moved into my space, ghosting the end of the rope over my chest and down my stomach. "So beautiful. Looking at you makes it hard to breathe."

My breath caught then, everything in me drawing tight.

"Will you kneel for me?"

Pure grit coated Kol's question, but it also did something to me. The asking—not demanding. And it made giving myself over to him all the more powerful.

Wetness gathered between my thighs as I sank to the carpet, my breaths coming quicker. Not in panic but in anticipation. And the fact that he was fully dressed while I was completely naked only added to it all.

"Lean back on your heels. Arms behind you," Kol instructed.

I did as he asked. My skin and muscles began to tingle because I so badly wanted whatever came next.

Kol moved in behind me, trailing the rope down my spine. "If anything is too tight, too painful, you say. Okay?"

"Yes," I agreed instantly.

"This is art. Painting your beauty in different shades. In all the colors of release."

My body instantly understood as Kol began wrapping the rope around my wrists, creating cuffs that he then tied together. With my hands bound, he ran the rope up, knotting it along my spine at different intervals. My brain soon followed. Release came from ceding control. And Kol and I gave that to each other—give and take in equal measure.

But now was my time to let go. To give Kol the reins. And in turn, he would let me know it was safe to do it.

The rope gliding against my skin made sparks dance beneath it. He moved with expert speed and grace, and soon, he was bringing the rope to the front of my body. He crisscrossed it into a figure eight knot that fastened just at my breastbone, a few inches below my throat.

Kol's gaze locked with mine. "How do you feel?"

"Like I'm humming," I whispered.

One corner of Kol's mouth tugged up. "You're fucking gorgeous."

He bent, dropping a kiss to that most intricate knot on my chest. And then he was back behind me, weaving the rope around my arms and pulling everything even more snug. With the rope rounding my shoulders and my arms behind me, I could not move the upper half of my body at all. The binds tightened, and I braced for panic to come. Only, it didn't.

Everything felt too damn good. I pushed against the ropes, feeling the way they held me in place. The bite of the fibers had more wetness gathering between my thighs.

Kol's fingers moved one more time, and then they were gone. He stepped back, circling me before stopping behind me. "Fuck. You, like this? It's everything. Burning it into my memory."

I pressed my thighs together as my arms strained against the ropes.

Kol moved again, coming in front of me. "Aching?"

"Yes," I admitted.

"Need to come?" he growled.

"Please." The word was a pant.

His lips parted on a silent inhale. "Love being able to give you what you need."

Kol knelt in front of me, still so much taller, bigger. His finger circled my nipple, teasing, toying. My muscles quivered as I arched into his touch.

In answer, Kol pinched the bud between his fingers, making me cry out. "Still," he ordered. "Let me take care of my girl. Give me that control."

I battled against my body and mind, coming to rest on my heels again.

"Spread your knees wide," Kol rasped. "Show me my heaven."

I swallowed, my mouth going dry as I moved my knees apart.

He sucked in a sharp breath. "Fucking glistening."

My lips parted, the need to beg for more hovering right there. But still I waited.

Kol's thumb circled my nipple. "How do you feel, Phoenix? Knowing you've given me everything?"

"Like I'm going to fly," I whispered. It didn't make sense that these bindings would set me free. That letting Kol choose my pleasure would let me truly reach release. But both were true.

One hand lifted to my chin so that our gazes locked. "Nothing more beautiful than my girl wild and free."

Then that hand dropped between my legs. Kol's knuckles skimmed across my already sensitive flesh. It was the barest of touches, but I couldn't help crying out.

"You need me?" he coaxed.

"Yes. Please. More."

They were our words, the ones that said I was ready—that I needed all he had to give.

Kol's gaze heated as he slid two fingers inside me. My jaw went slack as I fought the urge to move. The pressure of his fingers against my walls was so different like this, my body bent and bearing down.

He swirled those two fingers inside me, and I let out a soft mewling sound—almost animalistic need.

"Stay with me," Kol commanded. "Don't let go yet. Gonna fly so much higher if you hold on."

My breaths came in quick pants, and I somehow managed to beat the orgasm back. But as Kol circled my clit with his thumb, edging toward that tiny bead, I wasn't sure I could take much more.

"That's my girl. Fight it," he praised. "You're doing so good. A little more."

Kol slid a third finger inside me, stretching me, circling.

I cried out, almost losing it but barely holding on.

"Eyes on me, Phoenix," he growled. "I need that silver."

I forced my eyes open, ordering them to lock on Kol. It all happened at once. Kol pressing down on that spot inside me, his thumb ghosting over that tiny bundle of nerves, his other fingers twisting my nipple.

There was no slow tipping over the edge; there was only a collision at full speed. My body bowed as my arms strained against the ropes, tipping just into flickers of pain, but it only drove the pleasure higher because I couldn't escape it—I had to take all Kol had to give.

Tears spilled down my cheeks, my body looking for every release it could find. Tears of relief, of finally letting go, of knowing that I trusted someone this much, enough to give them everything.

I arched, fighting against the urge to buck, but I never lost Kol's gaze. Those beautiful, dark-hazel irises held on to me as he wrung every last wave of sensation out of me.

Just when I thought it was over, Kol would build me up again. Until finally, my body began to tremble. With one last crash, Kol pulled his fingers from me.

I collapsed against him, everything in me still humming as I was faintly aware of Kol releasing my binds. A second later, he scooped me into his arms.

I looked up at him, that beautiful face coming into focus.

"Thank you," he croaked.

My brows pulled together. "For what?"

"For giving me what I need."

I lifted a hand, ghosting my fingers over his jaw. "You gave it right back to me."

I tucked my legs under me as I hugged the bowl of ice cream to my chest. I felt like a limp noodle. But the best kind, if that was possible. I tried to load the streaming service but kept getting an error message. The Wi-Fi must've been out again.

"Yeah, that sounds good," Kol said, the phone pressed to his ear. "We'll be over in the morning."

We might've lost track of time after our evening escapades, which ended with a nice, long shower and made us almost miss calling Sky before lights-out at Owen's. Thankfully, we'd made it just in time.

My lips curved as I sat back on the couch and studied my ice cream, memories from earlier in the evening washing over me.

Kol ended the call and set the cell on the coffee table, then tugged my feet into his lap. "What are you smiling at?"

I grinned at him. "I love being kinky with you."

Kol's mouth quirked as he began massaging my foot. "Kinky, huh?"

"I mean, I feel like what we did qualifies," I challenged.

He let out a soft laugh. "Fair enough. You still feeling good?"

"I feel way better than good." I met his gaze and didn't look away so he would know I was giving him the whole truth. "I feel free. I can't explain it, but it helped erase something for me. Helped me reclaim what it means to let go of control, even just for a moment."

"I love that, Phoenix. So damn much."

And it was then that I realized it. I was happy. Even with all the darkness swirling around us, I was blissfully happy. More than that. I was at peace.

My phone dinged, and I fought the urge not to scowl at it. I didn't want anyone intruding on my happy bubble. I muttered a curse as I read the text.

Cora: *At the gate.*

"What is it?" Kol asked.

I winced. "I forgot I told Cora to come over after her shift. I wanted to make sure she was okay."

Kol simply smiled and reached for his phone to open the gate. He stood and bent to kiss me quickly. "I'll make her an ice cream sundae, too."

God, he was too good to me. So damn understanding.

I set my ice cream down on the coffee table. "Do I look like I just had sex?" I called into the kitchen.

A low, rumbling chuckle was my answer.

I grumbled something under my breath as I dipped into the hall bathroom to check out my reflection. Another wince. My cheeks were pink, my hair resembled a bird's nest, and my eyes looked slightly glazed.

Pulling out my hair tie, I tried to remedy the only thing I could. As I stepped out of the bathroom, I heard a door slam outside. *Oh well.* This was the best I was going to get.

A scream tore through the air, freezing me in midstep. Then a shout. Another scream.

Kol was in the entryway in a flash, his feet sliding into shoes as he yanked open the drawer on a hutch along the wall. He retrieved a black box and pressed his fingers to the top. It popped open, revealing a gun.

My stomach dropped as fear swept through me.

"Stay inside," he ordered.

"Kol," I choked.

"Stay inside," he begged.

I nodded quickly.

Kol jerked open the door, and just as he did, Cora stumbled up the front steps, holding her side.

"What happened?" Kol barked.

A bloodied switchblade tumbled from her hand and landed on the front porch with a clatter. She looked up at us in panic. Blood seeped through her pale-blue shirt. "He stabbed me," she choked out. "I got him back, though," she wheezed. "Started…carrying…for protection."

"Get her inside," I yelled. "We need to check her wound."

Kol moved then, helping Cora inside as his gaze jumped around, looking for her attacker before locking the door. But all that was left was a bloody switchblade on the front steps. We hurried to help her onto the couch.

"Shit, shit, shit," I said, seeing the blood seeping in earnest now. "Get a towel."

Kol dipped into the kitchen as I gently lifted Cora's shirt. Her features contorted in pain as I took in the angry slash across her abdomen. It was deep. I didn't think it was deep enough to injure an organ but certainly deep enough to cause a hell of a lot of bleeding.

I looked up as Kol returned, tossing me the towel. "Thank you."

His gaze locked on Cora. "Who?" Kol demanded. "Who was it?"

Pain lanced Cora's features as I pressed the towel against her cut. "That reporter. It was Reese."

Chapter Fifty-Two

KOL

My whole body vibrated, fury making my muscles tremble with the force of holding myself together. I should've known. Some part of me had—I knew, but I should've pushed harder. Had Dex do another sweep into the creep's computer.

But I hadn't.

I'd been too focused on Travis. So sure he'd escaped death and come back to destroy us all a second time. Or some twisted copycat sparked to life by his crimes.

Fucking hell.

I wouldn't let this monster escape. I wouldn't let him go on to ruin someone else's life.

"Nova," I clipped, moving toward the front door.

Panic lit her features as she looked between Cora and me. "Hold this to your wound," she instructed her friend as she pushed to her feet and hurried toward me. "What are you doing?"

I rifled through the drawer in the hutch, finally landing on what I needed: a tactical flashlight. I grabbed it and tested the beam. Batteries were still good.

When I was sure I had everything, I turned back to Nova. "Lock the door after me. Set the alarm. Call 911 and then my brothers."

Nova's hands snaked out, gripping my forearms. "No. You're not going out there. Wait with us. Wait for backup. Mav and Orion, at least."

I shook my head. "The longer I wait, the colder the trail gets. I'm not letting him get away. I'm not letting you or anyone else live in fear any longer."

"Please," Nova begged, gripping my arms harder. "Please, don't leave me."

Those silver eyes filled with unshed tears, and I knew they were tears of love. They still killed me—more lethal than any blade. I shoved the flashlight into my pocket and cupped her face. "I will always come back for you. Always."

A tear spilled over, tracking down Nova's cheek. "You did before you even knew me."

My throat tightened, an invisible rope winding around it. "It's like I knew you before we ever met. Some part of your soul called out to mine."

"Kol," she croaked.

"You make me feel worthy when I'm not sure I ever have before. You give me peace even when the outside world rages. I love you, Phoenix. And that's a forever thing." It was a vow without asking or pushing. But I needed her to know.

Nova cupped my face now. "You're the best person I've ever known. All I want is forever with you." And then she kissed me. It was far too brief, but it was a vow of her own.

"Call the sheriff's department. Call my brothers."

"I will," she choked out.

"Lock the door after me. Set the alarm. I have my phone if you see *anything* wrong."

She nodded.

The last thing I wanted to do was leave her. But I knew I had to. I had to end this. For all of us.

I stepped outside, gripping my gun in one hand and the flashlight in the other. I didn't turn around, but I waited until I heard the lock click into place. Nova was safe. She'd set the alarm, and my brothers would be here in minutes. Even Orion, at a time like this.

Walking down the steps, I listened. Nothing but the wind. I swept the beam of my flashlight over the gravel. Blood. A scattering of drops. Then something glistened.

A knife.

It was much larger than the one Cora had held. Blood coated the blade, and the sight had anger welling up inside of me.

My flashlight beam circled wider, but there was no sign of any more blood. Reese likely had one of his hands pressed to whatever wounds Cora had left him with. And the gravel made it hard to track things like footprints.

I gritted my teeth and studied the landscape. I would have to approach this another way. Taking a deep breath, I channeled the things I'd learned from Orion and Mav. They were geniuses at reading the land, Mav the forests and Orion the way every acreage knit together. Geographic profiling but from another angle.

What would Reese want now?

He'd go for coverage. Because, psychologically, that would make him feel safe. But he also wasn't stupid. So he'd want a means of escape.

The ranch road leading away from my house was too open. There wasn't enough coverage. Same with the pastures behind my house. There were forests to the east, but the question was: Would he go north or south along that forest?

I closed my eyes, picturing a map of our property, one of the many Orion had painstakingly created. It still didn't give me the answers I needed.

There were no roads or paths in the forest. Not even a river or stream that people would sometimes move toward when lost or confused.

I forced myself to look beyond our borders: Aster's family's ranch.

My spine snapped straight. There was a ranch road between two pastures that butted up against our east fence to the south.

I was already moving, breaking into a jog as silently as possible. I flicked off the flashlight since I didn't want to give away my position, and I knew I wasn't likely to get tracking clues until I was in the woods, where clothing could get caught on branches and bushes, and where you could see a human path through the underbrush.

My ears stayed tuned for any signs of movement as my eyes adjusted to the low light. Within a handful of minutes, I slipped between the trees. My pace slowed as I looked for landmarks that could point me in the right direction but also as I assessed what path a wounded man might take.

Not over a series of fallen logs but where the trees weren't as thick instead. I followed a game trail through the underbrush, thinking Reese would likely do the same.

As Aster's ranch came into view in the moonlight, my pulse picked up. I could see the road in the distance but no signs of movement.

And then I saw it.

A form slumped across the path. I broke into a run, shoving my flashlight into my pocket as I gripped my weapon with both hands. I had no idea if Reese had a gun or if he'd lost his only source of defense when he dropped the knife.

My lungs burned, and my muscles ached. I skidded to a stop, breathing hard.

The man on the ground groaned so faintly, I knew he was near death. I rolled him onto his back and pressed two fingers to his neck. Thready. Weak. He didn't have long. He needed medical attention sooner than now.

I recognized the blond hair, the blue eyes. The hipster beard. Only now his skin was far too pale. My phone was already at my ear, calling in his location to dispatch, telling them to send EMTs and deputies.

But as I studied Reese's wounds, the sense that something was wrong swept over me. I flicked on my flashlight, sweeping it over him. And that's when it hit me. The blood soaking his shirt… It wasn't fresh.

An untrained eye wouldn't know that, but I could see. It was starting to dry on the outskirts of the stain, turning to a more reddish brown as opposed to a deep red, which meant one thing: the blood had had time to dry.

Icy dread swept over me. Something was wrong. Deadly wrong.

The dispatcher on the other end was asking if I was there. "Kol? Are you all right?"

I was already running. "Send everyone you have. Send them to my house."

But terror had ahold of me now, my demons. Because it could already be too late.

Chapter Fifty-Three

NOVA

I watched Kol through the darkness, his flashlight moving over the ground in a nonsensical pattern. But I realized it was only a mystery to me. Kol read the ground like it was one of Orion's maps. His flashlight beam swept over the gravel again, and then he was jogging toward the trees.

About halfway to the tree line, his light cut out altogether. I tried not to let anxiety win as a wave of dizziness overtook me. "Alive. Breathing." I whispered the touchstones to myself as I forced my feet to move, away from the door, away from Kol.

Cora needed me. I had to call the sheriff's department and Dex. He'd tell the rest of the brothers.

I moved through the entryway back to Cora, who was now sitting up, the towel pressed to her wound. Her face was more than a little pale, adrenaline likely being replaced by shock.

"It's going to be okay," I assured her. "Kol will find him, and I'm going to get help."

I reached for my phone, but Cora's hand snaked out and grabbed my arm. Her fingernails digging in. "Don't."

My brows pulled together, confusion washing over me. "I need to call the sheriff's department, get you some EMTs."

"You don't, actually." She moved faster than I'd ever seen her before, shooting to her feet, the towel slipping away. And then something else was in her hand.

A knife.

The blade glinted in the light of the living room, sparking another memory.

"You need to bleed." The man's voice cut through the dark, and then the light flashed on. The brightness hurt as I scrambled back toward the wall, pressing my back against the cold cinder blocks.

He hauled me up by my hair. The knife sliced across my ribs, and a scream tore from my throat as white-hot agony ripped through me. Then the blade jerked along my other side, and I doubled over, the movement ripping my hair from his grip.

So much pain. Everywhere.

"Better?" Travis asked.

The question was for someone else, I realized. Someone I couldn't see.

The responder's voice was garbled, or maybe I was too close to passing out to hear them exactly. "For now. She needs to suffer."

And then the blackness claimed me.

I blinked against the memory. A little grainy like film that had been left out in the sun. But so damn real.

Cora surged forward, gripping my hair in a vicious tug, pointing the knife to the underside of my chin. "It's time for you to finally pay, bitch. Because you cost me everything."

My breaths came quicker now as my gaze darted around the room. I needed a weapon. A phone. Something to get me out.

There was a fireplace poker if I could get to it, a good dozen feet away. My phone was only a couple of feet away, too, but Cora was blocking the way and wielding a knife. Another wave of dizziness hit me.

I tried to fight it back. *Breathe.* I pictured Kol in my mind. I'd been learning about countless tools to help me in moments like these. But it was Kol who was truly my grounding stone. I conjured him now, leaning on the endless memories we were creating, the life we were building.

"Cora," I croaked. "Whatever happened, we can deal with it together."

"Oh, we can?" she mocked. "Can you bring the love of my life back from the dead?"

Another memory slammed into me.

The room was pitch-black. Water dripped from the only source in the room. My stomach cramped from lack of food. How long had it been since the man had given me something to eat?

I sat upon the thin mattress, hugging my knees to my chest. I missed Brae. Owen. How long had it been since I'd seen them? A month? Two? The passage of time had gotten so confusing.

Something rustled. Clothing? An animal?

I froze, panic digging in as a shape emerged from the shadows. But it wasn't the one I was used to seeing. This figure was smaller. Feminine?

My breaths came in short, quick pants.

"You're nothing," the voice growled.

A woman. But one who had rage flowing through her veins.

"You're stupid. Ugly. Fat. Not going to let you into the kitchen again. You're worthless."

An open palm connected with my cheek just as I saw a flash of someone. They wore some kind of goggles. Something that allowed them to see in the dark? *The thought was gone in an instant as my head snapped back in a vicious crack.*

It connected with the hard wall, and I fell to the mattress. Everything sounded like it was underwater then.

"Disgusting little slut. Fat whore. You'll pay."

Spit hit my cheek. But the world was swirling. And the darkness claimed me again.

I blinked rapidly, trying to blend the past with the present, trying to finally see. "You," I rasped. "You were there."

Cora started laughing. Like she was so damn amused with herself.

"You know, I kept waiting for them to come for me after you were found. Don't get me wrong, I knew your brain was fucked up, but I had no idea you remembered nothing."

An invisible fist closed around my throat the same way Travis's hands had so many times. It made breathing nearly impossible, like sucking in fiery air.

"But no one came. Such a weak little bitch. Couldn't even handle living in the dark for a year. Do you know how long I was in the dark? Nearly all my life," she snarled, gripping my hair tighter.

"Please," I whispered.

"Shut up," Cora snapped. "You don't get to beg. You ruined everything."

"I didn't do anything."

She shook me like a rag doll, so much stronger than I ever knew. This woman I thought was a friend. This woman I thought was a victim, just like me.

"You just couldn't die like you were supposed to," she clipped. "Just *had* to get found. For a while, I thought you'd stay this fucked-up version of yourself. And something about knowing you were so broken worked for me. Helped. But then you had to start on your healing bullshit. You had to try to remember."

It wasn't my time in that dark hole I was trying to remember now; it was every interaction I had with Cora in the here and now. I tried to view it through this other lens, the one that would help me see things as they truly were.

"Who kept you in the dark?" My voice was raw, emotion clogging it, but I managed to get the words out.

Cora yanked my hair harder, taking me back several steps with her fury. "You think you know the dark? You have no idea. My cunt of a mother would lock me in my room the second I got home from school and not let me out until it was time to leave again. She'd starve me. Make me piss and shit in a bucket. If I hadn't had Travis, I would've starved."

I sucked in another pained breath. Brokenness didn't happen in a vacuum. It sprouted from abuse and torture and pain. It festered when one mind twisted another. And a part of me felt empathy for Cora. A young girl so abused.

But that wouldn't stop me from doing what I had to do. And when she shoved me back, I'd gotten closer to the poker. Closer to a way to defend myself.

And I *would* fight. I might've given up before, back when Kol was the only person keeping me in the land of the living. But now, I wanted to live. And I wanted to live fully.

"I'm sorry." I let the honesty bleed into my voice. "I'm sorry she hurt you."

"You're sorry?" Cora sneered, yanking my hair again as she pricked the underside of my chin with her knife. "You don't get to be sorry. I don't need your fucking sympathy because I had Travis."

A light dawned as we moved a little closer to the poker. "What did Travis do?"

A smile stretched across Cora's face. Not a twisted one like earlier but a sweet one. A woman in love. "He helped me kill her." The smile grew. "He mixed her favorite drink with a few little additives. It only took thirty minutes for her to start convulsing. It was something to watch. And I didn't take my eyes off her. I made her see me when she died. Know I was the one who did it."

Cora's green eyes danced with glee. "Then we took her high up into the mountains, off Three Creeks Canyon Trail, and we buried her. No one ever found the body; we buried her so deep. And everyone felt *so* bad for me. They were all, *Oh, Cora, how can we help? Poor Cora, what do you need?*"

She scoffed in derision. "I'd take their handouts. Someone paying my rent through graduation. Another keeping my water and power on. More dropping off food. But Travis, he realized he liked the aftermath even more than the kill. He wanted to be in the thick of it while all the morons didn't have a clue that he'd caused it."

Everything started to come together, how abuse and cruelty had kicked off something in the two of them that could never be stopped once it was started.

I swallowed down the swirling panic. "Where's Piper?"

"You'll never find her. They'll never find her. She's going to rot," Cora snarled.

No. She wasn't. I'd never let Piper suffer my fate or worse.

I used that to spur me on. I threw myself to the side, yanking my hair free with a painful snap. I dove for the poker, but I wasn't fast enough.

The blade plunged into my side, and I could only do one thing.

Scream.

Chapter Fifty-Four

KOL

A scream tore through the air as I ran for the house. I knew that scream. It was different than the one I'd heard at the hospital all those months ago, but I knew the owner was the same.

I pushed my muscles harder, my lungs burning like I'd inhaled pure flames. I took the steps two at a time and then skidded to a halt. I didn't have the goddamned key. A million curses flew through my mind.

And then I simply acted. I punched my fist through the window next to the door. Fiery pain licked along my hand and arm, but I didn't care. I reached through the broken glass just as the alarm started to sound.

Good. That was good. Law enforcement would answer the call. My brothers would get alerts on their phones. They would come.

I would get to Nova in time.

Hauling open the door, I ran inside, my gun poised and at the ready.

I knew there was something off about Cora's story. I knew the timing wasn't right with Reese's wounds. But still, when I saw Cora holding Nova by the hair, a knife to her throat, shock rocketed through me.

She was the last person I would've expected to be behind all of this. And it was still possible she wasn't alone. My gaze swept the space before coming back to her, to Nova.

She had a split lip. Her breathing was labored. And there was blood—fresh blood—pooling against the tee she wore beneath my flannel.

A whole different sort of pain speared through me. Nova. My phoenix. Someone was trying to burn her to ashes again.

"U.S. Forest Service, lower your weapon," I said, my voice taking on a robotic tone.

Cora scoffed. "Like you should be holding that badge. You've been fucking your witness from practically day one."

It was interesting that Cora didn't use the term *victim*. Because to her, that wasn't what Nova was. And she was right in a way. Nova had taken flight from ashes that would have suffocated most people. She'd built a new life for herself. She'd found her way again.

"There anyone else here, Cora?" I swept the room again with my gaze. Because I still wasn't sure if Travis was in play or not.

Fury swept over Cora's features as she shook Nova. I could see the pain in Nova's expression, the way her skin paled even further. *Fuck.* I needed to move faster. But I didn't have a clear shot. Cora was using Nova as a human shield.

"You think Travis is going to pop out and shoot you in the head?" Cora snarled. "I wish. But you fucking killed him."

"It wasn't me," I told her, trying to keep my voice even. "You know that."

"But you were a part of it. You would've killed him if you'd had the chance. You didn't try to save him."

"He went into the river, Cora. There was no saving him," I said, trying to soothe.

"Bullshit. You could've if you'd wanted to. And if it wasn't for you and your nosy-ass brother, everything would've been fine. We would've kept going just as we were," Cora argued.

I tried to shift, stepping slightly to the side, but Cora answered my move with one of her own. Nova was wheezing now. Something was wrong. Seriously wrong.

"It wouldn't have stayed the same," I said. "Travis was escalating. It wasn't enough to kill them. To insert himself into the investigations. He was getting reckless."

"He was helping me!" Cora shouted, the knife sliding across Nova's neck. Not deep but enough that a trickle of blood slid free as Nova cried out in pain.

"Let's all take a breath, okay?" I stilled the trembling in my hand. "Let's just talk. Tell me what you need."

Cora's mouth twisted into an ugly smile. "I'm giving myself what I need. Just like Travis did for almost all my life. And now, I'm righting the wrongs done to him. I'm finishing his work."

I tried to pull the threads, tried to paint the picture in my mind. "So you took Heidi Ingram."

"She was in our place. Trav and I used to camp there all the time, and I go there to remember him. He would've taken her for me. Killed her. Because she looked just like my mom. Dark hair, pale skin. She was perfect."

"But you held her somewhere," I prodded.

Cora's eyes narrowed on me. "And I'll never tell."

"She has Piper there," Nova croaked. "Piper's still alive."

Cora moved the knife for a split second, slicing it across Nova's arm. Nova cried out, trying to double over, but she couldn't, not with the grip Cora had on her hair.

"Shut up, bitch."

"What about Piper? Why her?" I pressed.

"You think you're going to shrink me?" Cora mocked. "Please. No one gets in my head. Piper was a brown-haired bitch who wouldn't stop talking about how in love she was. She needed a lesson."

"And is that what Reese needed?" I asked. "A lesson?"

"He deserves to die. Printing all those lies about my Trav. He deserves almost the worst."

I didn't share that she'd likely get her wish if emergency services didn't get to him soon. Instead, I tried a different tack. "You can still walk out of here. If you push Nova toward me, I'll catch her, and you can run out. You know the sheriff's department is already on the way. But it will give you a head start."

Cora's green eyes went dead, as if there was no humanity in them at all. "You think I care about living when Trav is gone? I don't want to be on this earth without him. I'm just going to take as many of you traitors with me as I can when I go."

I saw it now. The plan she had. She never meant to make it out alive. And that made her the most dangerous creature of all.

Chapter Fifty-Five

NOVA

Cora was going to kill me, and she would try to kill Kol if she could. Anyone else she could get her hands on, too.

But I wasn't the same woman she and Travis had taken. I wasn't the same one who'd given up, even in the face of rescue. I'd found my strength. My *true* strength.

And I wouldn't let anyone hurt me again.

I tried to call on the self-defense class Brae and I had taken at the YMCA in Oakland. The knowledge was rusty and faded at best, but I remembered they'd said to go for the most tender or breakable points.

The teacher had given tips about going for the groin and eyes most often, but she was referring to male assailants. And Cora didn't have balls that would feel the brunt of a knee, even if I could whirl around.

But she did have one tender spot I was *very* aware of. The wound on her stomach. Whether she'd given it to herself or gotten it in an actual fight, I wasn't sure. But if I could get to that, I might have a shot.

I remembered the self-defense teacher instructing us in how to execute a combination. A foot coming down on the other and then your elbow slamming back. Cora was wearing sneakers, and though I was only wearing slippers, maybe if I brought my foot down as my elbow went back, it would work.

Anxiety swept through me as Cora went on about all the people she wanted to end. Roger for not standing by his friend. Dex for killing him. Brae for not leaving me to rot. Her knife was still at my throat, but in her diatribe, she'd moved it slightly. Away and then back. Not in huge motions, but enough that maybe I wouldn't get sliced if I timed things right.

There was a rhythm she didn't recognize. But I did.

My gaze locked with Kol's. At least I'd be able to see his face one last time if this didn't go well. But I had to try.

I love you, I mouthed.

Kol's entire frame tensed.

Be ready, I added.

I just had to hope he'd take the shot when he could get it. I had to hope that what we were fighting for would carry us through. Because I wanted a big, beautiful life with Kol and Skylar. I wanted ridiculous breakfast creations and over-the-top tea parties. I wanted evenings in the twilight with Kol and movie nights on the couch as a family. I wanted to live.

With that last thought, I felt the blade move slightly away. My foot came down as my elbow went back.

Cora let out a garbled sound of shock as she doubled over. I whirled, fisting my fingers and punching her square in the jaw.

Disbelief bloomed in her eyes, but it was quickly replaced by fury. She slashed out with her knife in an uncoordinated move. I tried to move out of her path, to jerk backward, but my foot caught on the edge of the rug, and I stumbled. Cora lunged forward, and the tip of her blade slid across my belly, but it wasn't nearly as deep as the other wounds.

Then she launched herself at me. It was pure hysterical rage. No thought, simply reaction.

Cora hit me full force, taking me to the floor. We rolled as I tried to keep her knife-wielding arm away from me. She was stronger than me. There was no denying it.

I still hadn't regained all the strength I'd lost while I was held captive, but I had adrenaline on my side. And I had the knowledge of all I was fighting for.

I brought my head up in one swift move, trying to connect with her nose.

It wasn't a direct hit, but Cora still cursed. "Just die already, you stupid fucking bitch."

The knife moved precariously closer as we rolled again, moving too quickly for Kol to get off a shot. I was trying desperately to slow us down. To still Cora long enough that Kol could fire.

Another roll, and I brought my legs up in a curl, ready to kick her off me. Long enough to give Kol what he needed.

But as my knees came up, my hold on Cora's wrist faltered. It slipped.

The knife slammed into my side. White-hot pain lanced through me as I kicked my feet out. And for a moment, Cora was airborne.

As she flew, two shots rang out in quick succession. Shock played out over her face. And it was as if time were suspended. Her and me. In some ways, we'd both become prisoners of the monster she'd created. But I'd gotten free.

And even as Cora disappeared from view and my pain engulfed me, I felt that freedom. Because I'd fought for my life. And I'd never stop fighting.

Chapter Fifty-Six

KOL

The blows were vicious. One after another as each woman battled for the upper hand. I tried to focus solely on the task in front of me. Trying to get Cora in my sights. A clear shot with no risk to Nova.

My phoenix.

I couldn't let myself think about everything she'd been through. All she was *still* going through. I could only think about ending this.

Nova's knees came up, and as she let out a pained sound, Cora flew into the air. I didn't wait. Two shots. Center mass.

She crumpled to the floor, but I was already moving, my gun trained on her. She let out a series of wheezing breaths. A stuttered cough. Then nothing at all. Cora's green eyes were wide and unblinking.

A brutal sort of pain, the kind that came from the heaviest

responsibility, crashed through me as I bent to press two fingers to her neck. No pulse.

Nova let out an agonized noise, and I whirled as sirens sounded in the distance. And that's when I saw it. Cora's knife, protruding from Nova's side.

Everything in me ran cold, as if my blood itself were slowing.

"Kol," she croaked, her face unnaturally pale.

I sank to my knees, taking her hand in one of mine as I tried to assess her wounds with the other. "I'm right here. I've got you."

"Take it out," Nova rasped. "Please."

It wasn't pain and responsibility swirling now; it was pure agony. "I can't. I'm so sorry, but that could make it worse. We have to wait."

"Oh...kay..." Her breaths were more labored now. Her eyelids fluttering. But the way she gave me her trust, even when I was causing her pain? It sliced me open.

I squeezed her hand hard. "Stay with me, Phoenix. Hear those sirens? Those are for you. Help's coming."

"Fighting...not...giving...up..." Those eyelids closed fully then, stealing the silver from me.

Panic speared through me, and it felt like icy claws piercing my heart. I bent down, leaning over Nova. No breath sounds.

I didn't let myself feel that. I turned it all off so I could act.

One hand covered my other as I settled them along her sternum. I began compressions. Everything about it felt wrong as I pressed hard on bone and muscle, sinew and organs. Hurting Nova more in the hopes of saving her.

My mouth came to hers in two rescue breaths. Then my hands were back to compressions.

Her body shook with the force of it. But I had no choice.

"You're alive," I rasped. "You're breathing."

And I would keep breathing for her until she could breathe on her own.

The chair in the tiny reception room wasn't meant for someone my size. The hard plastic felt like it would split in two at any moment. But I didn't care.

It had been too long, hours since we'd arrived at the hospital by ambulance. Hours since Nova had been wheeled into surgery.

And we were all just…waiting.

Waylon and Orion had stayed with Owen and Skylar at the ranch. But the rest of us were here. Aster sat, face pale as she stared at the floor in front of her. But I didn't miss the way Mav's gaze traveled to her every so often, as if to make sure she was okay.

Wylder sat one chair down from her, his expression completely closed down. I knew Cora meant something to him, and him not seeing who she truly was would carry a weight I knew he wouldn't recover from anytime soon. I wanted to go to him, tell him none of this was his fault, but I couldn't get my body to obey.

My gaze flicked to Brae and Dex, then quickly away. It was too painful to really look at Brae. Her face was tear-streaked, and her amber eyes were bloodshot. But it was the agony clearly ravaging her entire body that shredded my chest. Because Nova was her family.

My fingers tightened on the arms of my chair, the plastic creaking at the force. I'd scrubbed them in the bathroom, but I could still see tiny flecks of blood in places. Tiny flecks of Nova.

It nearly broke me, every last part of me coming so close to fracturing under the weight of it all.

Footsteps sounded, and my head jerked up. I was hoping for the surgeon or even a nurse, but instead, Roger filled the waiting room doorway. He wore that mask most of us in law enforcement had perfected over the years, but as his gaze traveled over all of us, just sitting and waiting, he sucked in an audible breath. "Any news?"

Maverick shook his head. "She's in surgery. That's all we know. We heard the reporter is, too, but they won't tell us anything because we're not family."

Roger jerked his head and came to sit one chair down from me.

"Anything on your end?" I asked, my voice robotic.

"We found Piper," Roger said. "Got Cora's location data from her phone company, and there was an old cabin about five miles from the campsite where she was keeping Piper and Heidi. One that's not on record. Piper's got some bumps and bruises and was dehydrated, but the docs say she'll be okay."

She would be okay. I only had to hope Nova would be the same. Because there was no other option. "Good. That's good."

"Found some journals. Got officers going through those now. We're going to see what we can pull together from those."

That was good, too. Only I didn't care. Maybe that made me callous, but the why of it all didn't mean a damn thing to me. All I knew was that Cora and Travis had caused untold pain.

Footsteps sounded again, and this time, a woman filled the doorway. Her black hair was pulled back into a bun, and she looked exhausted but tried to hide it. "Nova Monroe's family?"

"Yes." Brae and I spoke and stood at the same time.

The doctor nodded. "I'm Dr. Jeong, Nova's surgeon."

My hands fisted, nails digging into my palms as I held my breath, waiting.

"Nova made it through surgery and is in recovery. We'll be moving her to the ICU in just a few minutes."

"Is she—?" Brae swallowed hard. "Will she be okay?"

The doctor's expression gentled. "We need time. Nova's body hadn't completely recovered from her first ordeal. It makes recovery now more difficult. But she's a fighter."

It seemed so unbelievably unfair that Nova's chances of survival were lower because of what she'd already endured. But maybe the doctor was mistaken. Maybe all she'd been through had already taught her to fight, readied her for this battle.

"I can take one of you up to ICU where they are moving her," Dr. Jeong continued.

My gaze collided with Brae's, holding for a moment. Her eyes filled. "It should be you. You've become her anchor."

Fresh pain crashed into me. This gift from the person who meant the most to Nova was everything.

"Thank you." My words were barely audible and covered in grit, as if the inside of my throat had been rubbed raw with sandpaper.

Dr. Jeong nodded. "I'll show you the way."

Everything felt hazy as I followed her. Down a hall and toward a bank of elevators. Up a handful of floors and then down another hall.

She paused to douse her hands in sanitizer before swiping her key card, and I did the same. The alcoholic solution stung in places, my cuts from breaking the glass making themselves known. But the pain was a respite in a way. It helped distract me from the organ in the center of my rib cage, the one currently in pieces.

"This way," Dr. Jeong said quietly, leading me down a hall.

A younger man in scrubs exited a room and gave the doctor a nod. "They're just getting her settled."

Her.

Nova.

Supernova.

Phoenix.

All those names had one thing in common—they were each powerful beacons of light in their own ways. Not the kind of thing that could be snuffed out easily.

Beeping sounded from almost every direction as we waited, a disjointed cacophony of sounds that grated against my eardrums. Just when I thought I couldn't take it for a second longer, a woman stepped out of the room and nodded at us. The action made her tight braids swing. "She's all ready for you."

Dr. Jeong turned to me. "There will be a tube helping Nova breathe, another keeping her lung inflated, an IV, and wires connecting her to a heart monitor that will measure her heart rate, oxygen, and blood pressure. None of it is hurting her. You can still hold her hand, talk to her. Studies show that all of that helps."

I forced my head to nod, but the movement felt slow and clumsy, like I was moving through molasses. But I kept going—through the sea of darkness and into the light.

The beeping got both louder and quieter as I moved into the hospital room. Nova looked dwarfed by the hospital bed. So tiny. Delicate. Breakable.

My lungs cried out in protest as I realized I wasn't breathing. Sucking in air, it felt like I was inhaling shards of icy glass. Still, I kept moving forward.

Some part of me was aware of sinking into the chair next to the bed and taking Nova's hand. "Phoenix."

Her name was a guttural plea ripped from my throat.

She'd given me a place to simply be. A place of acceptance. Of safety. Something I wasn't sure I'd ever truly felt until her. And I didn't want a world without her in it.

My heart spasmed as I carefully lifted her palm to my mouth. I spoke against her skin, my lips forming the words and hoping she would hear them in two ways. "You're alive. You're breathing."

And I didn't stop saying them until sleep claimed me.

Chapter Fifty-Seven

NOVA

Hard voices. Not anger but frustration.

My brain tried to place them—the owners of the voices, what the words they were saying meant.

"You need to go home. You've been here for ten days straight." Male voice. Something inside me said *Dex*.

"You're starting to smell." Maverick's voice.

"I showered this morning, asshole." That voice. It reached something deep inside me because I knew it like no other. Yet it lacked emotion, despite the biting rebuttal. A deadening.

"Come on, man. This isn't good for you," Dex said, his voice gentling.

"I'm not leaving her," the other voice growled. "I wasn't there when she needed me." His voice cracked. "I'm not leaving her again."

Kol. The voice was my Kol. I battled against the heaviness of my eyelids. I needed to get to him. Tell him it was okay.

"You know this wasn't your fault, Kol," Maverick said carefully. "You didn't know."

"I shouldn't have risked leaving her."

The vehemence in Kol's voice, the self-hatred…they had me fighting harder.

My eyes fluttered the barest amount. Tiny glimmers of light pierced my vision. They hurt, like little ice picks to the brain, but I kept fighting. Even as Dex and Kol went back and forth.

"Uh, guys," Mav cut in.

"What?" Kol snarled.

"I think Supernova is waking up."

"Get the nurse," Kol barked.

And then hands were curling around mine.

"Phoenix?" he whispered. "That's it. I'm here. I'm right here. Just waiting for you to open those eyes so I can see that silver."

I took on more of the light, letting it burn me, and then climbed out of the ashes and into pure beauty. Kol's face was there. So close to mine. Those dark-hazel eyes. The deep forest and the pure gold.

"Hi," I rasped.

Kol's eyes filled then, his massive shoulders shaking as the tears began to fall.

My big, beautiful warrior was crying. Weeping. And I could feel it all. The pain, the relief, the love.

"Come. Here," I choked out.

He shook his head. "I don't want to hurt you."

"You won't." My side ached, and my throat was raw, but all I wanted was to feel Kol around me.

So carefully and gracefully you would've thought he'd been a ballet dancer in another life, Kol climbed onto the bed. He slid one arm under my neck while gently cocooning me with the other. "You're alive. You're breathing," he whispered against my temple.

"I'm alive, and I'm breathing. Because of you."

Kol shook his head. "I fucked up. I wasn't there."

"You were. Every step of the way. Because you reminded me that I could be strong. You taught me to live again."

"Phoenix."

"I gave you a warning, Boss. I'm never letting go. So you don't even get a choice in the matter."

Kol's big body shook, but this time, I knew it was a mixture of laughter and tears. "I love you."

"Convenient. Because I love the crap out of you," I said.

He pulled back, his knuckles skimming my cheekbone. "You're here."

"I'm here." I swallowed hard. "Piper?"

"They found her. No serious injuries, and she's home and recovering."

Relief swept through me, but it battled the tension still living there. "Cora and Reese?"

"Reese is alive. He's a couple of doors down. It was touch and go, but they think he's going to make it."

"Cora?" I pressed. I knew it wasn't fair for me to make Kol talk about her, not after everything we'd been through. But I needed to know.

"She died on the scene. I killed her."

There was an emptiness to Kol's voice, but I wove my fingers through his and squeezed with all my strength. "You saved me," I whispered. "There's a difference."

He nodded, the movement a little jerky, but his head came to rest against mine, and we simply breathed. I knew this wouldn't be something he'd be able to let go of easily. That wasn't the sort of man Kol was. But I would be with him every step of the way.

"Kol Archer. What are you doing in my patient's hospital bed?" a female voice demanded, but a hint of humor laced her words.

Kol winced as he pulled back. "Sorry, Zuri."

"You should be," she clucked as she headed my way with a tablet.

"Don't make him go," I pleaded.

Her expression softened, and lines formed in the dark skin around her eyes as she gave me a gentle smile. "I'll pretend I don't see him climbing back up there after I'm done checking you over."

My own mouth curved. "Thank you."

"How's your pain on a scale of one to ten? One being a walk in the park, and ten being the worst you've ever felt?"

"Four?" I hedged.

Zuri arched a brow. "Now I know you're lyin' at least a little."

"Six," I grumbled. "Can I have water?"

Kol was already moving, pouring me a cup and putting a straw in it.

"Little bits at a time," Zuri instructed. "We need to see how your stomach does."

The cool water was a balm to my throat, and I had to fight not to gulp it down. But the last thing I wanted was to throw up.

Zuri moved around the bed, checking the machines and then peeking at a dressing on my abdomen. "You're healing nicely. Your lung collapsed, but it's staying inflated now. Took you a bit longer to wake up than we usually like, but everything's looking good now."

"She always has run late," a new voice said from the doorway.

My gaze cut to Brae, but she was already rushing toward my bed, her eyes glistening with unshed tears.

My breath hiccupped as I struggled for control. "I'm sorry I kept you waiting."

"You should be," Brae clipped, wiping beneath her eyes. "But you're here now."

She moved in closer, bending to hug me but waiting to make sure that was okay. I closed the distance, ignoring the slight flicker of pain. "And I'm not going anywhere."

"Promise me?" Brae asked, holding on gently.

I released her and looked between the two of them. Brae and Kol. The people who meant the most to me in the world. "You're both stuck with me forever."

Chapter Fifty-Eight

KOL

FIVE DAYS LATER

"A LITTLE TO THE LEFT," I ORDERED AS DEX, MAV, WYLDER, and I shifted the bed in the room that had once been my office. Nova would be home this afternoon, and I wanted her recovery to go as smoothly as possible.

I'd moved the contents of my office into storage and ordered one of those beds where you could adjust the head and foot to create whatever position was the most comfortable. And using my office meant she wouldn't have to go up and down the stairs.

"You just had us move it to the right," Dex grumbled.

Wylder cursed. "This thing weighs like ten thousand pounds."

"Swear jar, Uncle Wy," Sky called from outside in the hall.

"She moves like a ninja, silent and deadly," Wylder muttered.

"Okay, set it down," I said.

The bed hit the floor with a heavy *thunk*.

Maverick stepped back, studying it. "You think it might be a little off—"

Dex smacked him upside the head. "Finish that sentence, and I'll drain your bank account and send love poems to all your coworkers' email addresses."

Mav gaped at him. "Who woke up on the cranky side of the bed?"

"Me," Dex clipped, his glare cutting my way. "Because this *tyrant* has had us playing HGTV since dawn."

"Oh no you don't, Buttercup," Brae said, sweeping in with Owen and Skylar on her heels. "We are making this room perfect for Nova."

"Hellion," Dex said, gentling his tone. "She's going to love it. You didn't have to test five different sets of sheets and three different blanket options."

Brae dumped the armful of bedding onto the mattress, her hands going to her hips. "You don't think she deserves the softest sheets known to man after what she's been through? A blanket that's both warm and breathable?"

Dex's gaze jumped around the room.

Mav held up his hands. "Don't look at me. Little Badass scares me."

My lips twitched. "Your fiancée is awesome."

"This is offsides or something. You're all ganging up on me," Dex complained.

Owen grinned at him. "You gotta know when to give up, bruh."

Dex let out a huff. "Fine, fine."

The only one who didn't join in the fray was Wylder. He'd been quieter than usual these past couple of weeks. We'd all tried to talk to him at one time or another, but he wouldn't get into anything about Cora. Instead, he threw himself into working at the Boot and helping out the crew at Dex's house, like he thought if he didn't slow down, he wouldn't have to think about it all.

"Daddy, Supernova's gonna love the purple. And look at the flowers Miss Aster helped me pick out," Sky cut in, holding up the vase she'd made for Nova.

I ruffled her hair. "I bet these are her favorites yet."

Mav's gaze cut to the door before Aster even moved through it, as though he had radar attuned to her. She bustled through, holding two grocery bags and crossing to the minifridge we'd put in the corner. "I got water, juices, some protein shakes. Snack packs that will be easy to grab if she's hungry but doesn't want to go to the kitchen. And a jumbo-size bag of wild berry Skittles, of course."

"You didn't get me anything, Ice Queen?" Mav asked with a grin.

"Take a flying leap, Satan," she shot back.

His grin widened. "You only fight with me because you care. If you didn't, you'd ignore me."

Aster's mouth slammed shut as she turned to me. "Whatever you do, do *not* put me on Nova duty with that caveman."

A low chuckle left my throat. "Noted."

"I'll just have Dex hack into the schedule and put us together," Mav interjected.

Aster whirled on Dex. "You even think about it, and I will come for you."

Sky giggled. "Auntie Aster is a baddie."

Aster held out a hand for a high five, and Sky smacked it. "Sisters before misters," Aster said.

"Okay, guys." I clapped my hands together. "We need to move. I'm supposed to pick up Nova in an hour and a half."

That got everyone into gear. Brae and I made the bed while Sky and Owen finished the Welcome Home sign. Mav and Dex helped Waylon with meal prep in the kitchen while Wylder went MIA, but when I walked out to check on everything, I nearly collided with Orion.

His dark eyes met mine as his throat worked. For a second, I thought he might speak. And then he raised his hands to sign, *"I'm glad Nova is okay."*

I lifted my hands to sign as I spoke. "Thank you. And thanks for helping out with Sky so much while I was at the hospital."

Orion moved his head in a jerky nod. *"I made Nova a cake. It's in the kitchen."*

As Brae had once said, chocolate was Orion's love language.

"I think she might like that even better than those Skittles she's always eating."

Orion ducked his head but not before I saw the barest twitch of his lips.

"Daddy! Come up here," Sky called from the top of the stairs.

I glanced at my watch. I had exactly fifteen minutes before I needed to leave. Taking the stairs two at a time, I let my daughter tug me toward her bedroom.

"You're missing one thing for Supernova," she said with complete certainty.

"What's that?" I asked.

She shoved a tiny, beaded object into my hand.

"What's this?"

"A ring. So you can ask Supernova to marry you." Skylar was completely nonchalant, as if this were the most obvious thing in the world.

I struggled to swallow. "You want that?"

Sky let out an exasperated sigh. "Duh. She'd be like the best mom in the history of moms."

A laugh startled out of me at that. "I don't disagree, Little Princess."

A throat cleared, and I turned to see Waylon in the doorway.

"I might be able to help with that," he said, his eyes a little misty. He reached into one of the pockets of his overalls and retrieved a small wooden box. "Been carrying this around the past couple of weeks, waiting for the right moment. This was my mother's. But there's something about it that just seems right for you and Nova."

I sucked in an audible breath as I opened the box and gazed at the glimmering stone. "It's like twilight. Like Nova's eyes."

"It's a silver sapphire. You don't have to use it. I just thought—"

"It's perfect," I said, cutting Waylon off. "Thank you. For everything. Now and always."

Waylon pulled me into a hug. "Love you. So damn proud of the man you are."

My throat constricted. But Skylar saved us. "This is cute and all, but you still gotta put a dollar in the swear jar, Grampa Way Way."

Chapter Fifty-Nine

NOVA

"I HAVE NEVER BEEN HAPPIER TO BE HOME." I TOOK KOL'S HANDS as he helped me out of the hatchback. He'd driven my car so it would be easier for me to get in and out of it. He was always thinking of everything.

A soft smile tugged at Kol's lips, even as he watched my every movement for any signs of pain. "I like hearing you say that. *Home.*" The curve of his mouth faltered for a minute. "You're sure it'll still feel that way after everything?"

I squeezed his fingers with as much strength as I could manage. "This will *always* be my safe place. It's where I started to live again. And where I was brave enough to love."

"God, I love you."

"I know." I took a step, testing the movement to see if it caused any pain. Even with two weeks of recovery, I was still tender. But I knew being here, surrounded by the people I loved the most, I'd heal faster.

"Are you sure you're okay with me taking over your office?" I asked.

Kol pinned me with a stern look. "Don't ask stupid questions."

"Boss, careful. Skylar will ground you if she hears you call me stupid."

Those hazel eyes flashed. "I'd never call you stupid. You're one of the smartest people I know. But I am gonna call that fuckin' question stupid. Because I've been making a place for you since the moment we met. Why do you think I made the space above my garage into an apartment? We didn't need that."

A soft smile curved my mouth. "I wondered, but I wasn't sure."

Kol shrugged as if it were nothing. "I could see you felt hemmed in and were looking for a way out. I wanted to give you a place to go." One side of his mouth kicked up. "And it got you closer, didn't it?"

My eyes started misting. "Kol…"

"Don't you dare cry, Phoenix. Our whole family's in there, and if they see you teary, one of my brothers is going to punch me for sure."

That startled a soft laugh out of me, and I found it didn't hurt as much as it had even a day ago. "I like you calling them that. *Ours*."

Kol's knuckles grazed across my cheek. "They are that. Ours. In every way that matters."

"I love you."

"Love you with everything I have." He bent and brushed his lips featherlight across mine.

"Excuse me," Skylar called. "I like the kissing, but we're all waiting here."

I chuckled against Kol's mouth. "I think we're in trouble."

"She scares me a little, so we should probably go inside," Kol whispered.

"Good idea."

He took my arm, walking with me. We were old hat at this, doing loops around my hospital floor on the regular. But the reward at the end of this trek was so much sweeter.

Skylar beamed up at me the moment we stepped through the door. "I'm glad you're home. It wasn't as good when you weren't here."

My eyes burned. "I love you, Sky. And I missed being here with you."

Her hazel eyes glistened. "You do?"

I nodded. "With my whole heart."

"I love you with my whole heart, too," Sky sniffed. "Is it still no hugs?"

Kol opened his mouth, I was sure to say yes, but I shook my head. "I think it's the perfect time for a gentle hug."

Skylar slowly walked toward me and looped her arms around me in the most careful embrace. I hugged her back with all I could muster.

"Best hug ever," I whispered.

"Me, too."

"Fuck, I'm crying," a new voice said from the doorway.

I grinned at Maverick as he wiped under his eyes.

Dex clapped him on the shoulder and squeezed. "*The Notebook* get you again?"

Mav scowled at him. "I shared that in confidence. It's not nice to use it as a weapon."

"Don't worry," I assured him. "*The Notebook* makes me sob like a baby."

"Thank you," Maverick huffed.

Dex smiled at me. "Welcome home, Nova."

"You have no idea how happy I am to be here."

He reached out and gave my arm a squeeze. "Thanks for fighting. Brae and Kol would've been a wreck without you."

I found myself fighting back tears again but battled through to smile. "Thanks for loving my sister so well. And for being the best brother to Kol."

"Okay, now I'm *really* crying," Mav said, throwing up his hands.

Kol took my arm again. "Let's get you inside before Mav drowns you."

"Rude," Maverick shot back, but he made way for me.

"Bed or couch?" Kol asked.

"Definitely couch. I've been stuck in a bed for weeks."

Kol led me toward the living room and more familiar faces.

Waylon was arranging some snacks and a wrapped box on the coffee table, while Brae had her arm curved around the shoulders of a subdued-looking Owen. I could make out Wylder just outside as he stood there with Orion.

I understood it. Wylder didn't feel like talking to anyone, so it didn't surprise me that he'd chosen the company of his silent brother. I was worried about him. But I knew he needed time more than anything.

My gaze returned to Owen. "Hey, Bubs. Think I could get a hug?"

His gaze dropped, but he crossed the distance toward me.

I reached out and squeezed his hand. "Anything you wanna talk about?"

He looked up, eyes watering. "Are you gonna go away again?"

My heart broke, but I pulled him to me, ignoring the flare of pain. "I'm not going anywhere. You're stuck with me. And I'm going to give you big, embarrassing hugs and huge, sloppy cheek kisses at drop-off and pickup all the time."

"You promise?" Owen sniffled.

"I promise."

Brae wiped at her eyes. "Love you, Supernova."

"Love you to the moon, B Baby."

"Again?" Maverick complained, wiping at his eyes.

"Okay, let's stow the tears and have some happy. Open your present," Waylon ordered.

I grinned up at him. "I can do that." I looked at Sky and Owen. "Want to help?"

They were eager to assist. We dispatched the ribbon and the Bigfoot-patterned wrapping paper. And then I lifted the lid.

The clock was a stunning riot of colors. A rainbow of purples, pinks, and blues, and had a little leprechaun, animals, and mushrooms. "It's beautiful."

"Just wait," Waylon said. "This is what happens when it hits the hour."

He tapped a button on the back, and wild berry Skittles shot out of a fairy, spilling into a dish disguised as a pond.

"Waylon," I whispered. "You made me a Skittles clock?"

He patted me on the shoulder. "You've earned it."

I leaned back against the chaise on the back deck, staring up at the sky from under a heap of blankets. I'd taken an afternoon nap and wasn't ready to go back to bed. I needed the stars, the endless infinity of the sky. It reminded me I was free.

I knew I had a lot to process ahead of me. But I also felt peace. And that was a wonderful discovery.

The back door slid open, and Kol moved across the deck to sit at the end of my lounger. "How are you feeling?"

My mouth curved. "I feel almost guilty for saying it, but I feel wonderful."

"Why should you feel guilty?"

I lifted a shoulder and let it fall. "There are still people being taken out by all this. Aster and Wylder both feel like they missed signs they should've caught. Owen is uncertain whether I'm here to stay. This community had yet another of their own turn on them. And me? I'm…happy."

Kol leaned in over me, kissing me softly. "You have earned that. Every single bit. Aster and Wylder will heal. Our community, too. And Owen? I'm pretty sure the fact that he wanted to see your 'war wounds' and was calling you a 'bad booty operative' by the end of the night proves he's resilient."

That last part made me chuckle. "You might have a point there."

"Thank you," he said, kissing me again. His knuckles skimmed across my cheek. "Didn't feel like home without you here."

"Kol…"

"Gonna ask you something. And it's okay if you're not ready."

My heart started hammering against my ribs.

"But I know what I want. And so does Sky. We want forever with you." He tugged a box from his pocket and opened it slowly.

I gasped at the stunning ring. A smoky blue-gray stone that was almost haunting in its beauty.

"It was my great-grandmother's. It reminds me of your eyes. And it reminds me of finding you in the twilight—of all the twilights we've shared since."

My eyes filled, and I knew the answer before he even finished speaking. "How about a forever of twilights?"

Kol's throat worked as he swallowed, sliding the ring onto my finger. "Can't think of anything better."

Epilogue

NOVA

FOUR MONTHS LATER

I STRETCHED MY ARMS WIDE AS I LEANED FORWARD ON MY mat, my body twisting. "Feeling the stretch of warrior two," I guided my class, as the early spring sun streamed down on us and a soft breeze picked up. "Keep breathing. If feelings come up, acknowledge them and let them flow. There's no wrong feeling, and no feeling is final."

It had taken time, but I'd come back to yoga. It was actually my time in equine therapy with Marly that helped me find it again. The horses had helped me get comfortable with stillness, quiet, and *feeling*. And then I'd been able to find my practice again.

Now, I taught three days a week as part of a program that Aster ran on her ranch. And another four classes at a small studio in town. I still worked two days a week at the Boot, but I wasn't sure how much longer that would last. There was more and more demand for me to do additional yoga teaching.

Wylder was still struggling. He hid it pretty well, but I could see the shadows he covered with easy smiles and ready jokes. My go-to had been drowning myself in adrenaline, but Wylder did it with acts of service, helping others to the point of running himself ragged. But it was something he'd have to figure out for himself.

"Coming out of warrior two, let's windmill our hands back down to the mat and move into downward dog, then lower ourselves into child's pose when ready. Nice, deep breaths. Think about letting go of whatever came up during the practice today."

I held the pose for a minute and then straightened, placing my hands on my knees, taking in the class and the gorgeous surroundings of the field we were in and the ranch beyond. It was an absolutely dreamy place to teach. "Thank you for joining me today."

As I pushed to my feet, a few of the students came to talk for a minute or thank me, but my gaze kept traveling to the man leaning against the U.S. Forest Service truck. He watched me with a single-minded focus that sent my pulse spiking.

Kol had settled into a good routine at work. He had a team he didn't mind working with—after Pete got demoted and transferred for insubordination—and he and his brothers had been able to take on a number of new cases through the Hourglass Network after my case was closed, still working in the shadows but doing immeasurable good.

I'd been able to sit in on a few of their meetings now, and it was beyond impressive what they were able to accomplish. In the past four months alone, they'd been able to help close two cases and were still working on four others.

"Thank you for this, Nova."

I turned toward the deep voice, taking in Jack from the Compass organization. "I'm glad you're liking it."

"Never thought bending like a pretzel would be my thing, but here we are."

I chuckled. "Life is full of surprises."

Piper bounded up to us, pulling me into a hug. "That was the best one yet."

She had recovered remarkably well from her ordeal. And when her cowboy had heard what had happened to her, he'd ditched the rodeo circuit and made a home right here in Starlight Grove.

"I'm so glad you thought so."

"I need to go meet Sam for lunch, but maybe you and I can grab a drink this week?" she asked as she backed away.

"You got it." I just didn't mention that mine would need to be nonalcoholic.

"See you this weekend, Jack," Piper called. She had now gotten involved in Compass as well. And it was something that gave us all a much-needed purpose.

Jack waved to us both as he headed for his truck.

Before I could bend to roll up my mat, Kol was there, doing it for me.

"You know I can manage that much, right?" I challenged.

He grinned at me. "Gotta take care of my girls. All of them." Kol straightened, his hand coming to my belly. "How are you feeling?"

"Good. Just thinking about the fact that we'll now need two of everything."

Kol chuckled. "Maybe we can get a bulk diaper deal."

My mouth curved. "You ready to do this, Daddy?"

He took my mouth in a long, slow kiss. "Nothing has ever made me happier than growing our family."

"I love you."

"More than you'll ever know," he whispered. "Even enough to build you a she shed."

I pulled back, a huge smile splitting my face. "You started?"

"Framing's all done, and you and Brae will have a clubhouse for all your troublemaking within a month."

I kissed him again. "Have I told you that you're the best, Boss?"

He grinned against my mouth. "Never hurts to hear it again."

A whistle cut through the air, and we looked over to see Mav walking toward us, his arm around someone. I blinked a few times. "Is that *Aster*?"

Kol frowned. "Maybe she took a hit to the head and forgot who he is?"

A wave of worry swept over me. Aster had been through it lately, but letting Maverick touch her in any way was not on my bingo card.

"Hey…" I greeted. "What's going on?"

"Just enjoying this fine spring day," Maverick said.

I looked at my friend. "Aster, you do know Mav has his arm around you, right? Blink twice if he brainwashed you."

Maverick scowled at me. "That's rude, Supernova. And honestly, I'm surprised you're shocked. It's pretty normal for fiancés to show a little PDA."

My jaw went slack. "Fiancés?" I squeaked. My gaze dropped to Aster's left hand, and there was a *massive* diamond on her ring finger. "But you hate him."

"That was just foreplay. Right, Kitten?" Mav cooed.

I was pretty sure Aster stepped on his foot as she gazed up at him. "You know it, Pookie Pie."

I looked up at Kol as if he had answers, but he was staring hard at his brother.

"Don't you spoil the surprise. We're announcing it at dinner tonight," Maverick warned us. "We want to tell the rest of the family ourselves."

"You don't need to worry about them being surprised," I muttered.

"Good," Mav said with a grin. "We'll see you two later." And with that, he guided Aster toward his truck.

I turned to face Kol. "I thought twin girls were going to be the dinner surprise."

He shook his head. "I don't think even quintuplets would have anything on Mav getting married to his archnemesis."

"Something's going on there, right?" I asked.

"One hundred percent," Kol agreed.

I laughed. "Never a dull moment."

He pulled me into his arms. "Regretting marrying into the most chaotic family on the planet?"

"Never," I said, stretching up to kiss him. "You keep me on my toes. I'd hate to have a boring life."

Kol's mouth curved against mine. "You gonna meet me in the twilight tonight?"

"Only for forever," I whispered back.

"Forever isn't nearly long enough."

Acknowledgments

I can't begin to tell you how excited I was to write Nova and Kol's story. From the moment I began writing book one in this series, scenes with these two were playing out in my mind. But when it came time to start plotting, I panicked. I couldn't figure out the right character trajectory for Nova.

She had been through an incredible trauma, but it didn't feel right for her to be meek or hiding out. As I thought about the two parts of her that seemed to be at odds, I really struggled. It was in talking it out with a friend and realizing that Nova's trauma could spark recklessness, thrill-seeking, and LIVING to the fullest that Nova really became unlocked for me. So my first and biggest thank-you has to go to my partner in wording crime, Elsie Silver, for helping me figure it out.

Creativity doesn't happen in a vacuum, and for me, it has to be tended and cultivated. Maybe that's why I've also recently entered my plant-mom era. Regardless, none of the magic of creation happens without a community around you. And I am beyond fortunate to have one of the most amazing ones. I'd like to give an extra little shout-out to friends who help me find my way whenever I'm lost: Devyn, Sam, Laura, Elsie, Rebecca, Kandi, Ana, Lauren, Amy, Willow, Mia, Jess, and Paige. Thank you for all you do and all the ways you show up for me. I love you all.

To all my incredible friends who have cheered and supported me through all the ups and downs of the past few months, you know who you are. Romance books have given me a lot of things, but at the top of that list are incredible friends that I am so lucky to have in my life. Thank you for walking this path with me.

To my incredible betas, Anna, Glav, Elle, Jess, Jill, Kelly, Kristie, and Trisha, who read this one at various phases and helped find the characters when I was struggling. I'm so lucky to have you all in my corner.

And to the most amazing hype squad ever, my STS soul sisters, Alice, Hollis, Jael, Katrina, Laura, and Paige, thank you for the gift of true friendship and sisterhood. I always feel the most supported and celebrated thanks to you.

The crew that helps bring my words to life and gets them out into the world is pretty darn epic. Thank you to Devyn, Jess, Tori, Glav, Rae, Kelli, Paula, Chelle, Jaime, Julie, Cat, Mary, Stacey, Katie, Jenna, and my team at Lyric, Kimberly and my team at Park, Fine & Brower Literary Management. Your hard work is so appreciated!

To my team at Sourcebooks: Christa, Gretchen, Katie, and so many others, thank you for helping these words reach a whole new audience and making my bookstore dreams come true. And to my team at Evermore and Century in the UK, especially Claire, Jess, and Rosie, thank you for bringing the stories to stores across the globe.

To all the reviewers and content creators who have taken a chance on my words…THANK YOU! Your championing of my stories means more than I can say. And to my launch and influencer teams, thank you for your kindness, support, and for sharing my books with the world.

Ladies of Catherine Cowles Reader Group, you're my favorite place to hang out on the internet! Thank you for your support, encouragement, and willingness to always dish about your latest book boyfriends. You're the freaking best!

Lastly, thank YOU! Yes, YOU. I'm so grateful you're reading this book and making my author dreams come true. I love you for that. A whole lot!

Also Available from

CATHERINE COWLES

Starlight Grove

Across the Vanishing Sky

Into the Fading Twilight

Beneath a Midnight Moon

Through the Gathering Storm

Within the Starry Silence

Sparrow Falls

Fragile Sanctuary

Delicate Escape

Broken Harbor

Beautiful Exile

Chasing Shelter

Secret Haven

The Lost & Found Series

Whispers of You

Echoes of You

Glimmers of You

Shadows of You

Ashes of You

The Tattered & Torn Series

Tattered Stars

Falling Embers

Hidden Waters

Shattered Sea

Fractured Sky

The Wrecked Series

Reckless Memories

Perfect Wreckage

Wrecked Palace

Reckless Refuge

Beneath the Wreckage

The Sutter Lake Series

Beautifully Broken Pieces

Beautifully Broken Life

Beautifully Broken Spirit

Beautifully Broken Control

Beautifully Broken Redemption

Standalone Novels

All the Missing Pieces

For a full list of up-to-date Catherine Cowles titles, please visit www.catherinecowles.com.

About

CATHERINE COWLES

Writer of words. Drinker of Diet Cokes. Lover of all things cute and furry. *New York Times* and #1 Amazon bestselling author Catherine Cowles has had her nose in a book since the time she could read and finally decided to write down some of her own stories. When she's not writing, she can be found exploring her home state of Oregon, listening to true crime podcasts, or searching for her next book boyfriend.

Stay Connected

You can find Catherine in all the usual bookish places…

Website: catherinecowles.com
Newsletter: catherinecowles.com/subscribe
Facebook: facebook.com/catherinecowlesauthor
Catherine Cowles Facebook Reader Group:
facebook.com/groups/CatherineCowlesReaderGroup
Instagram: instagram.com/catherinecowlesauthor
Goodreads: goodreads.com/catherinecowlesauthor
TikTok: tiktok.com/@catherinecowlesauthor
BookBub: bookbub.com/profile/catherine-cowles
Amazon: amazon.com/author/catherinecowles